*For everyone who has been
waiting for their time.
It's now.*

HEAT LEVEL AND CONTENT WARNINGS

Before starting this novel, I encourage you to first read this section to determine whether it's the right fit for your personal circumstances.

This book is closed door romance, which means there is innuendo, kisses are descriptive, and characters don't shy away from their attraction.

There is mild to moderate use of cuss words, particularly in emotional moments. However, there is no use of f-bombs, religious blasphemies, or known ableist terms.

The heroine was dumped by her boyfriend before the start of the book, and there is implied cheating with one of her friends. There are allusions to past bullying that the hero experienced from his childhood being an orphan. There are moderate depictions of stalking that may be uncomfortable.

Visit my website mariloyal.com for general content warnings that apply to my books.

CHAPTER 1
HOPE

Sometimes life throws you a curveball so wild, so unexpected, that you can't even take a swing at it.

Every year, my college buddies and I get together for Friendsgiving down in Miami, where we met as far back as seven years ago. At least half of the group lives out of state now, which didn't seem too terrible at first until life happened. We have a nurse, a future orthopedic surgeon, a personal trainer to celebrities, a brand influencer, and more. The one common thread is that basically none of us have work-life balance. Work is life.

I'm one of the worst. As a junior athletic trainer for a professional baseball team, I work twelve-hour days for basically all but two months of the year. Friendsgiving is essentially the start of that down season for me, and I look forward to it every year.

Sun, good food, drinks, and friends gathered together in the McMansion owned by the hosts, Kelly and Mitch. It sits by a lake and if that wasn't enough, it also boasts an infinity pool courtesy of Mitch's banker salary.

There's only one downside to Friendsgiving: Dawson Clark. A.k.a. my one and only ex boyfriend.

I park my yellow Jeep a few houses down from the McMansion because every spot in its vicinity is taken. Turning the rearview mirror my way, I'm met by a shocking view. Maybe leaving the roof off during the entire drive down from Orlando was a bad idea, especially when paired with keeping my hair untied. I make a weak attempt to comb it with my fingers and give up pretty quickly. I'm diving right into the pool after this, so what's the point?

After hopping out of the car, I pluck my overnight bag from the backseat and hoist it over my shoulder. One of Daddy Yankee's classics about evil exes plays in my head and I whistle it as I head over to the McMansion.

Okay, Dawson isn't some two-bit villain from a song, and I'm not secretly pining for him or anything. Since we originally started out as friends from *this* group, we decided to remain friends for the sake of the collective. Too bad I kind of lied when I said I was cool with it, because I want to punch him in the neck every time I see him.

"It's fine," I tell myself as I ring the McMansion's doorbell. "I'm fine, everything's fine. It'll be fun."

Pool. Cocktail. Those mini quiches Kelly makes. Catching up with everybody else. Clubbing with Amy later. Ignoring Dawson. Two days of this is totally doable.

The door swings open and there's Kelly with her wide pageant smile, blonder hair than usual framing her face, and the biggest pregnant belly I've ever seen. She spreads her arms wide and brings me for a tight hug. "Hope, you're here!"

"Wait." I try to push away but homegirl must be seriously working out because I can't. "Your belly—"

"I know! It's one of the biggest news this year." Finally, she frees me to frame her belly with loving hands. With her floral dress and perfect makeup, she looks like a model for a southern magazine. "I was waiting for everyone to be together to break it—the news, I mean, not water."

I blink. It takes me a second to get the joke and I snort. "Well, congratulations. You're positively glowing."

"Thank you." She hooks her arm with mine and pulls me into the foyer, where she calls out, "Hope is here!"

Music drifts from the backyard along with the smell of burgers on the grill. A few voices cheer for my arrival, while others continue their chatter. I don't know if it's just me but there seem to be more people than usual, which probably means some people found significant others since last year.

Vaguely, I wonder if Dawson is one of them. How should I react to that?

I tune out most of Kelly's tale about the pool upgrades— now with an integrated jacuzzi!—while I try to search for an answer. I can't find it in me to be happy for Dawson, even if his new beau turns out to be sweeter than sugar. In theory that would mean he found someone better than me while I'm still super single. Not exactly a palatable prospect.

But then, I also can't show any sort of negative reaction in front of the group. That would make things weird—and *weird* is what we've been trying to avoid so carefully.

I realize I'm looking down at the floor when a pair of men's boat shoes attached to some legs appear in front of me. My eyes rise and I have to stifle the relieved sigh when it turns out to only be Mitch.

"Wow, you look like garbage" is my greeting to him.

Sighing, he says, "Hope to see you too." He blinks slowly as if half asleep on his feet, which checks out with the dark circles around his eyes.

I don't have the heart to ask what he even meant and instead turn my attention to his wife. "Is work killing him?"

"No, I am." She smiles.

"She tosses and turns all night when she's sleeping. Or wakes me up with some weird craving." Mitch offers me a one-armed hug before shifting to drop a kiss on Kelly's forehead. "I'm going upstairs to take a nap. You're in charge."

"Always." She pats his butt as he wades away and I shake my head, trying to mask all the feelings roiling in my stomach.

Mitch and Kelly were the other couple from the friend group. I really thought I'd have what they have by now—the McMansion, the college sweetheart husband, and a little one on the way.

Instead, I'm single because all I do is work, yet the money's not enough to afford even a condo so I'm forced to live with roommates. At this pace, I should just marry my student loans because they seem to be the only constant in my life.

"Hope, is that you?"

I know that voice. I drop my duffel bag on the living room floor and pick up the pace toward the French doors. Bare feet pitter patter on the terracotta tiles until Amy McFadden, my college roommate and bestie, appears in all her bikini glory. Squealing, she launches herself at me as she usually does.

We both giggle and stumble, but my quads don't lie. I hold us steady until she pulls away and gives me a once over. "Va va boom, mamacita. You look hot."

"Pfff." My face heats up. There's nothing hot about a ratty baseball T-shirt, old shorts and Crocs that have seen better days, my go-to outfit for a comfortable three-hour-plus drive. Rather than explain all that, I divert the attention back to her. "No, *you* look hot."

"I do, don't I?" Her smile morphs into a lip bite and a furtive glance at Kelly. "Did you tell her the news?"

Behind me, the hostess says, "No, I'll leave that up to you."

"Ah." Somehow Amy seems disappointed.

"What news?" I cock an eyebrow. "Don't tell me you're

pregnant too." Her stomach looks as flat as ever, but maybe she's just found out. It'd be funny if my two closest girl friends from college are pregnant at the same time. And by funny I mean weird. I can't picture the same for me right now.

"Ha, no. It's less exciting, I guess."

"I sure hope that's the case." Kelly clears her throat. "Anyway, I think the cheeseburgers are ready, anyone want one?"

Amy runs a hand through her caramel brown hair, enhanced by expensive highlights. I know that tidbit because she's been dying it at the same upscale salon in Miami Beach since college. And for some reason, she's now avoiding my gaze.

"Why are you two acting weird all of a sudden?" I ask.

"Mojito as usual?" Kelly volleys back at me instead, fully knowing I'm a rum girlie.

I tuck my tongue against my cheek and fold my arms, because clearly I'm becoming my dad and these two are acting like my brother and I when we were hiding something.

Kelly drops the hostess act, maybe even the happy act, because her pretty face twists into an expression of unfiltered annoyance. "Just tell her, Amy. It's better that she finds out now from you than from everybody else."

When Amy starts biting her lip, I know whatever this is about can't be good. I don't change the Dad pose because it's already making them crack, but meanwhile I run through every possible scenario in my mind. Is Amy moving out of state? Or is she sick? Did her crush on my brother come back? No, that one can't be. He's been happily married for years now.

"What?" I all but bark when I can't take the silence or my theorizing anymore. "What happened? Are you okay?"

Boy, this must be big because Amy takes a shuddering breath and hugs herself before even opening her mouth. "The thing is—"

"Hey."

We all freeze at the new voice.

It sounds just like it did all those years ago, like a surfer boy who is cool and in no hurry to show it off. Worse still, nothing else has changed. That's the same mop of blond curls on his head, the toothpaste commercial smile, the same brown eyes that glint under the sunlight, and the tanned body that tells me he still plays water sports year-round.

Dawson.

"Hi," I respond curtly.

And then I zero in on the one thing that has changed. His arm snakes around Amy's waist, pulling her against him to rest his hand low at her hip. Possessive. The same way he used to hold *me* for years.

No one needs to say anything else. I get it now. And however I react will dictate the course of this weekend—maybe beyond.

I take a moment to process this, even if it feels like every pair of eyes is fixed on me. My mouth tastes odd, and I wish I could wash that down with the mojito I wasn't quick enough to accept.

The bitterness rankles deep into my soul, not just because Amy has broken some kind of girl code that I can't formulate coherently right now. But also Dawson's gesture is a blatant attack on the delicate balance we struck for two years. *He* is the one shitting on the group dynamic, but if I make that clear by showing any displeasure, he'll blame *me* for the awkwardness that is already ensuing in my silence.

This is why I'm glad that he dumped my ass—yeah, even though I was the dumpee. It made it feel very final and that distance from him allowed me to start seeing his true colors. He's a master manipulator and now it seems like Amy is his new victim. I feel sorry for her just as much as I'm pissed at her.

Knowing there's only one course of action, I turn to an annoyed Kelly and hook my arm with hers again. "Let's go make that mojito."

"Great, I bought the rum you like!"

"Cacique?" I gasp in an exaggerated way. "You sure know the way to my heart."

We leave the new couple behind us, but it doesn't mean I'm not boiling on the inside. For the first time I wish I hadn't joined this Friendsgiving, and I vow that next year I'm going to bring a new damn boyfriend that will erase the pity on everybody's faces.

CHAPTER 2
CADE

FEBRUARY

Nothing like spending St. Valentine's at a swanky restaurant waiting not for a hot date, but for your sports agent. I'd have preferred to hit a bar downtown, see if I could score a date for tonight, but Lou was adamant that we meet. For a guy who mostly ignores me, I figure this has to be important.

So, either I'm about to get sacked by my team or by my agent.

Judging by how late he's running, I hope it's just the latter.

I check my watch. It's half past six. Then I lift up my phone and click around until I locate his text message—it indeed says to meet here at six.

Sighing, I lean back on my chair. He'll show up eventually, even if it means waiting with a lukewarm glass of water for two more hours. In the meantime, I do my usual rotation of doom-scrolling through socials, stop to watch a whole two-minute video of a panda playing on some swings, and catch exactly zero sightings of my face or name on the profiles of sports channels and magazines. *SPORTY* gave me a feature in the offseason that made me hope my time was finally arriving, but the answer has been no. I am, in fact, still not arriving—just like my agent.

Now in a crappy mood, I put my phone facedown on the table and look around for entertainment. Of course this fancy ass place doesn't have any TV screens showing games. There's some jazzy music in the background drowned by the quiet hum of polite conversation and the occasional laughter. The tables around me are overwhelmingly taken by couples because of freaking course, except it's easy to tell if it's a long-enduring couple or a new one.

For example, the two in the table off to my right, closest to the bar. They both wear wedding rings, and it seems like they've reached the stage where much conversation isn't necessary. They've either learned to communicate telepathically or the relationship is in the rocks—no in between. I calculate they've been going at it for about fifteen years.

Then there's the couple on the left, in the row by the wall. These ones are clearly on a first date. How do I know? Because the guy is doing all the talking and the woman sits ramrod stiff, oozing awkwardness through her pores.

My phone buzzes with a text from Lou that says one single word. *Traffic.* That can mean he's near to arriving and the half hour delay was due to the fact that Orlando is one hour away from Orlando, or it could mean that I have yet to wait an indeterminate amount of time. Guess I'll just take it as W that he's really on his way.

For lack of anything to do, I take the glass of water and glance at the first date couple over the glass rim. He looks like he put some effort—his shirt is ironed and hair freshly gelled, not like he came straight from work. But she must have not been on the same page, going by the simple polo and trainers she's wearing. Maybe she didn't look up what kind of restaurant this was—the rich people kind—or this is her way of saying she's not really into it without using actual words. With women you never know.

Stomping feet distract me and there's only one person I know who walks like he has a vendetta against the floor. Lou makes his way through the tables, bumping into a couple of people and not bothering to apologize. You can take a New Yorker out of New York, but can't take New York out of the New Yorker.

Meanwhile, I'm from Texas. I make eye contact with the two offended people and say, "My apologies. Sorry for my friend." The *My* still comes out like *Mah*, no matter how many years I've been away from Texas because clearly the same adage applies to me. People will pry my *y'all* from my cold dead hands.

Huffing, Lou dumps himself in the chair across from me. "I hate this town. Everyone says living in Florida is like being on vacation year round and that's bullshit."

The corner of my lips lifts. "Good to see you too."

"You should've ordered for me," he says while taking the menu for a quick scan. "I only have a short moment before my charter flight to Miami."

"Well, I feel special now." The bulk of his clients are actually there, so if he came in person to see me this can't all be bad, right?

"You should, I came to—"

Of course, this is the exact moment the waiter chooses to drop by. "Welcome, would you like to see the wine menu?"

Lou drops the food menu like it burns and says, "Oh, yes. That would be great."

"I thought you have a flight soon?" I mask a snort with a polite cough.

"It's in two hours." He waves a hand at me and gleefully receives the drinks menu. As the waiter retreats to give us a moment, Lou says, "I assume you're not drinking, right? Spring Training starts soon so you better be in shape."

"Right." I fold my arms over the table and lean forward. "Speaking of, is there going to be a Spring Training for me?"

That pulls his attention away from the idea of booze. "What the hell do you mean? Of course there is."

"Just checking." I clear my throat. "So what are the news, then? Am I getting traded? Or fired?"

"Fine." He rolls his eyes as if I was being impatient and not him being late. "No, you're still with the Orlando Wild. No trades in your future."

I stay quiet because I don't know if to file that under Bummer or under Yay. My run with the Wild hasn't been exactly… wild so far. And not because I've played like shit or anything—I've been a damn fine closer pitcher. But that's not enough for me, and the team hasn't been enough for the fans. Last season we ended up near the bottom of the league.

This is why the *SPORTY* feature felt like such a big deal. I was kinda hoping it would lead to a trade into a better team. Except in that case I might've been relegated to pitching relief. Or maybe sent to the minors. So, lose-win?

"The big news is…" His lips twitch like he's holding back glee, and immediately my heart rate escalates. "Williams is the one getting traded."

I blink. Lean back on my chair. Hold the water glass for emotional support.

"Huh."

Despite my lukewarm reaction, I'm hootin' and tootin' in my heart.

This is major freaking news. Ben Williams has been the starter pitcher for the past couple of years. What edged him in the position over me is his annoying curveball that he can control at will. But other than that, he's not really a better pitcher than me. He gasses out on average one inning less than I do, and his fastballs are pretty average. But somehow he's managed to command the attention of our GM and the media much better than me, even though he's a grade-A doucheturd.

"Where to?" I ask, even though it's not my main question.

"The Denver Riders," he responds, now fully smirking. "Guess what that means for you?"

"A chance?"

"*The* chance." He laces his fingers in his classic shush-boy-I'm-about-to-negotiate-on-your-behalf pose. "That's why I came in person. I spent the afternoon meeting with your coach and GM. You're next in line for starter pitcher *if* you perform well during Spring Training. And it will come with a salary increase too."

"If," I clarify and he nods. "What happens if I don't wow them?"

"Are you planning to play like some pee wee, or something? What kind of question is that?" He blows a forceful puff of air. "Obviously in that case they'll trade in some other hotshot. This is your chance, Starr, so don't screw it up."

"A'ight, I won't."

I catch movement from the corner of my eye. The guy from the first date table gesticulates widely with his hands and his face is a mask of annoyance. A voice distracts me again.

"Are you ready to place your orders?" It's the waiter again.

Lou pushes away from the table before reaching for the pocket in his jacket. "Actually, I just checked the time and need to head out. Can you put whatever he wants under my card?"

"Certainly, sir." The waiter takes the card and heads over to the register.

"Geez, people are going to think I make a terrible date," I drawl.

"Your string of Annies tells me otherwise—Which reminds me, focus on baseball more than on women this season, yeah?"

"Right."

Lou tips his head. "I mean it, Starr. Don't blow this chance."

The waiter saves me from having to acknowledge that by gliding over. "Here's your card, sir."

Lou packs it away in his wallet and gives me one last look before stomping his way out of the restaurant. This time he doesn't run into anyone, though.

"Sir, are you ready to place your order?"

I tamper down my expression into placid disinterest. "What's the most expensive item in the menu?"

"That would be our marinated wagyu beef with truffle mashed potatoes, and tender vegetables with house aioli on sourdough."

So, an average meal made to sound pretentious. Perfect.

"Two of those to go, please." And just to be annoying, I add, "And a glass of orange juice."

To his credit, the waiter remains impassive. "Certainly."

That's when first date guy throws his napkin on the table and shoots to his feet. I haven't seen him exchange credit cards with any of the wait staff, which gives me the impression he's not only leaving mid-date, but also saddling her with the bill. What an asshole.

"Excuse me." I turn to the waiter leaving my table. "I'll also pick up her tab." I point at the stunned woman still sitting ramrod at her chair.

"Ah, y-yes. Of course." First time the waiter's not smooth like the house aioli, but I guess it's not often he sees a woman get dumped on a first date at this joint.

As he pivots away, I zero in on any signs that she may be crying or something. That's always uncomfortable as hell because I don't know how to make anyone feel better, and maybe it's best if I don't even try. She might want to pretend like tonight never even happened. Fortunately, Lou will foot the bill of her mistake because she shouldn't even have accepted the invitation from that waste of hair gel.

Finally, she turns to grab her purse from the back of her chair, and we make eye contact. She freezes.

Meanwhile, I can feel my lips curve.

"Well, well, well. What do we have here." I fold my arms.

None other than Hope Garcia, athletic trainer of the Orlando Wild Baseball Club, who opens her eyes as wide as they go.

"Starr," she all but hisses my last name.

"Garcia."

Her dark eyes check the exit. "Did you see that?"

"Every bit."

Her shoulders slump. But after one breath, she straightens back up and lifts her chin. "What can I do to make it so that the whole team doesn't find out about this?"

"Please, darlin'." I place a hand on my chest delicately. "I would never."

"Wasn't you who told everyone that Rivera cried while watching Titanic?"

"In my defense, that was right after he dyed my eyebrows in my sleep."

"Starr." She frowns.

"Your secret is safe with me, woman."

"I don't believe you for a second."

"Here is your order, sir, and the check." The waiter places a large bag on the table, along with a fancy little folio with the check. "Oh, I'm afraid I nearly forgot the orange juice. I'll be back in a second."

"Thanks," I say absentmindedly, running my eyes through the tab. Garcia's jerk of a date also ordered the wagyu and was going to make her pay for it. Meanwhile, she had only ordered the side caesar salad.

I scribble a decent thirty percent tip and crumple the receipt in my fist.

When I look up, Garcia's by the register. Someone gets in the way again and it's my waiter with the to-go drink. I use him as a cover to gather my stuff and high-tail it before she realizes what's happened.

CHAPTER 3
HOPE

"Are you taking notes?" Steve asks over his shoulder with the same air of polite indifference people use to say *bless you* after someone else sneezes.

He's my boss, though, so I have no choice but to offer a serious nod and reply with a well-timed "yes, sir." The question is extremely annoying when he assigned me to update the player charts in real time while they get their preseason physicals. That includes not just fitness records but also nutrition, because as the youngest and only female in the whole athlete care department, I'm obviously responsible for all the menial tasks.

Obviously.

On the outside, baseball has been making big strides to be more inclusive and recognize that it doesn't have to continue being the boys club it's always been. Heck, there are female umpires now. I wouldn't have gotten my athletic therapist job if I'd applied ten years ago—although I was in high school but that's not the point.

On the inside, though, The Show is still very much run by boys for boys.

Aside from me in the training staff, I can count on one hand the women who aren't in HR or accounting, and that includes my two roommates. One of our fave pastimes is sitting in our living room with a fancy little beverage each, and talking shit about the men we work around. Which definitely includes some of the players.

Unfortunately, I can't complain about the one I'd most like to. Fortunately, he seems to have kept his yap shut since the whole dinner date fiasco a couple weeks ago. Or he's biding his time to spill the beans at the right moment when I'll be the most humiliated, I don't know. Cade Starr is hard to read.

Ugh, speaking of…

"Starr, looking good." Steve stops by the treadmill that Starr is running on while wearing an altitude training mask, and motions at me to look at his stats.

I feel a pair of bright blue eyes follow me as I walk around the treadmill to peek at the screen. Firing my iPad back up, I jot down his heartbeat, oxygen levels, speed, and everything else that the chart asks for. The software we use immediately compares to the previous measurements and everyone and their mom will be pleased by this development. Starr is in the best shape of his life right when the team needs him the most.

That sucks. Here I'd have preferred that he got traded and took my little secret away with him.

My boss jerks his chin toward the next guy and I'm happy to follow along this time. Five other guys are on the treadmills, being analyzed from every angle by the entire operations and medical teams. Some fifty people stand behind a window over-looking the training facility, as some twenty of us in the larger medical team perform the checks.

Among them, I spot the owner, Charlie Cox, parked in a corner, splitting his attention between his phone, his assistant, and the players spread out through the gym.

Cox is one of those so called billionaire-philanthropists

who donates metric tons of money to the local arts every year, and apparently bought this baseball franchise three years ago because of his childhood fascination with the sport.

Three years happens to be as long as I've been employed by the organization. Rumor has it that I was a diversity hire to make the new owner look good. Seeing him here brings back the supreme annoyance I felt when my coworkers dropped that little tidbit. I'm sure Cox has no idea that I even exist, and I don't intend to catch his attention right now.

I follow behind Steve and I'm not above using him as a shield as we navigate the grounds.

Up next is Logan Kim, the best catcher in the team, also running with an altitude training mask. I don't know who started that fad, if Starr or him, but the two keep shooting each other these competitive looks that almost make me shake my head. I log Kim's data and compare it to his previous readings. This guy's also improved a lot, especially his pulmonary capacity.

That seems to be a recurring theme in most of the guys we evaluate after Kim. Aside from the handful of guys who still need to do more PT work during Spring Training, it looks like most of them have taken good care of themselves during the offseason. And maybe losing our star pitcher has fired them up.

"Nuh-uh, hold up," my boss says and I freeze, until I glance up from the player charts and find he's not talking to me. "Put that back on, there are ladies present."

He points at Lucas "Lucky" Rivera, our shortstop, who is in the middle of taking his shirt off to get his fat percentage measured.

Sighing, I mutter, "It's okay, Boss. They all look like pieces of meat to me."

There's a snort behind me, followed by a deep *and* deeply annoying voice with a Texan accent saying, "Is that so?" Up next, he walks by me while peeling off his sweaty shirt to queue behind Rivera. And because the team is singularly composed of only class clowns, one by one they all do the same. Even Kim, who is usually the most serious of the bunch.

It's not my first rodeo and these stooges don't know I was raised in a family of mostly men—Dad, older brother, and an army of boy cousins. My trade is literally studying muscles in an analytical way. To paraphrase Shania Twain, abs don't impress me much.

I open my mouth wide into a yawn so exaggerated that I manage to bring legit tears to my eyes. I even go as far as smacking my mouth a couple of times like I just woke up.

Rivera breaks through the quiet with a snort, and he smacks his buddy's arm. "Looks like you didn't impress her, Cowboy."

As more laughter and ribbing ensues, I say in a dead-panned way, "Can we get back to work before I fall asleep on my feet?"

Steve's eyes shift to the window, reminding me of the vow I made earlier with myself of not attracting the owner's attention. I cast a furtive glance his way and almost sag in relief when I find that he's vanished, his spot taken by my roommates.

Of course they choose to make their way over from the admin building in time to witness this little scene, but better them than the alternate scenario of the owner questioning whether a woman in the medical staff was a good idea after all.

And why the hell is Cade Starr half smirking? That's not the expression he should have on his face after he just got owned.

Wait. Does he think *he* owned *me*? Or... is he thinking about my disaster date?

"Hey, Garcia. Can you show me Kim's stats for a second?"

one of the analytics guys asks, and I'm all too glad to make my way across the floor as far from Starr as possible.

I hand over my iPad and fold my arms tight as I wait for this guy to review the catcher's chart, my foot tapping the floor with pent up energy. Normally I'm not fazed by a little teasing from the guys—that's just part of survival here. But not today. I glance over my shoulder at a certain shirtless pitcher, standing on a scale. He's nodding to whatever Steve's saying next to him, which is great news because it means he's not using his mouth to tell everyone what a terrible date I make. Rivera, his buddy, isn't paying me any extra attention, which gives me the hope that he also doesn't know.

Despite my name, though, I'm a firm believer that hope doesn't make for a good strategy. I spent almost two weeks worrying all on my own that Starr might've spilled the beans to the whole team and when I discovered that he didn't, I developed the hope that maybe he had just forgotten about it.

Until that freaking smirk a second ago.

I don't trust him as far as I can throw him—which means not far at all, because he's 6 foot 4 and two hundred one pounds of solid muscle. I have to find a way to shut him up for good.

Except obviously I can't kill him—that would get me fired, tempting as it is. I can't bribe him either because that would also cost me my job. What can I possibly do?

*

The opportunity presents itself during lunch break. One thing most male specimens have in common is how their logical brains shut off when presented with food. With other stimuli too, but those don't figure in this situation.

What this means is that once we park ourselves at a table to eat our lunch, my boss and coworkers forget my very existence. None of them notice how I pick a seat that allows me to keep a strategic lookout for my target: one Cade Starr, prospective starter pitcher for this season.

I wait like a lioness among the bushes until, halfway through lunch, Starr pushes his chair away from the table and stands. Leaning to one side discreetly, I confirm that there's still food on his plate, which can only mean one thing in the world of ravenous athletes: this man is going to the restroom.

And now so must I. "Excuse me," I mumble as I stand, but my colleagues are too enthralled by the chicken tacos to acknowledge me.

I take the exit closest to the kitchen and dawdle in the hallway, because it's not like I'm gonna fully stalk the guy while he does his business. I pluck my phone from my back pocket and check my email as I slowly inch closer to the restrooms. I'll save some special time later tonight to feel bad about being such a creep, but right now my focus is on survival—because I'd really expire if he decides to run his mouth.

"Whoa."

I lift my eyes, stopping abruptly when I find myself face to face with Starr. Turns out I moved a lot closer to the men's restroom entrance than I intended, and he almost bumped into me on his way out.

"Are you stalking me, darlin'?" he asks, still drying his hands with a paper towel. All the points I could've given him for hygiene poof upon his words.

"First of all, *darling* doesn't figure in the name field on my driver license." I fold my arms and spread my feet at hip width. "And second, yes. We need to have a word."

He blinks those bluish eyes of his slowly. "In the restroom?"

"We're outside of it."

"Semantics."

"Starr." I frown. "What the hell was up with that smug look earlier?"

"Garcia, I'm gonna need you to use more words than that." He waves circles in the air as if encouraging me.

I take a deep breath. "Are you planning on holding my humiliation over me forever? Or worse, are you waiting for the best moment to mock me in front of the whole team?"

"Huh?" His brow twists in pretty convincing confusion.

I check the hallway. Confirming it's still empty except for us, I speak through gritted teeth. "About the other night."

After one second of processing those words, Starr's face morphs. To my surprise, it's into annoyance. "Wait, you really think I'd make fun of you for suffering through a bad date?"

I tilt my head, waiting for the catch.

Nothing comes and now I'm the one who's confused. "Huh?"

Starr shakes his head. "The answer is no, I'm not going to give you any crap about your bad date."

"For real?"

"Yeah, no need to follow me to restrooms about it."

"We're outside," I repeat, huffing. "Anyway, you won't change your mind?"

"No," he deadpans. "Can I go finish my tacos now before the vultures polish them?"

"Sure…" I fall back as he passes me by and for some reason, blurt out, "I'm watching you, Starr."

He halts and slowly turns to look over his shoulder. Sunlight spills through the windows down the side, making his eyes look like turquoise glass mosaics, and for a second I'm mesmerized. Until he opens his mouth. "Apparently even in the restroom, huh?"

"Ugh, just go." I swivel on my heels and pretend like I intended to go to the women's restroom all along.

Inside, I meet my red face through the mirror and press my

lips tight. "Pitchers," I spit out like it's a curse. They all tend to be annoying and I thought we'd got rid of the worst after Ben Williams got traded. But now I don't know how I'll survive a whole season of Cade Starr when I keep putting my foot in my mouth in front of him.

CHAPTER 4
CADE

Closing my eyes, I take a deep breath and hold it in my lungs until the scents are imprinted in my brain. Sweat, grass, sand, leather, and a faint touch of Icy Hot seep all the way into my system. It's not like I stop training during the offseason, but it hits different to do it at a gym or in my house than at the team's training field. And what makes this even better is that today is pitching practice, baby.

"Starr."

I twitch just a little but I'm sure he notices. Logan Kim isn't an All-Star catcher for no reason. His eyes are scary because they don't miss a thing and they have the power to light up an outfielder all the way from home.

"Are you aware what us forming the first battery in practice means?"

Popping an eye open, I say, "That I'm finally being recognized for my talents?"

"That we're shit out of luck and stuck with you." He nods sagely and I shrug. It's kind of a dig but at the same time it isn't —the truth be like that. "So, keep in mind that everyone's watching and pitch your best ball from the get go or go home."

"I can't run home if I'm pitching," I shoot back, dripping with sarcasm.

He makes a big show of sighing while he puts on his catcher's cage back on his head. Even stops halfway to look back at me once more, shaking his head like a whole drama king. Maybe once his knees make him retire he can audition for a play.

As he settles back in his place and does some minimal stretching, I toss the ball in the air without paying much attention to it. I don't need to move my head to catch sight of the onlookers in the periphery. This is supposed to be pitching practice, but none of the other pitchers are even close to ready for the mound. They're huddled under the shade with the pitching coach, all watching me.

On the other side, the manager, at least half of the training staff, and part of the medical team, also have their peepers trained on me.

I lift my glove to hide half of my face so they don't see that I'm smiling like I should star in a horror movie, pun intended. After clearing my throat, I wipe my face clean and hide the ball with my glove.

Everyone and their mom knows that I pitch a mean and clinical fastball. It's the reason I was drafted straight out of high school into the minors, and moved up to the majors in a year and some change. But being able to land a hundred miles per hour fastball wherever the hell I want as a southpaw isn't as effective as someone may think against professional batters whose sole purpose in life is to hit it out of the park.

Sadly, I've struggled a lot more with the curveballs. It's why I've been a closer most of my professional career. Most starters have about three different balls they can play mind games with, and I've managed to secure a couple of serviceable curveballs that get me enough strikes and outs to justify my five-million salary. The problem is that I just haven't mastered one enough to make it a real weapon.

However, my personal trainers and I have been busy in the offseason. Rather than pitching something reliable but boring, like my fastball, I'm better off showing them what I've been working on—even if it's far from perfect.

"That's been way more than fifteen seconds!" a female voice shouts from the dugout.

Slowly, I turn to Hope Garcia right as she hides behind her boss. She's been avoiding me ever since the cozy restroom chat the other day, like she's embarrassed at her own actions. I guess she couldn't contain herself anymore, huh?

"Yeah, dude. This isn't the nineties. Just throw the damn ball," Lucky heckles with his characteristic megaphone voice. That's when I notice that the fielding practice hasn't even started, and they're also peeping like little kids around the fencing.

It's like the whole team wants to know if I can cut it as a starter or not. Ha, another pun right there.

I take my sweet time winding up like there are cameras trying to capture the motion of every muscle group. My pitching form is a bit weird, like me I guess, because I naturally lift up my right leg a lot more than average. It helps me hide my hand from the batters to really make them guess where the release point is going to be. But it also makes it hell for catchers.

Not this jerk, though. Kim's glove whips up right in time to catch the best pitch I've thrown in years.

I land half turned away from him, which means the first reactions I gather are from the bench.

Ah, damn. No one's impressed.

Wait, Garcia is. Her eyes are as wide as a cartoon's. Maybe this wasn't terrible.

Except that Kim rips off his mask, throws it in the dirt with way more aggression than necessary, and gets up to stride over. His eyebrows are so tight that they form three vertical lines in between.

That's not the expression of a happy catcher. I spread my feet wider to brace myself for impact.

Good call because he smacks my chest with his glove hard enough to topple a building. "A *cutter*? Really?"

"Yeah?" I ask, confused out of my mind.

"Since when can you pitch a cutter?"

"Man, I don't know. I woke up one morning right after Christmas and said, you know what my life needs right now? A cutter for my knife set."

"Shut up, clown." He runs his free hand down his face. "Are you telling me you've only been pitching this for two months?"

I hide my face with my glove, because this is pitcher-to-catcher only. "Of course not, you bonehead. I've been trying to make the cutter happen for like two years. I'm just finally getting the hang of it."

Somehow that calms his tits a bit. "Oh. Okay, that's better. I was about to drag you for messing up your form this close to the season."

"Nope, same form as always. In fact, that's why it's not fully game ready."

He cocks an eyebrow. "I knew that was a fluke."

"And yet I bet on it working. Fifty-fifty fluke."

"This is why I can't stand pitchers," he mumbles with a slow shake of his head. "You're all cocky bastards."

"Bless your soul."

"Excuse me, do you need some tea for your little chat?" Rob Beau, our manager, calls from the bench. In case we misunderstood, he mimics the act of pouring tea into an imaginary teacup.

"Fine," Kim grouches. "Give me only cutters. I'm going to

personally write a report on whether you have what it takes to carry the season."

"Just don't miss them. I'd hate to write a report on how *you* don't have what it takes to be my catcher." I smirk.

He tosses a middle finger and once he gets in position, we get to work.

I wish I could say I threw one perfect cutter after another, but that would be a lie and lying is bad manners, which is one of those things orphans get in more trouble for than anyone else. Like I guesstimated, about half of my pitches are absolute tire fires that would've cost us bases or runs. By the string of expletives coming out of Kim's mouth, I'd say runs.

The other half, though, were solid strikes. And that's good enough odds for me.

Larry Socci, the pitching coach, calls it for me once I've hit my average count. I can keep going but there's no point in pushing myself this early. I'm not one of those reckless dare-devils who have to be dragged away from the mound. I'm not in this for short term success.

Beau rubs his salt and pepper beard, eying me like he can't quite tell what species I am as I approach the bench.

"Cool down your shoulder," is all he says as I step under the shade, his attention back on the rest of the pitching practice.

Boo hiss, I think to myself. Where are my words of affirmation, coach?

"Wait."

We all turn to the female voice.

This time it's not Garcia, who pauses from pulling the shoulder ice pack from a cooler. Instead, it's Rosalina Mena, our social media girl.

"Can I record a couple of videos with Starr before he takes off his shirt?"

I refrain from asking if it wouldn't be better to record them after that, because I'm a damn gentleman.

"Fine." Beau nods at her before turning to me. "But ice right after."

"Yes, sir." I pick myself up and stride after Mena.

"Hey, Garcia. Come here," someone else calls from the field and she takes off so fast, she cuts through my path.

Back to avoiding sharing oxygen, I see.

I continue following Mena until she points at me to stand at a random spot in the grass. Or not so random, when she trains her camera so that the fielding practice—and not the pitching area—shows behind me.

"Okay, so this is going to be for a few different clips, so I'll try to get you at different angles to pretend like it was shot on different days."

"Efficient, I like it." I tip my cap to her.

She offers a brilliant smile, the kind I've heard won her a Miss Florida pageant while she was in college. "Great. So, question one: if you had a sister, who would you let her date from the team?"

"No one," I say right away, not only because I don't have a sister that I know of, but also because every guy on this team is a dirty horndog.

"Geez," she mutters amid chuckles. She shifts to the side, motioning with her finger for me to follow. Now the fences are behind me. "Question two: who from the team has the most game with the ladies? And you can't say yourself."

"Hmm." I press my glove between my elbow and my ribs to free my hand, and remove my hat to comb through my sweaty brown hair while I think. "Probably Rivera. The accent drives them wild."

Mena doesn't remark on my spectacular pun, instead she says, "That's funny, the guys were pretty unanimous in voting for you on both questions."

I reel back. Pretending like I'm not as shocked as I am, I ask in a casual voice, "Oh yeah?"

"And Rivera also pointed out your accent. He said the whole southern gentleman thing you have going on gets you all the ladies without even trying."

Maybe. Until they get to know me a bit better and figure out that I'm not husband material. Or family material, for that matter.

I can feel my face splitting into the smile that I offer to fans when they catch me in the last moment I want to be perceived —like say, in the restroom. "Why, I guess I should thank the team for the compliments. Are there any other questions?"

"Yes, last one." She takes a quick look around and I guess she doesn't find another decent background in the vicinity, because she settles for zooming closer to my face. To the camera, she says, "Question three: if you could have any girl-friend in the world, who would it be?"

This is the question that stumps me.

As much as I like women, I don't actually dream of being with any single one long enough to call her *my girlfriend*. Maybe I should name drop some impossible celebrity, but some fans have a way of spinning that way out of control. Maybe I should just name a random quality in women instead and call it a day.

Hope Garcia dashes across the green on her way back to the bench. It inspires me to say, "I want to date a woman who keeps it real no matter what." That's the first thing that flashed in my mind when I saw her. The second one was powerful thighs, but that kind of answer would probably have made Lou want to quit from being my agent.

There, generic and still decent. Mena's eyes lift from the camera to my face, her mouth opening until she changes her mind. After a moment, she tucks the camera away and says, "That's it for now. Thanks, Starr."

"Welcome, princess." I put my hat back on and head over to get my shoulder iced.

CHAPTER 5
HOPE

Maybe I should stop scheduling dates during rush hour or in the downtown area. Or both.

The Orlando Wild training facilities are nearby, so it's convenient to me and I'm always the first to arrive. Unfortunately, I've been waiting long enough that I'm beginning to suspect that the wait might not be due to traffic.

Today's guy has been the worst so far. Allegedly he works at the University of Central Florida, all the way on the east side. I know there's no practical way of getting here without experiencing the worst of traffic, but couldn't he at least give me an ETA? Or even text an OMW?

I tap my fingers on the table hard enough to cause ripples in the third water glass. I'm starting to feel the need for a bio break after so much water.

At least the weather is amazing today.

It's still a bit on the chilly side, so I'm wearing my Orlando Wild jacket for winter, unzipped because I'm worked up after an entire day of running around the field and training grounds, catering to the needs—small and large—of overgrown, muscular babies. I turn my face up to the sun, closing my eyes behind my sunglasses like I'm at the beach and not sitting in a terrace patio, surrounded by tall buildings and with cars blowing invisible plumes of smoke nearby.

Even then, this is the most relaxed I've been in weeks. Maybe it's best if this guy doesn't show up after all.

"Excuse me, are you still waiting for someone?" a woman asks beside me.

I pop an eye open and barely manage to stifle a sigh at the impatience of the waitress. She glances over her shoulder and I follow her line of sight to the big group of banker looking dudes waiting at the door to be seated. The fact that they look like carbon copies of Mitch makes me grind my molars, a reminder of last year's disastrous Thanksgiving and how I basically lost my entire group of friends in one fell swoop.

The waitress is still waiting for an answer, though. I lift my phone off the table and notice that I've been waiting just over an hour like a fool. There's no way that freaking jerk is showing up at this point.

"I guess not," I mutter, stuffing my phone in the pocket of my jacket and pushing the chair back to stand. I look around me and other than the glass of water she kept filling up, there are barely any vestiges that I was there at all. "Sorry that I didn't end up ordering anything."

As her expression softens with understanding and sudden sympathy, I decide that it's exactly how I'm going to treat this. As if I was never here.

Leaving her to tidy up, I weave through the narrow space between tables occupied by people using this café as an office, or those who have already left their workplaces for a little happy hour. I approach the door where the money bros stand, and one of them smacks his buddy's arm and points at me with minus one hundred percent discretion.

"Pfff, I bet she's not even a real fan. Women just don't understand baseball."

Luckily for him, I'm too tired of men to deign him with an answer. However, I'm not above bumping against him with my shoulder, hard enough that it makes him stumble. I assume that his buddy's chuckles means that they know he deserved it.

My loose hair blows in the wind while I make my way around the block to the far too expensive parking lot where my Jeep's at. That's the most annoying part about this whole deal, the sheer amount of money I'm wasting on bad dates with guys who don't even want to feign interest. Because I've had to foot my half of the bill every single time, and the entire bill on the two other occasions where my dates excused themselves to use the restroom and never returned. Except for that one time when a good samaritan saved my derriere at a fancy restaurant.

I catch a glimpse of my face in the rearview mirror as I twist to fasten my seatbelt. The top looks like I'm pissed off, complete with wrinkles between my tight eyebrows and narrow eyes that promise murder. But my lips are twisted in an exaggerated pout like I'm a kid about to throw a tantrum.

I punch the steering wheel once—that's as far as I allow myself. Otherwise I start wallowing in how much of a failure I am at romance, having only had one boyfriend ever who dumped me because I was boring, and who then decided to start dating my former best friend.

"This needs some angry hard rock." I find a playlist on my phone and jam to it the entire way home.

*

Some half hour later, I survive the traffic and pull into the gated community of townhomes in Winter Park, which is its own city smack inside Orlando, and is one of the nicest areas to live in. The only reason I can afford this place is because I room with Rosalina Mena, the team's social media girl, and

Audrey Winters, who works in the public relations depart-ment. The latter knows the owner and got us a massive discount.

I park by the curb and while unplugging my phone, notice that I have a message from whatshisface. Swiping the screen to unlock the phone, I read the message once. Twice.

"Hijo de su madre!" I scream in the quiet of the cabin.

I saw you sitting outside and you're not really my type. GL.

And of course I can't message him back with anything colorful for wasting my time, because he already unmatched me.

"Argh." With that neanderthal war cry, I throw myself out of my car and stomp my way up the yard to the house. I fling the door open with so much strength that it slams against the wall, and I snarl again.

Audrey startles from the kitchen but her shoulders relax when she sees it's just me. From the living room, all Rose does is glance up from her phone for a moment before turning her attention back to scrolling.

"What's got your thong in a twist?" Audrey cocks an eyebrow as I stomp my way to take one of the barstools.

"I don't wear thongs, they're too uncomfortable," I say as if that was what mattered here. Groaning, I run my hands down my hair, messing it in the process, and drop my head on the counter. "Why are men?"

"That's a really good question."

"Ugh. I know, right?"

I need to say no more for both of them to surround me in a second.

"Is this grounds for an HR complaint?" Rose asks from the barstool on my left. "Because I have them on speed dial."

From my right, Audrey snaps her fingers. "I bet it's Rivera. That guy flirts with anything that smells good."

"That's true." I snort, because Lucky Rivera has even

flirted with *me*, and I'm clearly a defective sample of the female species. "But no, this isn't work related."

"Oh."

"Hmm."

They sound almost disappointed, the gossips.

This is why I didn't want to tell them—not because I fear that the whole team will find out. My roommates are a lot more discreet than I figured Starr would be, and I was wrong about that too.

I just don't want to deal with the pity that no doubt will reflect on their faces. And yet, I'm so out of my depth that I clearly need help.

With a deep breath, I plunge into the waters of honesty. "My ex boyfriend is dating my now ex best friend and I've been trying all the dating apps to find someone I can show off to them for the next Friendsgiving, but my success rate so far is minus one hundred." I say all of this with my face smushed against the counter marble, like the grown adult I am.

There's only silence right after, which is no bueno.

Lifting my head up by a fraction, I peek first at Rose who strokes her chin, deep in thought. Then at Audrey, whose arms are folded, her eyes glaring at the distance.

"Yeah, okay." The latter is the first one who breaks. "You're not gonna get any advice from me. All men suck, no exceptions."

"My dad doesn't suck," I mumble and at the last second add, "but my brother does, yeah."

"I think your plan is flawless." Both Audrey and I fully turn to face Rose and she shrugs. "I mean, you're not actively hurting them by smearing them online or anything. You just want to show that you've moved on and are happier than ever with a new beau. There's nothing wrong in that."

"Ew, don't say Beau." I scrunch up my face at the thought

of me dating Rob Beau, the manager of the team. Last I checked he was still married to his wife of thirty years.

Rose rolls her dark eyes. "You know exactly what I mean."

"But her plan can't be quite as flawless as you imply if she looks this miserable," Audrey whispers every word carefully, as if I couldn't hear her because she's literally at arm's length.

With a great huff, I lean back on my seat. "Yeah, the flaw is men."

"Word."

"Totally."

"Or..." I cringe so hard that I my own shoulders rise to my ears. "The flaw is me."

"Absolutely not!" Rose smacks the counter hard enough that she hisses and cradles her hand close to her chest.

Audrey nods. "I agree. You're smart, driven, with a little accent that no doubt drives them wild, and super hot."

"Sure, I work out," I retort in a deadpan. "But I don't have the lithe body of a ballerina. I look like a weightlifter because that's what I am."

"Listen, I wish I had your tiny waist and huge butt without sweating half as much." She nudges me with her elbow.

"I'm partial to your arms," Rose says, wrapping her hand around my bicep through my jacket. "They have zero jiggle. I really envy that."

"I think men like some jiggle," I say, shrugging. "At least on account of how little they like me. Or maybe the issue isn't my body but me. After all, according to my ex I'm really boring to talk to."

"Where's all this negative self talk coming from, girlie?"

Another pathetic sound expels from my chest, but I respond to Audrey's question with the truth and nothing but the truth—abridged version. I touch on how Dawson was the only guy at college who looked past my muscles to the feminine side of me, up until it suddenly wasn't enough.

Aside from that, I include highlights from the dating apps like what just happened tonight—they also release cavewoman sounds once I show them the last message I got from tonight's would-be-date—to the one time a guy straight up ended the date after saying I could probably benchpress him, and the jerks who left me to pick up the whole tabs.

I'm so incensed that I keep running my mouth and say, "And the worst part is that Cade freaking Starr saw one of those go down. The humiliation was so strong, I even acted like a douche later and now I can't possibly face him ever again." I throw my hands in the air. "I'm sick and tired of men. I should quit my job and go work at a woman's college basketball team."

Rose grabs both of my shoulders, making my barstool swivel so I can face her. She's the more touchy feely of them two, which might be due to the familiarity of both of us being Venezuelan, even though we're not related. "I have an idea but I need you to really listen to it before you react."

"Go for it, at this point I'm desperate," I whine.

"Clearly both Audrey and I think you're amazing and short of giving you a little makeover, I don't think we can show you how to do much better at dating."

"Especially when neither of us are experts in the matter," Audrey says behind me.

Rose wrinkles her nose. She's the only one in this house who has game. Men flock to her gorgeous smile wherever she goes, and she dates enough of them to keep herself entertained. The problem is that she only has two kinds of stories to tell from this: horror ones, or tear-inducing ones. It puts her firmly on the same camp of what-is-wrong-with-men that Audrey and I belong to.

"Right. So I think you can benefit from an expert." Rose interrupts herself to press her lips in a clear sign of discomfort.

"And by that I mean, someone who can really give you insights from the male perspective."

I scrunch up my face. "So, a guy?"

"And not just any guy—one with such sex appeal that one little interview has gone viral and is resulting in thousands of marriage proposals from women on the internet."

"What?"

Behind me, Audrey starts chuckling. "Oh, that's genius."

"I'm gonna need you to spell it out for me," I say instead.

All that gets me is Rosalina's cellphone in my face, showing a quick little TikTok where Cade Starr talks about his ideal woman being someone who keeps it real or whatever. That sounds like a load of bull manure to me, because he's basically describing the half of the population who aren't like my former friends.

And then it hits me.

I jump from my barstool. "No way. I'm not asking Cade Starr for help."

"Think about it," Rose continues calmly. "You're probably going about this too tense because you have a deadline and all. Maybe what you really need is to know what to say to guys to get them to go on dates with you, and then what to say during said dates."

"Let's say you're right about that," I start, folding my arms and jutting my lower lip out. "But Starr is still the wrong guy for this. He doesn't have to go on dating apps to find an Annie for the night."

"Which is what makes him perfect because…" Her lips curl into an evil smile that paralyzes me. "He's the right person to turn you into the female version of him. No more apps. Just men flocking to you. You taking your pick. Doesn't that sound amazing?"

Audrey hums from her throat. "That does sound ideal."

I hug myself even tighter and say nothing. I don't have to.

We all know I agree with that. I've been making this monumental effort to put myself out there with randos from the internet for three months. Nine more of this would finish snuffing the spark of life from me.

But seriously, Cade Starr? The guy whose eyes I can't even meet because I'm so embarrassed?

Why couldn't Logan Kim be the one who went viral? He's a pretty decent guy who wouldn't tease the shit out of me.

Except… Starr didn't really mock me after the incident, did he? He seemed set on taking it to the grave until I made a big deal about it. In that regard, he's way better than most of the other guys in the team.

And it's also true that he turns heads wherever he goes. I've literally seen him stroll into some bar along with a flock of other fit men from the team, and be the only one swarmed by local women. It used to make Ben Williams, our former starter pitcher, gnash his teeth with open jealousy.

I picture myself being surrounded by men interested in me and—whew, it sounds terrifying. But at least I wouldn't be working so damn hard to find a decent one.

"Fine," I spit out as if the prospect of accomplishing my mission didn't make me want to barf. "Let's see if he even agrees to this little scheme."

CHAPTER 6
CADE

I stop in my tracks to yawn so hard that my jaw makes a popping sound. I rub my eyes, trying to clear the second wave of sleepiness that wants to crash over me thanks to my disrupted morning. Finally, I take the last step to hop on the treadmill to warm up.

Usually I catch the sunrise above the roofs of fancy ass houses while jogging around my neighborhood. My neighbor two houses down is this power suit middle-aged man, who usually walks his dog at a similar time. I say hey, he says hey back, and we ignore each other every other time we bump into the other again. Often, I also see this young mom jogging with her baby in a carrier. She always wears headphones and doesn't even go as far as power suit dude to say hey—straight up ignores me. It's a perfect arrangement for everyone involved.

Not today. Or yesterday.

Both days, I left my house in my training clothes, ready to do my circuit around the lake, and saw an unknown woman stretching around the corner.

That's not a big deal until the strange woman starts following you.

At first I thought I was being weird. Pfff, a woman, stalking *me*? What the hell for? I'm not a Hollywood star or even a household name in the league. I go to places in town and the vast majority of people don't recognize me. In fact, the handful who do are usually male baseball fans of the kind who can recall verbatim what my average was last year, the year before, and even in my last year in the minors. Even I don't know that shit, so we both get to enjoy flattering each other.

But women only ever approach me because I'm decent looking, and usually when they're imbued by liquid courage at a bar.

So I ignored her yesterday and finished my route. Except she was there again this morning, same spot, and with another friend. And this time, they were brave enough to make sure that I knew they were watching me. I've seen enough weird ish happen to other players to not chance it, so I made a stellar U-turn back into my house, grabbed my duffel bag and came over to the team facilities to train indoors instead.

I set a good pace on the treadmill and sigh, already missing the fresh air and natural light. But at least there are no weird women here.

Steps echo behind me. It's before seven and the place was empty until this point, but I wouldn't be surprised if staff starts arriving now. What is surprising is that the other person to join me is none other than Hope Garcia, and that she hops on the treadmill right beside mine.

Never mind, there *are* weird women here.

"G'morning, darlin'," I say with a voice raspy from disuse, but amused that I seem to have summoned her with my thoughts.

"Cowboy." She tips her head at me as if she was wearing a cowboy hat, and sets out on a jog. I kinda wonder why she chose the treadmill beside me and not one of the other dozen or so, but I'm not curious enough to ask.

For a peaceful moment, the only sounds come from our heavy steps falling out of sync and our breathing that turns heavier the more we increase speed, and in my case incline. I catch a little beep that comes from her bumping up her speed one more notch, and before I know what I'm doing, I do the same. Her eyes zero in on it, then on my face, and they glint like honey against the sunlight that hits us through the window. I'd never noticed that her eyes are so big or that maybe I should've nicknamed her honey instead of darlin'.

She snaps me out of that reverie by turning up her speed one more point.

My jaw slacks. Are we competing right now? Because if so, it's futile for her.

I run every morning just to wake up, and my actual workout follows after that depending on what I'm supposed to focus on each day. Today is leg day, and I'm happy to go harder at the run. I turn up the speed by several levels and give her a quick look that clearly says *stop trying to mess with me, darlin'*. I wish I could say it aloud but my lungs are busy.

Her eyes narrow and she jams a stubborn finger at the control buttons, speeding up until she's running like a gazelle. Her mouth arcs with stubbornness even as her nostrils flare with breathing that's as hard as a truck.

I snort a laugh.

We keep running like we're behind, bases loaded, bottom of the ninth, and we just batted a hit that could decide whether we win the World Series. However, we end up running the distance around the diamond several times over. I'm winded but I could keep going at more or less the same pace if I had to. Garcia finally gives it up and once she starts slowing down is when I follow suit.

"Breathe through your nose and not you mouth, darlin'."

I'm panting like a dog but still land the sarcasm, if I go by her glare.

She's on firm ground now, hands on her knees as she catches her breath. "It's your fault."

I resist the urge to snort again. I slow the machine all the way until I can step down. Reaching for two clean towels from the basket, I ask, "How so?"

"You kept turning up your speed!"

"So did you." I toss a towel so it lands over her head, casually drying my face with the other one while I watch her struggle with the cloth.

"Ugh, you're insufferable. Here I was working up my nerve to apologize."

I stop. "What?"

She huffs so hard that it makes her sound like a horse. Yanking the towel around her neck, and with a frown as deep as the Gulf, she says, "I'm sorry for being such a weirdo the other day when clearly you were just being nice about my horrible date."

For a moment, I don't react. Then I start blinking hard. "Huh. Okay."

Garcia presses her lips together, nods to herself, and swivels on her heels. After three steps away, she repeats the motion and comes back—closer than before. I jerk away in surprise.

"What now?"

She narrows her eyes up at me and shakes her head before leaning back. "No, nothing." I almost think this is the end of today's interaction with her, when she speaks again. "Actually, there's one more thing. I, uh… I have something of a wild pitch for you."

"Okay…?" My eyebrows rise.

"Wouldyoubemydatingcoach?"

"What?" I do a double take as if that could help me understand the weird barrage of words that spewed out of her mouth.

Garcia takes a deep breath. "Would you be my dating coach?"

It turns out I did understand her words, even if they make no sense.

"If he won't, I will."

We both turn to the third voice and have the opposite reactions. I relax seeing Lucky stride into the training room in his black joggers and a T-shirt with the flag of Puerto Rico emblazoned across his chest like graffiti. Garcia tenses instead.

He and I shake our hands, complete with fist bumps to our backs, and he turns to her. "But what do you need a dating coach for? Like, no offense but estás dura." I've heard him say this expression to women enough times to know it's a compliment.

If anything, it seems to make her more sour. "Can you please pretend like you heard nothing?"

We both know that's not gonna happen, though.

Lucky confirms this. "No can do, this sounds like way too much fun to pass up."

"Should I pretend I heard nothing?" I ask, shaking my head in confusion. "Because I have questions yet honestly don't need the answers."

Garcia ignores me. "Rivera, I feel like it's very pertinent for you to know that I worked part time at a steakhouse for a while when I was in college."

"What does that have to do with you wanting a dating coach?" He frowns.

"That I know how to use a knife on meat very well, and you'll discover that firsthand if anyone finds out about this."

Silence.

Slowly, he raises his hands and starts backing away. "I guess this conversation never happened, then?"

"That's right." She folds her arms and jerks her head, conveying that he should go away *or else*. And sure enough, dude backs the hell off to the treadmill on the opposite end. Her attention turns back to me and I kind of wonder if maybe I should've just put up with the stalker instead.

I spread my feet wide and stand straight. "No."

"Why not?" she whines.

"Why yes?" I run my hand through my damp hair.

"Because you got the dating thing down pat—"

I cut her off before she continues. "When have you seen me with a girlfriend?"

Garcia waves that away with her hand. "You're a smooth talker and women flock to you without even making an effort, which is exactly what I need."

"Oh, so you want women to flock to you? I didn't know you batted that way."

"I do not." Her brow darkens even further. "What I want is the equivalent. Men flocking to me without me having to suffer so much for bread crumbs of attention."

I hum from deep in my throat, considering all this random information that I didn't have on my bingo card. "I still don't think I'm the right person for the job, especially because I don't want to."

"Yes, you are! You just said noncommittal things to Rose and that video has gone viral. Thousands of women on the internet want your babies." Her hand closes in a tiny but powerful fist and she adds, "I need some of that."

My little jock brain puts two and two. This must be why I've suddenly earned a stalker.

I scrunch up my face. "Wait, what? Women want my babies and you want some of that?"

"No!" The horror in her face almost makes me laugh. I have to stuff my hand against my mouth to stop myself. "What I want is some of your easy charm."

"So I have charm," I repeat, cocking an eyebrow.

"Do not make me find my steak knife."

"Still no." I sidestep her, swinging my towel around my neck and holding onto the ends, heading to the mats to start some lunges.

"I'll pay you," she says, following right behind.

"The Orlando Wild organization pays me a pretty fair compensation already," I toss over my shoulder.

The hardheaded woman persists. "I'll do your laundry."

"You really don't want to do that."

All the way across the room, Lucky says, "Word."

"I'll ice you before everybody else."

"That will get you in trouble with your boss." I whirl around and she stops in her tracks an inch before colliding against me. She has to crane her neck back to look up at my face. I lower my voice so the eavesdropper doesn't hear. "Listen, you don't need any help, least of all mine. The right guy will come along when you least expect it."

"I don't need 'the right guy,'" she says with air quotes, startling me even though I school my face not to show it. "What I need is options and I need them quick."

I take a giant step away. "I still can't help you. I don't know if you've heard but something called Spring Training starts in a week and I'll be busy with it."

"But—"

"Good luck, darlin'." I toss my towel to a hamper basket and get in position.

To my surprise, instead of insisting once more, Garcia expels a breath that deflates her shoulders and walks away toward the weights wall. I watch her for just another second, wondering if she'll come back to keep pleading her case, and I'm oddly disappointed that she doesn't.

CHAPTER 7
HOPE

I am what anyone would consider a morning person. My alarm goes off at five thirty every morning and I'm ready to eat the world—or my stomach is. I'm in and out of the bathroom in five minutes, do a high-intensity interval training in my bedroom, shower in another five minutes, and make a protein shake or veggie smoothie that I can drink on the way to work.

Not today. Today I wake up rolling on my bed like a panda, and looking like one too. All thanks to a late night conversation with a dating prospect that stalled at three in the morning, and then the jerk unmatched me with no warning.

I'm not in and out of the restroom in five minutes. In fact, when I emerge from brushing my teeth, I can't even fathom the thought of sweating. I skip the shower, skip the healthy smoothie, and instead grab a breakfast burrito from the canteen at work. Maybe I shouldn't have stayed up so late for a jerk when today is day one of Spring Training. I hate it when there are consequences to my own actions.

"Good mor—" The words die in Steve's mouth once he takes one look at the dark circles around my eyes. He takes one giant step back. "If you're coming down with something you need to stay home."

"I'm not sick. I stayed out late uh, reading." He doesn't need to know it was text messages and not something more erudite.

"Oh." My boss's entire body language shifts back to the easy going vibe he first walked into the prep room with. "The good news is that you'll be able to take a nap on the bus later. How's prep going?"

My burrito wrapper lays discarded on a table that is otherwise full of snacks and drinks I've categorized by player. The nutrition team takes care of planning their main meals and managing player's health, but I'm tasked with making sure their before, during, and after game snacks are on point. It's always tricky because one guy loves strawberry flavors but hates other berries, another guy is the opposite, or you have the ones who only accept one brand and straight up won't even open another one. Plus allergies, intolerances and plain boredom. They riot if I give them the same snack two times in a row.

"Almost done," I respond, resisting the urge to sweep my arm over the table where I have pouches with player names emblazoned to hold protein bars, protein chips, and bottles with electrolyte drinks. On a different topic, I add, "I also got the trunks ready."

The trunks are packed with all the equipment we need to help players stretch and warm up, tape them up, ice them, stave off pain, and make splints with. They're also picky about which brand of muscle pain relievers they like, so I keep a stock of everything that exists under the sun is FDA approved.

Otto, my coworker, strides in a whole fifteen minutes late and gets a handshake from Steve rather than a scolding. He takes a look at all the work I've done and opens his mouth. "Looking great. Any snackies for me?"

"Help yourself." I offer what I hope is a casual smile but make sure to point at the fridge with my index and not middle finger, as I'd have preferred. I'm paid to take care of athletes, not him.

"Aww, Hope. You should be more of a team player and get something for staff too." Sighing as if this is the end of the world, he drags his ass toward the fridge to poke his head in there. Unfortunately he keeps using his mouth. "After all, it's such a long drive to Clearwater."

I turn my back on him to start collecting all the pouches and put them in a massive cooler on wheels, muttering, "It's barely over two hours."

Steve probably hears this because he clears his throat. "Anyway, where's everyone else?"

"Dom and Jimmy took up some of the trunks to the buses," I answer.

"Great. Otto and I will take the rest. Do you have this covered?" Steve points at the snacks.

"Yep, I got it."

My mood improves just a notch when both of them wheel the rest of the trunks out of the prep room, and I can keep working in peace and quiet.

Unfortunately my mind destroys any such notion when it reminds me again of the douche from last night, and how suddenly Otto has a bit of a point. A two-hour drive all the way down I-4 on a bus full of men sounds like a horrible nightmare. I wish I was back home, snuggled in my bed and making up for all the time I wasted on a random guy who didn't deserve it.

Alas, I drag my feet and the cooler behind me all the way out to the parking lot. The sun has no right to be as bright as it is today, and after a quick pat down of my pockets I come up empty for sunglasses.

"Great." This day can't possibly get worse, can it?

"Whoa, what's up with that grumpy raccoon face?" The obnoxious voice of one shortstop by the name of Lucas "Lucky" Rivera comes from the left. Worse, he's joined by his buddy, Cade "Cowboy" Starr.

I stare at him. "I prefer panda face."

"You're not sick, are you?" Starr asks.

"No," I grouch.

"Then what's up, Garcia?" Rivera points at me with his chin. "We don't need that bad juju to start Spring Training, you know?"

"It's not bad juju, it's just men." I huff and wave a hand toward the bus. "Anyway, hop on. We don't have all day." Other players and staff members bypass us on their way to the nearest team bus or the ones farther back.

"Ah. So this is about the dating issues again," Rivera says with a Mr. Miyagi nod and stroke of his imaginary beard.

There's plenty of loud chatter around us that I hope has covered his words. But just in case, I ask, "Did you forget about my steak knives?"

Rivera's eyebrows take off into the sky. "You know what, until this very moment I had."

"Let's go, you jerk." Starr puts a big paw on his friend's shoulder, trying to steer him away.

However, the Boricua seems to have other plans. He plants himself firmly and folds his arms. "Listen, my offer still stands. I can definitely help you with that issue."

And I guess I must be so out of sorts between the poor sleep and the anger roiling in my gut, that for a second I contemplate it.

Honestly, it doesn't have to be Starr who coaches me into successful dating. He's right in that we've barely ever seen him with the same woman twice. But Rivera had a solid girlfriend a couple of years back.

I mirror his exact stance down to the wide feet. "Okay, what do you have in mind?"

Slowly his lips curve into a little smirk that has the odd effect of making me want to punch his face. "Date me instead. I can treat you right."

"That's it," Starr announces and grabs a whole fistful of Rivera's shirt and hauls him away. "One more word out of your yap and I'll be a witness against you in the harassment lawsuit."

I snort through my nose.

Rivera gesticulates wide with his hands as he gets dragged to the bus. "I'm just trying to help, man."

The pitcher pushes him into the bus and right as he climbs the first step, Starr stops to glance back at me over his shoulder. The bill of his cap casts a pretty prominent shadow across his face, but I can still tell that he's studying me like I'm the batter for a rival team. He shakes his head and finally hops on the bus.

¿Qué diantres fue eso?

I file that one away to replay it in my head whenever I manage to land my head on a pillow again. For now, I take a seat on the cooler and wait until the team is fully boarded before I start my little round.

I check my list with the seating chart and take a grocery bag from the cooler, stuffed with the snacks for the players in the third bus. It takes about ten minutes to distribute them to everyone and I rinse and repeat with the next, and finally with the last bus. My eyes immediately fall on the two stooges, Starr and Rivera, sitting together toward the back, and I'm immensely glad that my seat isn't on this one.

"Kim," I call our main catcher's name and toss his snack pouch at him. He catches it easily, which is apropos.

"Miller." Snacks go to our first baseman.

"O'Brian." Another one to the right fielder. I keep going until I make it to the back.

"Rivera," I say in the most deadpanned way possible. This time he's more excited about the prospect of food and drink than on teasing me.

I reach into the shopping bag for one of the last pouches. Since Starr is right beside me, instead of tossing it I just dangle it on his face. "Starr."

He plucks it from my hand and I move away to reach the last three guys at the back. But suddenly a big, calloused hand wraps around my wrist and I freeze.

Turning my face, I stay still as Starr puts his snacks between his thighs and reaches into his pocket with his free hand. I try pulling at my wrist but his grip tightens enough to prohibit it, but not to hurt.

Then he produces a piece of paper from his pocket and slips it into my hand, finally releasing me, and tackling his snack as if nothing happened. I blink at the top of his purple cap with the Orlando Wild logo in yellow.

Somehow my body doesn't betray me. I stick my hand back in the grocery bag and dump the note, grabbing the next snack pouch to finish my job here. And luck is finally on my side because the last three guys have their full attention on a single iPad that is playing who knows what, and they barely even notice I'm trying to feed them.

I keep my eyes toward the front of the bus as I make my way out. There are no sassy comments from anyone, which means that really no one saw that. My heart hammering in my throat is the only vestige of what just happened.

And why the hell is it even working that hard? Yeah, it was surprising. But c'mon, it's not my first time a guy touches me. *It's just been a long while,* I think once I take my seat a row right behind my boss.

I unwrap the plastic bag from around my fist and stretch it

out. The note is crumpled up inside. After a quick glance around, confirming that literally no one gives a fudge about what I'm doing, I take it out and spread it open.

Let's talk about this after the game.

That's it. Not even a signature.

I fold it back up and face the window, racking my brain. Talk about what? What is the *this* he's referring to? Does he have a complaint about my snacks? No—I guess he'd broach that openly during office hours.

Then what? Is he truly worried I'll sue Rivera for kind of asking me out?

Or… I rest my elbow against the edge of the window, and jam my fist against my mouth. Has he changed his mind about being my dating coach? Did I look pathetic enough this morning?

Great, now I have to wait the two hours plus of the bus drive, another couple of warmups before the game, and then some three hours of playing ball before I can get my answers.

CHAPTER 8
CADE

A hand falls on my shoulder and stops me right as I intend to climb out of the dugout. "Hold on, son."

I turn to Rob Beau, our manager, and he motions me to the corner, so we can let a couple of the outfielders out. Beau folds his arms, and the coarse nylon fabric of his purple and yellow team jacket crinkles audibly. I fiddle with my cap while he observes me in complete silence, only chewing gum like a cow eating pasture.

"The trainers tell me you're in top condition."

"I feel good." Immediately the old timey song starts playing in my head.

His head jerks in a nod. "Good. But no cutters today."

The song comes to a scratching halt in my mind. "But—"

"It's still not refined enough and I'm hoping it can be a real weapon when it counts." He points a firm finger at my face. "No cutters today, Starr. Am I clear?"

"Yes, sir." I sigh in my heart—can't show anything else but obedience to the boss on the outside.

"Now, go out there and do some damage." He pats my

shoulder strong enough that it forces me to pivot back to the exit.

I let the momentum keep me going until I emerge into the sun. It's funny how out here the atmosphere is drastically different. The shade of the dugout right before the game starts is a crush of people trying to do last-minute things, setting up equipment, doing some stretching, saying prayers, talking strategy, watching film on iPads, even spraying on sunblock.

Outside, the sun blares bright and hot right above the field, and the perimeter is packed with fans from either team watching your every move. All the anxious energy inside the dugout turns into real pressure out here.

And I live for it… because I'm a massive weirdo.

"I don't like the look on your face," Logan Kim says as I approach the mound, where he's waiting for me. The Orlando Wild doesn't have an official captain but if we did, it'd be this asshole.

"Well, I don't like your face," I spit right out without much bite.

His mouth twists in annoyance. "You're too calm. Why is that? I don't like it."

I bend my glove against my chest, trying to soften it up after traveling inside a duffel bag. As response, I shrug and say, "Would you rather see me freaking the hell out or what?"

"Are you? Secretly freaking out, I mean?" He narrows his all-seeing eyes at me and gives me the same studious look as Beau.

"No." I blink real slow. "It's game one of Spring Training, there's no reason to panic. Besides…" I lift my glove to cover the lower half of my face. "No offense to the Sacramento Badgers, but they're not necessarily the hardest team to play."

Kim hums from deep in his throat and gives me a side eye. "I like this even less. I'd rather see you nervous than underestimating your opponent."

I tip my head toward the the home plate. "I'd love to keep chatting about our feelings but the umpire's giving us the stink eye."

"Get more tense, Cowboy. The last thing I want is for you to give this game away to one of the weakest teams in the league."

"Me?" I gasp in mock outrage.

"Yeah, *you*. Don't forget that we're starting you because we're shit out of luck."

I bob my head. "True, now that the great Ben Williams is gone we don't have a superstar pitcher. But guess what?"

"Don't say it." His expression tightens.

I still say it. "We have a Starr now."

"I hate you." Kim turns around and stalks away to home.

I hide the grin on my face behind my glove, not just because I don't want the Badgers to see that I'm not too concerned about them, but because I probably look like a possum baring its teeth.

Kim exchanges a few words with the umpire before lowering his mask on his face. The leadoff batter walks up to the plate and the umpire shouts, "Play ball!"

The crowd gets a bit rowdy and it makes my limbs tingle. It's really hard to feel tense or worried when I'm bursting at the seams with happiness. This is my freaking dream come true, to be a starting pitcher for the team. This is what I've been working for since the moment my middle school teachers figured out the only thing I was good for was playing baseball.

Kim signals for an easy fastball and I nod. There's no point in overthinking the very first pitch of game one, and the pitching clock is ticking. I make the kind of windup I'm most comfortable with, big and flashy, hiding my pitching hand behind my head, and release the ball right at the last second.

"Strike!"

The batter goes through the motions of sweeping the dirt

with his cleat and Kim returns the ball to me with a bit more strength than necessary. I can feel it convey a 'don't you get complacent' message as it thuds against the palm of my glove. What he doesn't know is that I'm giving him the middle finger inside my glove. Just keeping it PG for the little fans out there in the stands.

This time when he crouches, he calls for an easy curve that should fool no one. I guess we want to give some action to the infielders, and that's cool by me when we have no runners. The Badgers aren't known for power hitting either, so I nod once and position the ball in my glove for a run off the mill 12-6.

"Strike!"

That fell perfectly at the bottom of the strike zone, where the batter could've at least swung. He didn't even try, so either the guy is paralyzed by fear, or… the Badgers are just watching me.

Bleh, so this is why I can't do cutters.

A third strike is called after another curveball and I lift my index finger so everyone in the field can see we have one out.

"C'mon, give me some sugar," Rivera calls out from close to third base.

From first base, Miller says, "Give me something to justify my salary."

Even the guys in the outfield make some noise, urging the game to be more interesting than this. But the inning ends just like that, three outs and no runners on base. The stands are fairly quiet as we head over to the dugout.

"Good job," says Larry Socci, the pitching coach. "Looking good out there, Starr."

"It's just the new pants," I joke as I walk by him, producing a snort in reward. I grab the nearest free iPad I can find and before I can even fire it up, a big paw snatches it from me.

One obnoxious catcher drops right next to me. He taps at the iPad not to look at my pitching form, like I intended, but to zoom in on the batters. A crease appears between Kim's eyebrows for a moment until it finally clears. He tosses the device at me and I catch it in the air.

"What?" I ask.

"They're not studying you. They're just bad." He leans back against the wall and folds his arms.

"How do you know?"

He snorts. "They all reacted." Apparently that's all he means to say.

I prod him with "I need a few more words than that, you caveman."

"The Badgers don't have the balls to swing big but they twitched at every one of your pitches. If they were just watching, they wouldn't have even blinked."

"Meaning…"

"Your balls are enough." He nods to himself, not seeing the problem with his words.

I suck in air through my teeth. "Really trying not to quip with a that's-what-she-said joke here."

We both get jerked out of our riveting conversation at the unmistakable crack of a bat. Rushing to the barrier, we join the team to watch Rivera's first hit—no. A home run?

"Asshole," Kim mumbles. "Should've saved that for a bases loaded situation."

"No complaints from me." I nod all magnanimous as the ball finally lands on the grass behind the outfield fence. A few fans abandon their picnic blankets in pursuit of the home run ball.

"Yeah!"

"That's right, baby!"

"Rivera, you beast!"

More hoots and hollers come from the dugout, almost competing with the noise from the stands. The Boricua raises a fist as he jogs around the diamond, stopping to step on the bases in a very deliberate way. Last season, an umpire ruled he hadn't stepped on third base and therefore didn't score the run. He's probably still annoyed by that.

"And *that's* how it's done, lady and gentlemen." Rivera strikes a tough macho pose with his arms as he approaches, and it takes a second for my brain to click.

Lady? I glance over my shoulder and spot Hope Garcia coming out from the tunnel. She's wheeling a trunk that looks big enough to fit me inside, but doesn't seem to struggle with it. And of course she wouldn't, when her thighs are so sculpted that I can see her muscles ripple beneath the white fabric of her clothes. Has no one thought that maybe she should be allowed to wear different pants?

She notices me watching and for a brief second I'm annoyed to be caught.

I swivel my attention back to the front. While our second batter steps up to the plate, a couple of staff members remove the gear from Kim's legs and chest. He's our best batter and that, plus his catcher acumen, make him absolutely insufferable. I really have to solidify myself as *the* starter pitcher of the team so I can shut him up.

"Do you have it?" one of the guys asks behind me.

Garcia's voice responds with, "Tall glass of Bengay coming right up."

Annoying chuckles come after that. I peek over my shoulder again, this time as she's lathering up someone's bare shoulder. It's way too early in the game for that shit, but it's none of my business. At least she's wearing gloves.

The ball hits at another good angle and the sound gets my attention again. Our third batter is taking off to first base and gets there safe, right in time for Kim to walk up to the plate and get the crowd surging with excitement. I smirk as he misses the first ball by a mile, but he hits the second pitch hard enough that it almost goes over the fence. As the outfield rallies, our third batter makes it all the way home and Kim to second base.

"Yep, the Badgers suck," I mumble to myself.

The Orlando Wild, as a team, is decent. We don't have a star studded lineup now that Williams has deserted—aside from our catcher, I guess—but even with the two of them as a battery, we still fell short of the postseason last year. I'm not really used to the power dynamic we have in this game.

Yet, we end our first inning up by three runs. I shut them out in the next inning, and we score one more run with the middle of our batting lineup. I concede a couple of hits in the third inning that get our infielders running wild, one of them ending with a double play that will make the social media highlights. Kim runs me through a combination of fastballs that include some nasty ones close to the batter's chest, and also an array of curves that produce a few more hits. Sweat trickles down my face and my spine, more because of the sun than from the game itself.

However, I don't know if it fools Beau because as I walk to the dugout after the sixth inning, he declares, "Starr, you're done for the day. Get iced."

I open my mouth. Close it. There's no point in arguing with the man, and even if I didn't pull any spectacular plays that can secure my spot in the roster, it was a decent showing.

"Yes, sir."

"G'job, Cowboy." Rivera pats my back as I walk deeper into the bench.

More pats and similar words are tossed my way. I'm glad this inning starts with Kim's at bat because one look at my mug, and he'd be able to tell I'm disappointed.

I plop on the bench, finally releasing a heavy sigh.

"Shirt."

Garcia looms over me with the shoulder ice pack in her hands.

"Gee, darlin'. At least buy me dinner," I deadpan but still make quick work of my shirt buttons. I dig for the seam of my compression undershirt and peel it off over my head, tossing the yellow garment on top of the purple shirt.

Rolling her eyes at me, she says, "I probably couldn't afford it."

I slide my arm into the opening of the ice pack and hold still as she fastens it, first around my arm, then grabbing the loose strap that goes around my chest. She leans closer to circle the strap around me and I keep my eyes firmly on my lap because I'm a damn gentleman—who still can't help but notice that she smells like vanilla and something else. Something that should be bottled up and sold for top dollar. My traitorous nostrils expand to catch one last whiff of it as she steps away.

"Any discomfort anywhere?" she asks. I lift my eyes slowly, first stopping at her waist, where her hands rest, finally making one quick swoop up to her face.

"Nope." I pop the p with gusto.

"Hungry?"

Since I'm a well-trained dog, my stomach gurgles loud enough that I needn't answer verbally. I grin as Garcia cringes.

"Wow, okay. Gourmet snack coming right up." Her pony-tail swishes as she turns to dig in one of her trunks.

Meanwhile, the team rotates back to defensive positions. I watch as Thomason, another relief pitcher, takes to the field. Or maybe I shouldn't say another, because right now I'm not one and I'm manifesting that it stays that way. Thomason is a good kid, straight out of the minors, but not among the top of our pitching staff. I have no idea what Beau and Socci are thinking about, but the fielders are gonna be busier now.

"Here you go." Garcia's back next to me, offering a brown shake that does not look appetizing at all.

"Wow, looks better than a burger." Unfortunately that

makes my stomach roar again, and I have no choice but to start chugging the weird concoction.

She folds her arms. "So, you wanted to talk?"

I choke. Somehow I manage to not spew a brown deluge out of my guzzler, but keeping it in does make the recovery harder. The good news are that first, I don't die, and second, nobody seems to care about my close call. Everyone is focused on what's happening on the field. At least Garcia has the decency of handing me a towel to clean whatever spillage is on my face.

"Yes," I rasp out. "But not while I could die from it."

"Pitchers are such drama kings." She shakes her head slowly, clicking her tongue at the same time.

I grimace. "Shouldn't you be nicer if you're the one asking me for a favor?"

Her mouth opens. She takes a seat next to me and places her hands on her knees, all demure like. "Wait, does this mean you changed your mind?"

"Not quite." I make what I know is an obnoxious pause to drink some more of the protein shake. "I just have one question."

"Yes?" Her eyes open wide, shining with eagerness.

I slide farther from her because that whole energy's weird—much more eager than I'm equipped to handle. She slides closer again and I lean away.

"If Lucky hadn't tried to flirt with you, would you have taken him up as your dating coach or whatever?"

Garcia blinks several times and also leans away. "Yes, probably."

"So basically, anyone can do."

"Not anyone. It has to be someone who knows what they're doing."

"Don't you have friends for this?" I ask.

Something hardens her expression. "Not really. Not anymore."

Oof, there's a story there. Not that I care, but some weird shit has to happen for a woman to be desperate enough to find anyone to teach her about the dating world. And that's the problem—as much as I'd rather say no again because I have no skin in this game, she could end up with someone who has ulterior motives. Worse than Lucky, who's just a harmless flirt.

I rub my chin, feeling the rasp of facial hair. "Fine, let's talk again after the game."

"What? I've been waiting for this conversation for hours and you want me to suffer for longer? No, say it right now, Cowboy. Are you in, or not?" She presses her lips in a stubborn line and stabs her finger at the bench to punctuate her words.

I have a feeling the next one stabbed will be me if I don't finish this conversation now. After another swig of protein shake, I say, "Okay, I'll help you. But there are two conditions."

Her expression cracks and some panic seeps through. "I was actually kidding when I said I could pay you. I can barely afford rent and my student loans."

I ignore that and raise my index finger. "First, my priority is baseball, no matter what." Then I raise my middle finger. "And second, no falling for my southern charm and making this all awkward."

She sticks her tongue out in the universal expression of *yuck*. "That's easy."

"At least have the decency to look more heartbroken."

"I'm not one of your Annies, Cowboy."

I shudder. Unlike the stalker around my neighborhood, Garcia could probably catch up to me and tackle me to the ground.

She frowns. "Okay, no need to look so disgusted at the idea."

I bark a laugh. This time it does garner a few looks of

curiosity. Huffing, Garcia gets to her feet and strides over to her collection of equipment. When it's clear that I've been dismissed, I reach over for a discarded iPad to run through whatever film we got of my pitching while I finish up my drink. The coaches were right in not letting me throw any cutters today, especially because I don't have the form down pat yet. I'm trying to see if the cutter form has seeped through my normal one when a shadow descends over me.

It's Garcia again. She grabs my wrist and jerks my hand toward her, slapping a piece of paper on the palm of my hand before walking away. Confused, I rub it open and read.

We're not in middle school, you bonehead. Here's my phone number.

Smart girl that she is, she wrote it in pencil. The digits won't smear with my sweat once I stuff the note in my pocket. I temper my face to hide a smile and focus on the screen again.

CHAPTER 9
HOPE

The team won the first game and I have secured a dating coach. No one should blame me for dancing to some salsa in my hotel bathroom while I blow dry my hair. The cord stops me from doing a full spin, but I keep humming an old timey song I remember seeing my parents dance in the kitchen when I was a kid.

My clown of an ex used to make fun of me when I sang or danced from a tune playing in my head. At first either he made it seem like he was laughing with me, enjoying my joy out of the goodness of his heart—or that's simply what I wanted to believe all on my own. Thinking about that asshole, I dance even harder and work up a sweat even though I just showered.

"Whew." I shut off the dryer, leaving still a lot of wet hair to just air dry while I watch TV and order some room service.

We travel tomorrow morning bright and early to the next away game, which is going to be in the middle of Kansas. I have no doubt several of the players are going out to enjoy the nightlife of Clearwater, but I have zero desire to join them. What's in my future is salad and a brownie—a perfectly balanced menu—and HGTV.

I make an Olympic jump and release a little squeal at how much I bounce on the soft mattress. So what if I have the hotel's tiniest room with a twin bed because I'm the only woman who regularly travels with the team? At least I don't have to share with anyone stinky. And when Rose is allowed to travel with the team for certain games, where we do share rooms, I have no complaints because she's *not* stinky.

I paw around the bed until I find the remote and click the TV on. Right as I find the channel I want, my phone buzzes on my nightstand. After a brief moment of no further buzzing, I figure the text can wait and focus on the show with the cute twin brothers who flip houses. And then my phone buzzes again.

"Ugh." I drop my hand on the phone and pick it up.

ANNOYING COWBOY

Evening, darlin'

Would you like to start our lessons now?

I sit up straight, heart hammering in my throat.

ME

What?

NOW?

ANNOYING COWBOY

No time like the present

Come down to the lobby

ME

What if I had plans already?

ANNOYING COWBOY

If it was with anyone else you wouldn't need me

ME

With MYSELF

His three dots come and go several times until he sends a string of texts.

ANNOYING COWBOY

Oh

You're right

I shouldn't have assumed that wasn't a valid option

Good night

"Ugh!" I slap my forehead. I know I'm right in taking a stance. Even if we have a working arrangement, he needs to be considerate of my time too. But he is the one providing the favor, and I'm privy to his schedule and know we won't have another fairly chill night like tonight for about a week.

ME

Okay wait

I'll make an exception

After hitting send, I realize how much of a jerk I sound and I freeze. So does my brain, because apparently I can't think of a single thing to patch that up a bit.

ANNOYING COWBOY

See you in the lobby

Of course, this is when I realize that I'm in my sports bra and boy shorts, and I sincerely doubt Starr or anyone else will want to see that.

I bid a heartfelt goodbye to the television and turn it off to go in search of something to wear. I don't pack a lot of options because I'm not a fan of a heavy suitcase, and most of my clothes are official apparel, but I did bring a pair of faded boyfriend jeans and three basic tops from the GAP. White sneakers, wallet chained to my jeans, some chapstick, my phone and the room card, and I'm making my way down the elevator in record time. I tap my toe against the elevator's panel wall, urging it to go faster.

My limbs tingle with nerves because I have no idea what Starr has in store. He could either come outright to say that he's changed his mind and that I'm acting ridiculous and need to grow up—which, fair—or pull a worse move like standing me up just like some of the app dates have.

"Nah," I mumble to myself. "Starr seems more standup than I thought."

The elevator dings to signal the arrival and my heart seems to jump in my throat. A busy lobby at seven on a random Thursday night feels odd, like maybe what I expected was to find Cade Starr standing by himself waiting for me.

I step out and almost get ran over by a couple exiting the other elevator. The laughter of some dude bros gets my attention, but they're not any of the Wild players or staff so I ignore them. I sweep my eyes around, trying to find a cowboy-shaped pitcher, and instead spot our catcher at the reception. He's explaining something in that calm, measured way of his, but I don't think the receptionist is paying any attention to his words. She looks completely besotted at the sight of a Korean American baseball superstar with chiseled features and deep eyes. I'm so glad I didn't strike the coaching deal with Logan Kim, because maybe I'd look just like the receptionist.

"Over here."

My spine stiffens at the familiar voice with a twang. I veer left and it gets me out of the shade of some tall potted plants, and there's the cowboy. With the Boricua.

I stop, still with a whole yard between us. "This isn't an ambush, is it?"

"Of what kind?" Starr's eyebrows knot in confusion.

"Never mind, but what is the flirt doing here?" I gasp before answering my own question. "Don't tell me you brought him here to make me practice?"

"No, I was promised a beer in exchange for my presence," Rivera explains.

I stare at him for a long moment. "Oh yeah? Did the nutrition team approve that?"

"Well…"

Sighing, Starr says, "We're not in our turf. Anyone who sees the two of us alone might draw the wrong conclusions. Whereas three of us will look like friends."

"I don't think that show has held up well," a different voice adds from behind me. Logan Kim walks towards us, hands in the pockets of his jeans. His jaw length straight hair is half tucked behind one ear.

Rivera blows a raspberry. "Dude, no one's talking about the show."

"Then about what?" the catcher asks, standing next to me.

"Nunya."

"Oh is that your latest girlfriend?"

Meanwhile, Starr takes his phone out of his pocket. "Look at the time, it's I-want-to-get-the-hell-away-from-these-stooges o'clock."

I snort a laugh that somehow is what makes the other two stop their nonsensical conversation. Clearing my throat, I answer Kim's original question. "My uh, two buddies here and I are going out for a non alcoholic drink. Am I right?" And at this I level A Look at Rivera.

"Right." He jerks his head in a nod.

"Then I'll join," Kim declares. "I need to make sure this puppy of a pitcher stays out of trouble."

"What about me? Is it okay if I get in trouble?" Rivera puts a hand on his chest.

"Puppy?" Starr scrunches up his face but falls into step beside Kim. "Couldn't you say something more interesting like leopard cub? Or even a baby shark?"

As Rivera walks between them and drops his arms on their shoulders, saying, "I hate that song."

I rub my temples.

It's already pretty hard to have a conversation with Starr where I don't end up humiliated, but now with those two in tow this is a disaster waiting to happen.

"Aren't you coming, darlin'?"

I snap my head up. At some point, Starr fell back and is just a few feet from me, waiting. Kim and Rivera are already out the door, still visibly arguing about something I'm sure belongs to a comedy skit. Where's Rose to capture them at their silliest moments like this? As much as they annoy me, fans would love to hear their banter.

"Yeah, I'm coming."

We walk in blissful silence across the lobby until joining the other two. Rivera is still ribbing the fairly stoic catcher for sport, but Kim lobbies back some dry sarcasm that I can respect.

"So, here's my idea," Starr says beside me.

I finally look at him—really look at him. He's wearing a nondescript gray cap backwards, and a strand of smooth brown hair escapes from the hole to curl over his forehead. He's in a matching Henley, black jeans, and black high tops with white trims. The guy put zero effort into his look and still looks fresh out of a catalogue.

Oops, he's still talking. "—To see how you rate on the scale of good to bad."

"Huh?"

He stops and turns his eyes away from his teammates to

me. "You weren't paying any attention, were you?"

I open and close my mouth. Open it again. "I admit I got distracted." I'll never admit that it was by his fashion sense.

"Pay attention or I'll flunk you." He flips a strand of my loose hair with his fingers, which somehow makes the hair fly into my mouth. I'm too busy spitting it out to even consider any sort of revenge. "Anyway, as I was saying ever so patiently, we're going to a bar and I want you to find some dude there to flirt with."

I stop moving. "*What*?"

All three of them halt their steps too.

Starr rubs his freshly shaved chin. "You thought this was just going to be theoretical with no practical component?"

"I—Well… Kinda?"

"Fess up," the commanding voice of our catcher says. "What is it that you two are really up to?"

Points to Starr for clamming his mouth right away. But Kim is the nearest one in the team to the human version of a vault, and if Rivera hasn't told the four winds, Kim won't either. I wave my hand in the air to signal to Starr that it's okay to say it.

He jerks a thumb at me. "Garcia here asked for my help with dating."

"Why *your* help? You never keep the same girl around for long." Kim blinks as if confused. "Actually, none of the single guys in the team do."

"Yourself included?" Rivera nudges Kim with his elbow.

The latter shrugs. "Sure."

"Listen, beggars can't be choosers," I quip with a slow shake of my head.

"Ouch." Starr puts both hands above his heart.

"Plus," I add, "he went viral and now can't get a stick large enough to beat women off with. *That* is the energy I want, but with guys."

Kim scrunches up his face. "You don't want many men around you, trust me."

"That's what I said too," Starr chimes with.

"I know, men tend to suck, no offense—"

"None taken."

"Yeah, no. It's a fact."

I shake my head and finish saying, "But as a heterosexual woman, I'm shit out of luck."

"That's rough, friend," Rivera says in a heartfelt way as if he wasn't part of the population that makes dating so miserable.

"So what's the plan? Let's hear it." Kim jerks his chin at Starr.

The pitcher responds with a shrug and, "I just wanted to gauge what kind of game she has, see where I can advise. I want her to find a target, walk up to him, and talk him up until he gives her his number."

To my surprise, Kim doesn't shoot down the idea right away. "Not bad. And if the guy turns out to be a douchebag the three of us got her back."

"And that is the real reason I tagged along," Rivera says, expression all serious even though I don't know if I can believe him.

"But…" I desperately grasp at any way I could get myself out of this, and only come up with a flimsy argument. "I'm already not good at this. I'm going to be so much worse with an audience."

Starr cocks a supremely annoying eyebrow. "Didn't you admit to needing help? Because the next step is actually doing shit, you know?"

Damn it. It's like he knows exactly which buttons to poke. I may not be an elite athlete like them, but I sure am just as allergic to being seen as weak or cowardly.

"Fine, let's do this."

*

"Anyone yet?"

I nurse my unsweet iced tea closer to my chest and shake my head. The irony of the situation is not lost on me. The second the four of us walked in, half of the pairs of eyes zeroed in on the three tall, well-built ball players, and more particularly on the pitcher with the gem-colored eyes. Literally no one cast a second glance at me.

To add insult to injury, the three of them have stuck like velcro to me, pointedly ignoring the women who would have no qualms with chatting them up, but also ensuring that I don't run back to the hotel.

However, I am not a coward. I *can* be a failure, though.

Again, I make an attempt at spotting any candidates, but either the men are paired up or are in groups, and there's no way I'm walking up to a bunch of people to single one out and express my interest. I would simply become the first registered case of human combustion.

"Nope," I respond to Starr, popping the p the same way he did earlier.

Something in his expression suggests that he thinks I'm not trying hard enough.

"Cowboy, I'm pretty sure your eyes are way better than mine and can confirm that there are no single men in this place right now."

"How about red shirt in the bar?" he tosses right back.

All of us turn to the man. Luckily his back is to us, or he'd have freaked out at how creepy we look.

"He's sitting beside a buddy." I point at blue shirt next to him with my puckered lips.

"They're not friends," Kim says right away.

"Yeah, they haven't said a single word to each other since we walked in," adds Rivera.

"Oh." I bite my lip. "I genuinely hadn't noticed."

"Garcia." The fact that it's my last name and not his little nickname for me what comes out of Starr's mouth is what tells me he's serious. "No one's gonna force you to do this if you really don't want to. But you have to shed some of that fear if you want to make this work."

"I know." I scratch the top of my head and, taking a shaky breath, I ask, "But what do I even say?"

They all exchange blank expressions.

"Wait, wait." Rivera shifts his weight to one leg. "¿Me estás diciendo que no sabes hablar con los manes?"

Like magic, his question makes me wish for lightning to strike me.

"It's n-not that I don't know how to talk with guys." I clear my throat way too loudly. "After all I'm talking with all of you. Every damn day."

"Yeah, just not when it's romantically," Starr says, fully revealing what I left unsaid.

I'm pretty sure my face is so red that it may be bordering on purple now.

Kim hums from his throat. "I get it."

We turn to him and I ask, "You do?"

"Yeah, it's diffcrent. The stakes are higher."

"Thank you." I open my eyes wide to convey my sincerity.

"How's this…" Starr twists to place his sweet iced tea on the high top behind him. "You try to strike a conversation, don't even try to flirt. Just get some response back. I'll be next to you pretending to order something, ready to bail you out if you screw up."

"When," I mumble.

"If," he repeats with a sigh, then adds, "Or if you're just freaking out you can just poke my arm and I'll pretend you're my long lost cousin I hadn't seen since aliens abducted you."

"Solid plan," Kim deadpans.

My lips twitch. Unfortunately Rivera takes that as a cue to say, "I think she's ready. Camera, roll, action!"

No one moves.

Starr gives me a literal push. "C'mon, Garcia."

"Ugh."

I'm petty enough to stomp my way between the tables. I know the cowboy is somewhere behind me by how people's heads turn a moment after I pass. As glad as I am that he's offered himself for possible rescue, I'm mortified knowing I'll need it. They'll never let me live it down, and yet I'll be way harder on myself if I don't even try.

"Hi," I say boldly once I stop beside the test subject.

The guy jerks his head up from his phone screen and I'm relieved to note that he doesn't seem drastically older than me. He's also normal looking, which should make this easier than if I was trying to chat up some Adonis. The only reason why I'm immune to the baseball boys is because I know how much them and their gear reeks after a game.

"Uh, hi," the guy says, glancing around to make sure I'm talking with him.

The Texan accent sounds behind me. "Excuse me, sir, could I have a soda water with lemon?"

"Right on," says the bartender.

Apparently, I've taken too long to add anything to the conversation and red shirt shifts his attention back to his phone, where he seems to be watching the news. The news always suck so that's the last thing I want to ever talk about.

The weather? No, that's so cliché it's actually embarrassing. Besides, the Clearwater weather in February is chilly but boring.

"Um..." The sound spills from my mouth before I even find a sequitur, but even then the guy doesn't seem to even notice.

My eyes follow a line over his shoulder and fall on the

figures of one Orlando Wild catcher and a shortstop, both of whom are using the same freaking signals our base coaches use to tell a runner to keep going. I have the strongest urge to signal them back with a bird.

Heat nears behind me and suddenly, a too-warm voice whispers in my ear saying, "Just ask if he's a local."

My lips part in a gasp. Of course! How did I not think of that? Then I can ask him for some touristy recommendation or something.

"So…" I hear myself saying with a voice that doesn't sound like mine. I lean my elbow on the bar, trying to look casual even though I'm shaking in my sneakers. "Are you local? I'm looking for some recommendations."

That tears his attention from his screen. "Oh, I'm not. I'm just here on business." And back to his phone he goes.

"'Kay, thanks. No worries. Bye." I swivel around and freeze.

Starr is way closer than I expected, and our chests don't brush by a millimeter. He tilts his face down so I can receive the full blast of his disapproval via the subtle shake of his head. At least he has the heart to rescue me from this awkward situation, and I gladly allow him to pull me back to our group by my elbow.

He takes a casual sip of his new drink and announces, "She sucks worse than I thought."

"Yikes."

"Ay, bendito."

Groaning, I throw myself at the high top table. "Kill me now."

"No, I would like to keep my clean record, thanks," Starr says and even though half of my face is smooshed on the table, I clearly see him take his cap off, run his hair through the perfect wave of his hair, and put the cap back on. The picture of exasperation.

Kim claps Starr's shoulder. "Well, better you than me."

Okay, he's officially not my favorite of the three anymore.

"I've always said pitchers are patient people." Rivera nods in a sanctimonious way. "That's why you're the right guy for the job."

"Gee, thanks, guys," I say, sounding very much unalived.

Said pitcher studies me as if I was an animal trapped in a glass cage. "Yeah… this may be a bit harder than I thought."

And somehow that's the comment that hurts the most.

CHAPTER 10
CADE

The absolute best thing about living by myself is… that I can do whatever the hell I want in my house. A rave? Sure. Pool party that doesn't get contained to the pool deck? Totally. Boozy book club? Hell yeah.

But I mostly employ this freedom to start shucking off my clothes the second I walk home.

After almost a week on the road, we have a couple of upcoming games within comfortable driving distance. I push my suitcase away, not even minding where it stops, and rip off my jacket to toss it over my head somewhere in the vicinity of the couch. Who's gonna tell me I can't do that? No one, that's who. I also leave my sneakers in the foyer and slide on my socks all the way to the kitchen.

Carmen, my housekeeper, keeps it stocked depending on my schedule. When I'm going to be away for a long stretch, she makes sure the fridge isn't teeming with stuff that's gonna go bad. When I have a few days at home, she stocks it with all my faves. I grab a carton of orange juice, uncap it, and drink straight from it.

Again, who's gonna tell me no?

I return the carton back to the fridge and peel off my long sleeved shirt, then scratch my side for a second while I think.

"I stink. Thus, I shall shower," I declare to the void and the void doesn't answer back.

My kitchen is pristine, every granite and steel surface gleaming with some sort of lemon scented polish. The counters are clear of any debris, aside from a basket with fresh fruit. It's like no one lives here and yeah, that's kind of the case. All those parties I joke about don't happen because aside from Carmen, and the odd plumber or electrician, I never have anyone over. Not friends, not girls.

This is the result of growing up in the system and never having a space I could unequivocally call my own.

That changed in my second year in the majors, and only because it took me a year to build this house to my very particular specifications. Unlike normal houses, I wanted my parcel to be fully fenced in, with no possibility to be seen from the outside. It's why I can walk around my house buck ass naked if I want. That's my revenge for having been the zoo animal at school.

"Look at the orphan kid."

"Ew, I bet he has cooties."

"I heard if you touch Cade you might lose your parents too."

Those were some of the things I heard in middle school, at peak shitty-kids age. Now they watch me from TV screens and I get to show them what I'm really capable of.

And look at me now, on my way to a full walk-in shower with jet streams that come from every direction.

I pause in the hallway to discard my socks. My jeans take marginally more effort so I can empty the pockets on my bed, but then I ball up the garment and pitch it like a fastball to the chair on the corner. By rote I grab my phone and walk into my massive bathroom and get the shower going to build up some nice steam.

My phone goes off with yet another spam call and I take a moment to block it. It's been getting worse lately, no matter how many privacy protection services I try to join. A quick scroll shows me that today alone I've got upward of fifty.

"Maybe I should hire someone to manage my phone," I mumble, my voice still echoing from the tiles.

Whatever. I'm going to relax and go to bed early. I don't play tomorrow but I did today, and since I already had dinner, all I want is this shower and to slide into my silk bed sheets.

My whole body relaxes under the shower spray. This is luxury—not having to rush through a shower because there are a million other kids waiting for the one stall to clear, or because I'm an athlete on a tight schedule while at the team facilities.

Of course, the second I start lathering up is when my phone starts ringing again, and no matter how loud the shower is I can still hear it. I should've left the damn thing in my room.

I wait, muscles locked, until it stops making noise. "Finally," I grouch and turn my face up to the water spray.

Then the freaking phone starts going off again.

"That's it." I turn off the water spray and, still dripping suds, slide open the shower door and walk around to the vanity where I left the phone.

But instead of turning it off like I intended, I do a double take at the name that appears on my screen and before I can think, I answer the call.

"Cowboy?"

"Uh, yeah. You called me, remember?" Staring at myself in confusion through the mirror, I run my hand through my wet but still unwashed hair. "Everything okay, darlin'?"

"No! Yes. But actually no. Everything is most definitely *not okay*." There's something like a screeching quality to her voice that immediately puts me on edge.

"Okay," I say slowly, in a low tone of voice to not spike this wild animal on the other side of the line. "I need you to explain to me what is wrong so I can try to figure out something."

"My freaking ex is what's wrong!"

My eye twitches.

I remove the phone from my ear because another scream like that will send me to urgent care, and instead I set it to loud speaker and put it back on the vanity.

Now that I have confirmed this isn't a nine-one-one type of emergency, I ask, "What about your ex?"

"He's getting married! To my other ex!"

"Other ex?" My eyebrows rise all the way.

"Yeah, my ex best friend. They just—ugh, I can't believe I found out through Instagram. That like, adds insult to injury."

"So let me recap. You called me in a panic because your ex is getting married to your other ex, almost giving me a heart attack in the process, and interrupting my shower?"

"I—Sorry, what? You were showering?"

"Yeah, and I'm starting to get cold. Can I finish that and call you back?"

Garcia's voice sounds several notches higher as she says, "Oh. Yeah. Of course. I'm uh, sorry. Yep."

"'Kay, talk to you in a bit." I hang up and this time make sure to put my phone in Do Not Disturb, which I should've done all along. Live and learn.

I can't get back into the relaxation headspace I was in before Garcia's call, though. Instead of taking forever and a half to enjoy my two-seventy-degrees water streams, I end up rushing through it as if I had just finished a game and was getting ready for a press conference. As I towel off, I remember I meant to shave as well but that's gonna have to wait until tomorrow now.

I get dressed in record time and flop on my soft bed, towel hanging from my head, to call Garcia back.

"Sorry about that," is her greeting the second she picks up. "I momentarily lost my mind."

"Momentarily?" I tease and receive a huff in return.

"I admit I've been in a fugue ever since I found out the two of them got together."

"Hmm." I bend my arm to use my hand as another pillow. "I assume that if you called me it's because you want me to do something about this."

"You are very clever, Cade Starr. Has no one ever told you that?"

I snort. "No need to butter me up, darlin'."

"Fine, I'll get to the point." She proceeds to make a long pause where she does not, in fact, get to the point.

Picking up my phone from the pillow I tossed it on, I confirm the call is still connected. "Garcia?"

"I'm here," she says a lot quieter than before. "You already saw how bad I am at the whole flirting thing. Twice."

"Right…" That's all I dare to say because she's legit worse than *bad*. A cartoon robot probably has more game than her, but I'm not gonna be cruel in pointing that out.

"So, I really need your help to speed up the timetable."

"There was a timetable?"

"Thanksgiving. It's uh, a long story."

I tuck my tongue against my cheek and take a look around my room. The clock on the night table reads eight something, close to nine. And I mean, c'mon, my plan was already derailed and Garcia is clearly upset by this ex or whatever.

Shrugging to myself, I suggest, "Wanna tell me over a drink or something?"

This immediately snaps her back into professional mode. "No alcohol for you, mister."

"There are non alcoholic liquid things in this planet, you know?"

"I… Actually, I shouldn't bother you anymore. You need to rest, I'm sorry."

I volley with, "I don't play tomorrow."

"But—"

"Garcia, I'm bored." I surprise myself with this truth that suddenly decided to tear out of my chest. My amazing house, with its expansive rooms, amazing views to manicured gardens designed with native Florida plants, the pool that flows up the property like a human made river, the perfectly kept kitchen…

It's all empty. Lonely.

Swallowing hard, I add, "And honestly, I think hearing the story will help me be a more effective coach. It's like when you're training us and you need to figure out what exercises will work best to fix any issues or whatever, you know?"

"Then I'll drive closer to you. What neighborhood are you in?"

"Winter Park."

"Oh, me too." She then adds, "Then I'll text you a nice place we can meet at. See you in like twenty?"

"Roger that. Ten four," I say like this is the army and hang up.

I jump out of bed to find socks, shoes and a hoodie. My sneakers squeak against the marble floors as I retrace my steps out of the house, and I pause outside to lock my front door with my phone.

Rustling sounds behind me freeze me on the spot. I turn my face, slowly, expecting I don't know what. It's quiet again except for the gentle brush of the leaves with the wind. The lights around the yard illuminate a clear grass that twinkles with moisture, but I don't spot anything human shaped anywhere.

"Don't be a fool, Cade. This is why you fenced up the

whole lot," I say to myself. The only creatures that can reasonably scale up the walls are cats.

Stretching my shoulders, I make my way to the garage and fire up my pickup, eager to distract myself from my own mind, and drive over to this little ice cream joint at a strip mall in a hipster area of town.

When I arrive, Garcia is already sitting by the window.

CHAPTER 11
HOPE

"*Ahora sí he perdido la cabeza*," I whisper to myself in the dark of my car, parked by the curb of the townhouse I share with Rose and Audrey. The lights are off and their cars nowhere to be seen, so for all intents and purposes I'm alone right now. This has to be why I've gone and lost my marbles and called Cade Starr.

While he was in the shower, no less.

I rub my temples. I kinda wish he hadn't told me, so I didn't have to imagine him sopping wet and naked, but I also understand his need to make me understand how unhinged I am.

Surely anyone can understand that seeing something like *this* is enough to make your brain pack its shit and screw off in a long trip away from your head socket.

I lift up my phone again and swipe the screen. The Instagram post greets me again, looking like something out of a stock photo website. Amy cut her hair into a bob and wears a floral dress that stands out against the stark white decor of her living room. Dawson, in contrast, hasn't changed his hair one bit. It's the same curly blond that looks beach swept. He's wearing a khaki suit with a white button shirt that matches Amy's dress—and also the straw vase in a corner. Like he's trying to fit in her life in a way he never did with me, or like Amy wrestled him into compliance in a way I never could. And behind them, golden balloons shaped like letters read ENGAGED.

Everything I ever wanted but never dared to demand of him.

What's worse, I know I should feel happy that they found the right fit in each other, the perfect combination of personalities that makes dating for a few months feel like such a definite shoo-in that marriage is the only possible next step. Good for them.

I hate it.

Just as I'm about to put my phone away and turn the Jeep back on, a text pops up on the screen and gets my attention because it's in all caps.

KELLY

ARE YOU OKAY????

This is the second person tonight who asks me this. The true answer still remains the same in both of my languages: no.

My thumb hovers over the screen. Kelly has tried reaching out for months and I've been ignoring her, except to congratulate her on the birth of her baby in December. But this text is a fresh reminder of every one of her attempts to check in with me.

I let my emotions sweep me all the way and I'm a go big or go home girlie, so instead of texting her back I straight up call her. The second she picks up the phone, I blurt out, "No."

"No shit." Next, she curses even worse than that, and takes a deep breath to say, "This isn't about me, though. How do *you* feel?"

I run my hand through my hair and grouch, "Is this

conversation going to get to the ears of a certain newly engaged couple? Because I can't possibly take any more drama than this."

"No, I promise you. Not even to Mitch's ears or the baby's if you don't want to."

I shut my eyes tight. My hurt has clouded me so much that it's not just that I no longer know who to trust, but that I no longer trust myself too. I can't help wondering how I could've been so wrong in my judgment of Dawson and of Amy, that I wonder if I've been wrong about Kelly all along too. Maybe even about Rose and Audrey and Cade Starr and anyone not last-named Garcia.

And yet, Kelly has only ever been a ray of sunshine. She's spent months trying to make sure I'm okay. That was Starr's second question after I cold-called him a few minutes ago, if everything was okay. I'm sure my roomies would drop kick me if they found out I've been thinking this way. There's a different level of trust with people you do laundry loads with.

"I… I'm feeling a lot of things," I start in a hesitant whisper.

"Anger? Fury? Ire?"

A corner of my lips lifts. "I think those are all the same."

"Well, I'm not sure any of them really fit what I feel right now." There's some shuffling on her end and the distinctive click of a door closing. "I want you to know I told Amy this was a bad idea since the moment she first told me she and Dawson went on a date."

"Why did you never tell me?"

Kelly sighs. "We didn't want to hurt you—or I didn't. I think Amy's motive simply was that she didn't want to be stopped."

"I see," my voice shaking slightly. "When was that?"

She hesitates for a brief moment and finally responds, "I think their first date was um, two Decembers ago."

"What the…" I do a double take in the dark of my car. "That's only a few months after we broke up!"

"I know. This is why I couldn't say anything. It just wasn't right."

Something inside of me feels like glass crashing on the ground, and one of the shards pierces the last thread of my sanity. I burst out in guffaws that hurt even my own ears. Half gasping, half laughing, I ask, "So basically you're telling me that Dawson broke up with me so he could date Amy? Is that it?"

"I'm so sorry, Hope." She grunts in frustration. "I tried to stop them but—"

"Yeah, there was no stopping that. I sure couldn't. And you wanna know what the shittiest part of all of this is?"

"What?"

"That asshole had the cojones to gaslight me into not being able to show my hurt, to not tell everybody how I bent myself over backwards to keep our relationship afloat when he didn't even care—all on the excuse of not affecting the friendship group. And I agreed! I went along with this flimsy-ass reasoning because I'm apparently more spineless than a squid. And you're telling me that all this time it was so he had an open field to pull moves on one of my friends?" I bark another harsh laugh and shake my head at myself.

"Wow, I have no words," Kelly whispers and to her credit, her voice vibrates with anger. And that's still nowhere to the levels of virulent rage I feel right now.

"I'm gonna go now."

"Talk later?" she asks.

"Later," I say, at least having the presence of mind to accept that it's not Kelly I'm upset at, even if in a smaller way she also hurt me.

The enemy is Dawson. He clearly didn't give a flying turd about me, or he wouldn't have done something like this. And

Amy's a fool if she thinks she's safe from his scheming. What I need to do is show them I've moved on and don't give a turd about them in return, and this is why I need Cade Starr. I turn on my car and drive off.

*

I get to the ice cream shop a whole five minutes before Starr, and I take that time to unfollow everyone from the friend group who is giving effusive congratulations to the couple, and the two jerks themselves. I'm archiving any picture I have on my social media where they appear, when the bell at the door dings with a new arrival.

I lift my eyes to Cade Starr's entrance and my stomach dips at the disappointment in his face as he strides over to me. It feels like I'm being kicked when I'm already down.

But he toes the chair beside me to turn it my way, plops down with his massive legs spread out around me and leans his elbow on the counter by the front window. "A yoghurt ice cream place, really? And here I was excited that you were gonna let me cheat on my diet, darlin'."

My lips part and I release a soft breath in relief. He wasn't disappointed to see *me* but the healthy treats. Well, healthier—this still has more sugar than he should be consuming at this time of night.

"You have a whole season ahead of you, Cowboy."

He twists around, setting those weird blue eyes of his on the overhead menu. "Can I at least get the chocolate syrup? Your treat, obviously."

"Obviously," I repeat in a deadpan but push away from the window counter. "Fine, but I'll get you the kid's cup."

He looks up at me, eyebrows scrunched up in annoyance and lips curved into a pout. "Meanie."

I shake my head and leave the man-child behind to place

our orders. I'm not ready to start this conversation until there's some dopamine in my system, so I hang out at the cashier's until one of the two employees returns with our order. With my left, I carry Starr's smaller treat, and on my right mine.

I place them in front of our seats and his eyes bulge. "Excuse me but what happened to equality?"

"I'm the one who's suffering tonight," I mumble as I sit down and stab my spoon into my large swirl with strawberries, bananas, chocolate syrup, and caramel monstrosity.

"Fair." His attention shifts to his and he grabs his spoon. "How did you know I like peanuts?"

"It's part of my job. I know what each player absolutely can and can't eat, and what they should or shouldn't avoid."

"Oh yeah? What am I allergic to?" His eyebrows lift as he puts a spoonful in his mouth, his lips closing around the spoon.

"Nothing at all. You could probably eat a rock and be totally fine," I respond, doing the same.

"I'm impressed." A corner of his lips lifts, even with the spoon still in his mouth.

I shrug one shoulder. "You're one of the easy ones."

Once he's done swallowing his cold mouthful, he asks, "What about you? Any allergies?"

"None, I'm easy like you."

His lips twitch but he has the decency of not turning that into an indecent joke. "So tell me, Garcia, why is it that we can hold a low key conversation like this and you can't do the same with dates?"

My mouth drops open. Belatedly, and only because his face lights up with barely contained laughter, do I realize my mouth is full of food. I turn away for a moment to swallow without scrutiny and wipe my mouth with a napkin just in case.

I swivel back around. "Who's the meanie now?"

He observes a strawberry that hangs precariously on the rim of my cup, and I motion at him to just take it. "Thanks."

This makes his eyes light up even more and he carefully spoons the fruit and shoves it in his mouth. It's a very different look compared to when he's on the pitcher's mound in the middle of the game, radiating so much intensity that it even translates into television screens. Or compared to how he is when flirting with women at a bar.

"Anyway, I just wanted to illustrate the point," he says while eating. "You don't really need me."

"But I do," I whine bad enough that the two store employees glance our way. Ducking, I continue, "You don't count. I go completely blank when it's a stranger, like…"

"Like?" Starr prods.

"I lost my confidence," I admit for the first time in almost two years. "Dawson, my ex, he destroyed it. He said—He said…" I interrupt myself to clear my throat when my eyes start to sting. I refuse to shed a single more tear about my jerk of an ex boyfriend, and especially not in front of Cade Starr.

But the latter surprises me by taking a clean napkin from the pile between us and offering it to me. No pity in his expression, no empty platitudes tumbling out of his mouth. Like he's fine either way if I cry or not, but like he cares if I do just as smidge.

I take the napkin and lightly blot my eyes. Two small wet dots remain on it, proof that I'm nowhere near as strong as I wish. Sucking it all up for almost two years has led to this, so I try a different tactic. The one where I open up at least a little.

Biting my lip, I whisper, "He said he was no longer attracted to me because I'm boring, like one of the boys. I hate to admit that his words swirl in my head every time I try to talk with a guy." I push away the half eaten, quickly melting ice cream away. "Every single time without fail, I worry that the guy finds me too bulky, too loud, not cute enough, not feminine at all. Or worse, boring. And guess what? So far my dating track record confirms that."

"Hey." His voice is harsh enough it snaps me out of my funk. Starr leans his face lower to meet my eyes. His hair is wet and he's not wearing his usual baseball cap, so the while halogen lights make his eyes glint like the waters of the Caribbean sea. "Cut that shit out."

I snap my mouth closed.

"You don't let a bad ex take you away from yourself."

Oh no, my eyes are welling up for real now.

I only have enough strength to contain the quivers of my chin, but tears start streaming down. Starr reaches for the pile, sees my fists balled up around the hem of my windbreaker, and pats my face dry himself.

After the worst is over, he leans back on his chair, sighing and running his hand through his brown hair. "I have a very simple question."

I sniffle. "What?"

"Have you ever thought about just maybe… dressing more feminine?" He lifts his hands as a protective barrier the second I start glaring. "I'm not saying you should change yourself or anything like that, just that maybe you should try some armor. Just like how our team uniforms are the armor we go to battle with, you know?"

"I think the issue is deeper than what I wear." I fold my arms.

"And I don't see an issue at all." Starr shakes his head. "I wear an Orlando Wild uniform by day, sweats by night—" here he pinches the fabric of his hoodie, "—dress suits for galas, cowboy boots at a bar. And yet I'm the same Cade Starr every single time."

"I get your point." I huff and tighten my arms around me.

"Men are simple, in both good and bad ways," he says, resting his jaw against his fist. "The first thing we notice is what we perceive with our eyes. I just think if you hold your date's attention that way, you'll have an easier time unwinding and showing who you really are."

"And then if he doesn't like who I really am anyway?" I ask, getting to the core of the issue.

"You throw the whole man in the garbage can where he belongs," Starr says with a lopsided smirk. "Then we find a new candidate until you succeed."

I run the tip of my index finger down the wall of the plastic cup, following the trail of condensation like it's another tear I'm trying to clear. "Or we give up."

"We're the Wild, darlin', we never give up even when all the odds are stacked against us."

That springs a small smile on my face. Historically, we've been one of the bottom feeder teams of the league, with more hecklers than fans. And yet the lineup consistently tries their best in every game, even when facing superstar pitchers from historical franchises like New York or Los Angeles.

Taking a deep breath, I extend my hand. "You're right. I won't give up, but that means you'll have to put up with me longer for literally nothing in return. Are you in?"

Starr studies my hand, as if deciding whether to tie himself up to someone who is clearly not normal. But then he shrugs. "It's more entertaining than TV, so I'm in." He wraps his much —*much*—larger hand around mine for a strong handshake and I pretend like I don't notice the calluses in his hand, the texture and heat of his skin.

Pretending like this isn't the huge deal it actually is.

CHAPTER 12
CADE

"Another one like that," Pirela, our second catcher, says as he stands to throw the ball back at me.

I catch it, annoyed as hell that he has me on a fastball regime. I think I have the pitching form for the cutter down, and every cell in my body itches with the need to test it in a real game. Except that won't be today because I'm under clear instructions to not play. We started out one of our reliefs, followed by a prospect that still can't grow facial hair, and two solid guys from the minors.

My whole role today is to be in the bullpen throwing fastballs for the last two innings of the game just to screw with the opponent's mind. Unfortunately, I'm the one whose mind is being screwed over by the audience flanking the bullpen.

"Show us something worthwhile!"

"This is embarrassing, Starr. You should be making us proud!"

"Is a boring fastball all you got?"

"Boo!"

"Can I have your autograph?"

"Do you have a girlfriend?"

"My grandma pitches better!"

"Hell, my grandma has more balls!"

I do my best not to roll my eyes because I have no doubt some eagle-eyed fan would notice. And normally I wouldn't give a rat's furry ass about hecklers—or actually, I do. They fuel the very strong pettiness in me and push me to shut their yaps. Which I can't really do when I'm here and not on the mound of this very unimportant game that's happening in my hometown.

And that's the crux of my real annoyance. I really wanted to throw the cutter here as a very clear way of telling everyone here *bless your heart, asshole*.

Pirela crouches down again, extending one leg out probably to stretch his knee. He signals for another fastball, this time right against the chest of an imaginary right-handed batter. At least this isn't a coward's pitch, so we're starting to get somewhere.

We don't have a pitching clock here so I take my time positioning the seams of the ball where I can throw the nastiest pitch. Let's see how they like that.

The noise around me fades into a dull, unrecognizable cacophony in the background. I keep my eyes on the catcher's mitt as I wind up, my right leg rising high for a full extension. My arm's like a whip that puts a downright dirty backspin on the ball that shoots off from the tips of my fingers like a bullet. I land, keeping my eyes on the white blur as it slams with a violent sound and enough force to make Pirela reel back—and land on his ass. Not my fault he wasn't in the proper stance to catch.

But it was a strike for freaking sure.

I straighten myself up and after that, the next to recover is Pirela. He whispers, "Wow." And the word seems to echo because suddenly the audience has gone quiet.

I run my thumb under my nose to collect the sweat that's pooled above my lip, and straighten the dirt with my cleat.

"Whoa, how fast was that?" someone from the audience asks.

My personal record is one hundred two point five miles per hour. This one felt better. So maybe one-oh-three.

Pirela swings back to his feet and lifts up his mask. He opens and closes his mouth, shakes his head, and decides to walk over here instead. He deposits the ball on my waiting hand gently and looks up at me.

"I'm gonna have to ice my hand after this, you jerk, but that was cool. Don't do it again."

I snort. "You sound like you're hanging out with Kim too much."

"He's not wrong, you pitchers need to be reined in." He wrinkles his nose. "Back to normal fastballs, okay?"

"Bleh." I sneer.

Pirela taps my chest with his mitt before heading back to his spot and I have no choice but to suck it up because catchers are the boss on the field, and if I step out of line they tell on me with our grand-boss, our manager.

The game ends with a close win for us and I head back to the dugout next to Pirela, leaving behind the hecklers and cheers. This town hated my very existence when I was growing up—white trash abandoned orphan that I was—and now even the cheers and admiration feels like a personal insult. I didn't ask for any of it when I was a kid, but is this the only way to earn some respect? To throw a ball really fast? What will happen the day I retire? Will I go back to being the dreg of this town?

I'm not a spitter, but I hack up a good glob and launch it at the ground before reaching the dugout. I can't wait to brush the dirt off my shoes and get on the plane out of here.

A couple of innings of light pitching don't require much

upkeep after, aside from a shower. The debrief is quick because we have to drive down to the airport right away, and frankly I'm so eager that I'm the first one out of the facilities. Which is a mistake.

"Cade! Over here!"

"Can you sign my ball?"

"Let's take a selfie!"

"Would you sign on me? I promise I can keep it real for you, babe." This one is a woman who pulls down at her top to a hefty expanse of her chest. A mom nearby physically turns her son's head away from the display.

I rub my eyes, asking the heavens for patience—which is what I should've had in the first place. If I'd waited for the rest of the team to come out, I could've used them as cover from the crowd. But I also shouldn't show any cowardice to these people, so I have no choice but to play nice.

Not boob lady, though. I turn my back on her and pick a kid who's waving his regulation ball toward me.

"Hey, little cowboy," I say as greeting, crouching like a catcher so he doesn't have to stretch his tiny self over the fence.

The kid must be six years old and his smile has more gaps than teeth. "Cade, you're my favorite pitcher in the whole wide word! My momma says you're from here and that I can be like you when I grow up."

Er, hopefully not. Hopefully he grows up better.

"Whole wide world, sweetie. Don't forget the l."

The kid puckers his mouth to try again. "Wuo—would—world?" He manages, but the word sounds garbled and uncomfortable, and for the first time all day I want to laugh.

"Here." A woman's perfectly manicured hand appears in my field of vision, a million bracelets dangling from her thin wrist as she holds out a black Sharpie to me.

"Thanks." I pluck it and take the ball from the boy's hand. "What's your name, little cowboy?"

"Jerry with a J." Toothy grin follows.

I can't help but returning it. "Nice to meet you, Jerry with a J." I make quick work of my sloppy signature, which includes a sloppier star, and dedicate it to Jerry with a J, although I'm nice enough to omit the last three words. "Here you go."

"Yay!"

"Thank you," a man's voice says, and that's when I notice both parents standing behind the child. I rise up again, capping the Sharpie to return it to the mom, when I finally lift my head and freeze.

I recognize their faces. They made sure I memorized them when I was in high school.

She has the iron balls to smile at me. Megan, my first girlfriend and first ex. "Hi, Cade. Long time no see."

"Maybe we should take a selfie to commemorate this special moment, huh? Back together again after almost ten years." And he—Jimmy—has even more gigantic balls to say that, as if he hadn't been the one to lead the bullying campaign that resulted in Megan dumping my ass because, and I quote, she had just gone out with me for charity. And as if the two of them hadn't turned the whole school against my sorry fifteen year old ass up until the moment I became a varsity player and he didn't.

I wish I didn't care, and normally it's easy to pretend that I don't. After, all, I hadn't thought about these two since graduation. But something about being back in this place has me feeling raw.

I stuff my hands in the pockets of my joggers and narrow my eyes as if I didn't have one of the best eyesights in the team. "Oh, I'm sorry. Should I know you?"

I can tell this is the best diss I could've come up with without resorting to f-bombs in front of their innocent kid, because their faces turn into two masks of stupefaction.

While Megan is making an effort to recover, a different

voice sounds behind me. "Hey, Starr. We're gonna leave you behind if you keep dallying."

I turn over my shoulder and whatever the look is on my face visibly weirds Garcia out so much that she blinks hard.

"Coming," I say to her, and then to the little kid I add, "Stay out of trouble in school and be a good kid, okay, Jerry with a J?"

"Yes!" He gives an enthusiastic nod of his head and I wave at him, and only at him, before turning on my heels

To my surprise, Garcia waits for me. As we head together for the bus, she asks, "What was that?"

"What?" I ask.

She motions at her face. "That goofy ass look on your face."

"Oh, that was me being a damsel in distress. You were my knight in shining armor out there, darlin'." I smirk.

But Garcia, being the intense person she is, doesn't take this as the joke I intended. Instead, she pulls at my arm until I stop right before the bus entrance. "Starr, did they do anything to you? Do you I need to call security?"

I debate the merits of calling security on people who hurt me a decade ago—sure would've loved to have any backup back then—but even in my addled state I can see how there's no point.

Freeing my arm, I put it around her shoulders to steer her into the entrance. "Nah, let's just get the hell out of dodge." Without looking back, I climb onto the bus.

CHAPTER 13
HOPE

Hmm. I don't know about this one.

I twist my head as if that could help me discern whether to swipe right or left. It's not about his looks, the guy is pretty normal looking. Dirty blond, slightly thinning around his temples, with normal clothes that don't scream dude-bro-douche, an unassuming smile, and a decent build. He works out, maybe not with high intensity, but frequently enough to give him some definition. Which should mean he wouldn't feel too intimidated to see I'm well beyond a gym rat.

Moreover, he's a high school chemistry teacher, and even includes a couple of fun pictures his students must've taken while he was doing an experiment in class. In one, whatever it is was in the middle of exploding, and rather than surprise or anger there's a childlike glee on his face that automatically makes him more attractive in my books.

My thumb hovers for another second until I just swipe right. Confetti rains down the screen, announcing that we're a match.

Good to know that the teacher has taste.

A shadow falls over me. I lean my head back on the backrest of my chair and nearly jump in my skin at seeing the gorgeous upside down face of one Logan Kim.

"Whatchu up to, Garcia?" he asks because he clearly wants to hear it from my mouth, even though his eyes are pointedly trained on the screen of my cellphone.

Something nudges my foot and it turns out to be Starr, taking the chair next to mine on the left. On my other side, Rivera does the same.

I press my phone against my chest. "Rather, the question is what are you all doing?"

"Sitting. I thought it'd be obvious." Starr cocks an eyebrow at me and I kick his foot under the table.

Rivera rubs his hands. "Are you kidding? This is the best table in the house to catch the exact moment the hotel staff serves the dinner buffet. You have a good eye, Garcia."

"Not sure 'bout that," I mumble, checking my screen again. It's not like any of my picks so far have turned out to be *good*.

Kim walks around the table to sit across from me. Once he's situated, he extends his hand out to me. "Let me see that."

Like a child, I try to hide my phone again. All he needs to do is motion at me and I guess I'm not at all immune to a pretty face, because I cave. Sighing, I stretch over the table to give him my phone.

The other two stooges scoot closer to the catcher and huddle like they'd do around an iPad in the dugout, trying to analyze some play or look at stats. Instead, they quietly examine the match I just made after looking at dozens of prospects, swiping left at least at half, and not matching with a quarter of them. I'm exhausted already and it's not even eight in the evening.

Finally, Kim offers my phone back, saying, "You can do better."

"He's too normal, it freaks me out." Rivera sticks his tongue out like it even gives him a bad taste.

Meanwhile, Starr leans back, rubbing his chin and staring at me like I'm the lab experiment. "Why did you choose him?"

I shrug. "I don't know."

"As your dating coach," he says in a quiet voice that I can hear clearly because this area of the lobby is quiet. "That's bullshit. I bet there are one hundred reasons."

Huffing makes a strand of my hair fly in the air for a second. "You just want to know to make fun of me."

"Am I laughing here?" Starr's expression is the most dead-panned I've ever seen.

Like him, Kim and Rivera look more curious than eager to give me crap. I guess I'll put that to the test.

"Fine, but if it leaves this table I know who all leaked it and I'll slash your tires."

"Fair," Starr says.

Rivera shrugs. "Yeah."

All Kim does is nod.

I lean forward and they do the same, so I can lower my voice. "For starters, he's not a ten."

Rivera bobs his head and says, "Yeah, don't need a high school degree to figure that out."

"Why the hell would you pick a three at best?" Starr scrunches up his face.

"Please." I blow a raspberry like *he* is the one who knows nothing. "Any guy who is a four or higher is after a ten. I have a much better chance with the threes and under."

If anything, this makes his expression grow even more sour. "Don't tell me you think you're a two or something?"

"Am I the only one who is mildly disturbed by how we're measuring people in an arbitrary number scale instead of for who they are?" Kim asks, folding his arms and leaning back.

It's Rivera who responds. "That's what you have to do when you literally don't know them. Eyes first, brains later, heart last."

"Welcome to modern dating." I slump forward, dropping my chin on my hand for my arm to prop me up. "Anyway, in the non numerical scale, this guy falls under normal. Decent looking but not enough for him to be obsessed with his own reflection, respectable job, within my age range, and normal hobbies like cooking and running."

"Bo-o-ring." Rivera pretends to yawn.

"Give me that thing." Starr drops his hand on the table, palm facing up.

"You're not gonna unmatch me, are you?"

"No, I'm going to find you better options, darlin'."

I whine from my throat but fess up and hand over the device. He's only lifted it to take a first look, when another shadow falls on the table.

"What do we have here?"

I stiffen at my boss's voice. Even worse, he's brought Otto in tow and I wish I could grab my phone and make a dash for my room. Or better yet, out of the hotel.

But the device is still prisoner in Starr's hands and—wait, what is he doing? Why's he pocketing it?

"Hey Steve. Otto," he greets my boss and coworker with a tip of his head and he's just missing the cowboy hat to fully play the part. We're no longer in his home state but I guess you can't ever take Texas out of the cowboy.

"Guys." Steve nods at the others before turning his attention to me. "What are you all doing together?" The question sounds friendly enough, his expression placid, but given how it's only directed at me, I detect that it comes from authority-Steve, and not off-duty-Steve. So if I take his question and apply subordinate logic to it, the veiled accusation implies that the four of us shouldn't be hanging out together.

I'm scrambling to put together something that sounds casual and not absurd, which is definitely the opposite of *oh I was just showing my dating app matches to three hot baseball players who aren't tens, but a solid one hundred each, and trying to get their advice. Nothing big.*

But Starr comes in to pinch hit. "We're just talking about how much playing the field has changed nowadays." Technically not a lie, but with a drastically different core subject than the other trainers probably suspect.

"Fielders have never been busier since batters produce more hits, huh?" Steve jerks his chin at Rivera. "Speaking of, how's your knee?"

"A-plus-plus," says the Boricua with a thumbs up, before pressing his lips tight to hold back laughter. We pay special attention to his knees after the scare he gave us midseason last year.

"And yours?" My boss shifts his attention to the catcher.

"In mint condition." That's also a lie and we all know it. Catchers' knees are their weakest point and we've been extremely fortunate that Kim's haven't started acting up yet, even though he's already been playing in the pros for eight years.

"And your shoulder?" Steve asks Starr. He's never injured it, but it occasionally pains him enough that he can't hide it.

The pitcher lifts his arm to flex his bicep and I'm surprised it bulges even through his thick sweater. "Ready to throw some cutters right this second."

Otto looks down at me with a smirk before addressing the guys. "I'm curious about what Garcia can possibly be teaching to three professional ball players, though."

"She has an unbelievable amount of facts about each of us stored in her brain." Starr taps his temple. "It's pretty wild, actually. Pun intended."

My lips part.

And then Kim adds, "She's probably the most observant staff member and honestly, as a catcher I admire that."

Oh my gosh, is he for real? Or is that just to make Otto and Steve go away? But Kim's poker face is world famous, so it's impossible to glean the truth from his expression.

Maybe I need to stop staring at him, though. Going by how the cowboy's eyes narrow on me, I think he's starting to clue into the fact that I enjoy basking in the visage of Logan Kim.

"And she takes no bullshit, so she keeps us on the straight and narrow." Rivera raises his palm and there's no way I can leave him hanging after the compliment, so I high five him.

"Er, good." Steve clears his throat. "So, I guess we'll go sit at the table over there since there's no room here. Let's go, Otto."

The latter looks dissatisfied with the direction this conversation took, but he picks himself up and follows after our boss. Fortunately, they sit at a table by the window that is removed enough to not carry our voices to them.

"Whew." I slump on my chair.

Meanwhile, Starr takes my phone out from his jeans pocket. "Unlock this thing, please."

Rolling my eyes, I comply only so I don't have to dig any further holes for myself. It's weird to see my phone in his hand, though. It looks tiny and—

"Wait, who did you just swipe left on?" I ask, leaning forward.

"A finance bro."

"Yuck. Good job, Cowboy," chimes Rivera.

"Yeah, no bros for her." Kim frowns at my phone. Apparently he can see well enough from his vantage because he says, "Right on that one."

Starr lifts up his face. "What, is he your type?"

"He's a doctor," is all Kim says.

While I marvel at the fact that he can even read the

description from that far, both Rivera and Starr nod like they agree. And Starr swipes right without further ado.

By the time dinner is finally ready, I end up with nine new candidates to try with when I'm back home in Orlando. Hurray for VPNs, am I right?

CHAPTER 14
CADE

Back when I was called up from the minors, the one thing I enjoyed the most after pitching practice was the circuit. It's the one drill that brings the whole team together in unified suffering. Right now, usual regulars and competing prospects follow through the exercises divided into sections under the watchful eyes of the trainers and coaching staff.

Today is what I'd define as a perfect day, cool enough that we're still breathing air and not water, puffy clouds trekking slowly in the sky, the sun bright but not stabby. I even forego my sunglasses for the drills and twist my cap around. The field is filled with the sounds of whistles, cleats racing on dirt and grass, shouts of encouragement or heckling, the grunts of players pushing themselves hard, and of young prospects hacking up in a trash can. Welcome to the majors, kiddies.

I rub the sweat off the palms of my hands on my pants and stay low, waiting for the whistle. Once it comes, I take off like a raging bull is right behind me, working my legs until my thighs burn. Flanking me are three other guys and because we're professional little shits, we try to outrun each other. I'm nowhere near the fastest runner in the team—that's Lucky, actually—but I put up a damn good fight and make it in second place.

The hip rotations next would almost feel like resting in comparison, until you realize your thighs don't want to cooperate anymore. I grunt at the quick pace of the drill, sweat dripping down my face enough that I can see my own droplets fly around my face as I move. After that, prisoner squats really start testing my endurance. Especially because this is my fourth time around the circuit.

"Faster, Cowboy," says a familiar voice beside me. Garcia claps her hands, urging me. "That's it, keep going—O'Brien, you're cheating and I can see it!"

"Ah, shit." He huffs and puffs.

Somehow, I manage to find the strength for my lips to twitch, yet they don't form a full smile. Garcia is famous for being the toughest of the drill sergeants, like she genuinely enjoys seeing elite athletes shed tears. She also sticks to us every step of the way, which is a workout in itself.

Honestly, my respects.

The next one is relatively easy, side sprints with an elastic band. I pick the first one I find discarded on the grass and put it around my waist. The nearest trainer is precisely her so we have to partner up.

"Faster, darlin'," I tease back as she jogs over, and I appreciate how her little face tightens.

She slides into the circle of the band, securing it around her waist and spreading her legs to brace herself. "Less yapping and more running, Starr."

I give her a salute and start the drill before my heart rate goes down. I'd never admit this aloud because she'd no doubt inflict serious bodily harm on me, but the first time I was in a drill like this with her, I had serious concerns that I may somehow hurt her. Until I learned she holds stronger than a grudge. Obviously, my movement jerks her out of position and she has to dig her heels deep into the soil, but she still makes it impossible to topple her over. My deepest respects to her thighs.

I sure appreciate how her quads stand in stark relief under her leggings. They taper up into wide, shapely hips that are meant to be grabbed. By someone who is not me.

I best lift my eyes before she realizes I'm checking her out like a creep.

Once I switch to my other side, I fix my attention on literally anything else, which ends up being Lucky by the dugout, coaching a prospect into learning how to breathe again after a round of vomiting.

Finishing my reps, I step in to let the elastic band fall and Garcia does the same. I turn my head toward her and she's lifted her cap with one hand, wiping the sweat off her forehead with the back of her other hand.

"You doing okay?" I ask.

She looks up at me, surprised though I don't know why. Then she recovers and the trainer-in-session expression falls back on. "No dillydallying, c'mon."

I snort through my nose. I'll take it that she's fine, then.

I jog away to join the next drill and the following after that, until finally I'm deserving of a break. My legs feel heavier than usual as I make my way around the perimeter of the circuit where players are still going at it. There's a cluster of people around the drinks composed of none other than Garcia, Lucky and our annoying main catcher.

The only person I'm ever rude with is Lucky, because we have earned the privilege of this treatment from each other. He's chirping about who knows what when I approach from behind and jerk him back by the collar of his shirt.

"Hey!"

"You're obstructing business," I say, elbowing the rest of my way to grab a bottle.

Of course, he pays me back by squeezing *my* bottle while I'm drinking. Water explodes in my face. The bad news is that I don't manage to drink much of it. The good news is that I feel refreshed.

I wipe my face calmly. "Thanks, man. I feel so much better now."

"Sure you do." He guffaws.

"You clowns are embarrassing me," Kim says, drinking from his bottle in a civilized way.

Garcia checks over her shoulders and uncaps her bottle. "Actually, this might not be a bad idea." Then she pours water on her face.

Happy to report I'm not the only one whose jaw drops.

However, I do wonder if I'm the only one who lingers. Thank the heavens that her shirt is purple and not white, because it's already sticking to her chest in some typa way.

Kim clears his throat. "Since when did you decide to join these barbarians?"

"If you can't fight 'em join 'em and all that," she says, wiping excess water from her chin.

"Es lo que hay." Lucky offers his fist and she bumps it with her smaller one.

See? This is why I struggle to comprehend why this woman doesn't have men begging on their knees for a morsel of her attention. She's weird and fun, not to mention those thighs.

Her brown eyes settle on me, straight up worrying me that she might read my mind. My only diversion is blurting out, "So, when's the date with the chosen one?"

"Oh, yeah. I was wondering about that." Lucky cocks an eyebrow. Even the catcher appears interested in the answer.

"In two days," she responds after a deep inhale.

"Wait." I look up to think for a second. "But in two days we're on the road—we play whatshisface."

The other two grunt. No one in the Orlando Wild organization wants to utter the words Ben and Williams together, like the full name of the traitor has become the newest jinx we need to beat. In two days we face him for the first time against his new team, the Denver Riders, and Beau already declared that I'll be the starting pitcher.

Like the fool I am, I've had a grin on my face ever since. Until now. Pretty sure my mouth is a flat line right now.

"Yes." Garcia bobs her head, long ponytail bouncing behind her. "I'm off this entire weekend."

"That's great and you definitely deserve a break," I say carefully, scratching my chin and realizing only now that I forgot to shave this morning. "But I mean, how do we work out the logistics here?"

She tilts her head. "What do you mean?"

"I was thinking it would be a good idea for us to be there too."

"Huh?"

"Now that's an idea." Kim gives me a look that makes me think it's his first time realizing I'm a sentient being.

"Like, eavesdropping?" Lucky frowns in confusion.

I open and close my mouth. "Well, it'd be like when you —" I point first at Garcia and then at the field, "—are here following us along as we do the drills to make sure we're not screwing up, right?"

"Right..." She drags the word but doesn't seem totally against the idea.

"We could even use the PitchCom to send you plays to execute during the date," I say directly out of my ass because I honestly hadn't thought about this as hard as I am right now. Though the idea of observing from another table did occur to me before, inspired by that mess at the bar in Clearwater.

"Wow, dude. That's genius." Lucky points at me, shaking his hand in the same way he does when he's scored a run and is headed to the dugout to celebrate.

"Are you on board with this crap?" Kim asks her.

"Considering how much of a disaster I am at this whole thing, yeah… maybe?" Garcia scratches the back of her neck, pressing her lips tighter. Her eyes lift to mine. "Actually, this is probably the most brilliant thing you've ever said."

"Geez, I don't know if to be flattered or offended."

"Both," Kim mutters.

"But the problem is that we'll be flying back from Kansas right after the game," Lucky muses aloud, removing his cap to run his hand through his curly hair. "What time is your date?"

"Originally it's for six." The three of us groan because that's cutting it too close to our arrival, and she continues, "But it's probably no issue to reschedule for an hour later."

"Plus, you can always be late." Lucky rests his elbow on her shoulder. "That drives guys nuts. It's never a bad idea to cause some tension."

"We can't use the team's PitchCom for this, though." Kim folds his arms, adopting the air of responsibility of the unofficial captain, but not fully shooting down this ridiculous idea of mine.

"Eh, no worries." I shrug. "I bought one to test it with my private trainer last year. We can use that."

"Great, we have a plan." Lucky nods once.

"You know…" Garcia's eyes narrow slightly into a wistful expression. "Sometimes I wonder what even is my life."

A corner of my lips rises. "You mean not every girl has three hot studs helping her navigate the dating world?"

She shakes her head but there's no hiding the spark of amusement in her eyes.

A whistle goes off nearby and Beau's voice booms. "Break's over, kids! Time for some fielding practice."

Said three studs leave our bottles on the table to join the actual party. The circuit was nothing compared to what's waiting for us.

"Starr?"

I jerk to a stop and glance over my shoulder. Garcia still stands by the water coolers, her hands clasped in front of her all sweet and innocent like, even though she's the most hardass in this entire field.

I cock an eyebrow once enough seconds pass that this is starting to get awkward. She clears her throat and says, "Thanks."

I smile. "You're welcome." Then I turn my cap back to the front and go get my glove to resume practice.

CHAPTER 15
HOPE

have no idea what I'm doing.

While the team is out playing for their lives, I'm home staring at my wardrobe in my underwear. Basically the entire top rack is covered wall-to-wall by sweatshirts, windbreakers, hoodies, and jackets. Why do I even own so many jackets? It's only chilly like two weeks out of the year.

The bottom rack is taken by leggings of all colors—especially black—joggers, sweatpants, and a handful of jeans in black and different shades of blue. Not a single dress in sight.

I wish Cade Starr was here so I could tell him that his great plan of making me more dateable by wearing more feminine clothes has a huge hole already. Fortunately, he's not here to witness me in my boy short panties and training bra. That'd be hella awkward.

"Hmm."

I run my fingers down the tips of my freshly blow dried hair. I was pretty sure I had at least a couple of dresses. I recall a teal one and a floral thing. Didn't I wear them to go clubbing with the girls not that long ago?

"Oh!" I step into the mess to rummage through the shelves

where I keep my linen and smaller gym clothes. There, under a pile of undershirts, I find the two dresses all balled up.

I guess Starr's plan continues ahead. However, a new little problem has been unlocked. The two dresses are more wrinkled than a raisin. At least they smell clean.

Feet bare, I pad out to the living room. Rose sits on the couch with her Mac, and by the look of concentration in her face I surmise she's in the throes of editing videos for social media. Meanwhile, Audrey's in the kitchen, her back turned to us while she waters the serpent's tongue plants by the kitchen window. Beyoncé is the final member of the household, singing a country song in the background.

"Does anyone have an iron?" I ask, interrupting the quiet.

The two of them turn my way. No one's shocked at my state of undress—we've all seen worse at one point or another. But what captures their attention right away is the two dresses that hang in a crumpled cascade from my hands.

Rose points at them. "Whoa, what is that?"

"Dresses?" Audrey narrows her eyes, mouth open wide enough to let flies in.

"No need to be so shocked," I retort in a deadpan.

"Since when does Hope Garcia wear dresses?"

I shift my weight to one foot. "Since she's trying to make a bare minimum effort."

"Fair." Rose grins. "I can lend you some more interesting pieces."

"Please, I'm not a million-feet-tall former beauty pageant, I can't pull off anything in your wardrobe."

"I'm sure I have an iron somewhere." Audrey sets the watering pot down on the counter and pats her hands dry with her sweatshirt as she makes for the stairs.

Rose continues as though uninterrupted. "You can definitely pull off whatever you want. But I hope you have cuter underwear?"

I snort. "Literally no one's going to see it so what's the point?"

"The point is for *you* to feel like a million bucks, not to show it to anyone at all if that's not what you want."

Steps echo behind me. "'Kay, it's not an iron. It's a steamer."

"I'm sure that's fine," I say, turning to receive the device. It looks like some kind of tiny kettle and I immediately know that I have no idea how to even make sense of it. "Er, help?"

The two of them fully abandon what they were doing to help me get ready. I end up going for the teal dress because it's a simpler number—I'd describe it as a tight, short-sleeved T-shirt that reaches down to the middle of my thighs. With white sneakers, and a light coating of mascara and lip gloss, I feel like I've tried enough that it shows, while not making myself uncomfortable.

"How's this?" I ask the girls as they surround me in front of my floor length mirror.

"Not bad. Simple but cute." Audrey nods.

Rose hums. "I wish there was more cleavage or something."

"Just for the record, I'm wearing it to go to my brother's for my sister-in-law's birthday. There's literally zero need for cleavage there."

"Oh, okay."

Audrey side eyes me, tucking a strand of her blonde hair behind her ear. "What if one of your relatives brings a hot friend over?"

"In that case, having my boobs firmly secured under fabric will make me less nervous."

"Pfff." Rose shakes her head and leaves my room with the air of someone who gives up. All Audrey does is pat my shoulder before walking out too.

I grab my mini backpack, one of the jackets haunting my wardrobe, and blow kisses at them on the way out the door.

*

My brother, a whole grown man, father of two children, and five years older than me, spits out his beer when I walk into his backyard.

"Qué carajo?" he wheezes the question out between hacking coughs.

His wife calmly tears a square off the kitchen roll on the plastic table where the enormous Publix birthday cake sits, and passes the tissue to her man. Her name is Virginia Hernandez and she is a saint. Also a very smart woman for keeping her last name so she can pretend like she doesn't know Eduardo when he acts like a fool. Such as the present moment.

She leaves him behind to come give me a bone crushing hug that I return. "Ignore the little pest," she says.

"Been doing that since I was born." I lean away to offer the gift I got her. "Happy birthday, I hope you like them."

"Oh, thank you! Can I?" I nod at her to open the baggy and hold my breath. But her eyes light up when she sees the box containing my favorite earbuds for exercising. They clip over the ear shell as well as staying firm inside the ear, and one time she saw me wearing them she mentioned that she needed them for her morning runs. I knew she'd like them, but I didn't know if she had already bought them for herself and it seems like I knocked it out of the park. "This is perfect, thank you so much, Hope!"

"You're welcome. I hope they help you ignore my brother more effectively." We both have a good giggle about that, but then my baby niece starts the little gurgling sounds that precede fierce wailings. Virginia makes a move for her but I stop her. "Let me get her. Consider it another birthday gift."

Her shoulders slump in relief. "Oh, thank you. I was really hoping to get drunk off my rockers tonight."

"I got this." Nodding, I bypass the jerk I share half of my DNA with and reach for the baby. "Ohh, look at you, Emma! You're huge already." Carefully, I wrap her in my arms and hold her against my chest, bouncing her slightly and shushing her.

"Tía!" Eduardo Jr, a.k.a. Junior, a.k.a. my nephew, spots me from within the bouncy castle among other little kids, and waves frantically at me. I free one hand to wave at him, but that disturbs baby Emma and I have to seriously focus on the shushing now.

"Mija." Dad appears in my field of vision with a cold Polar in his hand. He might've left his homeland of Venezuela well before I was born, but Polar is still the only beer brand acceptable to his palate. Dad frowns at my mostly bare legs. "I was hoping you'd join my pickleball team against your cousins, but not wearing that."

And all at once I recall why I just don't do dresses. My life revolves around too many activities where I don't need to be flashing anyone.

Sighing, I mumble, "Should've told me in advance."

"My bad." Dad grins.

"Don't worry, sis. I can lend you my sweatpants."

I grimace and stick my tongue out. "No, thanks. Who knows when's the last time you washed them."

Eduardo rolls his eyes. "Fine, a pair of my wife's sweatpants then."

"Oh, now we're talking."

My girly look lives on for all of ten more minutes, as long as it takes us to find Virginia by the coolers full of Venezuelan beer bottles, and then for her to fetch a pair of well loved sweatpants for me to borrow. The dress turns into a T-shirt after that and I join Dad's team against my brother and one of our one hundred boy cousins. My hair also starts getting in the way and I use a hair tie permanently housed around my wrist to gather it into a bun atop my head.

Dad and I win the game because of freaking course. He did come to this country to play professional baseball after all, and out of his two kids, I'm the one who took the lion's share of his athletic genes. The other team had no chance.

"Okay, I'm ready for a drink now," I declare to my dad, and he hooks my arm and steers me to the goods. He grabs two ice cold bottles for us and uncaps them with his bare hand, like I've seen him do since I was a kid. I've tried, but maybe my hands are still too soft for it.

I wonder if Starr would be able to do it. His hand sure is calloused enough.

Dad exhales a satisfied *hah* once we take a couple of chairs by the back fence. A gaggle of kids run dangerously close to the cake, but literally no adult makes any move to protect it. There are groups of people chatting around a grill that my brother's manning. A few of my younger cousins have brought dates. And Virginia is laughing it off with her friends who were part of her wedding party years ago.

She and my brother were two years younger than I currently am when they got married, and my age when they had Junior. They were high school sweethearts too—a truly sappy and perfect love story like the kind I always dreamed of.

A sigh escapes from my lips. Why does everyone get this but me?

"What's troubling you, Hope?" Dad asks before taking another swig.

I debate what to say, not because I've ever been a daughter who hides stuff from her dad, but because I don't even know how to explain myself without dying of embarrassment.

"I'm trying something new, but I'm not sure how it's going," I start tentatively.

He rests his elbow on the armrest of the plastic chair and props his chin with the heel of his hand to observe me up close. "Dresses?"

I cringe. "Yeah."

"Why's it not going well?"

"It's just… too obvious that it's not me."

"Because of how your brother reacted?"

"Kinda." I'm pretty sure guys will see right through whatever dress I wear to my real tomboy self. But I'd rather not get into those details with Dad because I'd have to explain why I'm doing all this in the first place.

"He's just not used to it." Dad pats my hand, then adds, "Also, he doesn't have enough braincells to appreciate your beauty."

"Facts." My chuckles fade away as another thought enters my mind, and I dare voice it. "What do you think Mom would've thought?"

He's had a lifetime to get used to being without his soulmate, but even from the beginning, Dad never shied away from talking to us about her, sharing memories, showing us pictures and videos. Mom has never been a stranger to me, even if she never had the chance to get to know me.

Dad doesn't grow sad or quiet. Instead, he ponders quietly for a moment until he says, "I know she would've loved you just the same in sweatpants and dresses." My heart squeezes and I'm glad he keeps talking, because that way he doesn't notice the lump that has settled in my throat. "But she was a really girly girl. She talked about how excited she was to dress you up when you got older, you know?"

"I didn't know that," I whisper.

"I never said it?" His eyebrows rise, surprised at himself. "Shame on me. But yes, she wanted all girls from the beginning because of this."

I smirk. "Eduardo will love to learn that."

We laugh a little at my brother's expense. As if on cue, he pulls his attention away from the grill to give us a look like he knows exactly what we're up to.

Dad grabs my hand between his and claps it gently, as if he was making an arepa. "You can be whatever you want, Hope. I'll also love you just the same, no matter what, and believe it or not so will your brother."

"I know." I blink hard, my eyes glued on our hands. "I know."

And it strikes me right then that maybe the cowboy was right. I'll still be the same sporty, take-no-nonsense person whether I'm wearing sweats or cute clothes. Maybe I shouldn't be afraid of that, at least.

CHAPTER 16
CADE

release a caveman sound that offers zero relief. What would make it all better would be something greasy and cheesy with no nutritional value, or for Rob Beau to let me throw a damn cutter in this game.

"Still no," he says in response to my incoherent noises.

Huffing, I lean back against the wall to keep waiting for the inning to end. Not far off, a couple of staff members are fitting Logan Kim back with his catcher gear. He has seen the whole exchange and said nothing, which means he agrees with our manager and won't signal for any cutters this game either.

Neither man has ever been a pitcher. They don't understand what this prohibition does to a pitcher's mind. Mine is this close to breaking and resorting to begging or extortion. Not sure which one.

Finally the inning ends and I grab my glove. Kim and I jog together out of the dugout, and when he lifts his mitt to cover his mouth, I know he's about to drop some truth bombs the other team shouldn't find out about.

"Stop acting like a toddler pitching a tantrum."

Well, that's less exciting than I expected.

I cover the bottom half of my face with my glove too. "Look, you and I both know that my fastball and curve aren't enough to take on the Riders. Otherwise I'd have taken the starter spot from whatshisface years ago."

"That's correct but we still don't want the Riders or whatshisface to know what you're really made of."

I stop for a quick second, my lips stretching into a smirk. "What am I really made of?"

Kim knows I'm fishing for a compliment, which is why he responds, "Angus cow manure, straight from the heart of Texas."

"You couldn't just drop one measly compliment even if you didn't mean it? Right before I pitch this inning?" I click my tongue.

His face twists with disgust. "It's not like you're my girl-friend, Starr."

"Thank goodness. I'd be miserable."

The umpire gives us a pointed look and we both head over to our positions.

At the top of the mound, I take one look at the dirt under my feet and annoyance bubbles up my throat. I let it escape in a whispered curse. Whatshisface has always been a stomper, a real bull on the mound trying to mark his territory. He digs his toes deep with his support leg, and then drags his heel with the landing one, turning the dirt into an uneven shitshow I've never been able to stomach, since I'm entirely the opposite. My windup wastes too much energy with its big motion and I can't afford losing anymore with uneven footholds. Not to mention, it throws me the hell off because the holes in the dirt increase *my* risk of injury, not his.

And this is just one of the reasons why I can't stand his freaking face. For years, it felt like I was the only one with the problem, but now that he's gone other players and some staff are feeling a lot more comfortable with sharing stories. That's why I really want to defeat his fancy new team with my cutter. Alas.

Huffing, I take a moment to even out the dirt with my foot. Somehow I'll have to find the way to hold the Riders back with my old pitches.

Well, not just me. I lucked out in keeping the weapon that made Ben Williams the forty-million-dollar pitcher he is now. And that's Logan Kim.

He crouches down at the same time that the umpire calls play ball, and the first sign Kim gives me is a fastball with top backspin, the one I threw in my hometown that no one got to clock. The Riders are starting with the top of a lineup full of sluggers that won't balk at a good fastball, so I guess we're just going for a fielders game rather than a pitcher's game.

Fine. I have no real problem with that. I'm used to not being the star of the show, but it doesn't mean I'm giving up on that goal.

I nod and glance back for a second. The outfielders move in just enough, knowing that this is gonna be a whole ass carnival soon.

Facing out front, I wind up big time, sucking in air to give me even more explosive power. The ball slides out of my fingers in a way that leaves them tingling—in a good way. The ball crashes in a nasty thud against Kim's mitt, echoing around the stadium. I land right in time for the beautiful view of the batter swinging and missing so hard that he falls to one knee.

The crowd erupts as the umpire calls, "Strike!"

I stay stoic but on the inside I'm hootin'. That was fun.

Kim returns the ball and I pluck it from the air with my glove. I sweep around the dirt again and just in case, check the dugout. Apparently the success of that fastball worked against me because Beau shakes his head again, still no cutter.

Good freaking gravy.

Unfortunately, my All-Star, super trustworthy catcher calls

for a curve that leads to an unfieldable grounder and a runner on first. Another head shake from from Beau.

The contest is tighter with the second batter, but the three balls and two strikes situation ends in another runner on base thanks to a bit too much sweat in my hand. Grunting, I grab the rosin bag and toss it around until enough dust coats my hand. I blow the excess away and face my catcher once more.

Really? I wish I could ask him to his face. But another curve? He does know we're in the heart of the batting order, right? Like, it's only their best batter after this, another damn All-Star, and they already have two runners on base.

Yet, Kim signals for the curve again. And to twelve o'clock.

Like, I get it. I'm a southpaw. That angle's gonna be ugly for a right-handed batter, but these dudes can hit it.

"Here goes nothing," I sing song to myself without moving my lips.

Crack!

Well, look at that. We just set a perfect chessboard for the next batter, Miguel Machado, to step up to the plate and send us packing.

The crowd loses their collective shishkebab as the superstar slugger walks up to the plate. This ridiculous beast was last year's MVP for the whole league, and so far has batted four home runs even though we're only a month into Spring Training, with a .500 batting average and a .603 on-base percentage, on pace to break several kinds of records this season alone.

There's only one pitch in my arsenal that is noxious enough to give Machado any pause, and it's the one apparently Beau wants to preserve for a perfect world.

We are, in a succinct word, screwed.

Machado doesn't even whiff at the first pitch, a solid two-seam that would stump the bottom of the Riders lineup. But the next curveball does us in. The jerk doesn't even use aluminum bats, yet he hits it so hard that his wooden bat cracks and the ball still flies like a rocket to the sun.

I don't even have to turn to know it's a damn grand slam. I rub my ear as the Riders fans scream their throats raw, glorying in our obvious defeat.

Kim stands up and signals for the fielders to come over as well, and I sigh. It's only the fifth inning but I wouldn't be surprised if they want to pull me right this second. Meanwhile, the four Riders round the bases and step home in succession, jumping to high five one another like this is their show and theirs alone.

"Hey," Kim calls my attention.

I grunt in response.

"How you feeling?"

I marinate it for a second, and the strongest response comes from my midriff. "Hungry."

He does a double take.

Lucky leans his arm on my shoulder. "Guys, I think our pitcher broke."

"Maybe." I shrug him off me. "But if I'm not allowed to fight these guys with my best weapon, there's no other outcome than this. Instead, I'm really looking forward to dinner."

Miller, our first baseman, bursts into guffaws. "Practical as ever, Cowboy."

Kim tilts his head, studying me. "What do you want to eat?"

"Are we really going to have a food conversation in the middle of a game?" O'Brian, right outfielder, asks from behind me.

"Pizza," I respond clearly. "The greasiest pie we can find. The kind that turns the damn box transparent."

"Oh, man."

"That's the stuff."

Someone else's stomach roars.

"Tell you what." Kim steps closer and narrows his eyes at me. "I'll buy you that disgusting thing people pass off as food, but you have to do something for me in exchange."

I put a hand on my chest. "Keep it PG, man. There are witnesses."

He rolls his eyes at me. "What you're going to do is hold off the rest of their lineup this inning. And the next. And the next until you're subbed out. Can you do that, Cowboy?"

Silence befalls the team.

I blink, zeroing in on the dead serious face of the half Korean half Swedish all American catcher. He looks intense on a normal moment with his long hair, Sauron eyes that see everything, '70s goatie, and tattoos all over his arms. But he looks positively unhinged right now. Like he's testing me to see if I can hold up the end of such a steep bargain. Like maybe the asshole drove me to this corner to see if I break.

I want to punch him in his GQ face. I'm so pissed but amused at his clever tactic, that it all bubbles out in an unhinged laugh that no doubt will make the social media highlights of the game. Probably even more than the grand slam.

Pinching my glove between my left elbow and my side, I free my right hand to offer it to him for a handshake. "Deal."

He grasps it with his paw. "Transparent box."

"Triple cheese."

"Cholesterol infested."

"Stuffed border."

"Personal size or large?"

"Jumbo, you douchebag. Don't be cheap."

"You guys scare me," Lucky says behind me.

"This is the most bizarre battery this team has ever had," declares Brown, our third baseman.

Lucky pats my back. "Hang in there, Cade. Don't let that master manipulator play you like a fiddle."

Too late and we all know it. This is what makes Logan Kim

one of the best catchers in the league, that unmatched devious-ness of his. And I have no option but to dance to his tune during Spring Training if I want to make it as a starter pitcher.

But after that? I'm going to make his life miserable.

Once everyone returns to their positions, I raise my index and call out very clearly, "One out! For the pizza!"

"For the pizza!" the fielders shout in return, and we focus on the rest of the game.

CHAPTER 17
HOPE

"Do you remember the pitches?" the cowboy asks me once he has stopped his truck at a secluded corner of the parking lot, but with the same seriousness he exudes during an important game play.

"I think so." I tug at the sleeves of my cardigan, for lack of anything better to do.

"Run through them," the catcher suggests from the backseat.

I swallow hard, audibly. Starr unbuckles himself to turn slightly toward me on his seat and rests his arm on the top of his steering wheel. It strikes me for the first time right now, years after working with him in the team, that he's massive. He takes up so much space in this gigantic truck that feels like it's swallowing me.

But I glance back and Kim and Rivera also look barely comfortable in the spacious backseat, so I don't know why this would be a big deal.

I clear my throat. It isn't. My mind's just been momentarily addled by so much manly cologne wafting in the air.

"Pitch one," I start, "Play with my hair—tuck it, twirl it,

run my hands through it or whatever." I have to resist the urge to roll my eyes.

Starr nods. "Good. Pitch two?"

"Lean forward," I respond, folding my arms. This one's gonna be a challenge because my floral dress has a cleavage that's significantly deeper than I'm used to, which isn't a lot anyway. The key part is that I'm not used to it.

"Pitch three?"

"Find some natural way to laugh." I cringe a little. "Maybe let's not use that one too frequently. I don't have one of those cute little twinkling laughs that makes guys melt."

From the back, Rivera says, "Unfortunately this is more about him than about you. Guys like to feel like they're smart and funny, and getting a laugh is the way to know they're on the right track."

"Ugh," I grouch.

"Pitch four." Starr's still staring at me. We're only illuminated by the faint lights from the dashboard and the streetlights outside, and a beam from somewhere makes his eyes look almost unnatural. Like glass that shines from within. It's pretty freaky and mesmerizing in equal measures.

It takes a moment for my brain to restart normal function. "Right. That one is about asking him a question."

Starr bobs his head. "I'll use this one in the odd chance I see you talking most of the time. But pitch five?"

"The opposite. If he's talking too much, I should ask him if he doesn't want to know something about me."

"That's right. Be bold, Garcia," says Kim right behind me.

While I huff, Starr asks, "Pitch six?"

"Pretend to use the restroom to strategize with you weirdoes."

"Seven?"

"That's the wild pitch," I say, wrinkling my nose. "The one about doing something absolutely bananas to get his attention. If you call for this one I will break both of your wrists."

Starr's lips twitch. "Eight?"

I relax in my seat. "This one is you asking me for a sign in case I need to be bailed out."

"And what's the sign?"

"I'll tug my ear."

"Last but not least, pitch nine," he finishes.

"A heads up that you're bailing me out no matter what I think."

"Good girl." Before I can react, Starr reaches over and ruffles my hair like I'm a dog.

"Hey! My roommates spent hours getting me ready." I bat his paw away and comb my hair with my fingers, glaring at him all throughout.

"Is the receiver secure?" he asks as if nothing's amiss.

"Yes," I grumble, still glaring at him. "Rose used a million bobby pins to hold it in place just above my left ear and you almost ruined it with your greasy paw."

"Greasy? I'll have you know I showered."

Yeah, I know. They had a game today and no doubt showered before even hopping on the plane back. It's why their colognes have smelled so strong since they picked me up in Starr's truck.

"Ready?" Kim asks. "Like, no pressure but I really need to breathe fresh air."

"Me too." Rivera straight up opens his door.

Starr's face morphs into annoyance as he looks back at his bestie. "I told you to stop roughhousing while I was getting ready."

"Not my fault you spilled your aftershave all over yourself, butter fingers."

"Ohh, so this is why I've been almost choking," I say, also opening my door.

Kim grunts. "I told you, you should've showered again."

While turning off his car, Starr says, "Do you want me to turn into a prune like you, old man?"

I snort. As if Kim isn't barely a year older than him.

I slide off the seat and my feet land on the asphalt before my dress skirt settles back down. Twirling around quickly, I find that Starr's attention is still fixed on the backseat where more barbs are shooting his way. I exhale in relief, because it means he didn't see my comfy boy shorts underneath.

"Well, wish me luck, you guys." I clutch at the strap of the little purse Audrey lent me, but it gives me no strength back.

"You got this, mami," yells Rivera from the back.

"We got you," Kim says in contrast.

All Starr does is drag the sleeve of his bomber jacket up to show me the transmitter of the PitchCom around his waist.

This is the single most ridiculous thing I've ever done in my life: have someone else give me instructions on what to do in a date—and even more when they come from *a guy*.

But this is exactly what I've needed all along. I've sat paralyzed with fear of failure and fear of being hurt in too many dates. I admit freely that I don't know how this game works, and the only reason I ever had one boyfriend was because I already knew him. Or thought I knew him… semantics.

I take a deep breath that brings more of Starr's aftershave into my lungs and shut the passenger door. After smoothening the wrinkles off my dress, I make my way through the parking lot and walk into the restaurant.

A hostess immediately greets me with, "Welcome! How can I help you?"

"Um, reservation under Frank?" I hate the uncertain tinge in my voice, but I have actually come into a date in these exact circumstances, only to discover that the guy never made a reservation and of course didn't show up at all.

"Of course," she says in a peppy way, to my utter relief. "Please follow me."

Welp. Like it's a magic trick, my heart rate immediately rises as we walk across the restaurant. The hostess is taller than me and hides the view until we're close enough, and I recognize Frank the high school chemistry teacher sitting at a table, head bowed down while he reads something on his phone. Props to him that his thumb isn't swiping right or left while waiting for his date.

"Here you go." The hostess stops by him, motioning at the free chair that will have me sit with my back to the door. I won't be able to see the arrival of the three baseball stooges, but it is what it is.

"Hi." I try for a smile and a wave of my hand as the hostess abandons us—me, abandons *me*—but there's no reaction from Frank, other than blinking up at me. Slowly, I lower my hand. "Um…"

"Oh, hi! Of course. Hi." He jumps to his feet and offers his hand for a handshake like this is a business meeting.

I shake it because what else can I possibly do? But I don't like his hand. Not because it's clammy with the same nervous sweat that's coating my own, but because it's too smooth. More than mine. It's just so unfamiliar.

We both take our seats in uncomfortable silence. Audrey's purse falls over my thighs and I lift the strap over my head, twisting to hang it from the back of the chair. And I don't know how or why, but I lift my face and make direct eye contact with Cade Starr.

He has his chin propped on his hand, watching me. They've found a table clear across the floor plan, slightly farther up so my dating coach can catch all the action easily. I don't know if that's more unnerving or relieving, knowing that I'm not alone. But I really wish he was looking at the menu right now like the other two are doing.

Like it's no biggie and he does this everyday, Starr tugs at his sleeve and presses a button. Even though I know it's coming, I still stiffen at his recorded voice softly whispering the word *one* above my ear.

I tuck my hair behind my tingling ear and turn to my date. He's still blinking at me like he's seeing a ghost or something.

"So…"

That snaps him out of the trance and a slow grin takes over his features. He's cute in a boy next door type of way and the smile does him justice. "Sorry about that," he says while clearing his throat, "I was just stunned by how beautiful you are."

"Uh, thanks." My face twitches and I force a smile out. That is such a canned phrase that of course I only receive while I'm wearing a dress that's a bit too revealing. I wonder if he'd notice if I try to close the cardigan over my chest and over the open triangle that shows a sliver of stomach.

"I'm sorry if this is forward of me but I can't believe you're single." He leans forward and props to him that he keeps his attention on my face. "Can I ask why?"

"Why I'm single?" I repeat, my hand sliding towards the napkin I want to use for blotting the sweat of my brow.

"*Two.*"

A tiny gasp escapes from my lips at the instruction. I abandon the idea of the napkin and instead prop my elbows on the table to lean forward. Frank's eyes fly to my chest for a second too long, and I don't give a shit about Starr's instructions anymore. I lean all the way back against my chair.

"Hi, my name is Mandy and I'll be your server tonight," a woman says appearing beside us. "Are you ready to order or do you need a few minutes?"

I open my mouth but Frank is quicker. To me, he asks, "Since this is a seafood restaurant I assume you don't have any allergies, right?"

"Oh, yeah. None."

"Great." He turns to the server. "Then we're going to start with the oysters for two and the white Zinfandel."

Mandy gives me a quick look but I've turned into a statue. "Good choices, sir. Please call me if you need anything else." She retreats quickly.

That's when I notice my mouth has been hanging open this whole time. I snap it shut and glance down at the menu that I haven't even had a chance to touch.

Is it too early to tug at my ear? Because a guy ordering for me with no consideration for what I want is a red flag the size of Texas. And like, yeah, at least he checked that nothing here could send me to the hospital. But maybe he could've taken a second to ask if I even like the goopy things. Better yet, let me order for my own damn self.

I slide my hands below the table so he can't see how hard I'm squeezing my fists.

"So, why are you single?" he asks again, holding his chin like he's ready to hear my life story.

Not only do I not owe him that, I also have zero interest in sharing it.

"It's just how things shook up. How about you?" I ask in return, without even waiting for the pitch four call.

With a chagrinned expression, he says, "I'm just coming out of a long relationship that didn't work out…" He trails off, giving me an expectant look I can't decipher. "Aren't you gonna ask me why it didn't work out?"

"Oh." I squirm, trying to find a more comfortable spot on the plush chair. "No, I wasn't going to. That's private."

He laughs. "But isn't that what we're here for? To get to know each other?"

"I guess but—"

"She cheated on me." Frank sighs, shaking his head of thinning dirty blond hair. "With another teacher at my school."

"Oof, that's rough." I stretch my lips in a cringe of sympathy. I can relate more than he knows.

"Would you like to taste the wine, sir?" a different server says, holding a chilled white bottle wrapped in a white linen cloth, completely ignoring me. He must think I don't like wine, which is a mistake, or that I don't have a discerning palate—which isn't the point.

So what if I can't tell apart notes of oak barrel casket or grapes from California versus Chile? I recognize tasty versus yuck, so why am I being dismissed here?

While the male server and Frank do their tasting dance, I toss a glance over at the table with baseball boys. Kim's the first to react and smacks Starr's arm with enough force to make the guy wince while he's drinking water. He turns his attention to me and sees something in my face that has him pressing a button on the transmitter.

"*Six.*"

I shake my head slightly, like I'm the pitcher rejecting her catcher's call. It's not time yet to regroup.

"Excellent, very rich," Frank says in a way that feels rehearsed, and it occurs to me that he was here earlier than me. Who's to say he didn't rope the sommelier into this little theater to appear cultured and worldly?

I bite my lips, almost appreciating the effort. Literally not one of my other dates tried anywhere this hard for me.

I glance down. Is this the power of a little boob?

No, he couldn't have known I was going to wear this dress.

I wonder if he might've changed tack if I showed up in my usual sport polo and windbreaker, with joggers smeared in dirt from a baseball field or grease from some exercise machine. Probably not.

What if other dates also meant to make an effort and decided that I wasn't worth it based on how I looked? Like, obviously that means they weren't the right person for me all along. But I also don't want a guy who tries extra hard just because I'm wearing clothes that show off what my momma gave me.

The server pours two generous cups for us and the second he goes away, I take a healthy sip of the wine.

"So, Hope. What do you do for a living?" Frank asks, apparently not recalling that we already had this conversation via chat. Then again, he must be talking with twenty other women at the same time and can't get facts straight.

Annoyed but trying to replicate Rosalina's beauty pageant smile, I say, "I'm an athletic trainer for the Orlando Wild."

"Wow." His eyes sweep down and up my frame again. "No wonder you're so stunning. You must work out a lot."

This is dangerously close to a territory other guys have shown me they dislike. It's like they love a hot woman, but she can't be more dedicated to her fitness than they are because then she's self absorbed.

"Ah, yes. Nowhere near the level of elite athletes, though," I say carefully, trying to steer him away from delving deeper into my exercise regime.

"Anything going on with any of the players though?" he asks with a too-loud laugh. "Just want to know if I have competition, you know?"

"No, I'm a professional and so are they." Ish. He doesn't have to know that.

"*Three*," whispers the recorded voice of one such professional athlete over my ear. He must've guessed it was the timing, based on Frank's laughter. The last thing I want to do is pretend like this is a hee-hee-ha-ha moment because I'm so annoyed, but whatever. I drop an awkward chuckle to flatter him.

"Oysters for two." Mandy settles the whole paraphernalia on the table, a wide plate of oysters sitting on ice, two little plates with lime slices and some kind of sauce. A second server places a basket with steaming bread and butter cubes sliding down the crust slopes as well.

"Excellent!" Frank tucks in right away, grabbing an oyster and squeezing some lime on it and sucking it with gusto. I end up using a host of muscle groups in an effort not to cringe visibly.

Instead, I grab some of the warm bread and start with that.

"You need to try the oysters, they are truly incredible. Here." He takes one, squeezes lime juice on it, and offers it to me.

I guess it would be rude if I reject it right away. Leaving the yummy bread on my plate, I take the oyster. Maybe if I look at the ceiling instead of at the slimy insides I won't hate it as much. Bracing myself, I bring it to my lips and suck like he did.

Oh my word. I *hate* it. We should've gone to a burger joint or something. I thought I'd order some fancy ahi tuna, not *this*.

I set the empty shell on my plate and swallow without even attempting to chew. The quicker the feeling and the taste disappear from my mouth, the better. I reach for the wine to wash it all down.

Frank leans back, sighing. "Damn, you're so sexy. I could watch you eat oysters all night."

I choke slightly. It takes me a second to comprehend how his words can even relate to me eating a disgusting oyster. And then I realize it's because it requires sucking and my skin crawls to the point where I break into goosebumps. The really bad kind.

Calmly, I set the wine glass down and tug at my ear. When nothing happens right away, I tug twice more for good measure.

Like he doesn't notice my discomfort, Frank continues talking. "Did you know that oysters are an aphrodisiac? I never really believed it until this moment."

The oyster must've been alive because it's climbing up my throat—fast.

"Hope?"

I snap my face up. Never has Cade Starr used my first time, and never has it sounded more beautiful than in this very moment.

Behind him are Logan Kim and Lucky Rivera, and I've never liked these guys as much as I do right now.

"Guys!" I exclaim in a very exaggerated way.

"Fancy running into you," Rivera says, hands on his hips like he can't believe the surprise.

Frank gasps. "Wait, Cade Starr? And Logan Kim?"

Rivera points at himself but Frank pointedly ignores him, like he doesn't know who our shortstop is. If I wasn't sufficiently annoyed before, I'm even more so right now. Lucky's one of the best shortstops of the league right now and doesn't deserve the snub.

"Sorry to interrupt your date," Starr says with the kind of smile that could see him through presidential elections. "We couldn't help but saying hi to the best trainer in the Wild organization."

"Why don't you guys give Frank your autographs while I head to the restroom?" I say while pushing my chair away from the table.

"That would be amazing." Frank starts looking around for something they can sign, and Kim comes to the rescue.

He pulls out a small notepad from his back pocket and opens it to a blank page. "What's the name?"

I stand up and take my borrowed purse. Just as I'm side stepping around the towering baseball players, a hand shoots out of nowhere and grabs my wrist. I recognize the callouses even before I look up to find our starter pitcher, turned sideways from the table to slide his car key into my hand. I grip it tight and nod my thanks, and he lets me go.

I'm more relaxed than I'd have imagined for someone who is trying to escape a bad date. But then I get to the restrooms and start panicking because this is the stark opposite direction from the door.

How am I going to escape without Frank noticing me tiptoeing up to the front? There's only so much distraction three autographs will grant me.

"Can I help you, miss?" Mandy, our server, appears right behind me.

"Oh my gosh, yes. I need to escape that creepy guy."

She cringes. "Yikes, bad date, huh?"

"He said he could watch me eat oysters all night and did I know they're an aphrodisiac?"

"Sis, say no more." She casts a furtive glance around. "Come with me. I'll sneak you out of the kitchen."

I waste no time in following her, but the fact that none of the staff balk at some random chick walking between them through the kitchen tells me this is probably not the first time something like this happens.

Sure enough, Mandy leads me out of an exit that opens directly to the dumpsters in the back of the parking lot.

"Did you bring your car?" she asks me and I show her Starr's key in my hand. "Good. And don't worry, I'll pretend like I know nothing."

"Thank you so much." I widen my eyes, reacting a second later for my purse. "Wait, please let me give you a tip."

"You don't have to—"

"No, trust me. You're saving me from a big mess." I pull a Cade Starr and hold her wrist, leaving a twenty on her hand because that's all I have on me in cash. If I had a Benjamin I'd give her that. "Thank you."

"We need to have each other's backs." She reaches out for

a hug that I return enthusiastically and we part ways—her back to the kitchen, and me to furtively sneak into Starr's truck to wait for them.

CHAPTER 18
CADE

"Go, go, go, go!" Garcia motions with her hands like she's the base coach and we're runners to home.

The three of us climb into my truck with the same intensity and I only slow down to make sure everyone's seatbelts are fastened before peeling out the parking lot. The rearview mirror shows a clear coast, like the guy hasn't realized quite yet that his date bailed on him while he was distracted getting our autographs and selfies.

I grip my steering wheel tighter as we merge into traffic. "Where to? Home?"

"No," Garcia grouches and from the corner of my eye I catch her fold her arms tight like she does when she's upset. "To the greasiest food joint we can possibly find."

"Pizza?" Lucky and I ask at the same time.

"No," Kim cuts in from the backseat. "You didn't earn it."

"Dude." I sigh in exasperation. "I literally only let one more run through after the grand slam. Pretty sure I deserve pizza for that too."

"A deal is a deal and you didn't uphold your end."

"I don't know what the hell you all are talking about but I'd really love a pizza right now," Garcia says.

Since traffic is light, I jerk us to make a quick U turn.

"Starr." Kim's voice comes out like a growl. "Where are you taking us?"

"The lady wants pizza. Who am I to deny her request after she just had a bad date?"

"Good boy," she says, and since I'm driving I can't fend her off when she stretches over to mess my hair. Not that I would have, anyway. She deserves her revenge.

The difference, though, is that I don't bother fixing my hair after that. I probably look like I put my finger in an electric socket as I lead us into my favorite pizza place.

It works out great because what I like about it is that it isn't fancy at all. A bunch of bored college kids are at the counter, the kind that don't care about sports and would rather spend their time studying—and I'm not stereotyping, dude literally has a chunky physics textbook open by the register. And so, every time I come here I'm ignored and left to eat my greasy pizza in peace and quiet. It's perfect.

Someone shoves me with enough force that I have no choice but to step aside, and Garcia bursts through. She turns back to us, oblivious to how the college kid ogles her like she's the single hottest entity he's ever witnessed IRL. "Everyone okay with a meat lovers?" she asks.

"Oh yeah," Lucky responds.

Kim sighs. "Fine. But I'm not buying because Starr doesn't deserve it."

"I'll buy it." Rolling my eyes, I reach for my wallet in my back pocket and add, "Make it stuffed crust, though."

She turns back to the kid. "Extra large stuffed crust meat lovers. One large Coke, two large unsweet iced teas, and one medium sweet iced tea."

"Um, um. Yes. Will that be all?" He blinks hard.

"And a brownie." Garcia nods more to herself than to the kid and stomps away to a table by the window.

The kid is still staring at her as he says, "That'll be thirty seven and fifty two cents."

I slap a fifty on the counter and say, "Hey kid, you do know she's way out of your league right?"

"Oh yeah…" He drags the last word until he manages to snap himself out of his stupor.

As I head over to the table, I contemplate whether I should tell her what just happened, so she can clinically understand that her problem with dating isn't her. But as I take the last free chair across from her, I realize there's no way anyone's getting a headway in right now.

"Can you believe that?" she's saying, angrily waving her hands around. "Like I get that he's probably chatting up a bunch of women at the same time, but he couldn't even have the curtesy of rereading our chat to refresh his mind, instead of asking me something he was supposed to already know? Way to make a girl feel special."

Beside her, Kim sits ramrod straight, eyes wide as he glances first at Lucky across him, and then at me.

Lucky's also uncharacteristically quiet. I don't dare to move to see what he's doing, in case that attracting her attention will remind her that I'm male and therefore also guilty of the shitty things other men have done to her.

"And then!" Her voice shakes. "He had the cojones of ordering for me! Which already pissed me the hell off, but that's nothing compared to what I felt when it turned out to be oysters—which I hate—and he got them just so he could be a creep. Like, made me eat one and then started making comments about how sexy that was and that it's an aphro-disiac. Can you believe that shit?"

I slam the table and jump to my feet. The guys do the same, our chairs making an ugly scraping sound.

I zero in on the mean looking catcher. "Can you fight?"

"Damn right, I can." He cracks his knuckles.

"I hope that bastard is still there," Lucky says, followed by a string of words in Spanish that I can't comprehend but don't sound friendly at all.

Garcia takes a deep breath and barks, "Sit down. Now."

We freeze for a single second—then scramble to take our seats again.

"I appreciate the sentiment, but none of you are going to jeopardize your careers for me."

I run a hand through my hair. "I'm sorry, Garcia. I thought he looked the most normal out of the other ones."

With her elbows on the table, she drops her face in her hands and grunts. "Ugh. I think walking up to a circus and asking out the nearest clown would be better than this."

"Excuse me," the college kid says and she leans away from the table, tossing her head back with a pained expression like she has lost the strength to even hold her head up. Unfortunately that reveals a bit too much skin for the employee and he trips on his feet, almost spilling all the drinks on her.

I jump to catch the glasses right in time. Meanwhile, Kim does the same—except he's not reaching for the drinks. Instead, he's using his hands to obscure the view of Garcia's chest from the horny yet barely adult employee. Kim's glare sends him scrambling back to the counter.

Huffing, Garcia lifts her head back up and Kim and I settle down like nothing just happened. Beside me, Lucky stuffs his fist against his mouth to stop himself from laughing.

"I think I'm just going to give up," she declares all of a sudden.

"You're well within your right," Kim says, taking one of the large unsweet teas.

Lucky grabs the Coke, staring at Garcia's hand reaching for

the last unsweet tea and leaving the medium sweet tea for me. "Wait a second, how did you know our drink orders?"

"I know what all of you eat and drink." Her entire face is scrunched up in annoyance as she sips from her tea.

"Never mind that. What about Friendsgiving?" I ask, reminding her of her own goal.

She groans, her shoulders dropping in even more defeat. The sound unfortunately gets the attention of the employee again. I lean to the side so I can pin him with a very clear glare. It means *keep looking at her like she's food and I will screw you over*. He confirms my initial guess of him being smart by stabbing his eyes back down on his textbook.

"You're right, I can't give up. But what am I going to do?"

Kim stretches his arm behind her and rests it on the back of her chair. "It seems to me like dating apps aren't working though. Why don't you try something else?"

"Like what?" She lifts her face to him. I don't know if she realizes how close that puts them together.

"Meeting old school." He shrugs, his leather jacket almost gleaming under the white halogen lights. "At the grocery store, or at a game, or through friends. Something like that."

"I'm doomed." She turns back to me. "I don't have time to waste loitering at the store, waiting for someone to pick me up. And all my friends are at work, where I spend basically my every waking moment."

The employee comes by with the massive pie. To his credit, he pivots away before his beady eyes can find Garcia's chest again.

I rub my chin, pondering her words while Lucky's the first to tuck into the pizza. Kim grabs a handful of napkins from the side and hands them all over to Garcia, and to my shock, this earns him a smile.

My entire body grows as stiff as a plank at the realization. The answer has been there all along.

It's not the first time I catch her acting out of character in front of Logan Kim. Maybe the old school way he's suggesting is precisely this, for Garcia to simply date someone from the team or staff. And it seems like he's the one who catches her attention.

"Aren't you eating?"

It takes me two tries to tear my eyes away from the little smile on her face, and from Kim taking a slice to place it on her plate. More romantic than her date, already.

Slowly, I look over at Lucky. "What?" His cheeks look like a chipmunk that has stuffed a bit too many nuts, so instead of using his vocal cords he just lifts his half eaten slice in response. "Right, right."

I grab one for myself and take a bite, but it doesn't taste that great tonight.

*

I'm quiet as I drive us back to the Wild training facilities where the others left their vehicles. Garcia, Kim, and Lucky chat about who knows what, no words filter into my brain. My left elbow is propped against the window and I rub my chin, thinking about how I even am going to make this happen. Will Garcia kill me or thank me when she finds out?

I stop by the security gate and lower the window to swipe my badge. I spot Kim's Ducati first but keep driving. Then there's Lucky's Escalade, a couple other cars from people who must be working really late, and farther is Garcia's yellow Jeep.

"Tonight's been interesting," Lucky says, unbuckling himself. "Are we doing it again?"

"Hopefully not. No offense." Beside me, she also removes her seatbelt. She reaches into her hair, rummaging for a good moment until I realize what she's doing.

"Just give it to me tomorrow," I say.

"Thanks. There are just too many bobby pins." She shows me a whole pile already in her hand before opening her purse to dump them in. As she searches for something else, she mumbles, "Thank you, guys. I don't know what I'd have done without you."

I turn to look at the window, clamping my mouth shut tight.

"Any time, Garcia," Lucky responds instead.

"Yeah, and if you need to have someone beat up, just call us." Kim grunts.

"Good night, then." I hear her door open, the slide of her dress and skin off the seat, and then the door shuts.

Behind me, the guys open their doors and I spring to action. Jumping out of my truck, I grab a handful of Kim's leather jacket to hold him back.

"What the—"

"We need to talk."

His face twists. "What about?"

Lucky rounds my truck and finds us there. He does a double take at my grip on Kim's clothes. "Dare I ask?"

"No." I wave my free hand away. "We need to talk battery shit. Go."

"Gladly." Lucky pretends to wipe sweat off his forehead and heads over toward his vehicle.

I release Kim just so I can reach into my truck to turn it off. Meanwhile, the yellow Jeep drives by and the Escalade lights come on at a distance.

"This is starting to creep me out, Starr. Why do we need to be alone to talk about battery business?"

"Because that was bullshit. This isn't about work." Slamming my truck door shut, I stuff my hands in the pockets of my jeans and lean back. "This is personal."

Kim spreads his feet apart and folds his arms. "Is that so?"

Bobbing my head, I blurt out, "Are you single?"

For a long moment, the only thing that breaks the silence is Lucky's Escalade driving away with his stereo blaring some reggaeton that makes the ground vibrate.

Kim clears his throat. "What, are you interested?"

Slowly, I draw in a big breath and release it. "Listen, I know I like women with long hair, but just because you have long hair it doesn't mean that I confuse you for one."

"Oh, so this is about Garcia."

My eyebrows rise. "How did you guess?"

"Your question made me think two things. One, you were into me—thank heavens that's not the case. Or two, this is somehow related to this whole whacky night with Garcia. What's the deal, then?"

My fists tighten in my pockets. I have a short moment of hesitation. Am I doing the right thing here? Coaching her on how to act during dates is one thing, but this is entirely different. This is getting into her business. And yet, I can't help thinking that it's the best thing I can do for her. Like maybe it's not a bad idea, even though the pizza is rioting in my stomach.

"I hate it to admit it, but you're the most gentlemanly dude I know," I start with, speaking through my teeth. Kim's eyebrows rise and his eyes narrow, the picture of disbelief. "And it seems to me like you care about her to some degree. Enough to tag along tonight."

"Are you suggesting…"

"Yeah, you should go out on a date with her." Wow, saying it aloud is even worse than keeping it in my head.

"Hmm." Kim tilts his head as if that gives him a better angle to observe me. I stay still because I have no idea what he's looking for. I'm not joking here, I really think he's the best candidate for her.

I shrug. "Wouldn't that be the old school way you were talking about earlier?"

"Right." He tucks his tongue against his cheek. "Well, it's

true that I care about Garcia. She's pretty cool and she deserves to be treated right."

I nod, unable to produce even one word while I wait for the verdict.

"So… sure. I can date her."

My eye twitches. Dating her is different from what I suggested, which is taking her out on a date. But I guess that would ultimately be an even better result. With the way she looks at him sometimes, I'm sure she'd love to show him off at Friendsgiving this year and beyond.

"Cool, I'll arrange it," I say, my voice sounding all kinds of weird.

Kim rightfully guesses this conversation to be over. Without further ado, he walks over to his bike and I climb back into my truck.

I sit there long after Kim has left the premises, wondering just what in the actual hell I have just done. Even more, wondering why I feel like I'm gonna barf all over the dashboard.

CHAPTER 19
HOPE

Amy's first reaction when I started working for the Orlando Wild was gasping and saying, "Oh my gosh, you're going to be surrounded by so many hot men *all the time!*" Followed by squealing.

What she didn't know is that the hot men are sweaty *all the time*. With sweat comes a certain stink that you can't unlearn, and some of them don't shower properly so they have some B.O. that clings to them on and off the field. That's aside from how rank their uniforms and equipment get with use. This one time I made the mistake of cutting through the laundry area, and I haven't recovered yet.

And oh, guess what, Amy? Some of them fart while exercising. Sometimes a lot. I'm not gonna judge them for that because hey, so do I—so does everyone with intestines—but sometimes they compete over whose fart stinks the worst like middle school children. And sometimes such competitions make it really hard to breathe in here.

Like right now. O'Brian's face is redder than usual for an elite athlete who is only doing the last stretches for the day before hitting the showers, which very clearly signals him as the culprit.

Lucky Rivera can't stop coughing beside him because he was probably the receiver of the worst of it, and I never thought I'd feel this bad for the bubbly guy.

"Dude can you just point your gas hole in literally any other direction?" Lucky demands, pointing toward the window.

"Sorry, man. The breakfast burrito must've been kinda stale."

Somehow I find the strength in myself not to gag.

What probably saves me is that I get distracted by one of the younger guys half assing his stretches. I march over to him, thankfully removing myself from the area with the biohazard, and say, "You really need to get that full extension in. Otherwise you're teaching your muscles to stay tight. Like this." I sit down on the mat beside him, spreading my legs wide and reach for my big toes with both hands. "And then hold for thirty seconds at least."

"But…"

Slowly, I ease back up. The fact that he's avoiding my eyes raises a red flag right away. "Where does it hurt?" I ask with a calm tone.

He jerks his face up, eyes wide. "I—How did you know?"

"It's what I went to school for." I grin and it has the effect of relaxing his shoulders.

"I think it's my hamstring. It started bothering me after the sprint to second in the fifth."

That's baseball speak for he ran like the wind to second base in the fifth inning and has been hurting since. I didn't see him limp to the dugout after that, so hopefully that means it's nothing major. And I remember the play because it was quite spectacular, it got the crowd going.

"Try to flex your knee for me and tell me how it feels."

He winces a little but his leg moves pretty fluidly. It's good news but only leaves me with a basic course of action for now.

"All right, I'm going to go get an ice pack. Can you prop your leg up against that wall while I get it?"

"Okay." He sighs like this is the end of the world.

I pull myself back to stand and sort through a floor plan covered in men doing various stretching exercises, and trainers watching out precisely for things like this. Even as I walk with a clear objective in mind, I make sure that whoever I'm leaving behind is doing his stretching correctly. You'd think that men who have anywhere between ten and twenty years doing this seriously would know better, but you'd also be wrong.

Right as I'm about to walk into the training staff room, I get stopped by a hand around my wrist. I don't even have to wonder who it is anymore.

"Starr." I turn to glance over my shoulder.

The man himself holds my arm prisoner in his grip, and my eyes catch on the protruding veins traveling up his perfect arm. Perfect because he's not a dramatically bulky guy, but has the definition and volume every gym rat dreams of.

I guess it's not just his arm. He's in a short-sleeved compression shirt in Wild pruple that outlines every nook and cranny of his muscle fibers. I jerk my eyes up to his face, flushed from exercise, damp hair curled over his forehead, droplets of sweat tricking down his nose and chin.

"Garcia," he says in greeting. "Can you wait for me in the parking lot after we're done here? We need to talk about something."

My pulse goes from one hundred to a thousand.

It's never a casual topic when people say *we need to talk*, yet can't say whatever it is outright. But for the life of me, I can't think of anything bad that the cowboy might have to say, other than a variation of: you're too pathetic to consider dating anyone, so I'm quitting as your coach.

And I desperately need that to not be the case. I don't want to keep feeling like a failure forever.

Swallowing hard twice, I manage to say, "Sure. Not a problem. See you there. At my car. Or I mean, at the parking lot."

He seems to not find my twisted tongue any weird because he nods, drops my hand, and turns back to his spot to keep stretching his shoulders with a medicine ball. I watch him for a second, the muscles in his back working through the motions and rippling and tensing beneath the fabric. I shake my head hard at myself and continue into the staff room.

There, I collapse against a wall.

What the heck was that? His aren't the only pretty muscles in this building. I slap my cheeks hard enough to center myself back in reality.

After picking up the correct ice pack and my iPad, I return to the floor to take care of the hamstring situation. After fitting the young guy with the ice pack—and fortunately not getting farted in my face—I step aside to log this incidence in his file so we can monitor him. Steve will hold a team debrief while the players hit the shower, and then I'll be able to...

Go and wait for Cade Starr in the parking lot.

I keep my eyes fixed everywhere but on him, yet the thought of The Talk—whatever it may be—keeps my heart rate at one thousand. Or okay, I exaggerate, at nine hundred.

Once I'm finished for the day, I trod out of the building along with my coworkers and get in my Jeep to wait. My leg bounces as I watch Steve drive off through the rearview mirror, and then other staff one by one. This all happens in the span of maybe one minute, and yet none of the players are walking out yet. Maybe they're also getting a debrief from Beau and the coaching staff.

I open my door and climb out, pacing back and forth just to let off some steam. I'm on lap fourteen across the sidewalk when some of the players start appearing. Freaking Starr is not among them.

Did he forget? Should I text him? No, he has a right to be as slow as he wants. He could be legitimately busy, like if Beau has held him back to talk about tomorrow's game against Logan Kim's brother. What do I know.

"Finally," I mutter when his pretty head pops out of the building followed by the rest of him, this time clad in jeans and a sweatshirt that don't openly show all his guns. I sigh in relief —except it shouldn't matter. But it does. I am legitimately glad that I can't distinguish his body.

While I have that existential crisis, he waves Rivera off and veers toward me. He checks his phone for a moment but after pocketing it, his freaky blue eyes find mine and pin me in place. I don't have to check my Apple watch to know that my heart rate is skyrocketing the more he approaches.

When he's maybe ten paces from me, he opens his mouth and I cut right in.

"What? What is it? My anxiety is killing me!"

Starr halts, his eyebrows rising. "You have anxiety?"

"Not until you said the words *we need to talk*. Do you understand how stressful that phrase is?"

How dare his lips twitch.

"It's no big deal." He sets his duffel bag on the sidewalk and stands back up. "Hmm, or maybe it is."

"Starr, don't make me maim you," I say through gritted teeth.

He full-on grins now. "Wow, I don't think those are words that should come out of an athletic trainer's mouth." I raise my fist and he backs one step, chuckling. "Hold your horses, darlin'. This is about the dating stuff."

"You're not quitting, are you?"

"No. I just have a different idea."

I empty my lungs in relief and let my shoulders slouch. It feels nice compared to how tense they were. "Do you, now?"

He folds one arm, his hand holding the crook of his opposite elbow, and with the free hand rubs his chin like he does when he's pondering. Those all-seeing blue eyes of his grow more serious too.

"Hear me out. I really don't think the dating app scene is for you."

Like a child, I kick at an invisible pebble. "I know. I categorically suck at it but what else can I do?"

"You're not the one who sucks, the weirdoes you've dated do." That stumps me, but if he notices that, he ignores it and continues, "So the whole mess last night gave me an idea. What if I arrange a blind date for you?"

My jaw drops. Eyes bulge. Heart trips.

"W—Whoa—*What?*"

His eyes trace every one of my physical reactions and a corner of his lips tilts. "What if I found you the perfect date? And also helped you get ready for it?"

"I—I... I don't know what to say."

"The answers you're looking for are either yes or no." He bends down to pick up his duffel bag and shrugs it on. "Anyway, think about it and let me know. Have a good night, darlin'." He tips his head, even though he's not wearing a hat, and walks by me, leaving a waft of clean man that makes me shudder.

I look at the back of his head, at the strong column of his neck, wondering how much force would take to wring it. Honestly, I'm not even this murderous with my brother, but there's something about Starr that makes me want to... to... do something. I don't know.

I stomp a few steps back to climb into my Jeep, waiting until he drives off in his black pickup to start my drive home.

*

Unfortunately, I'm not faring any better once I'm home. Even the comfort of clean clothes, our plush couch, and a fluffy blanket haven't gotten me out of the funky mood.

"What's your deal?" Rose asks, sitting beside me with a massive bowl of popcorn that I guess is her dinner for tonight.

"I don't know, I've asked her like three times and she hasn't spilled a word," says Audrey from the reclining armchair that's usually hers. She has the uncanny ability of multitasking like no one else I've seen, which right now features her reading something on her iPad while minding us two unruly children.

"I was waiting for full quorum to talk," I admit and unfold my legs from beneath me. "I need advice. Boy advice."

"Oh." Rose's eyes light up. "That's my favorite subject."

Meanwhile, Audrey groans. "Can we literally talk about anything else? All we do at work is talk about or to men. A girl is tired."

"But she needs advice, we can't be bad friends." Rose chuckles.

Sighing, I say, "Trust me, I too wish to be thinking about anything else but the male species. The problem is that they're so. Freaking. Annoying."

"Drop 'em truth bombs."

"You're not wrong about that."

After we've recovered from our grimaces, I explain, "As we're all fully aware, my dating endeavors have been truly a disaster. So Starr has come up—"

"Wait." Audrey tilts her head. "You still call him by his last name?"

I do a double take at the topic change. "Uh, yeah. It's either that or Cowboy."

"Does he call you Garcia too?"

"That or darling in that Texan accent of his. Why?"

"I'd have thought that with all the time you spend together you'd have become friendlier."

While munching, Rose chimes in, "He calls me princess."

"Apparently I'm sugar." Audrey points at herself.

I clamp my mouth, my eyebrows tightening. I guess he has a cutesy southern nickname for every woman in his life.

"Whatever." I wave my hand. "For the record, I'm also hanging out with Rivera and Kim a lot and we're all still on a last name basis." I lean back on the couch. "Except maybe Rivera and Starr because they're besties. But anyway, this isn't the point."

"Sorry, you were saying?"

"Starr has a new idea that is pretty out there." They both lean closer in anticipation. I take a deep breath and blurt out, "He wants to set me up on a blind date."

Instead of garnering the gasps and outrage I expected, Rose reacts to ask, "With whom?"

Audrey's eyebrows go up. "Is it with himself?"

"No!" I shout and turn to Rose. "And I don't know! I have no idea. He just sprang this on me like an hour ago. What do I do?"

"First I'd ask with whom," suggests roomie one, the popcorn monster.

"But that would defeat the purpose," surmises roomie two, the armchair hoarder.

"I should say no, right?" I glance from one to the other. "Right?"

Audrey sets her iPad on her lap and steeples her fingers. "But what if—and I know it feels like a big one—what if he legit finds someone awesome? Like, he's not the kind of guy who'd pull a prank about this."

"Haa, I hadn't even thought about that." I shake my head. "You're right, though. He's a pretty trustworthy guy in that regard at least. But what if he finds someone weird?"

"Weirder than men on dating apps?" Rose asks without any malice, pure conjecture alone.

"Oof, yeah, no."

"The question is… What if he's the one who shows up to the date?" Audrey asks.

Wait.

Wait.

Why does it feel like someone snatched the couch and I'm falling into a void? I have to grab fistfuls of my fluffy blanket to make sure I'm still sitting in place and not experiencing real vertigo.

"He wouldn't," I say firmly.

"Why not?" asks roomie two.

I blow a raspberry so hard that I'm pretty sure she won't need to water the living room plants anymore. "Look, we've all seen baseball boys flirting at bars. They have the subtlety of bulls. Especially him. Like, if he was into me in any way shape or form he'd let me know, Rivera style."

Audrey snorts and Rose chuckles. This is the post-Rivera club, we've all been asked out by him at one point or another.

"Cade's more subtle," Rose says, reaching for another handful of popped kernels and we both turn to her. "In fact, he rarely initiates. Women are usually the ones who do."

"Oh?"

She shrugs. "What? You're not the only one who sometimes travels with the team."

"True." I fold my arms. "But anyway, it's not him. Maybe he wouldn't be as overt as his buddy, but Starr knows I spook easily and he wouldn't spook me."

Audrey gives me A Look. "So you trust him enough to know that but still can't call him by his first name?"

"It's just weird, okay?" I frown.

"My thought is," Rose continues all by herself, "You don't

have anything to lose by trying. In fact, it sounds less scary than meeting a total stranger from the internet."

We all mumble at that. The most terrifying aspect of dating someone you've only met on an app isn't that he might not show up or reject you in your face—like it's happened to me time and again. But that he may hurt you.

Thankfully *that* has never happened, but Rose is right. I really doubt Starr would pair me with some freak when he himself came up with two pitch calls meant to bail me out of the crappy date.

I roll forward, letting the cushions swallow me. "Should I say yes?"

"It's up to you." Rose chews on popcorn for a moment before adding, "But I'd definitely say yes."

"I wouldn't," Audrey cuts in with a deadpanned tone. "But that's because I'm done with men forever."

Staring at the ceiling, I'll say, "Well, I have an ex to show up so... I guess I'm in."

Later, after we've settled down and headed to our rooms for the night, I tuck myself in bed with my cellphone. After several deep breaths and much staring at a certain pitcher's name on the screen, I send a response that may or may not change my life.

CHAPTER 20
CADE

There's nothing peaceful and quiet about Spring Training—or the season, period—but we luck into having two days in a row with nearby games that allow us to sleep at home. It's the perfect time to schedule this date between Garcia and one obnoxious catcher who acts like an actual decent person around her.

I try not to gag as I lean against my truck, waiting for Garcia.

It was shockingly easy to arrange this whole thing. Once Garcia texted me back saying that she wants to try it, I just had to confirm to Kim and we agreed on a restaurant for tonight. Lucky's free like the wind, so the two of us will oversee the whole thing from a nearby table we already got reservations for. Garcia knows we'll also be there, but she thinks it'll be the three of us watching out for her like at the seafood place. I even lent her the PitchCom again to really make her think she'll be on a date with someone she doesn't know.

But before that, I'm going to give her killer armor and weapons.

Her bumblebee yellow Jeep pulls into the parking lot of a random pharmacy near the training facilities, where we agreed to meet so that no one else from work can see us together and assume shenanigans. Are we shenaniganing? Yes, but not like *that*.

She parks two spots from me and gets out. She's still wearing her team branded staff uniform of purple jersey with yellow trim, including the white joggers. A guy walking out of the store literally stops and stares at her behind. I lift my eyes and fulminate him with all the power vested in me from simply being a full head taller than the damn creep.

None the wiser, Garcia says, "Here I am. Where are we going?"

I jerk my thumb behind me, attention still pinned on the asshole who just won't stop staring. "Hop in."

"Okay." With a deep breath, she walks around the front of the truck until she disappears behind it. The sound of the door opening and closing is what snaps the guy out of his frozen state of stupefaction.

"Ya done?" I bark at him.

"I—uh. Sorry, man. Didn't know she was taken." If it wasn't because of how fast he scrambles, I'd have told him to respect women even when they're not taken, but with far more profanity.

I wait until he drives away to climb in my truck. "What took you so long?" Garcia asks me, fully fastened and having turned the A/C vents toward her. Her loose hair waves from the air blowing to her face.

"Nothing." I turn away to grab my seatbelt and put it on before firing up the truck. Wanting to forget that gross little episode, I say, "Anyway, we're going shopping."

Garcia groans.

I'm glad I haven't even pulled out of the parking lot. Slowly, I glance her way. The utterly pained expression on her face is very much at odds with the things that sound made me feel.

I clear my throat. "What?" The question goes both to her and to my body, to be honest.

"I *hate* shopping."

"Of course you do." My words come out garbled.

She doesn't seem to notice because instead she folds her arms. "What is that supposed to mean?"

"You're always in training clothes, official or not." After a pause, I add, "Well, I apologize for the assumption on my part. Maybe you do enjoy shopping for gym clothes a lot."

"No, I hate it too."

"Then I withdraw my apology." Somehow that earns me a smack on my arm. "Hey, what's that for?"

"I don't know, I just have been bottling up a big need to do you bodily harm, but I really can't satisfy that without getting fired. This is the least you could take from me."

I jerk my face away lest she can read what's going on in my mind. That groan of hers has really put me on a path that's probably worse than the creep who was checking her out earlier. My logical brain knows there's no real innuendo behind her words, but my lizard brain screams that I could take everything from her.

"All right," I say a bit too loud and squeaky in an attempt to shut down that train of thought before it departs the station. I click on the radio and Shaboozey fills the quiet.

"You okay, Cowboy?" I can feel her laser beam eyes on the side of my face as I finally set the truck in motion and merge into traffic.

"Yep."

That's literally the last word I manage to say for the entire drive. Garcia tries to drill me about where we're going and I don't respond, which she thankfully takes to mean that I'm being mysterious, without having any idea that I'm just having a war with myself on the inside.

Since when does Hope Garcia make my skin feel like it's on fire?

At a red stoplight, she's saying, "—And that's why I think dresses are a waste of time. Like, I get it, guys can see some gams or some other skin and that's fun for them. But for me it's no fun if I can't move around freely or if I have no pockets, you know?" And her words barely register because all I can do is look at her.

Her skin is a light brown that doesn't blush easily. What would it take to make it grow fully red? But the funny part is that her lips are naturally pink. And thick. I once dated a girl who had to see a plastic surgeon to get hers to look kind of like Garcia's.

Shit, she's still moving them. "Hmm?" I manage to ask.

"I said, I bet you wouldn't like it if your clothes had no pockets, huh?"

I snort and turn back to the front when traffic moves again. I tighten my hands around the steering wheel. The radio shifts to a classic from Shania Twain and Garcia starts singing along under her breath, so I use the controls in my steering wheel to ramp up the volume. As she sings more freely, I relax on my seat.

We make it to the Outlets, one of Orlando's most touristy attractions. A lot of the hardcore shoppers have already left for the day and we manage to find a parking spot near the entrance. After watching for traffic, we cross the rest of the parking lot and I make sure to keep a friendly distance from her. Close enough that any other potential creeps will be deterred, but not enough that she'll get weirded out.

However, the grounds are still teeming with people who speak all the languages under the blue sky, and it forces us closer.

Just as we're rounding a corner, a tween boy runs by and I pull Garcia against me a second before the kid rams into her. The little jerk doesn't even apologize.

"Whoa!" Garcia then says something in Spanish that I have no hope of catching.

"You okay?" I look down.

Mistake. When she leans her head back to glance up, it fully rests against my right pec.

"Yeah, thanks. You probably just saved me from needing new teeth." She chuckles and I notice that her body's still pressed against mine.

I release her arms and step back slowly but surely. Jamming my hands in the pockets of my jeans, I lift my chin in the direction we should continue on because again, I can't speak for shit. My teeth gnash as we resume the walk. The feeling of her butt pressed against my hip hasn't disappeared, but that's not even as bad as the weight of her head on my chest.

Maybe I've been single too long. Rather, I've never had a proper girlfriend and maybe it's time to consider that. I'll sure need a big distraction once this whole saga with Garcia is over and she's found someone to be happy with.

Finally, I motion toward the fancy store I chose for this. I heard one of the wives at a team party once mention that this was where she shopped when she wanted to impress Miller, her hubby. It was followed by a lingerie brand but my brain blocked out that part for my own self preservation. Besides, that's not a stop we're going to include in tonight's shenanigans before I deliver her to Kim. I will also murder him in cold blood if he tries to take it that far on date one.

All that flies out of my head when Garcia stops, takes one look at the store's display, and blurts out, "I can't go in there."

"Why not?" I manage to ask, proud of myself that I'm verbal again.

"That's way too fancy. I can't even afford it."

I stretch my hand across the air and say, "Outlet."

"But—"

"Don't make me pick you up and take you in, because I will."

Her shoulders droop and she drags her feet, but does walk in. She slows down to whisper to me, "See? The whole place is completely empty because it's so expensive. Not even discounts can attract people."

I grab her by the shoulders and steer her across the shop floor, bypassing elegant displays of mannequins with blank faces. At the back is where we find people—a single clerk who beams upon sighting us.

"Welcome, Mr. Starr. We prepared the selection you asked us for and have a dressing room ready."

"Great, thanks." As I gently push a now non-verbal Garcia toward the dressing room, I add, "Oh, and please put the dresses with pockets at the forefront."

Hope Garcia glances at me over her shoulder with shock in her expression. "Wait, Cowboy, did you just—"

Rent the whole store for an hour for her to shop their best selection of dresses for a first date that a woman who isn't comfortable showing off her body could wear? Yes.

"I'll wait here," I say instead, lowering myself to the tiny loveseat that barely fits me. "Show me if you want. Or not. Up to you." I shrug like I'm not interested at all.

"Oh. Um. Okay." Garcia casts an uncertain look at the saleswoman who only smiles placidly in return, until she finally disappears behind thick white curtains.

The clerk turns to me. "Can I offer you both any drinks? We have red and white wine, champagne, beer, ice tea and water."

"Red wine for me, please!" Garcia shouts from the dressing room. "Wait, no. What if I spill it? Water, please."

"Red wine for her and sweet ice tea for me, please," I say.

"Right away."

Garcia waits until the woman's steps fade away. "Starr, I can't afford to pay for a stained dress here."

"Then I suggest you drink carefully."

"Ugh."

The faint jazzy music in the store doesn't mask the rustling sounds of the Orlando Wild's only female athletic trainer changing out of her clothes. Fortunately my phone buzzes in my pocket and I thank the heavens for the distraction.

CATCHER BRAT

I know you're dropping her off but am I taking her home?

I suck in air sharply. I hadn't thought about that.

Her car is still at a pharmacy's parking lot near downtown. I guess if the date goes well she'll want to extend it as long as possible and have Kim drive her home. I could get Lucky to pick up her car and drive it to her place, or to the facilities. She could catch a ride tomorrow morning with Winters or Mena.

"Shit," I hiss to myself. There's something even more important than that.

ME

We'll figure that out later

You better not take your bike though

She's gonna be in a dress

I think Garcia wrapping her legs around Kim and hugging him from behind as they zoom through the city would be too much for their first date.

CATCHER BRAT

How do you know about that?

Right. I didn't tell him or Lucky about this stop first. Rather than fess up, I double down.

ME
Take your damn car, you prick

His three dots appear on the screen but that's when the curtains swish and Garcia walks out.

The first thing I notice is that it's funny that she's still in her sneakers. But then I see the bare skin of her legs and they're tanned, like maybe she runs in shorts everyday. How did I not know that?

I shake my head. Of course I wouldn't.

I force my eyes up. And up some more. That's a hell of a lot of leg. Finally I see the yellow dress she's in, it's tight around her torso but goes all the way to her neck and flares out down her waist.

She scratches the back of her neck and my eyes catch on her bulging bicep. "I really appreciate you for figuring out that yellow is my favorite color, but this is too short for my taste."

"In my defense, I didn't know it'd be too short," I say, my voice thick. I guess that if I can see the inner curve of her thighs, a dress is considered too short. "Try the other options, then."

"Ugh, we're going to be late to this date," she says at the same time as she turns around and gives me a heart attack.

The dress has no back. It's all skin and no bra straps as far as the eye can see.

Of course, this is when the clerk returns with drinks. "Here you go, sir." I don't even know how I find it in me to accept the glass of tea without toppling it over. The woman heads over to Garcia saying. "Oh my gosh, you look stunning!"

"Thanks." Garcia accepts the wine glass from the edge of the dressing room and leans forward in an exaggerated manner to make sure she can sip as far away from the dress as possible.

"Mr. Starr." I freeze as the saleswoman addresses me. "You must be so happy to be taking this beautiful woman out on a date."

Garcia and I choke at the same time.

The good news is that she does it gracefully without ruining the dress she's not going to buy. The bad news is that I spew black tea on my shirt.

Garcia snorts, laughter dancing in her brown eyes. "Serves you right." With that, she disappears back into the changing room.

"I'm so sorry! May I help you?" The poor clerk is the human version of Munch's The Scream. It's almost funny, except my stomach is cold from the spill.

Plucking the fabric between my fingers, I say, "I may need a new shirt."

"Of course. I can help you select one. On the house," she adds waving her hands.

It's going to be easier if I don't fight her on this, even though I fully intend to pay for it. "Thanks." I set the tea on the table beside me and try to stand, but she stops me.

"Please, I will bring you some samples. Would you like one in a similar style to what you're wearing?"

"Er, sure." It's a simple button up, so we can't go wrong with this. "I'm usually a size M, sometimes L."

"I think you'll be L from our slim fit with your muscular frame."

I try not to grimace because Garcia's hearing all of this and I'm sure she'll find some way to tease me about it. "Great, thanks."

A minute goes by while the woman is hunting in the men's section, but there are no signs of life from the dressing room. My phone is also quiet. Kim didn't respond in the end.

"Hey, are you alive?" I ask.

"U-Um." The curtains shift but she doesn't come out. "I can't show you this one."

My perverted mind runs through a host of possibilities why, all of which make me squirm.

"Why not?" I ask, clearing my throat.

"Because I look like a potato sack and you'll laugh."

I expel all the air in my lungs and uncross my legs to lean my elbows on my knees. "Listen, I must see this now as payment for all my efforts."

Shit. She groans again. I know it's supposed to be in complaint but I don't know what's happening to me, because it hits me very differently.

But then she slides the curtain open and—

I blow a raspberry and burst out laughing.

She huffs and folds her arms. It makes the thick, burgundy puffy dress deflate against her body. "I told you."

"Wait, wait." I grab my phone from the sofa. "I need to immortalize this."

"The hell you do." Quick as a rabbit, she hides back behind the closed curtain and prevents me from saving digital proof. It'll live forever in my mind, though.

"I found a couple of more casual button ups you can try," the saleswoman says, reappearing from my left.

One of the shirts is white and the other light blue, closer to the one I'm wearing. This time I do rise to take them. "Thank you. Can I use the dressing room next door?"

"Of course!"

I trod over and also hide behind some curtains. This store is so swanky that the dressing rooms are the size of my bathroom, complete with another little sofa, floor to ceiling mirrors on two walls, and more brass hangers than any other dressing room I've seen since I can afford to go to stores with them.

As I unbutton my soiled shirt, I can hear the slide of fabric against skin right next door. I lift my eyes to my face on the mirror. The stark hunger reflected there scares me—I didn't even know I had been suppressing it until it shows itself right this moment.

I run my hands down my face, forcefully rearranging my features to literally anything else. Garcia has trust me to be her coach, her glorified wing man. The last thing she needs is for me to betray that trust by trying for something else.

Sighing, I toss my shirt on the sofa and grab the nearest one of the options. More rustling sounds from next door as I slide my arms in the new shirt.

"Oh!" The inflection in Garcia's voice is weird. New. "I think this is the dress."

"Yeah?" I stop moving. "Let me see."

Unlike any of the previous times, she slides the curtains resolutely and I follow in her example. We walk out of our dressing rooms at the same time and both of us turn into statues.

Her long hair is swept forward over her shoulder, looking even softer than the fabric of the fancy dress.

But that's what she wanted me to see, so I shift my attention lower. I have no idea what this kind of dress is called but I'd define it as Oh Shit. It's tight. Everywhere. Every single of her curves is demanding attention and yet, the dress wraps her from her neck all the way to her knees. It's even long-sleeved. It only has one flaw, though.

"It doesn't seem to have pockets." Once more I'm proud that I can get clear words out, even though my mouth desperately needs another sip of that tea.

"That's not what's important here," Garcia says with an odd pitch to her voice. "Why the hell are you like that?"

"Huh? Like what?" I look up at her face.

The answer is in her pointing her finger at me. I look down again. "Oh." Right, I was in the middle of trying on this shirt and didn't even button it. I grab the bottom button and start working my way up without meeting her eye. "Anyway, is that the dress or do you want to try the others?"

She clears her throat twice. "No, I think this is the one. And the price tag didn't make me want to faint."

"Good." Once I'm done with the buttons, I work on tucking the shirt in my jeans and look back up at her. "Then, stay wearing it. We need to get you shoes now."

Her eyes fly from my hands, one holding my jeans so they don't droop and the other one doing the tucking, back up. "But doesn't it look okay with my white sneakers already?"

More than okay, but I still answer, "They have flats too, not just heels."

"Whew." She puts a hand on her chest in relief.

"You two look phenomenal," the clerk says as she walks back up to us. To me she says, "The stylist has also arrived."

"Stylist?" Garcia parrots.

"Great. Also, I think I'll just take this shirt," I say as I pop open the sleeve buttons and work on rolling it up. It registers after a long moment that there is absolutely no noise other than the fabric rustling of my sleeve, and the jazzy music.

And it's because both women are staring at my arm.

I stop moving. Yet they still don't react.

What's the deal?

"Uh, we'll also need shoes for her," I say tentatively. "Garcia, what's your shoe size?"

"A ten." She jerks. "What? No. I don't know why I said that. I'm an eight. Size eight—not me. I'm not an eight." Then she drops the world's most awkward laugh.

The clerk also unfreezes. "What style would you like?"

"Nothing with heel, please."

"I will bring you some options in a quick moment!" The clerk races back out to the floor.

Meanwhile, Garcia approaches closer. Her eyes get diverted for a second as I start rolling the other sleeve, but then she wraps her arms around herself. "Starr, are you getting me a full makeover?"

"No, I know you don't want any of that." I push both of my sleeves as far up as they can go, and walk back to my ice tea for a healthy sip. "You're not gonna get your hair cut and a full head of makeup or whatever. Just tell her what you want and she'll do it." Once I finish my little speech, I sit back down on the sofa where I don't intend to move until it's time to pay.

Garcia opens and closes her mouth, but the clerk returns not just with several options of what seem like sensible shoes, but also with a second woman in tow who carries a large case. They walk Garcia back into the dressing room to fit her with the shoes and makeup.

The saleswoman heads back out and I motion at her to take me to the register. I insist on paying for the men's shirt because it's not like it was her fault that Garcia stunned me so much that I couldn't keep the drink in my mouth. After completing the transaction, she hands me over a bag containing Garcia's work clothes and I do my best not to stare, even though my mind's eye can clearly picture Garcia taking them off in that dressing room.

I'm back on the sofa finishing my tea when the stylist comes out, her packed case in hand and tossing a daring wink at me as she leaves.

I glance around, searching for an explanation about that when Garcia follows.

I don't even pay attention to her shoes or the dress, and she doesn't look drastically changed. Maybe her hair's fluffier at the top. But there's something about her face that glows even more than usual, and her lips are redder than before.

I could kiss them.

I could also drop kick myself in the 'nads for thinking that.

"Well?" she asks expectantly, bouncing a little on her feet. Like she's excited to go on this date.

A date that will be with Logan Kim.

There's no hiding that I'm choked up as I say, "You look beautiful, darlin'. Do you feel like it?"

And of freaking course, this is when she chooses to blush all the way from her neck to the root of her hair. "Actually, I do. Thank you, Cowboy."

And of freaking course, this is the moment when I realize I'm absolutely, thoroughly screwed.

CHAPTER 21
HOPE

Starr has been acting weird. It's not that he's normally a chatterbox or anything—he leans to the quiet side and when he talks, it's to tease with that Texas drawl of his. But there hasn't been much teasing this afternoon. In fact, except for when I tried on the dresses, he's barely even looked my way.

It's almost as if he's nervous.

And okay, I'm a girl. I have hormones. Sometimes they addle my brain. I blame them for planting the seed of thought in my mind that maybe his weird behavior could be because he's my blind date. He's kind of dressed for it, too.

I stretch the fabric of my new dress lower down my thighs. A country singer crones about some long lost love as Starr drives me to the restaurant where the date will be. After having bought me a dress, shoes, a little purse for my phone and keys, and even hiring a stylist to come into a clothing store that he rented out for an hour. For me.

That's… that's… I don't think my hormones can be blamed on this.

I glance at him from the corner of my eye. The stoplight is

red and he drums the steering wheel with his thumb. His left hand rubs his chin, deep set blue eyes trained firmly on the car in front of us. A muscle in his jaw ticks, like whatever he's so lost in thought about is annoying.

Mierda.

This man is gorgeous.

Yeah, yeah, I knew that. He didn't go viral last month because of the words he said, but because he has an accent and a face that weakens knees. And his body too. I've seen him in various states of dress or undress over the years, regularly ice him, help him relieve cramps, and oversee his workouts. It lands very different to see all that when he's wearing his uniform or his training clothes. That's always felt like work.

But earlier today, with his shirt unbuttoned showing all that golden skin, taught with ripples of muscle and a smattering of light brown hair? And his forearm muscles flexing as he rolled up his sleeves? *That* hit different. Like a scene straight from his bedroom.

What if my date *is* Cade Starr?

I tuck my hair behind my ears and they feel much warmer than usual.

I can't possibly go out with him. First, he's already seen me at my most unhinged. If I'm not attractive to guys on my baseline setting, I'm downright repellant at my most intense. Second, dating anyone in the team would be like crapping where I eat. If something goes wrong, I'll be the one whose ass lands in the street.

Third, which by itself is as weighty as the first two points combined: the last thing I want is a pity date. And that's what he'd be offering, just like when Lucky Rivera immediately asked me out when he found out that I was desperate to find a guy. Starr has never shown any kind of interest for me in that sense anyway, which is how I'd know it's out of pity.

Well, until today. This whole afternoon has been some real

boyfriend shit. Or better, I guess, because my ex never treated me this nicely.

The truck stops moving and I look up from my hands. Starr speaks for the first time in at least half an hour. "Here we are. When you go in, ask for a reservation under your name."

"Um." I swallow. "My name or last name?"

He turns to me. "Hope."

I hope—pun intended—that he doesn't notice how my breath hitches.

"Okay." I unfasten my seatbelt and pretend to be way busier with that than I really am. Casually, I ask, "Aren't you coming too?"

"In a bit." He offers no further explanation.

And I don't know what else to say either. Thanking him for all the pampering right now would be weird if he ends up sitting across from me at the same table. I'm just going to play along.

Opening the door, I slide off his truck and he takes out his phone, ignoring me altogether. I close the door and round the truck to the front door of the restaurant. He still doesn't follow.

"Welcome," a young hostess says with a million dollar smile. "Do you have a reservation?"

"Yes, under the name Hope." My mind, ever so helpful, replays the voice of a certain cowboy uttering my name from his lips. My skin, ever so unhelpful, breaks into goosebumps all over.

"Right. Follow me."

I just figured out why these tiny purses are called clutches because I clutch mine for dear life as I follow her. The restaurant has some busy tables, so at least he didn't rent the whole thing this time. But it's still spacious enough that it screams money. The lighting fixtures are low over the tables, so that only the customers and their food are plainly visible. The rest of the decor is dark, intimate, walls made of glass with gentle cascades of water trickling down the sleek surfaces. Even a Coke here must cost a fortune.

She guides me through the place almost to the back, close to the bar, and when she steps aside it's to reveal my table.

It's not empty, though, like it would've been if Starr was trying to be all mysterious. Rather, there's a man already waiting.

And it's none other than Logan Kim.

My jaw drops so bad that the hostess has to clear her throat not to laugh.

Meanwhile, Kim gets up to pull out a chair meant for me. When it's clear that I'm incapable of any coherent thought, he motions at the chair with his head, his thick black hair coming loose from the hold behind his ear and falling to half obscure his face.

"Oh. Um." I scramble to take a seat and he pushes me gently toward the table.

I cast a confused expression at the hostess, but rather than offer any explanations she just takes her leave.

Kim retraces his steps, one hand sliding down his stomach to hold his tie in place as he sits back down. He hasn't even settled down when I blurt out, "What's happening?"

"I'm your date," he responds with his deep, smooth voice, dark eyes twinkling under the low light.

My hands are clutching at my little purse so tight that they tremble. I try to swallow but my mouth is dry as a desert. ¿Qué carajo me pasa? Why is my stomach in knots?

Water. That's all I need. I force my hands to relax and reach for the pitcher and my fancy little glass. Kim leans back, a tiny smile on his face as he watches me drain my glass like it's alcohol and I'm trying to get smashed as quickly as possible.

Ha, maybe I should order a stiffer little beverage.

"Wow, I'm speechless," I say, which kind of defeats the concept of being speechless, except there's nothing else that comes to mind. I can't even comprehend all that I'm feeling myself.

"How come? Were you expecting someone else?"

Yes.

No. I shouldn't have.

But I was.

"Um." I tuck my hair behind my ears again and mumble, "I was just expecting a complete stranger." That's not entirely a lie. It really was what I thought up until this afternoon.

"Is this better or worse?"

"To be honest, I'm not sure," I admit, which elicits a chuckle out of him. It has the curious effect of relaxing my muscles, and I finally settle into the chair. "We already know each other, and for example I know you'd never treat me like crap."

"Props to me." Kim grins.

"But on the other hand, you've also already seen me acting like a headless chicken, so I can't imagine you're sitting here with any real interest in me."

His thick eyebrows rise. "Who says that?"

I blow a raspberry. "Please, I've seen the women you've dated."

"C'mon, only one was a supermodel."

"Kim." I give him a look trying to go for stern, but I actually want to laugh.

"Call me Logan." He shrugs. "We're on a date after all."

"Logan." His name rolls off my tongue easily, even though it's the first time I use it. I spread my hands on the table. "Can we be fully honest here?"

"Always."

I appreciate the earnestness of his answer and it makes me smile. "We both know there is nothing that will come out of this date."

"Ouch." He places both paws over his heart. "This is the fastest I've ever been rejected."

"It's not that I'm rejecting you. If circumstances were different I'd be going wild over you."

Humming from his throat, he leans closer, elbows on the table. "What circumstances?"

Of course he has a big ego. I know that. The entire team and staff know that. Fans know that. Logan has exceptionally amazing genes because he comes from one of the most famous baseball families. His dad is none other than Jeong Guk Kim, the first South Korean to be inducted into the American base-ball hall of fame. His brother is Lewis Kim, an All-Star pitcher who breaks records every season. And his mother is Freya Backstrom, a Swedish supermodel famous for her ethereal beauty. Logan has as much beauty as he has skill, and is brim-ming with sex appeal. I literally don't know a single woman who is immune to him. Some men too.

But... "We're basically coworkers," I say and when it still doesn't seem to click with him, I add, "Dating coworkers is a historically bad idea for women, and I'd really like to keep my job. I have big student loans to pay off."

"Ah." He runs his hand through his hair, not messing it one bit. "So you refuse to date anyone in the Wild organization?"

"Yeah." I make a grab for my glass but it's empty. Before I can react, he reaches forward to refill it.

"So just to clarify, even if it's not me, you also won't date anyone else in the team?"

"Right."

"Hmm." He leans back on his chair and takes a moment to study me while I wash the rest of my nerves down with water. Finally, he asks, "Would you like to continue with the date anyway? I'd love to treat you."

I lift my chin. "Yes, please. I would love free fancy food." And my stomach roars in affirmation.

*

Logan and I walk out of the restaurant together, laughing easily about some prank the third baseman played on Lucky Rivera a few days ago in the locker room.

"I swear, I've never seen Rivera squeal so much," Logan says, shoulders still shaking with mirth.

"Oh my word, I'd have paid to see that." I wipe a tear off my eye. Unfortunately, that makes my eye sting somehow. "Ouch!" I stop walking and squeeze my eyes tight, but that makes it worse.

The amusement fades from Logan's voice. "What happened?"

"I think an eyelash went into my eye."

"Let me see."

I stand still and struggle to open my eyes. Two warm hands hold my head firmly and Logan looms closer than ever before. He searches my eyes—er, the one eye—intently, and in a parallel universe I'd wonder if he was going to kiss me.

Instead, he says, "Found it. It's actually not in all the way so I think I can get it. Can you keep your eye open?"

"I'll try." I grit my teeth and force myself not to move a millimeter as he leans much closer. One of his hands releases my head, the other one sliding to the back, through my hair to hold me in place. Carefully, his fingers grow impossibly large as they approach my eye and suddenly—sweet relief. "Oh, thank you."

He steps back and lifts the evil eyelash resting on the pad of his index finger to me. "Blow it for good luck."

I do and rub my eye. A second too late I remember the makeup.

"Oh, shit," I say in a truly unladylike way. "Did I just smear my makeup all over?"

"Nah, you're still pristine."

Not that it matters, but I still sigh in relief. "Okay, good."

He takes another step back and puts a hand in the pocket of his dress pants. "So, should I take you home or is someone else driving you?"

We both know who the someone else is. I glance over my shoulder, but Cade Starr doesn't jump out of the restaurant, ready to be my chauffeur again. Maybe he's not even here anymore, knowing that I'd be in great hands this time around.

"Actually, I didn't arrange a ride back. Can you please just drive me to where my car is parked?"

"Sure thing. After you." He motions in the general direction to his left and I fall in step.

I've never really paid attention to what he drives, but he stops by a fancy ass car I recognize as a Maserati, though I couldn't begin to guess which model or price tag. I don't know why it surprises me because Logan Kim is a flashy kind of guy, but it's like I half expected him to drive another pickup.

The car is so annoyingly low and my dress so tight, that I end up having to accept his help to slide into the seat, butt first, and then turn to tuck my legs in. Logan closes the door like an old school gentleman and the passenger seat absorbs me while he makes his way to the driver's seat.

"Whoa, dude. This is way fancy," I say once he climbs in.

He flashes a quick grin in the night. "Right? Makes me feel like I've finally made it."

As we strap in, I ask, "You needed a car to realize that, Mr. Highest Pedigree in the Land?"

"Yes, actually." There's a twist on his lips that is more sardonic than amused, but then him turning on the car distracts me because the engine sounds like a beast from the jungle, and off we go.

You'd think he'd have a need for speed while driving a machine like this, but Logan drives calmly through the streets, keeping the easy conversation flowing over some chill music that plays from his sound system. He delivers me to the pharmacy parking lot where my Jeep awaits, opening his car door for me again, helping me get out, and waiting until I'm safely driving away in my modest vehicle.

From the rearview mirror, I see his fancy ride take a left where I keep going straight. Finally, I feel alone enough that I can free myself.

My chest twists painfully and as if on cue, my eyes prickle with hot tears.

This was the best damn date I've ever been to. No one has been kinder or safer than Logan Kim, and I bet this is why Starr arranged it. Regardless of whether he thought this could turn into the real deal, the cowboy definitely knew I *needed* to experience something like this. Because he's learned enough about me to figure out that I'm starved for this—for a kind guy who treats me with respect.

And yet he's not the one who showed up.

I dab furiously at the tears trickling down my face, sure that my makeup is really getting messed up now.

It doesn't matter though—none of this does. If Cade Starr had been my date, the conditions would still be the same. He's still my coworker and therefore out of bounds. It still would've been a pity date to show me what a nice date would be like. He's obviously not interested in me, and the proof is that he sent Logan instead.

A sob tears from my throat. Unfortunately, that doesn't mean I'm not interested in him.

CHAPTER 22
CADE

Lucky and I rush to follow after Garcia and Kim once they start heading out of the restaurant. Halfway before the exit, I brake suddenly and Lucky slams into me.

"Dude, we have to pay first," I say.

Lucky steps back, saying, "Oh, right. Why don't you go ahead while I pick up the tab?"

"Thanks, I'll see you outside." I offer my fist and he bumps it before I keep going.

But Garcia and Kim aren't out of the premises yet. The hostess and another employee have detained them to take pics with Kim, pics that Garcia herself is snapping on someone's phone. I retreat a few steps and hide behind a tall plant. They both know I'm here, but I'm still trying to respect the fact that this has to feel like an actual date. I'm not going to interfere if they do, in fact, hit it off.

I force my fists to relax as I wait for the pleasantries to be over. My eyes zero in on Kim guiding Garcia out, his hand on the small of her back. The large doors swing closed behind them and when I step out of hiding, they're both laughing in the middle of the parking lot.

See? That's why he's the right guy for her. I can't think of a single time I've made her laugh like that. If anything she's always irritated at me.

"Ready?" Lucky's voice drifts from behind me.

I open my mouth to speak and that's when I notice how hard I've been clenching my jaw. "Yeah, let's go."

We trod out of the restaurant, still keeping a big distance behind the couple. I mean, Garcia and Kim. They're not a couple. Yet.

Then they stop and so does my brain, because Kim positions himself in front of Garcia and grabs her face.

"Oh shit," Lucky whispers with amusement, snapping his fingers. "They're gonna kiss, aren't they? Dude, they're gonna make out!" He smacks my chest with the back of his hand.

But I can't move. I certainly can't find it in myself to show any amusement.

Garcia's back is to us. I kinda wish I could see from her expression if this is all she's ever wanted. Maybe that would make it a lot easier to grab this weird feeling in my gut, shove it in a box, and toss it nearby in Lake Eola.

I swallow hard as they kiss, mentally cursing at myself for being such a damn good cupid, but also angry that I have the balls to feel angry in the first place.

Like geez, dude, what right do I even have to feel jealous? I have no interest in Hope Garcia. And if I did, that would make me a complete asshole anyway.

I barely register as Kim pulls away but next thing I know, Lucky's jerking me hard to hide behind a car.

"What the—"

"Shh," he says with a finger against his mouth. He stretches to peep over the hood of the car but when I try the same, he jerks me back down.

"What are you doing, Rivera?"

"Looking out for you, trust me."

Still crouching, I rest my elbows on my knees and bring my hands up to rub my face. My voice comes out garbled as I ask, "What do you even mean?"

A car roars by and when Lucky motions at me to stand again, it clicks that it must've been Kim driving away with Garcia on his passenger seat. I swallow down the bitter taste on my tongue.

Lucky observes me for a moment with his game face, not his usual clown grin that precedes some sort of prank—but like I'm a rival he expects to bat a nasty hit from that'll make him earn his sizable paycheck.

"You dipshit," he says at last.

I jerk back as if hit. "What?"

"Are you in love with her?"

"No!" I exclaim, my face scrunching, my palms sweating, my skin itching.

"Let's say I believe that. But clearly you feel some typa way over her. It's written all over your face."

"I told you not to have that second whiskey."

He shoves me. Hard. "Stop bullshitting, man. Why aren't you the one taking Garcia out on a date, then?"

"Because I don't feel anything for her." For the first time in a long time—and the last time was when I ate the last slice of his pizza—Lucky glares at me so I hard that I wouldn't be shocked if he socks me in the eye. "Trust me, I—I really don't."

"I've never heard you stutter before."

Grunting, I run both hands down my hair. "Fine. Maybe I do feel some typa way, like you said."

"Uh huh." He folds his arms and leans his head back to stare me down.

"But I'm not the right guy for her, man."

"Why the hell not?"

"You're kidding me, right?" I give out a dry laugh while motioning at myself. "What do I have to offer? Literally nothing."

"That's not how you use the word literally, you absolute fool. Literally—" he says in a sinister tone as he advances to poke my chest, "—means not even yourself, and last I checked you're single as shit."

I bat his hand away. "That's not what I mean and you know it."

"No, I *literally* don't understand you right now."

Exasperated I basically shout, "I have no family! No past. No legacy. I don't even know what day I was really born. I don't know if I still have parents. Or siblings. I don't know where I came from, what health issues I may develop, or worse. I—I..." I breathe hard, swallow with difficulty. "I don't know if my biological mother was hurt for me to exist. Or if she just didn't want me. I'm all alone, Lucky. I have *nothing* and she deserves *everything* she wants and then some."

Somehow his chest rises and falls with the same cadence as mine, as if we're running around the field instead of standing in the middle of a quiet parking lot.

Stepping back, Lucky lets out a shaky breath and a string of Spanish, aimed pointedly at me, which can't be any good. Then he says, "You do have a brother. *Me*."

My eyes pop.

"And you're not alone." He points a finger at my face. "You have a whole team behind you. You have fans."

"That's not the same," I say, my voice raspy after shouting like a fool.

"Yeah, it is. I bet some fans probably love you more than relatives would." He wrinkles his face. "And screw your parents. They don't deserve you, you're clearly too good for them."

I sigh. "Lucky, I get what you're trying to—"

"Shut up." That snaps my mouth shut. "Listen to me. You raised yourself better than most people are raised by their parents. I'm not gonna accept any Cade Starr slander, not even from yourself."

Casting my eyes down at the asphalt, I say, "Can we pretend like I never said shit?"

"No. I'm actually glad you spewed all that bullshit so it doesn't fester anymore. Look at me, gringo." I glare at him and he returns it even harder. "If you want her, don't let anyone take her from under your nose. And don't you dare talk yourself out of what you deserve."

"I don't *deserve* her," I grouch, balling my fists. "She's her own person and doesn't owe me crap."

"Argh! I really want to punch you in the nose right now."

Dryly, I say, "Fine, do it."

"No. Your hard head would probably break my hand." Grunting, he makes as if to walk away but then returns right back. "You fight for her, you hear me? And if you need help getting Logan out of the picture now, I'm here for you."

"Whatever."

"Not whatever." He claws at my shoulder and stops me. "I'm here for you, Cade. For better or for worse."

"Are you trying to marry me?" I joke to deflect.

Lucky frowns harder. "Clench your jaw tight because I'm gonna punch you now."

I shrug out of his hold and jam my hands in my pockets. "Keep yapping all you want, I'm going home."

He waits until I'm far enough, and right as a group of people are coming out of the restaurant, to scream, "I love you, man!"

I cringe and try to hide my face from the now giggling strangers. It makes me rush to my truck but then once I'm inside, the fact that I'm not safe here either punches me in the nose. And that is because of the lingering smell of vanilla.

My eyes fall on the empty passenger seat where a certain athletic trainer sat for a good part of the afternoon, enough that the scent of her skin still permeates the air. Unbidden, my nostrils flare trying to absorb it all in one go.

A weird laugh bubbles up my throat, and it doesn't stop. I've finally gone and lost my last marbles. Heat rushes up and settles on my face and I don't know if it's residual embarrassment, effort from the unhinged laugh, or what. I bury my face in my hands, waiting until the fit subsides, and rest my forehead on the steering wheel.

Muffled by my hands, I ask, "What the hell am I gonna do with myself?" But as I search for that answer, I have to make sure not to act weird around Garcia and Kim, no matter what it takes.

CHAPTER 23
HOPE

"Oh, yeah. That's the spot." Miller moans as I apply the right kind of pressure with the massage gun on the stiff spot of his trapezius. It made him throw weaker than a pee wee during a base steal an inning ago.

"Sit still, dude," I demand and he braces himself against the railing.

Behind us, the dugout is a mess of activity. The New York Eagles is one of the best teams in the league, and one of the oldest in the entire North American league. Playing for it was probably the childhood dream of half of the guys in our team, and the fact that we've kept them to zero runs in this game, when their lineup includes superstars like Lewis Kim, frankly has all of us losing our collective minds. It explains things like how my massage gun has never been more active during any other Spring Training game, because the players are just so tense.

I guess it doesn't help that we also haven't scored a single run. Even one such celebration would put us in a different mood.

But then Beau clears his throat, and that stops all the voices at once. I watch from the corner of my eye how he motions at someone behind me, and then speaks.

"Starr. Come here, son."

I confess that I pay a smidge less attention to Miller. I'm not too concerned about it though because he also sets his attention on whatever is about to unfold.

The air behind me stirs, leaving behind a scent I'm now very familiar with. It's warm skin, sweat, and the remnants of a spicy aftershave that I never noticed until one day he spilled too much of it on his clothes. Now I can catch it even when he's far from me.

Other players make way for Starr to reach Beau, who stands with one foot atop the stairs out of the dugout. Pitcher stops before manager and we all lean in. I turn off the massage gun so I can snoop.

"Are you ready?" Beau asks.

"Yes." After a second, Starr adds, "What for?"

Miller chuckles next to me. Meanwhile, I have to resist the urge to facepalm. The cowboy is a big fan of deflecting serious moments like this, even at the expense of appearing ditzy. But it's always on purpose, and I'm starting to wonder if it's to hide his nerves.

It's funny because two months ago I wouldn't have imagined him as capable of feeling nervous. He always seemed so confident, bordering on cocky.

As if reading his mind, Beau puts a hand on Starr's shoulder. "It's time to throw it."

"Oh shit," Lucky Rivera whispers from nearby.

Instead of pumping his fist in the air, Starr tilts his head and asks, "Why now?"

"Because we need a statement and this is the right team to make it with."

Our starter pitcher turns around, sweeping his eyes all across the dugout as if trying to gauge where everyone else is at. He gets nods, cheers, fist pumps, claps. It might be just me but he seems to pause for longer when his eyes find mine. A single sunbeam bathes half of his face, making that eye shine like someone's applying CGI effects on the man, while his other eye is darker. Goosebumps break all over my skin and I jerk my head in a furious little nod for lack of anything better to do. My lungs recover the ability to work when his attention moves on.

He points at someone at the end of the dugout. "What do *you* think?"

The noise quiets down as we collectively turn to who Starr is referring, and it's none other than our catcher. Logan is getting fit with his gear right after his at bat ended in an out.

"I would've liked to wait," Kim says with a little shrug. "But if our manager says you're ready, then I'm also ready to catch whatever you throw."

"Aww yeah!" someone shouts, and the commotion resumes.

"I'm good now, Garcia." Miller rotates his shoulder and stretches his neck. "I'm so ready to party."

"'Kay, but don't get hurt."

That's when the inning ends and it's time to go on the defensive. "Let's go," says Logan while picking up his helmet and mitt. He high fives the rest of the team on the way out and it distracts me enough that I don't notice when Starr leaves the dugout.

I glue myself to the railing, stepping on a stool that is here precisely for the shorties of the team and staff. Logan jogs over to the mound where Starr is fixing the dirt with his foot, and all the while the rest of the players take their positions on the infield and outfield. The Eagles's next batter is the first in their three-hole, and he gets ready as the Wild battery confers behind gloves. I've never been able to read lips but I know these baseball boys have eyes like, well, eagles, and can even steal signs if someone's not careful.

But how I wish I could hear this conversation.

It ends in both of them bumping their gloves on each other's chests before Logan heads over to the home plate and settles down. We're so quiet that the umpire's voice calling *play ball* reaches my ears.

The counter starts ticking and the first pitch ends up being a two-seamer close to the batter's chest. The Eagle player has to jump back to avoid it, even though Starr's control is so uncanny he's yet to beanball anyone in his entire pro career so far. The easy strike makes us all tenser, somehow.

Is the cutter next?

No. Another fastball. This time the batter doesn't swing and it ends up being a ball. I try to grab tighter onto the railing and my plastic gloves make an uncomfortable squelching sound. Sweat is pooling inside of them, yuck.

"Strike!"

Crap, I missed it.

No one's making a big deal out of it, so it couldn't have been the cutter, right?

Everyone's eyes are laser trained on Starr as he catches the ball from Logan. As the counter starts again, Starr shakes his head at Logan's signs not once, but twice. I swallow hard but that doesn't push my heart back down from my throat to its rightful cavity.

Good gravy, this man's gonna kill me. And since when do I speak like a southern lady?

"C'mon," I mutter to myself.

Starr's pitching form is a thing of beauty. A lot of pitchers focus on keeping their windups economical so they can last longer, but that's because they don't have the tree trunk thighs that Starr has. Not that I've worked for other teams, but we do have eight pitchers in the roster at any given time and literally none of them works out their legs anywhere as hard as Cade Starr. It's like the cowboy is training for a life or death race against a mustang. He's lucky also that his genes have given him calves that are also thick with muscle apt to keep up with the power in his thighs, and he has the most flexible joints in the entire team.

I don't exaggerate. Part of my job is to keep track of ridiculous things like that, and Starr is the most hypermobile in the team. The athletic trainers keep a special eye on him for this reason, to make sure he doesn't hurt his joints by hyper extending them during training or play.

Now, I watch him lift his right leg in a way that would make other pitchers exhaust themselves. His left foot rises to tippy toes that tip him forward. Meanwhile, his left shoulder and arm turn into a supple whip behind him and the ball shoots off his fingertips like a bullet. But it's dropping way too much to be the cutter I've seen in practice.

"Strike! One out!"

Mumbles travel up and down the dugout. Of course we're happy for a first out at the bottom of the sixth inning against Lewis Kim's team. Of course.

But where's the damn cutter?

The audience grows rowdier as the cleanup batter of the Eagles steps to the plate, doing some practice swings that are meant to intimidate our pitcher. This guy is a 6 foot 7 giant with all the power of batting the ball way out of the park and into the parking lot. He's already done it once during Spring Training.

"This is it," I say, because there's literally no one better to stump in this lineup than this guy.

The first pitch is the same curve that struck out the previous Eagle. My heart stops as the batter connects. I follow the course and relax. The line umpire calls a foul.

The batter settles for the second pitch and Logan crouches again to signal. Starr gives no response other than starting his windup with the exact same movements as every pitch before.

Except this ball doesn't drop.

And then a millisecond before the bat can connect, it drops like freaking lead.

Logan catches it square in his mitt, hovering a millimeter above the dirt.

"Strike!"

"Holy—" someone screams in the dugout.

"Dude, did you see that?"

"That was brutal!"

"Is there a replay?"

"Dude. *Dude!*"

If I was a cartoon, my jaw would hit the floor.

While the dugout is a flurry of euphoria, the stands are eerily quiet as Logan returns the ball to our pitcher. I squint, trying to make out Starr's expression. There is literally nothing in it, no sign of glee at throwing such a wild pitch that it has completely stupefied everyone in attendance.

Pitchers usually have several balls under their arsenal— often different types of fastballs and curves. Until now, Cade Starr had good enough weapons to keep him a regular in the majors. But I think I just witnessed the moment he really becomes a monster.

And because his battery partner is another monster, their third pitch is another cutter that makes the Eagles' cleanup swing and miss by a mile.

Literally every Wild player and staff member screams their throats raw—including me. I don't even know what I keep shouting, but I can't stop myself. If anything, seeing Starr lift his hand, index and pinky up to signal two outs to the outfield, makes me louder. My pulse races as the next batter steps up to the plate. Wedging one foot between the padded planks of the railing, I hoist myself up so I can scream through the clearing above.

"Go wild, Cowboy!" I yell.

He throws another two-seamer by the batter's chest that gets another strike. It feels like time or space are warping, because everyone else moves fast, the voices blend into a single scream, and yet Cade Starr is calm as he receives the ball and nestles it in his glove. He runs the palm of his left hand against his pants to wipe the sweat, and winds up again.

"Strike!"

"One more!" I shriek, my voice breaking embarrassingly.

Starr catches the ball again and he turns to the dugout. I know it's to watch for any signs from Beau, so does the rest of the team, but we're all feral in this moment.

"Kill 'em, Cowboy!"

"For the pizza!"

I have no idea what that's about but I also parrot, "For the pizza!"

Starr tosses a nod before turning back to Kim, who crouches down. They're an aggressive battery that doesn't tend to wait out the clock. And so Starr throws again and—

"Strike! Batter out!"

All I can do is scream the letter *a*. In Spanish. In English. Only *aaaaaa*.

This freaking asshole just struck out the Eagles' three-hole. Their best batters. Without conceding even one hit. In a game where he's completely shut them out for six whole ass innings.

I need to breathe or I'm going to faint from the excitement.

Our boys return to the dugout at an easy jog, as if they hadn't just basically declared war on the entire league. Logan says something that makes the pitcher smirk, and then they're greeted in the dugout by an avalanche of paws jostling them around.

"Starr," Beau barks. "Good job. Go get iced."

Starr's shoulders droop but he knows better than to chal-lenge our manager. However, one by one, starting by Logan, the nearby players clap Starr in the back on his way to the clubhouse.

I lower myself carefully back to the stool and then to firm ground, and the motion catches Rob Beau's attention because he pins me with a look. "Garcia, go ice him."

"Yes, sir." I check around me but the trunks are too deep into the dugout, where Steve and Otto are busy taking care of a couple of other players. So I guess it wasn't so much that moving drew attention to me, or even my screaming earlier, but the fact that I'm closest to the clubhouse tunnel. I head into it, sure that I have what I need in the clubhouse and don't have to fight through an unruly dugout for ice packs.

Most of the stadiums where Spring Training games happen are much smaller than regular season stadiums, some-times a little more rundown too—like this one. The clubhouse is smaller than our home one, the furniture less comfortable. I walk into the room right as Starr is pulling his jersey over his head. The fabric messes his sweaty hair, because he's already tossed his hat in his locker.

"Any issues?" I ask as I keep crossing the open space toward the small training room where the rest of our junk is. The walls encasing it are made of glass, and as I rummage around a couple other trunks, I can still see him peeling off the yellow undershirt.

"Nah, I'm good."

I stop. I can definitely say Starr está bueno, which literally translates to what he just said. Except in Venezuelan slang it means he's hot.

And uh, yeah. He really freaking is.

Sweat trickles down his back, sorting the ridges and valleys of cut muscle to disappear under the waistband of his pants. When he shifts to turn, I make sure to stick my eyes to what

I'm doing. I find the cooling spray he likes to be doused with before I fit him with the ice pack, but I don't find the shoulder pack itself so this will have to be a two-part job.

As I step out to the open, Starr is lowering himself to the chair by his locker, facing me. He throws his head back as he slumps and I have to tighten my jaws to not scream like I did a few minutes ago.

I don't care, I tell myself in my mind. *I'm a professional. This isn't the first time you've seen him shirtless. Nor will it be the last. And other guys in the team are just as attractive or more.*

Except I can't fathom that right now. Not while the thick column of his throat is exposed, corded muscles standing out as his Adam's apple bobs up and down. He props his forearms on the armrests, one leg bent and the other one stretched out —but both spread out confidently. His chest rises and falls with breathing that's still more labored than baseline, and a drop of sweat trickles down the hollow under his jaw to the deep ridge between his pecs that are dusted with almost blond fuzz.

Scratch that. I feel completely unprofessional right now. The things I want to do to that drop of sweat shock even me.

I clear my throat so loud that we both startle. Starr lifts his head, eyes widening in surprise like he forgot I was here too. Then he looks at the can in my hands and that reminds me of what I'm actually here for.

"Right, sit up straight."

"Yes, ma'am." His mouth twitches as he complies. Since he knows the drill, he turns away as I begin spraying all the way from his neck to his elbow.

I grab his heavy forearm with one gloved hand as I spray toward his back. His skin feels really hot even through my gloves. "You pitched a lot in the first innings. Any discomfort?"

"Nope." He squirms a little, as if finding a better angle on the ratty chair.

And then he winces a little.

I stop moving altogether. That could be because of literally any reason, but I wasn't hired by a professional baseball team for being pretty. In my mind, I retrace every single thing I've done. Lifting his forearm didn't cause that reaction, so there's no issue in his shoulder. But I just adjusted my grip for a second so I do it again.

There's the little wince again.

I do my best not to show any big emotions. This isn't the moment for that. Starr just threw the best pitches of his career so far and I'm not going to let them be the last.

Calmly, I twist to offer the spray can to him. "Can you hold this for me?"

"Sure," he mutters, taking it with his right hand.

Using the pads of my thumbs, I start kneading the thick muscles of his forearm. The same part of his anatomy that yesterday made a clothing store clerk and I suffer brain melt-downs. Starr rests his right arm again and turns to watch what I'm doing, which adds an extra layer of I-better-not-embar-rass-myself-right-now.

To keep my own damn mind centered, I ask, "Since when did you start feeling discomfort?"

He lifts those freaky eyes of his to mine. "I'm fine, really. Maybe just tense."

"Don't bullshit me, Cowboy."

"I wouldn't dare." His lips curve in a little smirk.

I focus back on his slick skin—or rather, on massaging his muscles. I trap his forearm between my elbow and my ribs so I can use both hands to work the flexors at elbow level. Starr grunts, no longer able to hide that this muscle group demands attention. They don't feel tighter than usual, so there's a solid chance it's a one-off. Maybe even the adrenaline of today. But even then, I'm not going to risk it.

I speak low because it feels weird to use a normal volume

when we're this close. "The good news is that it doesn't feel terrible—"

"Wow, that really makes a man feel special." There he goes again, deflecting.

I ignore that. "—But I'm still going to recommend putting you on light duty for the next few games."

He groans. "What? Right as things were finally getting good for me?"

"The team needs you in tip top shape to throw that cutter again."

This lights up his entire face and even though I cast a shadow over him, his eyes are as bright as a clear noon sky. "Did you see that?" His smile is contagious and before I can latch onto my professionalism, I'm grinning down at him.

"It was pretty wild."

"Yeah, that felt even better than at practice, actually."

"Speaking of, how does this feel?" I press into the knot of tendons in the crook of his inner elbow.

Reflex kicks in and he tries to jerk his arm away, so I tighten my hold.

"Whoa, at least buy me dinner first if you're gonna touch me like that."

I'm rolling my eyes at his attempt to camouflage the real discomfort he must be feeling, now that my fingers found the problem spot, when a third voice comes from behind me.

"Garcia, are you flirting with a player?"

Starr and I freeze. Wide blue eyes find mine.

"No," I respond through gritted teeth and continue massaging Starr's arm.

Stretching forward, Starr glances around me and greets my prick of a coworker. "Berger—" I momentarily enjoy that Starr refuses to call Otto by his first name. "—No need to feel jealous, man. I'm the flirt here, and if you need some attention just let me—whoa." He turns back to look at the spot where I dig my thumbs. "Do that again."

"Please," I remind him.

"Do that again, ple—yeahhh." Starr slumps back against the chair.

"Well, be glad it's me who walked in," Otto says as he appears in my field of vision. "Anyone else who heard you two would think something inappropriate is going on."

I gnash my teeth and refuse to meet his stare, even though I feel the laser beams on my face.

Starr speaks in a deadpan, "So glad."

"Why are you here, Otto?" I ask.

"Steve sent me to bring a shoulder pack, they're all in the dugout."

The pitcher traps the spray can between his thighs and extends his now free hand. "Thanks." After a moment of inaction, Otto hands it over to him.

"Anyway." Otto clears his throat in a phlegmy way. "You two behave while I'm gone, I'd hate to write you up."

As if he had the power to do that.

I turn a fulminating glare on him. "Screw the hell off."

"Just saying. You should be more careful than anyone else, Hope. You're a single woman among men." He shrugs in a petulant way and walks off to the dugout.

I huff. "Hijo de su madre."

To my surprise Starr glares after him and says, "Wow, I didn't know he was such a little shit. Does he treat you like that often?"

I switch my attention on his arm, starting by his rock solid bicep that makes me work extra harder. "You heard him, it's what I get for being the only woman in the player support staff. Go me, breaking the glass ceiling by face planting on it, I guess."

He mutters a big curse and looks up at me. "I'm proud of

you for standing up for yourself, though. And I just want you to know we'll have your back. Me and everyone in the team, especially Kim."

I pause. "Why Logan especially?"

He mouths the catcher's first name without producing a sound, and shakes his head hard. "Well, because you're dating now."

"What?"

"What?" he repeats, frowning.

"Who's dating who?"

"You and 'Logan.'" He uses his free hand to air quote, the frozen shoulder pack strewn over his lap.

"Uh… where did you get that from?"

If anything, he looks even more confused. "Didn't you kiss last night? Because that's a pretty solid indication that the fit is right and all that. At least enough to get a second date."

I lean back. Unable to hold his gaze, I do my best to focus on his arm. Slowly, I say, "Logan and I didn't kiss last night."

"But I saw you—I mean, Lucky and I. You were in the parking lot. He grabbed your head like this." He mimics it with his hand in the air. I don't know why it makes my pulse spike like I'm watching him strike out an Eagle with a cutter.

"Oh. He was just getting an eyelash out of my eye," I whisper. Starr whips his face back to me. "But anyway, no. We're not dating. There's no second date happening."

"Why not?" He almost whines.

"I appreciate the effort, Coach." Finally done with the massage, I gently lower his arm to the armrest and reach for the ice pack. As I work, I say, "But there's no way I can date someone in the team. Not without getting written up or worse, fired. You heard Otto just now, didn't you?"

Starr draws air sharply and when I meet his eyes he whispers, "Shit."

We don't speak the rest of the time it takes me to wrap the

ice pack around his shoulder and elbow, but all throughout he glares at a random spot on the floor. I almost apologize for ruining his plan of setting me up with Logan—not that it would've worked anyway. The catcher isn't the one catching my eye these days.

Starr throws his head back on the chair, right arm over his face to cover him from the light. I leave him there, returning to the dugout where no one else makes my heart race.

CHAPTER 24
CADE

A jerk snaps me awake and I immediately know something's up when I can barely open my eyes. It takes several attempts until I'm able to crack one open and I lay there disoriented for a long moment. There's light streaming from the bedroom window, which is weird. This time of year I usually get up before dawn. It's during the regular season, where games are at night, that my alarm goes off mid morning. Did the alarm not go off?

Wait, that's what the annoying blaring sound is.

Groaning as if I was trying to lift four hundred pounds, I manage to roll my two hundred pounds over to the edge of the bed. I swing my arm over, pawing around the night table until I feel the rectangle under my hand. I tap around the center of the screen, but the sound doesn't stop.

"What now?" I mumble with the same delivery of a drunk man who has screamed all night long.

I bring the phone to my pillow and crack the eye open again. No wonder the alarm wouldn't shut off—it's actually a phone call, and from my agent of all people. I swipe the green button, set the call to loudspeaker, and drop the phone on my pillow so I can pull my bed sheets over myself again.

"Lou."

"You sound like garbage," is his greeting. "Is that team of yours abusing you too much?"

I like that the *too much* implies that some abuse is fine. Snorting, I say, "No. They're even forcing me to rest against my will. Those villains." My voice breaks at the end and trying to clear it results in a few coughs.

"Well, good. The last thing we need is for you to play while sick."

"I'm not sick."

"And I'm Jason Momoa." I keep my trap shut because if a movie was made about Lou DiMarco's life, his role would be played by James Gandolfini. But I understand the sarcasm. "Did you see the team doctor?"

"No, Mom," I deadpan. "I got home last night, went to bed, and you just woke me up."

"Call them if you start feeling worse."

Lifting a hand to rub my bleary eyes, I can't help but being weirded out by this conversation. Lou isn't a warm and fuzzy kind of guy and I've never been at the top of his client list. So I voice as much.

"You're freaking me out, Lou. Why did you call me to mother hen me?"

The man huffs. "Side effect of having some good news for you."

"Oh?" I don't know if it's because I'm not feeling well or what, but I can't fathom what kind of good news my agent may have for me when I'm already happily employed and uninjured, if a bit under the weather.

"Thanks to that viral video of you talking about your ideal woman, and the spectacular pitch from yesterday, you've been pitched for a great promotional opportunity."

"Great pun," I mumble.

He ignores that. "*SPORTY* magazine has reached out to Orlando Wild PR and me to feature you, front page and full body spread. We both want you to say yes. We'll respect if you say no but I will judge you."

I snort.

"When you say full body, would I be wearing clothes?"

"Yeah, it just means they'll turn one of your pictures into a poster in the middle of the magazine."

I didn't know that still existed in this day and age, but there are still plenty of sports fans who enjoy collecting physical goods from their respective teams. One of the highest selling merchs from the Wild is actually Logan Kim's player card, after all.

"But with clothes?" I ask to confirm.

"I didn't know you were so modest. Aren't athletes used to being nude in locker rooms all the time?"

Yeah, but I happen to have one female coworker I don't want to horrify. I have a feeling she wouldn't meet me in the eye if I go around parading what my unknown momma gave me, consequently sacking me as her dating coach. And I don't want that. I committed to helping her until she finds the right guy to take to her Friendsgiving, and I'm a man of my word. I also enjoy keeping her around.

"There's a time and place for everything," I rasp out the words as I explain. "And my philosophy is that what happens in the locker room stays in the locker room." See, like yesterday. When Garcia was massaging my arm. If I even allow myself to think about it, things will go south. And by *things* I mean my blood.

"Fine. I'll put a clause about bare torso only."

"Thanks for protecting my modesty," I joke.

"Does this mean you're in?" he asks in his sharky tone that got me an extra million dollars in my previous contract, even though my performance was nowhere near what it is today. I owe this man basically everything I have right now, and I don't intend to short him for the commission that the *SPORTY* gig will get him, even if I'm not dying for it. I'm a professional athlete and not a model, after all.

"Are you sure they asked for me and not for Logan Kim? He's the pretty boy of the team, you know."

"So are you, you little shit. And they called me personally, using the combination of letters that make up your name."

"Ah." I bite my lips to suppress the laugh I'm sure would send Lou over the edge and turn his insults even spicier. "Then I guess I'll do it."

"Excellent! I'll review the contract, add that clause, and send it back for your signature once they have approved. Hang tight."

"When's the thing going to be?" I ask very belatedly, but I blame my addled brain.

"You're hot in social media trends right now, so they want it to be in a week. We'll coordinate with the team's PR to not interfere with your regular schedule."

"Great." I don't know if it's because I'm weak right now, or because I'm snuggled all comfy, but I let out the sappy Cade that lives inside of me for a second. "Thanks, man. You're the only one who really looks out for me."

And that stuns the great Lou DiMarco shark into silence.

Or maybe he's just so grossed out that he's had to mute himself so he can gag.

But then he clears his throat. "You're welcome, kid. Get better." And he hangs up.

"Wow," I mumble. By the awkward inflection in his voice, I'd guess he wasn't grossed out. More like touched. That's what he gets for being at the top of a very reduced group of people who watch out for me.

Lou, Lucky, my housekeeper Carmen, maybe Garcia? Probably not.

Both Lou and Carmen are in my payroll so maybe they shouldn't count. But Lou was the only one who caped for me so hard that eventually a team scouted me. Carmen brings homemade food for me, even when that's not part of her contract. I think this all goes beyond a paper relationship.

Or I just don't know what the real thing is. I close my eyes. Lucky's declaration of brotherhood still has me reeling. I had to look up what that even means online but I'm not sure I get it. Like, of course I know how to read—the logic is clear. But the real concept? I have no idea. It wasn't a sentiment I shared with other orphans I grew up with, maybe because it was always a temporary arrangement.

But one day Lucky and I will play for different teams. Or one of us will retire. Then what? Does the brotherhood go on?

And the same for Garcia. She'll find her guy soon. Maybe I get traded. Maybe she finds a different job. That'll be the end of our relationship.

I scrunch my face. What relationship, though? She's employed by my team to mind my physical health and that of thirty nine other guys. We're barely friendly now.

So if not people I employ or people I work with, who do I have left?

I swallow hard and turn to the opposite side, my face against the sun. I force my breathing to even, and my mind to focus on the feeling of my sweatpants against my legs, the sheets under my skin, the coolness of the pillow, and nothing else. Being on light duty means I can sleep in a little longer, get to the facilities and train a little less, and I decide to do just that.

*

This time I'm marginally more aware that my phone is ringing because of a call, and not the alarm. I roll over, intending to reach for my bedside table, when my cheek falls directly on my blaring phone.

"Shit." The sound is extremely annoying this close and I try to move away, but my body feels like lead. I barely manage to lift my head to free the device, or myself, depending on how I may look at it.

My eyes feel even blearier this time around as I try to focus them on the screen. It takes a moment for the caller ID to register in my brain.

Little Darlin'.

Huh?

I answer the call. This time I don't have the mojo to put it on loudspeaker, so I drop my phone on my face with the receiver on my ear. "Garcia? Why are you calling?"

"Why am I calling?" she shrieks. I wince, but there's no earthly force that can make me move more than that. "What do you mean why am I calling? Half of the team has been calling you!"

I half groan, half ask, "Why?"

"It's six in the evening! You never showed up for training. Of course everyone is up in arms."

"What the—Shit." Grunting, I pick myself up to sit. The bed sheets slide to pool around my waist and I take a look around. My bedroom is dark except for the faint light of the clock on the wall, and the sliver under the door that tells me Carmen must be around—and probably thinks I'm at work.

"You sound horrible."

"Thanks," I rasp out, running a hand through my hair. Grabbing the sheets, I push them away and sadly they don't go far enough, which is the moment I realize I really am sick after all.

She sighs loudly. "Are you home?"

"Yeah." I all but crawl to the edge of the bed and my head swims as I reach to turn on the light.

There's some rustling on her end, followed by her furious typing on a keyboard. "I'm putting you on the injured list for the time being. Get some rest and don't forget to eat properly."

"Ugh."

"You *did* eat today, right?"

The weird twist in my stomach reminds me, first, that no. I did not. And second, that I don't want to. Like, anything I put down the guzzler will come out like a fountain.

Maybe I should at least drink some water, though. I grab for the room temperature water bottle on my bedside table. Uncapping it feels like a feat and the water feels downright freezing once it hits my mouth. My stomach swirls the one sip like it's a blender, and I stop.

"Uh…"

"Starr."

"Garcia?" I wince.

"Do not make me force you to eat."

"Ha ha," I rasp out, and there's only silence on the other end of the line. "Oh, you were serious."

"Give me your address, Starr."

I blink hard, as if the dim light hurt. "Huh?"

"I will make you my dad's famous chicken soup and have you pitching cutters again in no time."

Something happens in my chest, like a fever is breaking out there and expanding across my entire body. But it's not uncomfortable. It doesn't churn my stomach or make my head spin. I want to lean into it, just the same as when I'm tired and want to lay on my pillows.

"I'll text you," I say, touching my free hand against my chest. My heart beats rapidly underneath.

CHAPTER 25
HOPE

"Starr is accounted for," I declare as I walk into the meeting room where the entire support staff is meeting, tucking my cellphone in the back pocket of my regulation pants. "He also seems to be down with a cold like Rivera and company."

That leads to some sighs, groans, and facepalms.

Yesterday, everyone was fine and playing their best. Today, no other than nine guys are down with what seems to be the same bug. The only difference is that the rest of them showed up to the facilities and gave training a try for a brief moment, until either they or staff noticed that they shouldn't be training at all and were sent home.

But Starr never even showed up. We've blown up his phone all day long, and his agent said that last he checked in the early morning, Starr was at home and just sounded tired. I don't know about the rest of the men in this room, but I've been freaking out that something really bad might've happened to him—like a traffic accident on the way, or something worse. I'm so relieved that he finally picked up his phone and it was with my call, that my body feels like it's floating compared to a few minutes ago. Not that I can say any of this aloud without having my words misconstrued. And especially not after Otto's little comments yesterday.

"He took your call?" said douche asks, cocking his eyebrow and cutting a look at Steve that everybody can read.

I deadpan with, "Yeah, maybe because I called him twenty times back to back, instead of you trying once and giving up."

"Thank you for the persistence, Garcia," Beau says, tossing a nod my way that placates me because upon his level response, Otto and the others can't stir the shit they wanted to. "Did he sound as bad as the other guys?"

"Slightly worse, I'd say." As curses and complaints rise, I add, "But maybe it's good timing. This way he can really rest his elbow."

Steve nods. "That's a good point."

"Now that all the players are accounted for, we can discuss how to reshuffle the team for the next few games. Thank you to the training staff for your support today." That's a clear dismissal from Rob Beau, which is great because I've been here almost two hours extra trying to locate one cowboy that now needs some soup.

I rush to pick up my bag and luck out that there are no Otto sightings on my way out. I make a mental note of being extra careful around him, even when I already trusted him as far as I could throw him. And I'm a quite strong girlie.

In my car, I check the text message from one Annoying Cowboy with not only his address, but a door code. I'm not surprised that his house is in one of those Winter Park neighborhoods where rich people live, and I set course for a nearby Publix to buy ingredients. His kitchen better be stocked with the tools I need, or else.

Or else I'll have to drive home to get them, and I'd rather not explain to my roommates why I'd be poaching pots or knives from our kitchen. I trust them a lot more than

Otto, but I don't want them to think this is a bigger deal than it is.

It's just that none of the other guys legitimately sounded as bad as Starr did, and the second he admitted to not having eaten anything my amygdala kicked in. I'm a fight type of person, which rather than anger, more often than not translates into having to do *something* so I don't feel useless.

Soup it is.

I probably break a world record of fastest grocery shopping for all the ingredients necessary for Dad's chicken soup. It's his bootleg version of the Venezuelan mondongo but only with one type of meat—chicken—and without spending two days in the preparation. It's still a pretty hearty everything-but-the-kitchen-sink recipe that cures everything but a broken heart. I tried it after I got dumped and it's the only time this soup hasn't fixed me.

The drive to his house is pretty quick, and when I shift into the brick streets is when I know I'm in the seriously moneyed area. Breathing here already increases my taxes.

"You have arrived," my GPS says, the screen signaling that my destination is on the right. But all I see is a concrete wall at odds with the open lawns on every other lot. I park behind two cars by the entrance of the bunker-like property and check that the house number nailed over the entrance matches the text message from him.

"Huh," I mutter as I step out of my Jeep. I pick up the bags of groceries from the back and head over to the door. I search everywhere for the keypad, and I don't know if it's because the streetlights are too dim, or if it's just that this door is too fancy, but it takes me a good moment to find the near seamless keypad.

The door gives out a fancy little beep as it opens.

"Oh, geez," I say to myself. Is this a bank or a home?

I walk into a yard unlike anything I've seen before. It's quite narrow but long—very long. There's perfectly manicured grass, and the walls are flanked by so many plants that it's easy to forget that the whole property is encased by concrete. But something in the middle of it makes me smile.

Starr straight up built a pitching mound with a strike zone painted old school against an end wall. The wall is stained with blows from what must be thousands of pitches he's thrown at it.

Shaking my head, I close the entrance door behind me and make my way across the narrow patch of grass to the house. In contrast to the property's perimeter, the house walls are made of crystal clear glass. Inside the lights are on and display decor straight out of a gallery room—large, modern furniture in earth tones, brass all over. But first, there's a front door I must defeat.

I wouldn't consider myself a genius of my generation or anything, but I key in the same code as before and this door also opens. I'd pat my own back if my hands weren't busy.

"Wow," I say once I'm inside, and my voice echoes in the empty chamber of perfect acoustics.

This place was clearly decorated by an expensive designer because even the light fixtures look intentional. The kitchen is pristine, only with a bowl of fresh fruit on the marble counters. There better be actual cooking crap behind the cabinets. I place the bags on the kitchen island by the farm style double sink, straight out of the renovation shows my roomies and I like to binge watch while dreaming of having house-buying money one day.

There's only one thing missing from this place, though. And that is…

Signs of life.

And I don't just mean because Starr wasn't waiting by the door to greet me. I mean that there's literally no indication that he even lives here. Where are the family pictures? The domestic messes? The mismatched mugs or even the Orlando Wild paraphernalia? This looks like a freaking AirBNB that costs a grand per night.

"Starr?" I call out weakly. Something about raising my voice in this house kinda scares me. What if my shrills break the glass or something?

I glance around again, as if he could pop out from between the couch cushions. The kitchen seems to be smack in the middle of the floor plan because the main entrance opens directly to it and to the vast living room, which I'm facing right now. I pad softly toward the opposite wall to the entrance, where massive crystal doors overlook a long pool that spans across the length of the property all the way to the back, where I assume the rooms are. It feels way longer than the front yard, and since I didn't see his car outside, I put two and two and deduct that it's because the front yard is cut short by a garage. The wall with the strike zone must be its side.

The property probably fits three of my dad's whole lot, except this is just for a single guy. He must throw some pretty wild parties in here.

I shake off the yuck that gives me and take out my phone from my pocket to shoot him a text. My *I'm here* goes completely ignored. Did he go out? No way to find out unless I snoop in his garage.

Well, since I'm here I might as well. I retrace my steps to the entrance, using the sort of mental map I've made of the place. There's a short, narrow hallway to the right of the entrance that I ignored when I walked in. It ends in a door and it unlocks to a dark, uncomfortably hot space. I feel around the sides until I find a light switch and flip it.

Voila, a massive black pickup truck is parked in the middle, surrounded by racks of tools, household goods, and baseball equipment. A.k.a. a garage.

I turn off the light and close the door. This tells me one

thing: Cade Starr is somewhere in this house, and he might be indisposed enough that he's passed out.

I gasp a little. "What if he needs urgent care?"

Screw decency, I need to find this guy right now.

My sneakers squeak against the marble floors as I pivot around the kitchen to the opposite hallway that runs by the pool. Somewhere behind the kitchen, it cuts perpendicular into a smaller hallway, but I try the very first door on the left instead.

Success.

If it hadn't been for the single lit up lamp by his bed, I'd have missed him and tried another room instead. His bed is massive, no doubt custom made for a 6 foot 4 giant like him. And there, in the middle, is none other than the house owner.

"Starr?" I whisper and he doesn't stir. Something really is up.

I approach slowly not to spook him in case he wakes up— but there's no need, dude's completely out cold. He lies on his side, facing the lamp, one hand on his cellphone maybe since we last talked.

The bed sheets lost the fight in trying to cover him at some point and they're balled up between his legs. Fortunately, he's wearing gray sweat pants. Unfortunately, no shirt. I'm not strong enough to stop myself from admiring the clear ridges of the serratus anterior muscles that cover his ribs. They're very pretty, okay? His brown hair is a complete bird's nest atop his head, and his lips are slightly parted as he breathes in and out softly.

But finally I notice his face. There's a bit of a scruff going on, and it doesn't hide the pinkness of his cheeks.

I've never in my life seen Cade Starr blush. He's one of those people who tends to grow paler while exercising, rather than pink. In fact, he even tans golden rather than pink, as shown by the clear tan lines in his arms.

Without thinking, I place the back of my hand against his forehead and he's hot. Like, not just attractiveness wise. He's legit burning up with a high fever.

Just as I'm about to pull my hand away, he traps my wrist in his hand.

I freeze. His eyes are still closed and there's no change in his breathing, like he's still unconscious.

I make another attempt at freeing myself and it backfires. Spectacularly.

With a grunt, Starr yanks at my arm with so much strength that it tilts me off my axis. I barely manage to suppress a squeal, focused on not crashing into him. My knee against his mattress stops some momentum, until he shifts to use his other hand.

Next thing I know, he flips me around until my back crashes against his chest. All the air leaves my lungs as he tosses a leg over my hip and pulls me flush against him. The lack of oxygen to my brain keeps me paralyzed as he settles his arms around me, the one under my neck wrapping around my chest, over my boobs, until his hand rests on my shoulder. His other arm falls over around my waist, his hand snuggling under my ribs.

Snuggling.

Cade Starr is *snuggling me*.

Mierda. Mierda. What the hell do I do?

If I move—if he wakes up—oh, this is gonna be bad.

But also, what if he *doesn't* wake up? I can't spend the whole freaking night in his bed. That would be worse!

Oh my gosh, I'm in Cade Starr's bed.

No. That doesn't matter. The issue here is that he feels like a log that's burning inside a fireplace. Sweat is already breaking all over the areas of my body pressed against his. That might also be because some of them are in contact with parts of

Starr's anatomy I never imagined I'd be in contact with. Or somewhat contact. Thankfully there are layers of clothing.

Welp. What if he was one of those guys who sleep naked?

In reflex, I jerk my head in a hard shake and that does stir him.

"Hmm."

That relaxed, almost delighted little sound from his throat sends my heart rate through his expensive roof. Worse, he wraps himself a little tighter, his arms closing dangerously around my chest.

I don't need to touch my hand to my face to know it's burning up worse than he is, but for an entirely different reason. Even when Dawson and I were still besotted with each other, I can't remember a single time he embraced me anywhere as deliciously as an unconscious Cade Starr. Imagine what it'd be like while he's fully awake and it's intentional?

I'd die.

He'd probably die if he wakes up and finds me here, though. If the roles were reversed, I'd scream bloody murder and call the cops.

I test the situation by touching his bare forearm, the one over my chest. It gets me no reaction, so I wrap my hand around the firm muscles and tug—and again, until his hold comes loose and I can lower his arm to the mattress. His knuckles collide with his phone screen, but that still doesn't wake him up.

Swallowing thickly, I try the same trick with his other arm. This one's more awkward because it lays above me, but with some effort I manage to rest it on his side without it sliding. His breath keeps fanning my nape steadily and when he makes no attempt at trapping me again, I begin wiggling away from him.

My traitorous nostrils widen almost impossibly, trying to capture his scent on the sheets. It almost makes me dizzy from how good it is, and I can tell that it's not from aftershave but purely from his skin.

I roll toward the edge of the bed and drop to the floor on a crouch, ready to hide under his bed if he opens his eyes. But no, he's still completely gone to the world.

I rise back up and lower one knee on his mattress again. Placing one hand against his chest, the other one balancing me over the mattress, I push him hard until he rolls to his back, arms spread wide. Huffing, I walk around to the foot of the bed to yank free the sheets that are tangled around his legs. I throw them over him, even going as far as tucking them into his sides to keep all the heat in. This way he'll sweat and finally break the fever.

Turning his head toward me, he suddenly mumbles, "Hope?"

And I stop—breathing, blinking, thinking.

His eyes remain closed, though. A little line appears between his eyebrows. Is he dreaming about me or am I in his nightmares? But he knew I was coming, so it probably means nothing.

I bite my lip, gently stepping away from the bed and retreating all the way out of his bedroom. My hands tremble as I grab the door handle and shut the door so softly that it makes no sound.

Then I run to the kitchen. So fast that my shoes don't even have enough time to squeak against the floor.

I only stop when I'm in front of the groceries, my chest expanding and contracting violently while I try to get enough oxygen to my brain. My whole body is a ball of raw nerve right now. I feel like such a perv because there's no way I should be thinking the things I'm thinking about a man who is so ill that he's not even aware of what he does or says.

But he said my name. Not my last name. Not darlin'. *Hope*.

Placing my hands on my steaming face, I try to reason that

it's not the first time. That time, during the PitchCom date disaster, he did call me out by my name.

It feels different now. Maybe because I was pressed up against him. And maybe because I feel—

"Who are you?"

I jump around.

An older woman wearing rubber gloves up to her elbows, and brandishing a dripping mop at me, stands at the end of the hallway I just came from.

Like I've been caught in the middle of a crime, all I can utter is, "U—Uh…"

"State your name and what you came here for before I call the cops." She pushes the mop closer to me.

I lift my hands. "Um, I'm Hope Garcia. Friend of Starr's— coworker. I'm in the team. Not a player. Staff. I came to make soup. He's sick."

"Oh." She blinks hard and the mop moves back an inch. Slowly, her eyes travel up and down my length, closing in on the team logo emblazoned across my chest. She clears her throat. "Still, I'd like to see a badge."

"I—Yes. Of course. May I reach for my phone in my pocket. It's also my wallet."

Somehow this softens the woman. "Miss, if you're that concerned about an old woman with a mop when you're clearly strong enough to take me down, you're probably not a weird stalker. But yes, please, show me your employee badge."

I quickly produce both my Orlando Wild employee badge and my driver license. She inspects them for a quick moment, watching my face like she works for the TSA, and finally sets the mop down on the pristine floor.

"So Cade's sick?" She frowns.

"Yeah, he's been sleeping all day."

"He's home?" Her eyes pop. Now she rests the mop against

the wall and works on removing her gloves. "Ugh, I should've checked. I'd have cooked him something."

"Um." I tuck my phone back in my pocket. Even though the woman is almost two feet shorter than Starr, and her features completely different, the air of protectiveness in her is so real that I ask, "Are you Starr's mother?"

"Goodness, no. You flatter me, Miss Garcia." She chuckles and then, like it's part of a joke, adds, "Cade's an orphan."

And just like a few minutes ago, my whole world tilts off its axis.

CHAPTER 26
CADE

Hope Garcia is in my arms.

The scent of vanilla envelops me and I lean even more into it. Her hair is soft and warm against my face. Or maybe that's her skin. I press my nose against it, desperate for more. Her curves are snug against me and it's all at once the most comfortable and exhilarating feeling of my life. Even better than striking out a cleanup batter with my cutter.

Wait. She feels rather flat. I run my hand across her side and except for some tiny wrinkles in her clothes, she's as flat as…

My mattress.

I crack an eye open.

Yeah, that's because Hope Garcia is, in fact, not in my arms. There's nothing in them but air, and I'm lying alone in my bed. Groaning, I close my eyes. It felt so real. I could've sworn I was touching her skin. In fact, my pillow kinda smells like her.

And then the door opens and *she* walks in.

"What the—" The two words spill out of my mouth like a

scream. Pure adrenaline kicks in and I roll away from her, trying to hide any possible vestiges that I was really enjoying that dream. By a stroke of luck, the sheets wrap around my waist. By an even bigger stroke of luck, they also prevent me from rolling all the way down the bed and crashing on the floor.

I balance myself against the opposite edge of my mattress and lift my head up. Her arms are folded and her tongue's tucked against her cheek. I squeeze my eyes closed but when I open them, she's still standing in the middle of my bedroom. Everything feels very real this time—the dip of the mattress beneath me, the hot bed sheets, the cool air—so I must be fully awake.

She tilts her chin down at me. "You may want to cover up."

Oh, shit. Did I make it all worse?

Swallowing hard, I rise even more to look down at myself. The bed sheets tug at my sweatpants dangerously, instead of erm, protecting my modesty. If anything, I'm showing a hell of a lot more skin than I was trying to spare. I clear my throat as I grab a handful of the sheets and pull them up to my stomach.

"I, uh. Sorry about that," I mumble in a rasp.

Garcia is cool as a cucumber, though. Which… yeah, it's annoying as shit. I know she works around buff dudes all the time, but would it kill her to show some reaction?

"Where do you have your comfy T-shirts?"

It takes me a moment to process her question amid the fog of hormones and annoyance swirling in my mind. "Second drawer on the right side of the dresser." That's the drawer I'm one hundred percent sure doesn't have underwear or jockstraps.

Her steps barely make any sound as she trods over to the dresser. Pulling open the correct drawer, she takes a look for a quick moment until she plucks out a yellow Orlando Wild T-shirt, with the team name in purple like it is in our alternate uniform. Then she tosses it at my face.

"Oof." I grab a handful of the fabric and remove it from around my head. "That was pretty good, Garcia. You could be our new relief pitcher."

"Get dressed and come to the kitchen when you're ready. You need water and food desperately."

I need other things that I can't mention aloud without scaring her off. Instead, I snap my trap shut and nod, watching her leave the room and close the door behind her.

Collapsing back on my bed, my ever helpful memory recalls the exact moment I created a door code specifically for her and texted it along with my address. That was probably a minute before passing out.

The clock on the wall says it's almost nine and on cue, this time my stomach gurgles with hunger. That's gotta be a good sign.

Straining, I manage to drag myself out of the bed, balled up T-shirt in my hand, and head to the bathroom.

Some ten minutes later, I emerge from my room wearing the T-shirt. My feet are bare on the floor, and there's a fresh smell of lemon that tells me Carmen was here today. She's not in the kitchen, though. It's just Garcia by herself, stirring the contents of a pot with a ladle while she holds the lid with her other hand.

I stop and stare blatantly. Whenever Carmen gives me food, it's because she's cooked it at her home since I hire her as a cleaner and not as a cook. The meal service I hire just delivers to my front door, and I barely ever make anything myself.

This is the first time anyone cooks in my kitchen.

I blink hard like my eyes are the shuttle of a camera, trying to preserve this moment in my memory forever. Garcia makes a little sound from her throat, like the smell of the food alone is enough to bring her satisfaction. My body is simultaneously too cold and too hot, and I have to steel myself against a shiver. My tongue turns into lead, though, and there's no way I can speak.

Garcia notices me at last. Her eyes lower to my now clothed chest, before flying back up to my face, and I realize that I forgot to comb my hair. I wish I didn't look like a sleaze right now. I wish I looked my finest.

But then again, she wouldn't be here if that was the case.

"Sit down, I'll fix you a bowl."

"Yes, ma'am." I drag my feet around the kitchen island as promptly as my weak ass allows. Grunting, I heft myself on a barstool.

Her back is to me as she reaches for a bowl she already had lined up by the stove. She must've rummaged through the entire kitchen to find what she needed, and I don't judge. I use it so little that I'd have done the same myself.

She's still in her daily training staff uniform, black joggers that hug her hips and her butt, and a tight purple long-sleeved shirt that clings to her tiny waist. My mouth waters, and it's not precisely because of the incredible smell of hearty soup permeating the air. Her ponytail is half over her shoulder, half streaming behind her and obscuring the column of her neck, and I could swear I know exactly how it feels like against my face to the point that it makes me itch.

Shit. I feel like an absolute fool—just the same as the rest of men. How the hell had I never noticed how gorgeous she is?

Maybe it's better this way. If I had, I'd have asked her out the second I found out she was looking, just like Lucky did.

Wait a freaking second. Does that mean he had the hots for her like, for real? Is that why he got so intense with me after her date with Kim?

I shake my head hard and that's when Garcia turns around

to bring a massive bowl of soup over, carrying it between oven mitts. "Careful, it's really hot."

Ya don't say?

I wait on edge as she slowly walks around the kitchen island, sucking in air as she places the bowl in front of me and whiffs me with her arm. I can't believe I'm angry that she didn't accidentally touch me.

"Right, water." She snaps her fingers. Now that she's free of the steaming soup, she's much quicker to skip over to the fridge. "I mixed in some electrolytes to hydrate you faster."

"Thank you," I say, overwhelmed out of my mind between the smell of homemade food, of her—her presence alone— how alive my whole house looks with her in it, how unexpected and hard that hits me. I blurt out, "I didn't think you'd come."

She twists her face. "You gave me your address." Then sets the drink on the kitchen island, sliding it over to me.

"Yeah, but I still didn't think you'd come." I avoid her eyes by grabbing the spoon. The bowl has soup, all right, but also an assortment of vegetables, corn, and pieces of chicken in it.

"Mrs. Gonzalez was also extremely shocked to see me."

My eyes whip up. "You met Carmen?"

"Yep. She thought I was a stalker at first because apparently you have no one else to visit you, ever."

I don't know why that combination of words gives me vertigo, like I'm sitting still but someone is slowly yanking the floor from under me and I can't do anything about it.

I try to distract myself by picking a spoonful of soup with plenty of chunks in it. After blowing on it slightly, I put it in my mouth and almost die right here. My tastebuds explode with flavor. I lock my throat so that no matter what happens, the nascent groan doesn't escape from it.

Garcia folds her arms and lowers them to lean on the counter, which is already much more than I can take in my weakened state when the move frames her chest so well. "I had to show her my employee ID to pacify her, which was fine, I appreciate that she looks out for you so much. Especially because apparently you have literally no family to do that for you?"

I choke so hard on the soup that I'm afraid a chunk of potato will come out of my nose.

"Drink," Garcia says breezily, pushing the water bottle closer to me from across the kitchen island.

I uncap it and take a healthy swig. After a bad coughing fit that burns my throat even more, and some more swigs of the drink, I manage to utter a weak, "what?"

Garcia looks almost angry. "I didn't know."

"Know what?" My brain is still not processing.

"That you have no family. What the hell? Why did I not know something as important as that?"

"I—I have no idea. It's not like it's a secret," I rasp out and squint at her. "Why are you even upset about it?"

"Because!" She throws her hands in the air. "It's a pretty big thing. I feel like a terrible person for having no idea."

"You freaking weirdo," I say with more shock than any bite. "It's on my literal Wikipedia page. I'll spare you the search. Cade Starr's early life: abandoned in the rain at the steps of a church approximately a week after birth. Absorbed by the Department of Family and Protective Services. Named after Cade Mathews, the director at the time, and last named after the lone star state. Extra r for funsies—I'm paraphrasing but that's the gist." I shrug.

Her voice grows even harsher. "So it's true that you're all alone in this world?"

"Yep." I dig the spoon back into the hot soup, looking for the tastiest morsel to chase away the bitter taste in my mouth. "Biological parents never showed up, was never adopted and ended up growing in the system. Lucky claims to be my brother now." In an attempt to lighten the mood, I add, "Maybe I should've asked him to make me soup instead."

"He can't. He's down with the same bug as you." Her chin trembles. Her eyes are glassy.

"Uh, Garcia… why do you look like you're about to—"

A tear rolls down her face. Then another.

My eyes go as wide as saucers. "Darlin'?"

Even worse, a massive sob escapes from her mouth, echoing around us. I sit frozen as she stomps around the kitchen island—toward me. What the hell?

And then her arms are around me, burying my face against the crook of her neck. She lands between my thighs. The spoon slides from my hand, clinks loudly against the porcelain bowl, and falls on the marble.

"What's happening?" I ask, stunned, my lips moving against her skin.

Her chest racks with another sob. "I'm sorry. I had no idea. And here I've been treating you like garbage all these years, thinking that you were just another self entitled prick of a man baby."

I bark a laugh. "Wow, tell me how you really feel."

"I'm serious, Starr." She sniffs and that's when I realize that her face is buried in my hair. "I feel really bad right now." She squeezes me even harder.

I'm not nice enough to put the distance she deserves. Instead, I fully go for it. Wrapping my arms around her, I bring her as close as can. I breathe deep to get as much of her scent as I can, and I command every molecule of my body to memorize the feeling of her in my arms. This is way better than any dream.

"It's okay, Garcia. I'm okay." My left hand travels up her spine, farther until I find the skin at the back of her neck.

She sighs against my hair and I'm undone. In a way I've never been.

But then she's pulling away and I have no choice but to let her. I tighten my jaw so I don't ask her not to leave. Her hands push slightly at my shoulders and I dare to lift my face.

She's biting her lower lip and a new tear rolls down her cheek. Her eyes are red and puffy, and so is the rest of her face. I've never seen anyone more beautiful in my life.

Swallowing hard, I run my thumb gently across her cheek to dry her tears. A visceral need grows in my belly, much deeper than the desire I already felt for her. And it's the need to ask her if I can be hers. If she can claim me. If she can be the one I need to never be alone again.

But I can't do that. She's been looking for someone who can offer her everything she wants, and here I am, just wanting to take more from her—when she's already offered her time and her presence when I'm sick. Especially not when she already explained that it would be too risky for her to date someone from work. It makes me angry at myself for wanting her.

"The… the soup is growing cold," I mumble.

With a little gasp, she retreats from the warm circle of my limbs. "Right! You need to eat and I, uh, I need to get going. It's super late."

I watch her scramble around the kitchen, dumping used things in the dishwasher, throwing out garbage—not looking at me at all, clearly uncomfortable. I force myself to keep eating the soup she made.

"There's plenty left over. Just put it in air tight containers and you can freeze it. I'm going to leave now but if you need anything else text me. Or call me. Not Rivera, though, he's also sick. See you later, Starr—No, I kinda hate your last name now. Cade? But that's also not really yours. Cowboy? Should I call you Cowboy forever?" Her eyes widen, as if she's only realized now that she just crammed a million words into five seconds.

I take my sweet ass time chewing some bits of chicken and

veggies, swallowing, and finally speaking. "Trust me, Cade's been mine for twenty seven years."

"Cade?" She breathes out.

"Yes, Hope?"

Her jaw drops. "So, uh. First name base?" I don't know if she means it as a pun or just misspoke, but I like it.

I snort through my nose softly. "You just made me soup and hugged me. That's definitely first name base."

"Okay." Her voice sounds weird even as she nods firmly. "Good night, Cade."

Even though she's firmly out of bounds, I can't help feeling buoyant at this moment. Smiling, I rasp out, "Good night, Hope."

I watch her leave my house, cross my yard, and disappear behind the entrance. And even well after she's gone, my heart keeps racing like a horse.

CHAPTER 27
HOPE

The moment I realized it's taken me twice as usual to get ready in the morning, I deduce something's wrong. The confirmation comes as I'm about to open the front door to head to my car, and stop for the most aggressive sneeze of my life. I'm pretty sure it's strong enough to wake my roommates up, even though it's an hour before their alarms go off.

Wincing, I do a U-turn and tiptoe back to my room, closing the door softly behind me. Looks like I didn't escape the great common cold wave that has crashed on the Orlando Wild. I doubt that hanging out with, um, Cade, in his house yesterday was enough. I'm sure I had it in my system already.

I lean my back against the door. Boy am I glad he's not the only one who's sick, otherwise explaining this to my boss would be a lot more complicated. I take my phone from the pocket of my joggers and dial Steve.

"Good morning." As I say this, I sniffle naturally because that's what you do when you get a sudden tickle inside your nose.

"Oof, let me guess. You caught the bug too."

"I think so."

He sighs. "Well, get some rest and come back if you feel better in a couple of days."

"Thanks and sorry." We know the drill, the players's safety is our top priority and any time anyone gets anything remotely contagious, we have to use our paid time off to stay home and protect them. It's part of what makes my job completely unpredictable, aside from all the travel I have to do with the team.

We end the call and I change gears. I dump my duffel bag containing all the clothes, toiletries, equipment, and snacks I usually cart back and forth to work every day in a corner of my room. Turns out I won't need it for a few days. Instead, I march to my closet to take out a different bag and dump some comfier clothes and a couple of books about kinesthesia that I'll finally have the time to read.

In the kitchen, I leave a message on the magnetic whiteboard tacked on the fridge to let the girlies know what's what, then I send a text to my dad.

ME

Heads up, I got sick and am OMW to spend it with you

MI PAPÁ

What kind of sick?

ME

The kind that can't be propagated to players any further

MI PAPÁ

But it's okay if I get it??

ME

Yes, sorry

I roll my eyes at his dramatics. If Eduardo and I didn't kill him when we were kids coming from school with anything between chickenpox and stomach bugs, a little common cold won't defeat him either.

But then his three dots appear again right before a new text.

Snorting, I shake my head. He's the one I get my early bird ways from, but even I admit that if the day comes that I can retire like him, I don't plan on waking up any time before seven in the morning. One extra hour of sleep is the least I'd deserve after a lifetime of working for someone else.

He sends me a thumbs up emoji and we have a deal.

The drive to my childhood home goes by quickly because traffic isn't brutal yet. His car is gone already, but I still park by the curb so he has the easier access to the front door. This one isn't some fancy model like the ones at a certain pitcher's house, and I unlock it with an old school key.

I drag my feet around the house the same way I used to when I returned home after school, exhausted and sleepy after studying all day and then doing my extracurriculars. I was in track and softball, because only one thing was never enough, and also because I figured learning to run would make me a better softball player. It worked, I guess, because I played in college. In fact, Dad still has a few of my medals hanging in the living room walls along with the family pictures.

I stop by one of Mom's that Dad must've taken himself. Newborn me is in her arms, while a small and cute Eduardo Jr. clings to her skirt. Geez, what happened to him to become exactly the opposite? My eyes return to Mom's face for a second, though, lingering on features that are now very clear on my face. The same defined eyebrows and dark eyes, the same kind of wide smile.

"Genes, man." I sniff.

I tear myself from the spot and keep trudging to my old room. After dumping my travel bag at the foot of the bed, I let myself drop on my bed face down. I kind of smush my nose but I don't care, I'm too tired to move now. I'm glad I was okay yesterday and could help Cade out a bit, though.

"Cade," I whisper, savoring how his name rolls off my tongue easier than it should. I bury my face against my mattress, although there's no one else here that I should hide my blush from.

Me muero.

I've been trying not to think about it since the moment I left his house, but I'm not that good at compartmentalizing. And let's be honest, that was pretty memorable. One thing was the accidental cuddling he clearly has no recollection of, but another entirely was me purposely hugging him.

An unidentified sound comes out of my throat, the result of embarrassment mixing together with the feminine urge to squeal and curse at the same time.

Because what the hell was I thinking?

I wasn't. I was overcome by so much emotion once Mrs. Gonzalez, the cleaning lady, put together the final piece of the Cade Starr puzzle. I apologized for having acted like a turd to him. And now I feel like I should apologize for being so much nicer after learning about this aspect of his life, when I'm sure all he wanted was to be treated as usual. And then I went and said I want to use his first name from now on?

"Ugh. *Ugh!*"

Of course he wouldn't say no. He was sick. His brain wasn't working as usual, as exemplified by the sleepy cuddles. I bet he was weirded out that I freaking hugged him.

I turn my face so I can breathe again, and there's a tickle in my nose that propels me—albeit slowly—to the bathroom to blow my nose. Afterward, I look at myself in the mirror and my whole face is a tomato.

"We can never face him again," I say to my reflection and she shakes her head back at me. "What would Mom have done?" I ask mirror-me, but she doesn't answer back.

Probably apologize, I think with a huff.

Slowly, I trudge back to my bed and this time I sit on it in a more civilized way. I stretch to remove my cell phone from the front pocket of my joggers, scroll and tap until I find his text message chat.

My thumb hovers without doing anything for a long moment.

"Mom, make me brave," I whisper and maybe it's placebo, maybe it isn't, but I finally go for it.

ME

How are you feeling today?

And now I wait for him to give me an opening. It's early and I'm sure he's going to sleep in while he recovers. I leave my phone on the bedside table, right next to the smiley face alarm clock that I spent weeks saving for in middle school. Shuffling without leaving the bed, I open my bag and pluck one of the kinesthesia books to settle into bed with.

I'm tucked in and comfy, only as far as page two of the introduction, when my phone buzzes. I chuck the book at my mattress and grab my phone.

ANNOYING COWBOY

Still sluggish

Thanks for asking, darlin'

I suck air through my teeth. These days that *darlin'* of his is hitting me differently, and I hate it because it's all in my head.

ME

Hope

Remember?

"Oh, shit," I mutter, smacking my forehead. I was supposed to be apologizing for that and not digging my heels further.

ME

Actually

Only if you want to

I don't want you to feel like I coerced you into dropping the last names just because you were sick

He sends the emoji with flat lips and a raised eyebrow.

ANNOYING COWBOY

Please darlin', I agreed of my own free will

I mean, Hope

It'll take some used to, is all

ME

Sure, I'll still call you Cowboy sometimes

Biting my lip, I tackle the other topic too now that the easiest one has been cleared.

ME

And um, also

I wanted to apologize for my behavior
yesterday

ANNOYING COWBOY

For making me soup?!

ME

No, I mean for um…

I hugged you without your consent and I AM
SO SORRY!!!! That should never have
happened. I literally don't know what came
over me. I totally understand if you don't want
to work with me ever again, I'll figure out a way
to get you assigned to Otto or Steve every
time. I'M REALLY SORRY and ohmygosh I'M
SORRY FOR TREATING YOU DIFFERENTLY
I'm sure you get so much crap from people for
your origins and I just acted impulsively based
on my own emotions without considering for a
second how that might make you feel. I made
you uncomfortable DIDN'T I?? Cade I'm sorry,
you don't need to forgive me just know that I
really regret it

I hit send on what ends up being the single chunkiest para-
graph I've ever written in my life. I press my curled fingers
against my mouth, waiting for a response.

The word *read* appears under my text, and his three dots
aren't showing up.

I run my eyes through the text, cringing at the horrible
punctuation and at how unhinged I sound, and try to put
myself in his shoes. He must be calling up his lawyer to get a
restraining order against me.

But then something terrible happens.

He calls me on FaceTime.

Yelping, I sit up so fast that the whole room spins. I check my reflection in the screen and the good news is that I'm not so red anymore, only my nose is. My hair's a mess because I let it loose, and I quickly comb my fingers through it before accepting the call.

Oh my—

A tiny squeak lodges in my throat at the sight that greets me. The cowboy is in bed, face down, his smushed cheek making his lips jut out. His hair's a rat's nest worse than mine and the scruff is scruffing way harder today. But the worst part is that I can see part of his shoulder and back and know he's shirtless again.

And that transports me to seeing him on his bed in that exact same state, and how that awakened every hormone that has been dormant in my body for the past two years.

That has to be why I acted like a fool in his kitchen.

"What the hell are you talking about, *Hope?*" The extra emphasis on my name with his extra raspy morning voice is weakening my legs. Good thing I'm sitting.

I sniffle and rub my nose with the heel of my free hand. "I thought I was very clear."

He scrunches up his pretty face. "What part of me hugging you back made you think I wasn't okay with that?"

"Well, you were sick and..." And I have proof that you weren't all in your usual state. But fessing up to how he cuddled me pretty intimately would make this conversation so much worse, so I stay mum.

"And I was totally fine with a little comfort." He moves the screen closer to his face and the closeup is about to give me a heart attack. "Hey, why is your nose doing that?"

"Doing what?"

"That." He points his finger at the screen when I sniffle again. "Are you crying or are you sick?"

Sigh, I respond with, "The latter. I've also been put off duty."

"That sucks." After a moment, he adds, "I have some soup that someone made me. Want some?"

My lips twitch. "I'm sure that person would want you to eat all of it."

"Yeah, she would. It seems to me like she worked very hard at it. One second." He sets the phone on the bed, facing up to his ceiling. All I hear is some grunting until the image swirls and he's back on the screen. This time he's face up, using one arm to prop his head higher on the pillow, which makes his bicep bulge beautifully. He must be holding the phone up quite high considering how much bare chest he's showing too. "So, what are your plans now that you're down too? Napping?"

I force myself to look at his face, but it's not like I'm immune to the scruff either. Clearing my throat, I utter a weak, "Maybe."

"Do you sleep half naked too?"

It takes a moment for my brain to process his words, and right when I think I must've imagined them, his lips stretch into a cheeky grin that shows all pearly whites.

"Cade Starr!"

"Oh, so we went from last name base, to first name base, to full name base?"

I splutter. "I meant basis. Not base."

"I kinda like base better."

I almost fold my arms, except one is busy holding the phone up. "And anyway, what's it to you?"

He shrugs. "Just wondering what to watch out for if I ever need to go rescue you in the middle of the night."

"I don't need rescuing. I'm a self sufficient woman." I close my mouth for a second. "Except for that one time with the horrible date."

"Of course." He coughs and it seems part of an act, until the cough keeps going.

"I shouldn't keep you any longer. Take a nap, Cade."

His eyebrows twitch but then his expression softens. "You too, Hope. I hope this doesn't hit you too hard. I also hope to see you at the ballpark soon."

"Hardy har har."

His smile now is dangerous, the kind that goes viral on social media. "Get some rest, darlin'."

"You too, Cowboy," I grouch because it's either that or swoon on camera.

We end the call and I collapse on my back, arms spread eagle across the bed, blinking up at the ceiling and wondering how that innocent little phone call could make me feel even more screwed than before.

CHAPTER 28
CADE

Out of an abundance of caution, the team physicians decree that everyone who's down with the cold should stay home for a week to ensure that we fully recover, and don't pass this along to the rest of the team.

It's great. I haven't had this much free time in years. Even during the offseason I'm too busy training to catch up on TV shows or whatever. I now know the name of every season winner of The Great British Baking Show. In theory, I should also be able to bake a very flaky pastry, but I don't want to try. My expansive but empty kitchen feels sadder than ever, and I've been avoiding it with all my might. Just go in, quickly heat up leftover soup, and dash to my couch to keep watching the show.

Or to text Hope.

In my defense, she's also been bored out of her mind now that she's read her kinesthesia books and gone through every photo album at her dad's place.

We FaceTimed once more, a couple of nights ago. Even though she sounded a lot more congested than the first day, and her features were more haggard, her eyes were as bright as two jewels as she told me about her mom.

"She had a total thing for skirts," she said, openly amazed. "In every single picture she's wearing one. The only exception was shorts at the beach in Margarita during their honeymoon."

"What's Margarita?" I asked, pronouncing it in such a Texan way that it made her laugh.

Once her amusement subsided, she said, "It's an island in my parents' home country. But anyway, seeing her pictures…" She trailed off to bite her lips, and I really struggled with focusing on her next words. "It just made me wonder how I would've turned out if she'd raised me."

I remember having to sit up at that point, concluding that maybe lying down on my bed while talking on camera with the woman I have a thing for is probably not wise. At least going by the very red blooded reaction of my body to just seeing her bite her lip.

Fortunately, my brain replayed her words and they annoyed me enough to snap me out of the haze. "Why is there some implication that you turned out wrong?"

"No—well." She shrugged, not noticing that the collar of her oversized T-shirt slipped off her shoulder. I did notice. "I might've just turned out girlier, is all. Then maybe the whole dating thing wouldn't have been so hard."

"Listen to me, Hope. There's nothing wrong with you not being girly."

"But—"

"Nuh uh. Don't make me mansplain how wrong men are."

That made her smile, which, with her hair wildly spread over her pillow, the bare little shoulder, the pink nose—shit, it did something to me.

A few more minutes of conversation followed and then we hung up for the night. And that was it. For over a day.

The problem is that she stopped responding to my texts two days ago and either she's grown bored of me, or something's happened. I'm annoyed at being so professional that I don't have her roommates's numbers to check in. I'm sure it'd look weird if I ask her boss for her digits. And if I ask Lucky and he does have it, I may blow a fuse.

So I wait for a whole day until today, my first day back to the facilities for light training. I speed walk across the parking lot and the building like it's also going to accelerate time until I can find out if she's okay.

"Welcome back," someone from the back office says as I walk in, carrying my duffel bag.

"Thanks, Joe. Everything good with you?"

"Yeah, also survived the cold."

"Good, good. Well I hope you have a good day." Mentally I wince at my inability to be more eloquent, but I'm really in a hurry here.

"Take it easy, man. We really need you this season."

That trips me up—literally. I manage to not faceplant by sheer athleticism alone. But dude's already walking away, taking words that were usually said to Ben Williams with him.

"Huh," I mutter. Shaking my head, I set course for the training area to see if I catch sighting of a certain Latina.

The second I walk into the locker room, I'm greeted with, "Hey man!"

"Welcome back."

"Missed your pretty face, Starr."

"I didn't. Your face annoys me."

The latter comes from Logan Kim, so I ignore him.

Lucky greets me with a handshake and a smack to my back. Pulling away, he says, "Bruh, I missed you so much that I got you a present."

"It's not a whoopee cushion, is it?"

"No, it's just socks." He pulls a roll of socks from his back pocket and places it on my hand. Already by the color I can tell that they're not normal.

Keeping my face straight, I unfurl them—and unfurl them some more. The things have to be knee high, if not higher. And… A few guys from the team burst out laughing.

"Remind me how old you are again?" I ask him.

He jams his hands in his pockets and gives me an innocent look. "Thirty, why?"

"Shouldn't you act a bit more serious for someone who claims to be my older brother?"

He waves a hand. "Nah, that'd be boring. Anyway, put them on."

"There's a punch line coming, isn't it?"

"Yes, but not until you're wearing them."

My eye twitches, but I know Lucky. He's as relentless at robbing bases—and he has the team's record to prove it —as he is with his practical jokes that belong to middle school. They're usually in the form of a challenge, always benign, sometimes annoying, often funny. I wonder which of the two it'll be this time, so I sit by my locker, remove my normal socks and push up the legs of my black joggers to the knees so that his absurd socks can be on full display.

"Pffff." He presses a hand against his mouth once I'm done with the first one, and completely loses it when I'm done with the second one. "See, Cade? That's what you get for skipping leg day!"

I groan as he guffaws, and some of the other guys join in. "Seriously?"

The only way my legs can look like as chicken's is by wearing these white socks that have a cartoon chicken's legs drawn at the front and at the back. I make a mental note of finding an even worse pair for him.

"Wait, wait, wait. Let me take a picture." He produces his

phone and I let him. "Guaranteed these pics will make chicks lose their minds far more than your *SPORTY* article."

"What?"

"Chicks?" He grins. "That's where I got the idea from."

"No, the *SPORTY* thing. You know about it?"

"The whole team knows. Audrey Winters from PR came looking for you a few minutes ago. She's waiting for you in Beau's office."

This annoys me even more than I already was at the constant distractions.

"Great," I mumble, getting up.

O'Brian stops me with a hand on my chest. "Dude, are you going in with those socks?"

"Yeah, I'm gonna wear them until they have holes on their toes," I grouch, never backing from a prank war with Lucky. If I remove these socks right now, I won't have a right to retaliate.

"There goes your heartthrob reputation."

Lucky hooks an arm around my neck and whispers into my ears, "The socks are also a reminder to not chicken out about other things."

"What things?" I frown at him.

"Going after the girl you like."

Every blink progressively sours my expression even more, especially when his shit eating grin widens more and more. He pats my chest and lets me go. No one else seems to have heard that, and if I don't dignify it with an answer, I can pretend like I also never heard his words.

Of course, the moment I walk into Beau's office and Audrey Winters looks up at me, the greeting sticks in her throat upon the sight of my brand new socks.

"They're funnier without the sneakers," I say in a deadpan.

She snaps her jaw shut and recovers. "Let me guess, Lucky Rivera."

"Bingo." I sigh and pull up the chair across the meeting

table from hers. "Good morning, sugar. I heard you wanted to see me about this *SPORTY* gig."

"I—Yes. May I suggest you don't wear the chicken socks for the photoshoot?"

"I will consider it out of the goodness of my heart." I lace my fingers together and place my hands on the table. "Can I ask you something else before we start on the topic of the photoshoot?"

"Sure." She tilts her head, shiny blonde hair falling over her shoulder.

"How's Hope doing?"

"Oh, it's been touch and go—Did you just call her Hope?"

I lean forward sharply. "Touch and go?"

"Well, she had to go to urgent care last night because—"

I jerk to my chicken feet so fast that my chair topples over. We both stare at each other in equal shock at my reaction. Clearing my throat, I pick up the chair and mumble apologies. When I meet her eyes again, there's a weird little glint to them.

Winters leans back. "I heard you're on light duty today, which is why I was hoping to hash out the specifics about the photoshoot with you but..." She shrugs most elegantly, if I may say. "I wouldn't mind if you had to step away from the facilities for a personal emergency."

My eyes narrow slightly. "Am I understanding this right? You're giving me an excuse to—"

"I know her dad's address, if you want to go see her."

I stand there, my heart racing under my sweatshirt, doing my best not to show outwardly how eager I am for this information. So I can go see her. And make sure she's okay. Return the favor, even. Although I don't know how to cook. But I could wipe her forehead with some wet cloth like they do in the movies, or something.

"And would that be okay?" I ask carefully. "Giving me her address."

"I think so," she says, bobbing her head with every word. "I have yet to meet a guy who is as kind and well mannered as you. But just so we're clear, I'll gut you with this pen if you hurt her." She lifts up a fancy pen, holding it like it's a knife.

"I respect that," I say, meaning it.

"Good. Now, write it down."

CHAPTER 29
HOPE

A block from my childhood home, there's a park where I used to come with my older brother to play ball together. In classic Florida fashion, it has a natural retention pond in the middle with occasional alligator sightings. Us Florida people don't really care, though, and we'll even put benches around the ponds like our main sport is waiting for a gator to show up to test our zigzag running skills.

Currently, I'm parked at one such benches, sitting cross legged and taking most of the span of it while I munch on some trail mix. Tomorrow will be my first day back at work and it'll kick off with a flight, so I need to store as much energy as I can.

The problem is that it feels like that's all I've done the past week, and I'm tired of looking at the same four walls all the time. So here I am, contemplating the immortality of a crab, as a weird saying in Spanish goes.

It's going very well, if I can say so myself. The afternoon sun is warm but there's a breeze, and a few birds nearby chirp in the cutest damn way. I almost feel like I'm in a Jane Austen movie.

Until someone abruptly shoves my leg and sits right next to me.

"What the—" The rest of the words die in my mouth—rather, it opens wide enough for a fly to come in. I freeze at the opposite end of the bench, shrank with my knees up and arms hugging my baggy of trail mix as if this was what the invader was here for.

Instead, none other than Cade stretches an arm over the backrest of the bench, manspreading obnoxiously as he watches me.

"What the hell are you doing here?" I shriek, starting to recover from the initial shock.

Propping his opposite elbow on the armrest, he rests the side of his face on his fist—still looking at me. "I should ask you that. Why aren't you at home if you've felt bad enough to go to urgent care? Moreover, why did I not know?"

I splutter for a moment, confusion reigning over my mind. "I—I was bored at—What urgent care?"

"Your roommate told me."

I don't even ask who, it doesn't matter. Shaking my head, I explain, "I did have to go to urgent care but it's because my dad hurt his ankle playing pickleball yesterday."

Cade's eyebrows take off like airplanes. "Oh. Is he okay?"

"Yeah, it just took forever to get checked and then fitted with a cast, and then the prescription for the pain."

"I'm glad he's okay." Clearing his throat, he shifts to sit up straight, his knees now at a normal distance that allows me to unfurl myself from my tiny corner. His turquoise eyes scan me from the baseball cap on my head, my loose hair, my gigantic sweatshirt with the Orlando Wild logo, down to my leggings clad legs, and my comfy sneakers I've had forever.

I look shabby, I know that. If I had a heads up that he was coming by, I'd have ran home and made some effort. Maybe ditched the sweatshirt.

"And I'm glad you look okay," he adds in a quiet voice. That's when I realize he wasn't checking me out, but making sure I'm no longer sick.

"Gee, thanks for the compliment," I say in a teasing manner just to hide my embarrassment at myself. "And you look…"

My attempt at deflecting works like a freaking charm, because he looks like a whole mess. I blow a raspberry and barely manage to stop the ensuing laugh by pressing a hand to my mouth.

He's wearing his cap backward, and has the dude version of my outfit except for the silliest socks I've ever laid my eyes on. They look like chicken legs.

A corner of his lips twitch. "Wait till you see the magic trick." Then he toes his sneakers off and I really bark a laugh. They really are chicken legs complete with chicken feet.

"Let me guess… Rivera."

"Who else." He leans back, turning his face up to the sun. "Wow, this is nice."

Sure is. I don't mind that the bench is a bit too small for the two of us, like at all. My thigh brushes against his and his arm is behind me. I have front row view of his neck stretching in the most inviting way, but all I can do is run my tongue across my lips and look away. To my trail mix. I put some more in my mouth just to keep it busy.

"Cade?" I ask while chewing.

"Hmm?"

"You haven't told me what you're doing here."

His arm brushes with my hair as he lifts it to hold the back of his head with both hands. "I was in a meeting with Winters when she mentioned the urgent care thing and I panicked a little. In my defense, I didn't hear back from you for a whole day."

He was worried.

Warmth spreads all over my chest.

"But anyway, this was in Beau's office and while she was giving me your dad's address, Beau walked in and ruined my plans of ditching."

"Ditching?" I gasp and smack his rock solid thigh with the back of my hand. "That can get you suspended, you clown." I pause before asking, "Were you that worried?"

He turns his head slightly towards me, eyes shifting to mine and it feels like they're pinning me against a wall. His lips part. I lean forward slightly, eager to hear the answer…

When someone else's voice speaks instead. "Is that Cade Starr?"

We both turn. A little old lady walking a chihuahua stands just a few feet from us, waiting for her tiny dog to finish its business, but her attention trained very much on my companion. Er, friend. I guess. Coworker? Bench partner.

"Yes, hi, ma'am." His southern manners kick in right away and he sits up straight, tipping his head at her.

"Oh, my goodness." She looks around herself. "I don't have any paper to get your autograph. Now my grandkids won't believe I met you."

"How about a selfie?" he suggests and it lights up her whole face so bright, she competes with the sun.

I'm not strong enough to not melt as he gets up from the bench in a hurry, eating up the distance in two easy strides. The elderly woman barely reaches his shoulders in height, and as she gives him her phone for the selfie, he crouches in his chicken socks to take the picture as close to her as possible.

Cade Starr isn't just a nice guy. He's one of the sweetest people I've ever met in my life, period. When I was alone, humiliated, and about to be scammed out of the most expensive dinner of my life, he swooped in without hesitation and without expecting anything in return. When, at my peak unhinged, I asked him to be my dating coach because I needed help, he agreed without much hassle. Now he makes small talk with a random stranger, even bending down to pet her dog because he can't seem to fathom the concept of ignoring even canine fans—and it is a fan, all right, going by how it flips its belly up to Cade's scratches.

A freaking dorable.

I swoon. I legit sigh so strong that I feel like I'm melting down and have to use both hands to keep my head upright. One day, Cade is going to make a woman very, very happy.

Why can't that be me?

The old lady gives him a hug that forces him to arch his body, and I hear her bless him like he's her grandson instead. After waving goodbye, she keeps walking her doggo and the baseball player heads back to my bench to sit again.

"So, where were we?" he asks.

I swallow thick. There's no way I'm going to remind him of the question I asked. He must have been that worried to make the trip here, yes. But that doesn't necessarily mean he has feelings for me or anything. He's just the kind of guy to drop everything for the people he cares about—or even his fans.

And I want… I want to be even more important. I want to be the person he worries about the most.

But I have no right. How incredibly awkward, even underhanded, would it be if I go from "hey, wanna be my dating coach?" to "hey, I'm firing you as dating coach because I want to date you instead." I never intended this to happen but that's how it would look.

Then, there's the bigger issue. The one where Cade has literally one best friend in his entire life who buys him chicken socks, and no one else. It would be cruel of me to demand more than he's willing or able to give, and then turn the whole work dynamic sour if things go wrong.

That's when it hits me that it was the exact same reasoning

Dawson gave to force me to not feel my feels. And now I'm doing the same thing to myself.

The trail mix churns unpleasantly in my stomach.

"Hope? Are you okay? You're making a weird face."

I'm lightheaded as I raise a hand to stop him. "Hold on, I'm processing something right now."

"Can I have some of your trail mix while you do that?"

"Have at it." I offer the bag and hold very still as he takes it, his hand brushing against mine.

There's no way in hell I'm going to let my douche of an ex win. That's the reason I even approached Cade in the first place. Yet I also know that the second I decide that yes, I do, in fact, have a huge crush on Cade Starr, I'm going to screw it all up. Between work being tricky and me morphing into an upturned turtle with no social skills in front of men I'm remotely interested in, it's a recipe for disaster. And I really don't want to mess things up with Cade.

So how do I navigate this?

"Oh. My. Gosh!"

Once more, we turn to the unknown voice.

This time it's a girl about my age with the tiniest waist I've ever seen, in a sports bra and shorts most commonly found in summer than this time of year. In fact, looking at her makes me chillier.

She places a delicate hand on her chest. "Cade Starr? *The* Cade Starr?"

"Uh, hi," he says, sounding dazed. And I don't blame him, she's very pretty. Button nose and thick lips type of pretty.

"I'm such a huge fan." Her smile could power an entire country's electrical grid. It only falters slightly as she spots his socks.

I bite my lips not to laugh. Also because she doesn't seem to notice me and if she's part of the fan demographic that is *deeply* interested in him, it might be best to not call attention to me.

"Thank you." Cade lifts his cap to run a hand through his hair. "Would you like a selfie?"

My face twitches, this close to grimacing. Why does this smack so different to the old lady?

"Yes, I would love one!" She immediately whips out her phone from her arm holder and hands it over to him as he approaches. He does the exact same thing, crouching lower so he can appear in the frame, and she glues her side to his, boob squishing against him and all.

Yep, that's why it smacks different.

Once the picture is taken, he straightens out again to return the phone, but she imprisons his hand in both of hers. "Just so you know, I'm a woman who keeps it real so if you're interested maybe I can give you a call later?"

Cade gives an awkward laugh. "Thanks, I just really have to focus on the season or my agent will kill me."

This is when she cuts a blatant look at me.

Fortunately, I have an alibi. I point at the logo of my sweat-shirt. "I'm just his trainer."

She lifts her nose a little and faces him again. "Or I could give you my phone for whenever you're bored?"

Well, she's definitely keeping it real, all right. As much as her interest makes my gut twist, I admire her cojones. I wish I could take pointers from her on how to be confident in front of men, but I suspect a lot of it comes from her genes granting her conventional attractiveness.

"Uh, sure." He palms his pocket and I watch, frozen, as he keys in the digits she dictates along with her name. Kiera spelled with i-e.

I use every ounce of self restraint in my arsenal to sit very still, show absolutely no reaction, as she jogs off in a way that makes her hips swing masterfully, and as Cade returns to rejoin me at my park bench.

But then the little shit pulls up his phone, goes to his

contact list, and deletes Kiera of the Great Genes off his contact list. Then he pockets his phone again and picks up the trail mix baggy once more.

The anger swirling in my gut ebbs away and my logical brain kicks in. He probably didn't want to cause some drama rejecting a fan romantically, especially now that everybody's a social media keyboard warrior. But also, it's not like he has a girlfriend to claim a stake on him either, and he's not a liar.

"You could've lied and said you're taken," I blurt out because maybe I'm not as good a person as he is.

"I could have." He tilts his head back to pour some nuts into his open mouth.

"Why didn't you?" I frown.

"Because I'm not actually taken yet. Can I finish this?"

"Go for it, you goof." I marinate his words, especially the *yet*. Like he does want to er, eventually become taken.

Could I? Could I be the one to snatch him off the market?

Sliding his feet back into his sneakers, he stands up again and says, "'Kay, I've seen that you're alive and well, so I'm gonna go before Kiera comes back around to ask why I haven't called her yet."

I roll my eyes in an exaggerated way. "Go, you stud."

"Thanks for the compliment." He smirks and reaches over to flick the bill of my cab.

"Hey!" My protests go ignored and he walks away with my trail mix, leaving me with a crush that threatens to burst at the seams.

CHAPTER 30
CADE

'␣ve been trying my best during most of this damn flight to keep my eyes on the cards, and not on Hope.

However, it's not my fault that I keep losing or that she stands just farther up the aisle, chatting up with Larry Socci without realizing just how freaking hot she is and how much attention she's getting from my teammates. They respect her enough that they'll never do or say anything untoward—or rather, they know she'd chop off their limbs—but clearly they still have eyes.

Yeah, I know I'm being a hypocrite. I too am transfixed by the slope of her lower back turning into a spectacularly round butt that would fit perfectly in my hands. And on my lap.

But—and this is the big difference—I'm at least trying not to stare. Miller two rows above me is fully jaw slacked, his face red because of who knows what he's thinking. Actually, I do know—I'm thinking it too—and it makes me want to commit teammatecide.

"Dude, it's your turn."

I make a gargantuan effort to turn away from Miller's slobbering face. Lucky motions at the Uno card on top of the pile and I check my deck looking for ones or yellows.

My traitorous eyes peek from above the fan of cards in my hands, right in time for Hope to run her fingers down her long hair. Most of it falls behind her but a strand escapes to caress her cheek, and I can't believe I wish I could be her hair right now.

Lucky clears his throat.

I throw my last yellow card at the pile. Logan Kim tosses a red one with the same number and mutters, "You're being too obvious, you knucklehead."

"Huh?"

"He means that if you keep staring at her the whole team will realize you have a giant torch for our only female trainer."

Kim nods at Lucky. "That."

I clear my throat. "Be quiet, you two."

"Then be less obvious," advises Kim.

I grumble an incoherent string of sounds and lower my face. Focusing on the game is still much harder than it should be, like I had a dormant Hope Garcia radar that can now pick up her presence no matter where she is. It figuratively beeps as she walks down my aisle, leaving a trail of vanilla that warms up my body from the inside.

"So…" I stretch out the word until it's almost uncomfortable.

Kim ignores me, though. "Uno." He puts a card on the pile and has one left in his hand.

"Kim." He finally lifts his eyes to me. "You never told me how your date with you know who went."

Dude cocks an eyebrow. "You know exactly how it went."

"Sure, from her side." I lift a shoulder. "But I'm also interested in knowing your side of it."

"If you're worried I may want to snatch your girl, don't. I'm not into her."

I don't deny for a second that that's my concern. Hell, I don't deny anything anymore. Lucky read me like an open book the night of Hope and Kim's date, and the latter is too sharp for me to even pretend.

"Why not?" I ask, more confused than annoyed. I didn't understand almost two months ago how guys can possibly *not* be attracted to her, and I still don't get it today.

"Because I'm not in the business of taking what's not mine."

"Then why did you agree to date her in the first place?"

Lucky nudges me again. I take one look at the card on top and already know I've lost.

Sighing, I say, "Pass."

"I win." Kim dumps his last card on the airplane table and stretches back, hands behind his head as he looks down his nose at me. "And the answer to that is simple. I was bored and I wanted to see your reaction."

"Wow, we'll never get along, will we?"

He offers a feral grin. "Probably not."

Lucky clicks his tongue. "You're such a catcher."

"What's that supposed to mean?"

"You're all sneaky like that. Makes me glad I'm not a pitcher."

"Lucky you," I deadpan at the Boricua. I push myself up to stand and stretch my back. "Anyway, I'm gonna go get a snack. Want something, you jerks?"

Kim tilts his head and gives me a look like he thinks the snack I'm talking about is Hope. And first, she's not a snack—she's the whole damn meal. Second, the snack is just an excuse to see her.

"Offer rescinded to you," I say to him, glaring.

Meanwhile, Lucky smacks his lips. "I'm a little thirsty, not gonna lie. Thirsty for some ac—"

"You also can go get your snacks yourself."

After stepping out of my seat, I walk a step in the opposite direction and smack the back of Miller's head.

"Hey! What the hell was that for, Cowboy?"

"You know exactly why, you stinking perv."

He blinks for a moment until it finally clicks. His expression turns sheepish. "Sorry."

I'd tell him to apologize to her, but learning that she has colleagues who leer at her would probably make her uncomfortable and I don't want that. Instead, I say, "Just don't do it again." Huffing, I swivel around and trudge down the aisle to the service area.

I push the curtain aside with my forearm and stop. Hope is right in front of me, leaning back on the service counter as she glares at her phone screen so fiercely that it's a wonder it doesn't crack.

"Everything okay, darlin'?"

"No," she responds right away, before even meeting my eye. "Look at this bullshit." She flips her phone so I can see the screen.

At first I'm not sure what I'm seeing, but at second I start making out words from what looks like a digital invitation. I step into the enclosed area, letting the curtain close behind me, and take the phone from her hand. And yeah, I enjoy the feel of her hand under mine, however brief the touch lasts.

I read aloud in my most bored drawl. "You are cordially invited to the engagement party of Amy McFadden and Dawson Clark, to be celebrated at blah blah on…" I look closer. "Oh, this is in less than a month. Didn't you say they started dating just last November?"

"Turned out it was since way longer," she spits out with annoyance.

The plane tilts a little and I have to spread my feet wider to not pitch. Just in case, I place a hand on the cabinet above her.

"You said you don't have feelings for him anymore, so why are you gnashing your teeth?" I ask, returning her phone.

"Because…" As she pockets it, she draws in a sharp breath. "At the rate I'm going, there's no way I'll find a boyfriend for Friendsgiving, forget within a month."

I close my mouth. Open it again. Close once more.

Boyfriend.

She wants a boyfriend.

The thing I've never really been.

I've dated. I've fooled around. And the only time I thought using the boyfriend label was fine, it lead to one of the most prominent episodes in my collection of childhood trauma. I don't need to get a psychology degree to know that it's the main reason why I never wanted to try again.

Except I really don't think someone like Hope, after everything she's gone through, would be satisfied with just being a date. She wants to be a girlfriend. Probably a wife after that. How the hell can I turn myself into boyfriend or husband material when I'm simply not?

"What if…" I trail off, trying to wet my suddenly dry mouth. "What if you keep me as your backup plan? You know, in case you don't find the boyfriend you're looking for in time."

"Oh." She blinks fast. This close I notice she has long eyelashes. "Um, would that be an option?"

"Sure." I shrug, acting much cooler than I feel, considering I'm so hot under the collar. "My pride as your dating coach is on the line. I won't have you show up empty—"

The word *handed* vanishes in thin air, replaced by the yelp that comes from her. The plane tilts forward, sharp enough that Hope loses the battle. She goes from leaning against the counter to crashing against my chest. My arms close around her and I've never been happier that I don't have actual chicken legs, because I'm able to keep our balance and not send us crashing through the curtain and to the middle of the aisle. Overhead, the beep that indicates we should be at our seats with our seatbelts fastened comes on.

But we stay put. Hope, probably because she's trapped in my arms. Me, because there's nowhere else I'd rather be.

"You okay?" I whisper, looking down at the top of her head.

But that's also when she tilts her head back. And our noses brush.

Her eyes widen and I can feel mine doing the same. Wiggling, she wedges her hands between us and pushes me away. "Yeah, thanks. You?" And steps back against the counter again, putting as much distance as the space physically allows her.

Um.

Excuse me but…

Ouch.

I run a hand through my hair. "Yeah, I'm good. We should probably take our seats, though."

"Right."

"Oh, wait. I was supposed to come in for a snack."

"Right," she repeats, turning her back to rummage in the cabinets. These charter planes aren't like a regular commercial one, so they're stocked with all sorts of nutritious and flavorless snacks fit for professional athletes. She hands me over an insipid peanut butter bar that tastes just as meh on the ground as it does on the air. "Here you go. Drinks are in the bottom cabinets."

"Thanks." I watch her disappear behind the curtains without meeting my eyes. Lifting an arm, I sniff my clean armpit. "Okay, I guess I don't stink. Then what's her deal?"

Did an accidental hug not fueled by pity make her so deeply uncomfortable?

Because if so, this whole girlfriending her thing might be a lot harder than I even imagined.

CHAPTER 31
HOPE

'm being tested. There's no other way to explain this.

First, I have to spend a couple of days exercising every muscle—literal and figurative—in order to act normal around the cowboy, especially because Beau still has him on light duty. Unfortunately, this means Cade's mostly working off the field. In the training gym. Where I also work most of the time. But fine, somehow I survived. It just involved me busying myself with other players and in the back office.

Today, though? A whole mess. We're gonna have to write it off.

Today is *the* photoshoot. Featuring Cade "Cowboy" Starr. In front of a lens. For *SPORTY* magazine.

Granted, *SPORTY* is a family friendly publication. This one won't pose him naked and with only a baseball glove covering his privates. However, now that my mind went there, I can't unsee it.

I shake my head hard and literally touch some grass. I'm sitting cross legged on the turf beside Audrey as the show goes on. She's in charge of the whole operation from the team's perspective, so she and some crew members helped the photographer set up on the field. Cade was split off from the team to come fulfill his contractual obligation and, instead of staying put for the post game training, Lucky Rivera rallied the troops to come watch. Staff, including me, tried to get them to return to training but to no avail. Thus, instead of keeping myself busy at the gym, I ended up here in prime position to ogle.

And ogle I do. Like I'm sorry. I'm a red blooded woman. He's freaking gorgeous, okay?

I dig my fingers in the grass blades and grab a handful. The makeup artist, a peppy girl with blue hair, has predictably been oiling him up for the part of the photoshoot where he'll be less, um, clothed. I'll give her props because she's wearing surgical gloves but I mean… she's still rubbing him up. Like, full on getting in the nooks and crannies. And her face is blood red because whose wouldn't?

Meanwhile, Cade has his face turned up to the sun, expression serene as though this doesn't affect him. But I have every indication to infer he *is* a red blooded man and this must be affecting him. If not the oiling up, then the hecklers in the stands.

"Yeah, babe! Get in there, don't miss the armpits."

"Wait, did he shave them for this?"

Laughter.

Cade's face twitches but he doesn't respond.

"What about his face?" Rivera wonders amid chuckles. "Is oiling it up going to make him look gross?"

"Nah, I think it's probably part of the sexy sweaty look that chicks will want."

"Hey, Starr! Don't forget to do the lip bite."

"Your left side's the best, bro. Get the pics from that side."

"Back side would be better."

Guffaws.

Beside me, Audrey snorts. "You know, none of them are wrong."

Except for the left side stuff. Cade's face is pretty damn symmetrical. In fact, he's a study in beauty with the straight nose, full lips that stretch into a wide smile, and the square jaw that could cut steel. He doesn't have to do anything special other than stand at the mound for *chicks* to go wild. Ask me how I know.

"We're set," the makeup artist squeaks out and I don't blame her. If I had to do her job, I'd faint the second my hand makes first contact. Glove or not.

"All right, I'd like to get some shots in the dugout," the photographer says. "Can you pretend like it's the middle of the game and you're drinking some water?"

"Make sure to spill some on your chest," Rivera calls out.

Cade cracks a little and sends a glare to the stands of near forty grown men screaming embarrassing things that go from middle school level to definitely-for-adults. But finally he disappears into the dugout along with the photographer, with Rose at their heels because she's been capturing video for the social media accounts, and I can relax for a bit.

"You doing okay?" Audrey watches me from the corner of her green eyes.

"Me?" I squeak like the makeup artist earlier. "Why do you ask?"

"You seem to be struggling."

I blow a raspberry. "Not at all."

Oh yes, super struggling. Mega struggling. I literally don't know how I'm going to be keep a straight face the next time I have to massage him or ice him. I'll be worse than the makeup girl.

Rose emerges from the dugout but still appears to be filming, she points both her phone and a camera toward the stands, and the guys from the team cheer for the video. She continues jogging the perimeter behind the home plate to join us.

Huffing as she sits down, she says, "I need a break in the shade. Whatcha up to, you guys?"

"I think we need a roommate meeting," Audrey declares with no warning. As Rosalina and I stare pointedly at her, blondie raises her hands. "It's nothing bad, just girl talk."

"Oh." Then I know exactly what the subject is. "I truly don't think we need any girl talk."

But then Cade steps out of the dugout, now wearing his team shirt but unbuttoned and his cap backward. He lifts his face and I stiffen, because he's looking directly at me.

Or not? He could be observing either of my roommates.

Except I can feel both of them turn to me, right in time to catch the heat crawling up my neck. He seems to watch me for a moment longer while he walks over to the mound, the photographer and his assistant trailing behind.

As they take action shots of Cade pretending to pitch with his shirt open—as if real games allowed that—Rose chuckles. "Yeah, it seems like we do need girl talk."

*

"What am I doing here?" I grouch from the middle of the couch, nursing a glass of wine and wrapped in my yellow fluffy blanket that makes me look like a certain cast member of Sesame Street.

"You, my friend, have feelings for a certain pitcher." Rose clinks her glass with mine and after a quick sip that makes her shiver slightly, she continues, "And I've been down that road before, so I think Audrey had the right idea in calling for this meeting."

"Wait, what?" I do a double take, my brain short circuiting. "You have feelings for Cade? Had?"

"Cade?" Rose's dimples show thanks to her little grin. "Since when do you call him Cade?"

From my other side, Audrey points out, "Notice how she didn't even deny it."

"Rosalina Mena," I say in a serious tone. "You need to tell me right now if you're interested in him, because if you are then I'm not going to stand in your way."

"Ugh, you adorable dork." She throws her arm around me and pulls me toward her. I release a little *ack* not just because she's kinda choking me, but I also have to make a huge effort to not let my wine glass overturn. "And no," she responds, pulling away. "I'm not after the cowboy. What I mean is that I've been to that rodeo of dating a pitcher, and I don't want you to make my mistakes."

"If not Cade, who?"

"Ben Williams." Audrey sips from her wine as we both watch her. "What? I saw him leave your room in the middle of the night once."

While Rose's jaw drops, I shriek, "What? How did I not notice that?"

"You sleep like the dead."

"Yeah, it's kinda scary."

"Okay, never mind that." I wave a hand. "But Ben Williams? Really? And are you still together?"

"Hell no." She leans back into the couch, sighing hard. "I dumped his ass."

"Go girl." Audrey snaps her fingers. "He did not deserve you."

"I know." Rose tosses a glorious curl behind her shoulder. "He's a cheating asshole and I feel like I can breathe again after he got traded. Good riddance."

My face morphs into a mask of disgust. "I always thought he was a self entitled prick, but cheating? On you? Girl, I'm glad I didn't know because I'd have maimed him."

"That's why I didn't say anything. Didn't want you to wind up in jail." She pats my knee.

"So let me guess"—I interrupt myself to sigh—"this is an intervention so I don't fool around with Cade."

"Yes and no," Rose says.

I turn to Audrey for answers. She drinks more wine.

"The cowboy is different from The Unmentionable," Rose starts, twisting slightly to prop her arm on the back of the couch. "For example, I doubt he'd keep you a secret just so that his other side pieces don't find out you're one of many."

My jaw drops.

"I will murder him."

"That's not the point. The point is that dating within the team… well, if it doesn't work out, it can be pretty bad for you. The irony is that what saved my behind is that no one knows we dated."

"I know," I mumble, closing my lips around the rim of the glass.

"But on the other hand, you've been searching and searching," Audrey says from her armchair. "And if the one you found is Cade then you shouldn't let life pass you by."

"Didn't know you were such a romantic," Rose jokes.

But our roomie shrugs. "I personally am not, but I call it like I see it."

"That's all well and good but this is me we're talking about." I place all five digits of one hand on my chest. "Super awkward, can't flirt for shit tomboy with no sex appeal."

"Pfff."

"Who the hell said that?"

"Every guy I've attempted to date ever?"

"Screw them." Rose sticks her tongue out in a universal expression of yuck. "That's all bullshit they said to compensate for falling extremely short in front of you."

"Let's say that's the case, but Cade's just my coach. In fact, we basically just became friends. It'd be weird if I suddenly go like, hey—"

"Let me stop you right there." Audrey cuts in, raising her hand. "You should've seen that man pale when he thought you went to urgent care. His lips straight up turned blue, that's how worried he was."

"Yeah, I've seen him staring at you too." Rose casually drinks from her wine like she also didn't just drop a bomb on me.

"*What?*"

"Uh huh, dude's as whipped as you."

In turn, I whip my head side to side, waiting for the moment they drop the punchline and say this was all a joke.

But Audrey leans forward, forearms on her knees like this is serious company PR business. "Ultimately the decision's up to you, but Rose and I got tired of watching you two do the bird dance with blindfolds on your eyes. Dating a coworker can be very tricky but what does that matter if this is the real thing?"

My mouth opens and closes. Tingles run all over my body, leaving flashes of heat and cold in their wake. I snuggle deeper into the blanket but the issue isn't the air conditioner. It's that I'm freaking the frack out. Straight up doing everything I can to not self combust right now.

With a thread of voice, I say, "But I don't know how to do this—get a guy."

"We can help you if you really want." Rose winks. "Need to turn your dating coach into your date? Easy."

"And if you don't want to, we can help you avoid him for the rest of your life." Audrey's smile is soft. "I have a PhD on that."

My face is absolutely flaming as I process the fact that I haven't been anywhere near as discreet as I thought. If they've noticed, who else has? Does Cade know that I have the hots for him? Heavens, I hope not. Not to be dramatic but I would simply perish.

"Thanks, guys. Can we talk about something that will make us pass the Bechdel test?"

Audrey cringes. "We work with only men and basically have no social life away from work, so probably not."

"The only way I know is to rewatch Legally Blonde. Who's in?" Rose asks, and it gets her a full show of hands.

CHAPTER 32
CADE

My childhood dream was to become the best pitcher in the entire world, earn millions of dollars, build a house big enough for twelve people, and be so successful that no one else could say "there goes the orphan no one wanted" anymore.

I have since revised the dream to be more realistic. Yes, I do make millions of dollars per year and have invested enough that I'll be able to live comfortably for the rest of my life in my very nice house. Also, barely anyone ever talks about my origins anymore, to the point where Hope—a coworker who has clearly never stalked me on the internet—had no idea. So in that sense, that childhood dream is fulfilled too.

But I'm middle of the pack when it comes to salary among pitchers though, because so far that's also what my performance has been. Until now. And I hate to admit it, but a lot of it has to do with Logan Kim.

I have only the deepest admiration for his ability to manipulate me—I mean, not letting me quit even when I think there's no more gas in me. I have no doubt that making a battery with him was the reason Ben Williams even reached the heights he has, because in his previous position of starter pitcher he got the lion's share of Kim's attention.

Right now we're in the middle of a game with the worst conditions for me. It's chilly and rainy, my uniform is soaked through and heavy, and my grip on the ball is shot. Yet Logan Kim won't let off me and keeps making one wild call after another.

The fact that it's working pisses me off the most.

When the inning ends with no runs, I do my very best to not sigh in relief because the ball didn't fly off my fingers wrong and kill anyone.

Because guess what? I'm competitive as hell and if he wants to goad me, I'm not gonna back down like a wuss. So I keep throwing my hardest to scare off all the batters.

"Decent job," he has the nerve to say as we job to the dugout.

"Screw you."

All that does is make him smirk. I'm starting to learn his patterns because there are different levels to his manipulations. Level zero is the one he applies to Hope and anyone not in the team: it's the one where he's legitimately a decent freaking person.

Level one so far is reserved for the prospects, and it consists of a few innocent sounding quips to drive their performance up. That "decent job" comment actually falls in this category, it's meant to piss me off and induce me into an "I'll show you decent" mentality. I don't know what it says about me because it works every time.

Level two is the much more subtle but nuclear shit like when *he* drove me into a corner by using Miguel Machado— a.k.a. a common adversary—to push me harder than ever before. The promise of pizza was just his way of letting me know what he had just done, and honestly if it wasn't because of that I wouldn't have even noticed that the whole scenario happened because of him.

So he's a master manipulator with integrity and I respect that, but I kinda wanna punch him in the face too. It's complicated, especially when I can already feel myself growing into the pitcher of my childhood dreams because of his calls.

The dugout offers a much needed respite from the rain. The swooshing sound behind me tells me it's bad enough that the umpires might consider pausing the game, and I'd truly love them for it. As it is, all I can do is change my clothes for the third time in the course of four innings. I pinch the fabric of my shirt off my body and it legit makes a gross squelching sound.

I look up to locate Beau or any of the other coaches, but instead my eyes fall right on Hope's. Her lips are peeled back in a cringe as she watches me, like she understands just how uncomfortable I am right now. I wrinkle my nose in return so she knows that yes, I am, in fact, *yuck*.

Socci appears in the corner of my eye so I tell him, "Be right back, going to change and to the restroom."

"All right, hurry up," he says while chewing gum like he wishes it was tobacco instead.

For a brief second I ponder suggesting to Kim that he should do the same, but he's getting the gear removed and someone holds a helmet out for him, which reminds me his at bat is next.

Shrugging, I head into the tunnel and instead of stopping at my locker to change, I go to the bathroom first because I'm a man of priorities.

Once I'm done and I'm washing my hands, I chance a peek in the mirror and confirm that I look like a wet rat, uniform clinging to every nook and cranny. Between this and what will be seen in the *SPORTY* magazine pictures, there's no need for anyone to imagine anything. I've basically shown it all.

I wonder what Hope thinks about that. Like, she did cringe earlier so maybe that's not a great sign. Or maybe she doesn't think about it at all.

"Hmm." But I want her to think about it. I'm starting to hope the rain doesn't stop—pun intended.

There's no point in drying my hands after I left a whole trail on the floor, so I walk out of the men's bathroom, thinking of ways I can tease the interest of a certain Latina, when I ram into someone.

Or rather, someone rams into me.

Someones.

"Cade! We love you!"

"Can you give us your autograph?"

My body freezes but my brain rapidly questions what in the actual hell are three fans doing *here?*

"Cade!" One of them clings to my throwing arm. Just before she closes her claw around it, I jerk it free and lift it over my head.

"Um, excuse me ma'am, you're too close to—"

Another one runs her hand down my stomach, trying to go lower. I step back and crash against the door. I'm torn between dashing inside for cover, but they seem invested enough that they'd follow me in and I know the door doesn't have a lock.

"Excuse me." I try to side step them but that's when the third woman tries to lasso me. She blocks the little space I could've weaseled out of, and this one reeks less of alcohol than her buddies.

She leans into my right arm, closing hers around it like a vise. "Hey, Cowboy. We've been waiting for a chance to talk."

I have a sort of out of body experience right there, of watching myself being harassed by some fans in a hallway in the restricted staff-only area, and taking a closer look at them. And this third woman is the one who strikes a cord.

Right now she's in an Orlando Wild jersey and jean shorts,

but I've seen her before in bright leggings and tops, running right behind me in my neighborhood.

I shut my jaw tight to not call her out. It could set her off—I don't know. I've never really dealt with stalkers and all I know is from what happens to celebrities.

Fortunately I have superb panoramic vision. Unfortunately I find that we're alone. I also can't defend myself the way I would if these were men.

And it's like they know it because they keep trying to grab what is not theirs to grab.

I make my voice firmer. "Ma'am, I'm in the middle of a game. Can you please step aside and let me go?"

"But—"

Steps approach and I look up for Kim's entrance. "Starr, did you get sucked in by the—What the—" He freezes for a quick second, eyes widening almost impossibly. Mine do too, trying to impart a message saying that we absolutely cannot lay our hands on fans but I really need help. He jerks a nod, sucks in air, and shouts over his shoulder, "Security! Can someone call security? Starr is being harassed by trespassers!"

The drunkest women giggle like this is all a joke. But the third one, the actual stalker, appears to be torn between fleeing or freezing. Except, as more people tumble out of the club-house, she freezes.

"Cade is what?" Lucky yells, charging like a bull until he sees what's happening and gets to the exact same conclusion as Kim and I.

Fans. Women. Can't. Touch. Shit.

"Calling security now," someone says.

"Excuse me." The familiar voice parts the sea of men from the team, and in comes one Hope Garcia and—what the hell is she doing? Why is she taking off her staff shirt?

She balls it up and slams it into Lucky's chest, who somehow manages to catch the fabric before it falls. We all watch her in complete silence because none of us have ever seen Hope Garcia in her sports bra. I wish I was literally in any other circumstance than this because…

Hot. Damn. She is *perfect*.

The muscles of her sculpted arms work as she pushes Kim away, her eyes trained on the women. And then, in the calmest voice, Hope says, "I'm security."

And in three more steps she grabs one of the fans by the elbow and yanks her with enough force that the woman stumbles back. The second woman tries harder to cling onto me and this time I cooperate, grabbing her wrists to pry her arms off my waist. Hope pulls the woman away by the jersey.

The stalker steps aside all on her own, hands up like she's being arrested. But Hope doesn't let her off, she jerks a thumb behind her, pointing at the stalker's buddies. "The three of you, against that wall. Now."

They stumble on their feet in their drunkenness and sag against the wall.

Hope's eyes are a blaze of fury as she sets them on me, and I stiffen under her scrutiny. It's when she starts turning away that I realize she's not angry at me, she was looking for signs of injury.

And that… is what nearly undoes me. I have to prop my shoulder against the doorframe so I don't swoon like a teenager with a crush.

"Socci and Berger, stay with me to keep an eye on these women while the rest of security arrives," Hope barks orders like a badass boss. "And Starr."

"Yes, ma'am?"

She jerks her head toward the others. "Go."

"Ah, right." I walk around her, keeping an eye on the strange women. The stalker avoids me now, which is great. I can't wait to never see her face ever again.

The guys suck me in among them, arms surrounding me

like a shield. I glance over my shoulder, where Hope has her arms folded as she glares at the strangers.

I'm not embarrassed that she had to rescue me, even though the expectation on men is that we never need rescuing. I just wish none of this had happened so she shouldn't feel as upset as she looks.

CHAPTER 33
HOPE

Silence reigns in the staff room after the game. We're all sitting around a massive table, coaching staff, trainers, other people from the operations back office, and even legal. Rob Beau sits at the helm as the manager of the team, but even he seems stumped for words.

It's like maybe this is the first time in their lives that all these men realize that yes, men can get sexually harassed to. The world can also be scary to them.

I wish I could tell them all the times I have—from randos telling me to smile while I'm winded after an hour of jogging, to a guy giving me a weird look in the line to pay for my groceries, and then having to wait until he leaves so he doesn't see what car I drive, to the drunk assholes at nightclubs who think that dancing is an invitation for them to get handsy.

I expel a harsh breath that invites the attention of a few of them, including Beau. He levels his sharp eyes on me as he scratches his cheek, and finally tips his head in acknowledgment.

"Garcia," he starts with his scratchy voice. "I want to thank you for your heroic actions tonight. We are truly fortunate to have you as part of our staff."

I swallow hard and blink even harder because my eyes start to prickle. These are words I never thought I'd hear in an organization that has never seemed to appreciate me.

Clearing my throat, I say, "My job is to look out for the players and that's what I did."

"You went above and beyond. You acted when the rest of us couldn't find how, and you were very clever about it." For the first time in my life I see Rob Beau smile like the sweet Black grandpa he is to his family, and not as the brilliant yet stoic manager he is to the team. "Taking off your shirt that says staff and not security won't give them any grounds to file a claim against you."

Socci nods to his left. "That really was a stroke of genius."

"But—" here Beau pauses to give me A Look, "—I hope there is no next time so you can always keep your shirt on."

Someone coughs. They start looking away. Heat crawls up my throat.

Yeah, I also can't believe I did that. But it wasn't like I had a SECURITY shirt lying around nearby that I could change into while the creeps kept groping Cade. I just took one look at his pale face, his throwing arm raised high to protect it, and instinct kicked in.

And that instinct was to protect *him* at all costs.

"Now." Beau shifts his focus on the operations people. "We need to make sure this never happens again to Starr or to any other player."

"Of course, we are on it. While the game continued, we discussed some enhanced security measures we will take. In the meantime, we submitted footage and testimonies to the authorities to press charges."

I nearly melt into my chair. Cade will be relieved to hear

about this. I bet he's going to be a typical guy and pretend like this was no biggie, but it's a biggie.

The operations guy continues, "The only testimony we're missing is Starr's since he went right back to the game and…"

And completely shut out the other team after that.

It's unbelievable. If anyone had doubts about whether Cade Starr is season starter pitcher material, they've effectively vanished. No one would've faulted him for being rattled enough to let a bunch of runs through, or heck, even pull away from the game entirely. But he went right back into the rain and pitched in such a stone cold way, that the other team broke their record of whiffs, and Cade broke a personal fastball speed record. It's almost like being upset made him play better.

Or seen from a higher level, like Cade Starr is so used to adversity that he just takes each one and sets it down like a new stepping stone on his way to greater heights.

And if that's not what makes a great ace for a baseball team, I don't know.

"I'll talk with Starr and his agent to see what they can do," Beau says.

"For now I think we have enough grounds to press charges for trespassing and disorderly conduct from the organization's standpoint, but that doesn't guarantee Starr's safety outside of the premises," explains the operations guy, rousing mumbles around the table.

I slide my hands under the table and tighten my fists. Those new security measures better be damn good, then. It's not like I'm going to be by Cade's side everyday, all the time, ready to beat off women who want to cross the line. I wish, but that's just not the case.

Since the rest won't be solved tonight in this meeting, Beau shifts the focus onto different topics, including the lineup for the next game, as well as sharing some pointers for Steve and the rest of his team to watch out for.

Players will be coming back from dinner any time to get started on their stretches, so he adjourns the meeting. We're kinda somber as we head back to the training gym and I make a beeline around different machines to sequester myself in the office. Maybe my boss and the other trainers sense that I need a moment to myself because they loiter outside, waiting for the athletes.

I sit on my chair and swivel around, my back to them, and let my face drop on my hands.

Trágame tierra. I cannot believe I showed everybody my bra.

The fact that it was for a noble cause doesn't let me feel much better. I'm just glad it was one of my newer ones and a black one. A lighter color would've probably shown a lot more than I already did. My chest isn't much to write home about but I never imagined a day like today would come, where it became a leading character at work.

Too bad there isn't a big enough hole to crawl under around here.

My phone buzzes in my back pocket. I leave it be for a moment while I slouch on the chair, but it shakes again. And again.

I deign myself to look at what's happening and it's just my roommates.

HAPPY ROOMMATE

Oh my gosh I just heard what happened

Are you okay?

MELLOW ROOMMATE

That sounds like an absolute nightmare. I'd sue

But if you or Cade want to sue please give me a heads up so it doesn't turn into a PR nightmare

HAPPY ROOMMATE

Hush, you corporate drone

HOPE R U OKAY?!

ME

Yeah, I'm not the victim here

And for that reason, I reserve the right to tell them about the bra situation when we're safely at home, where I can do my best to morph into an ostrich.

MELLOW ROOMMATE

What about your man?

"Shh!" I say aloud, even though she's not in the office. Then I type.

ME

Shush woman, he's not my man

HAPPY ROOMMATE

YET

ME

Anyway, we don't know how Cade's doing. He kept on pitching and hasn't come back from dinner yet

MELLOW ROOMMATE

HE KEPT PITCHING???

HAPPY ROOMMATE

And shut the other team out. I saw it with my very eyes

ME

Yeah he's... something else

A shadow falls over me, followed by a scent I could now recognize in my sleep. But it makes absolutely no sense because I'm alone in the office, and I would've heard a sound if…

Slowly, I turn my face up. Cade Starr leans over my chair, looking down at my phone screen until he shifts the bluest eyes to me. "Y'all are talking about me?"

I exceed my multitasking skills by hiding my phone against my chest, yelping, and pushing the chair away from him with enough strength that it crashes against the desk, rattling everything on it and also myself.

"Cade!" I sound breathless and squeaky, like someone caught in the middle of a crime.

He straightens up, hands on his hips, and that's when I notice what he's wearing. Just his undershirt, which is tight enough that it hides absolutely nothing and looks like it was sprayed by a can, and his baseball pants rolled up to his knees. No spikes or socks. No wonder I didn't hear him come in. His hair is still damp from sweat and the rain, and his lips have a tilt that annoys me.

Cade cocks an eyebrow. "So?"

"The news are spreading around. The girls were just worried about you."

"But you said I'm something else. What does that mean?"

One in eight billion. But also strange. Wonderful. Sweet. Annoying. Talented. Hot. Kind. Sneaky. Adorable. Tender. Strong.

Ugh.

I pick that last one. "Strong. No one can believe you went out to pitch after that and killed it."

"I'm a pro." He shrugs like it's easy pweasy lemon squeezy.

"Are you really okay?"

Cade's eyebrows rise a notch. "I am, thanks to you. That's the main thing I came to say."

"It's no—"

"Nuh uh." He lifts his index finger. "Don't say it's nothing. It was not nothing. You were my lady in shining armor and saved my ass out there."

"Lady in shining armor?" I let my lips stretch into a smile for the first time in hours.

"Your armor was kind of flimsy but hey, no complaints from me."

"Hold on." I start looking around. "I need to find something to throw at your face."

Cade chuckles and the fact that he's able to produce such sound after what he just went through does something to me. I'm glad it hasn't ruined his mood, but I'm also angry that he's not taking himself as seriously as he should.

And yet, who am I to tell him how to feel? So I clam my jaw shut.

"Anyway, there's one more thing." He puts his hands in the pockets of his white pants that have seen better days. "Beau said Thomason and I should get ice baths because we pitched hard today. But I saw the other trainers are busy right now, so I figured you could do it."

"Yeah, of course." I leave my phone face down at my desk just in case and get up. "Let's go." We walk out of the office together, my sneakers making a normal sound with every step, but his feet are shockingly silent for how large they are.

Not far off is the younger relief pitcher, Josh Thomason, hanging around waiting for us. I motion at him with my finger and he follows along right away. It's not like the players have ever been uncooperative with me before—in fact, fellow staff have been much harder to work with—but the eagerness stands out.

I hope it's because he knows I'm a go getter and not because he caught a glimpse of my boobs earlier.

We march into the space with all the massage beds and physical therapy equipment for anyone recovering from injury.

At the back, we have an area that looks like a bathroom, tiled floors and walls, with state of the art ice bathtubs that look like something out of a sci-fi movie. Years ago, staff had to cart buckets of ice to each tub and then fill them with water, old school, but now the machines take care of everything themselves. All I have to do is press a few buttons on a control panel to adjust the settings, and voila, they start whirring away.

Once I'm done, I turn around and open my mouth to say something. But now I don't know what. Both players are removing their clothes and I'm a professional—it should be whatever. Besides, the white ceiling lights are harsh and not flattering.

But Cade Starr doesn't need any cozy lighting to look amazing.

I'm almost sorry for Thomason, but he barely registers as he stands in his sports underwear, waiting for his tub, and chatting with Cade about their game today.

"—And when you threw that last cutter, I really tried to look at it and see if I can get some pointers, but man—"

Meanwhile, Cade's peeling off the undershirt, his muscles bunching like poetry in motion. I wish I could particularly congratulate him for his posterior deltoids. Chef's kiss, no notes.

Oh shit, he's taking off his pants.

I whirl around to check the screens. The ice levels are not high enough yet.

"It's all about the legs," Cade explains behind me. "Everybody thinks it's about the grip and of course that's a key aspect, but you put the power with your legs."

Thomason sighs. "Yeah, I gotta work on them. Mine are some of the scrawniest in the team." They're really not scrawny for anyone's standards, but it's true that his legs are the reason his stamina isn't where it should be, if he wants to shoot for the starter pitcher position.

"You have a great trainer here who can get you to that level," Cade says, followed by a very long pause.

They're both staring pointedly at me. "Oh, me?"

"No, the ice tub," Cade says, his words drawling even thicker with the sarcasm.

I'm happy that I can still recognize how annoying he is, even though he makes me salivate.

The tubs beep and I clap. "All right, boys. Hop in."

Thomason is already whining before his foot even touches the surface of the icy water. In contrast, Cade dives right in like this is a hot tub instead. He's not even trying to be macho about it, it's how he's always done it. The only sign that it does affect him is by how his body tightens with the temperature shock.

"Arms in, down to the neck," I command to him, because he's being sneaky by keeping his arms around the edge of the tub.

"Do we have to?" Thomason whispers.

"Yep." I fold my arms. "I'm not above pushing you down with my own hands if I have to." At that, the two of them do exactly as told and sink all the way down to their necks. "Atta boys. Now, I'm going to set my timer for fifteen minutes. Try to make it."

"Good luck," Cade grunts.

In contrast, Thomason squeaks, "You too."

Otto would leave and come back in fifteen minutes, not really caring that sometimes players get out of the tubs, lounge for a bit, and jump back in when they hear him coming.

Not me. I pull up a chair and sit between the tubs, facing the players. Thomason keeps his eyes shut tight, no longer capable of any chatter. He lasts for eight minutes and thirty four seconds before he allegedly feels like he's dying. He gets up shivering like a leaf, steps out of the tub, picks up his clothes and power walks away.

Shaking my head, I set about draining his tub and starting the self cleaning cycle.

Meanwhile, Cade rises higher and makes his ice water slosh out of the tub. "Hope?"

I keep my back to him on purpose. "Hmm?"

"I meant it earlier."

"Meant what?"

"Thank you." That works like a rope that pulls me back to face him. He has his right elbow over the edge of the tub, chin on his forearm as he watches me. "I really don't know what I would've done without you."

"I—Well—" I raise my hands to tuck my hair behind my ears, except it's gathered in a ponytail and I look like a fool. I lower them again. "You're wel—"

I get interrupted by the beep of my watch, signaling that fifteen minutes have passed. And then the worst happens.

Cade starts to get up.

Water sluices down his body, his skin gleaming as his muscles work with the movement. I try not to stare but I'm not strong enough. Instead, I drink it all in, his wide shoulders, his firm chest, the cinematic eight pack, the defined V that starts at his outrageously narrow hips and disappears down his underwear.

Oh my gosh. He's in his underwear. I need to lift my eyes right freaking now.

I do, right in time for him to step so close that I can feel the cold radiating off his skin. His expression is blank but his eyes searching. They roam all over my face, leaving tingles in their trail. For a wild second they settle on my lips—and the traitors part. I don't know if it's because I want to tell him to kiss me or if I'm just shocked.

But then his eyes rise to mine and slowly, like molasses, his lips lift into a smirk. That gesture alone sends a stab of need through me, traveling like heat all over my body until my toes curl in my sneakers.

Cade lifts a dripping hand, and one of his freezing fingers runs across my cheek for a second, then farther up behind my ear where he hooks a strand of my hair I wasn't aware of.

"See you later, my lady in shining armor," he whispers with a deep voice.

I steel myself against the shiver but his smirk deepens. Cade steps away and bends to pick up his clothes, and I'm ashamed to report that I do look at his perfect bubble butt. Without a glance back, he walks away leaving me a mess.

CHAPTER 34
CADE

"Do you hear me?" Kim demands from the shower stall next to mine, loud enough so I can't use the excuse of the water spray, or the noise all around us as a hoard of naked men soap themselves up and chitchat like school kids.

"Yes, honey," I respond as I rinse my hair.

From my other side, Lucky asks, "Who's the wife in this relationship?"

"Starr."

"Kim."

This gives Lucky great amusement, and good for him. I'd punch them both if my hand wasn't so valuable.

Sighing, I turn my face into the cold spray for a moment, gathering myself to speak in a civilized manner. "Yes, Kim. I will do more stretching at home before bed, and I will eat extra protein too. Quit nagging me. I don't give you shit every single day."

He's lathering himself with dedication as he says, "That's because nothing you say is going to make me a better player than I already am."

I stare at him, and I even feel Lucky step around me to also stare him down. Kim just shrugs those tatted shoulders of his.

"Wow, that's cold, man." Lucky shakes his head and returns to stand under his shower.

"Point taken, Mr.-All-Star-Top-Pedigree-Dog," I enunciate every word in a deadpanned way. "But one more annoying word out of your mouth and I'll drop this bar of soap right at your feet when you're not noticing."

Kim raises soapy hands in defense. "Hey, soap bar jokes in the showers are a step too far."

I flip him off and finish showering. In the end, I don't make him slip to his demise because I've never been a fan of getting in trouble with the law. It's just too much hassle.

That's also why I'm still thinking about whether to press charges against the three women or not. The punishment so far might already be enough. They've been banned for life, and thanks to the media, they've also been immortalized for posterity as part of the select Florida Women club of very public mughosts. I can't imagine that would go well with their employers and families.

The Orlando Wild organization left it up to me to press more serious criminal charges and I haven't decided. I have no proof that one of them has stalked me longer than the recent incident, so I think without that the case for a restraining order is weak. Lou said he'd back me up either way, but that also going on my first season as a starter pitcher with this hanging over me might have mental repercussions. I've never felt more like just a jock with a high school diploma until this moment.

For now, I'm going to let it be. Like the team is doing at the facilities, I'm also upgrading my home security system. I've installed more cameras than a bank.

I grab a clean towel from the rack and get to work. A couple of guys go by to grab towels too, and stop before me.

"Hey, Starr. Looking good out there."

I resist the urge to say *and in here too*. Instead, I return, "You too, man. Wild save you made at the bottom of the second."

"Ha! That's a good one."

We lift our chins at each other in farewell and keep doing our thing.

Once I'm mostly dry, I wrap my towel around my waist and take the bend around the showers to the lockers. Ever since we got our first female trainer, the management made some changes to the clubhouse so that we essentially have two lockers: these ones right behind the showers, and the ones outside. This area is smaller and by company policy, it's the only area in the clubhouse where we're allowed to be buck naked.

I put on my underwear here and wrap the towel around my neck before heading out to the open area. I don't like getting dressed here because the shower steam makes my clothes cling and I hate that. Besides, it's not like Hope Garcia, a full blown athletic trainer whose main hobby is reading books about muscle groups, clutches her pearls at the sight of some skin. In fact, that's why for the longest time I thought she was made of steel.

Until yesterday.

I may be just a jock with a high school diploma, but I know what the look on her face meant when I was getting out of the ice water tub.

Hope Garcia isn't as stoic as she seems and she definitely liked what she saw.

It was in the way her pupils dilated while she ate me up top to bottom, how her nostrils flared, her difficulty swallowing or even speaking, and for the first time in my life I saw color rise to her face.

I came *this* close to pulling her against my wet and freezing body, and warming up my lips with hers.

But considering what she's been through with one night-mare date after another, enough to ask me for help with coaching her through it, I'm convinced that she deserves some proper, old school romancing. Something to let her really understand that she's worth every effort.

On the other hand, slowly introducing the idea of maybe dating me, instead of some random guy from an app, can give her plenty of time to decide if she really wants to be with me. One thing is finding me attractive—which, yay—but an entirely different one is keeping me around long term. There's no precedent of that in my entire twenty seven years of life. The one girlfriend in my teens ditched me just as quick as we got together. Then I was a temporary stop for the rest of the women in my life since.

What I know for sure is that I never felt for any of them what I feel for Hope. That need to keep her safe, while also standing in sheer awe of her, and the visceral desire to have her pressed up against me in something more than a friendly hug.

I don't know what that says about me, that I was never capable of feeling this way with other women. But I know it means that she is the real deal for me.

And speaking of her, Hope appears through the door from the gym, eyes trained to the front as she strides with purpose toward her boss. Steve is talking with one of the younger players off to my right—dude's in a similar state of undress to me and she doesn't give him a second glance while she shows some piece of paper to her boss.

I'm extra slow getting dressed now, not because I want her to catch me in my underwear again like some sort of creep, but because every single system in my body slows down in her pres-ence except for two. My eyeballs, taking her in, the shirt slightly bunched at her waist, the way the black leggings hug her powerful thighs, her wide hips and her firm butt. And my heart, working on overdrive to pump blood harder than it does even in the middle of a game.

"Okay, thanks," I hear her say. She does the same chin nod as a farewell that the guys do, swivels around while keeping her back to me, and jets right out.

So cold. So fast. So purposely not looking at me.

"Hmm." I narrow my eyes at the doors swinging shut behind her, and this time I hurry up getting dressed. My plans for tonight were going home to stretch again and eat a whole cow, because I'm sure Kim will notice if I don't do as he says one way or another. But I'd much rather see if Hope would like some ice cream or something low key and still friendly.

Lucky strides out half dressed by the time I'm putting on a black T-shirt over my head. "So how about we—"

"Hey, be right back man." I bump his shoulder, grab the jean shirt I intend to put on top later, and walk right out of the clubhouse and into the training gym.

A few long strides take me to the bend at the right, where light streams from the inside of the trainers' office. It's too silent to be packed with the other trainers, but it could also mean that Hope ran all the way out and is on her way to the parking lot.

My pulse trips when I spot her in her office, but it's not because of the best reason. She stands on her tippy toes on a step ladder, trying to reach something on a high shelf. At the first sign of the step ladder tipping and her little yelp, my amygdala kicks in and I rush.

"Oof!"

That's the sound of air swooshing out of her lungs as she crashes against my chest. I cinch my arms tight around her waist to stop her fall. Her head falls back on my shoulder. As gravity tries to take her, her chest pushes against my arms and she gasps. Slowly, I let her slide down until her feet touch the floor. And then something truly weird happens.

None of us move.

Me, I know why. I'm trying to imprint this moment in my memory for the rest of my life. To savor the way every curve of her body feels against mine, the scent of vanilla that teases my nose and makes my mouth water, the softness of her cheek against mine, her hands squeezing my arms.

Shit, she's driving me wild and doesn't even know it.

But why is *she* not moving?

Wait, does she think I'm some random groper?

I loosen my hold on her right away, and I'd think she'd push my arms away the rest of the way, maybe roundhouse kick me next—yet she doesn't. Instead, her hands stay on my skin a moment longer and she speaks before even turning.

"What are you doing here, Cade?"

I blink slow at the back of her head, following the trail of her ponytail to the back of her neck. I wonder if it would taste like vanilla if I kiss it.

Shaking my head hard, I take a step back and answer, "Returning the favor already, apparently. That was really dangerous, darlin'." In more ways than one.

She grabs onto the shelving unit and climbs on the step ladder again. "Well, thanks. But I had it under control. It's not even that high."

"Please, you were just about to hurt your pretty behind," I say. Maybe my body's still ruling me here, but I place my hands around her waist and lift her up the rest of the way.

She gasps. "Cade! What—"

"C'mon, get the thing."

"Ugh." She reaches for a box of something. "You can set me down now."

But instead of lowering her to the death trap, I lower her down to the floor and this time she whirls at me fast.

Jabbing a finger to my chest, she whispers, "You shouldn't

have done that, no matter what happens to me. What if I got you hurt?"

I cock an eyebrow. "You can't possibly think that would be enough to hurt me."

"But what if?" She frowns.

"Nothing happened, though." I glance around. "My question is why are you even doing this in the first place? Shouldn't someone taller do it? Or at least use a safer ladder?"

She snaps her mouth shut and retreats a little. "Fair point on the ladder, but I'm the only one responsible for stock so that's why I have to do it."

"Only?" My eyebrows tighten.

"Yup. That's what happens when you're the only woman in the team and also the youngest."

My jaw tightens and Hope's eyes close in on it. I open my mouth, about to release a string of curses on her behalf, when my stomach roars like an angry lion instead. We both look down at it, almost expecting a beast to tear out.

The annoyance in her face is completely gone after that. "I guess you should go eat something, Cowboy."

Oh shit, that's an opening if I know one.

Casually putting my hands in my joggers' pockets, I ask, "What about you? Is your own lion roaring any time soon?"

"I, uh…" She clears her throat. "Mine's more like a kitten purr but it started a while ago, yes."

"Want to—" I don't even finish my question when a different voice interrupts.

"What's this?"

I move aside and face the newcomer. Rosalina Mena is bent down, picking up my shirt that I tossed aside when I made the dash to catch Hope. Right behind her is Audrey Winters, who steps into the trainers' office, takes one look at both of us and her eyebrows rise.

"Sugar. Princess." I tip my head at them.

"I assume this is yours, Cowboy?" Mena offers my shirt, forcing me to walk over to her.

"Yeah, thanks." I take the garment and unfurl it so I can put it on.

Winters shifts her eyes between Hope and I. "So…"

"Right." Hope gives me a little smile that I can't decipher. "The girls and I are going to dinner, and since your stomach just tried to attack us… wanna join?"

Do I wanna—

That's what I came here for. To find the way to stay around her a little longer. If that included fasting under a rushing cascade for a whole day, I'd do it.

I don't know how I manage to keep my tone and demeanor casual, as I respond with, "sure."

CHAPTER 35
HOPE

I don't understand what's happening right now, but I'm not complaining.

Somehow, I went from planning to hit our fave taco joint in Mills Avenue with my roomies, to hallucinating that Cade might've been about to ask me out for dinner, to ending up in a full group dinner and cramped in a too small booth…

Smack between Cade on my left and Rose on my right.

Rose has no chill, too. Like I know the booth is fairly small and all, but she doesn't have to keep pushing me into Cade so hard. The poor guy had to rest his right arm on the backrest to not get completely crushed. But it also means that I'm flush against his side, and it's shocking how well we fit. If I fully melt into his side I'll never want to leave.

Besides, he has no business smelling so good. I just knew it was him catching me when I slipped earlier by the scent alone. Then my body remembered that yeah, that was how it felt when he feverishly wrapped himself around me, and that was all the confirmation I needed to know it was him.

And these are all the reasons why I'm currently dying right now.

Across from us are Rivera, Audrey, and Logan. Audrey's also kind of crushed between the two huge men, but none of them look anywhere near as bothered as I am.

If Rose pushes me one more time… I send her a glare and she keeps her attention set on Kim in front of her.

"Great restaurant choice, Kim," Rose says with a cute little grin.

"Yes, plenty of protein." He motions at Cade's plate. "Why aren't you eating?"

"I'm trying but I don't even know where to start." Cade's voice rumbles through his body and as a result, through mine. It travels all across my skin and settles like a ball of fire in my chest.

Rivera motions at his plate, where he demonstrates how to use a fork and knife. "Watch this, bro. This is how you use utensils."

"Screw you," is the rapid comeback.

Meanwhile, Rose leans to whisper in my ear. "You may also want to focus on the beef on your plate and not the beefcake by your side."

"What he just said," I spit back.

Cade moves and I stop breathing. He brings his arm up around me and has to lean forward until the table's wedged in his stomach just so he can use both hands. He starts cutting up his massive steak and veggies to bite size pieces furiously, and next thing he's returning to the previous position against the backrest, turning himself into *my* backrest. He stabs a piece of meat with the fork in his left hand, and brings it up to his mouth.

Rose smacks my thigh with enough strength to smart. I know she's thinking what I'm thinking but I can't believe I'm even thinking it. Is the cowboy into this?

Because I'm really into it. And I hope we never have to leave this booth. Bless every single person that jam packed this restaurant and forced us to take a booth that sits six normal people, but not when three of them are massive baseball players.

*

Unfortunately, time goes by fast when you're having fun. Too soon we finish eating and we have to leave because more people keep arriving, and we do have a road trip tomorrow morning.

"Okay, I can definitely drive back the people who came with me, but I need to stop at the pharmacy on the way," Audrey tells the group once we're standing outside the restaurant. We came in two cars, hers and Cade's, all girls in one vehicle and all boys in the other. "So, if anyone has any issues let me know."

"Actually, I also need to stop by for toothpaste," Rivera says and turns to Kim. "Didn't you say you need baby wipes?"

Kim tightens his jaw so tight that we all see a muscle jump. "Right." I'm shocked he doesn't deny it.

"Guess we'll catch up to you, then." Rose looks at Cade first, then at me.

And that's when it clicks.

Did—Did the four of them just set us up?

Untucking his tongue from against his cheek, Cade looks at me and says, "Shall we?"

"Uh, sí. Sure. Let's."

I duck from everybody's sight because their attention is what's making my tongue tie up. At least they have the decency not to laugh at me as Cade and I walk away together.

Together, I say, even though we're like six feet apart.

Our steps echo in the quiet of the parking lot as I follow Cade to his black pickup truck. He unlocks it and I jump into the passenger seat in a flash, and Cade pauses outside, watching me with eyes narrowed in thought.

Confused, I wait until he also climbs in to ask, "What was that?"

He hums from his throat as he buckles up and turns on the truck. "I was just wondering if you like to open and close car doors yourself or for the guy to do it."

My heart rises and threatens to kick my brain off its socket, but brain prevails. "Oh, is this a date coaching moment?" I stroke my chin in thought like I see him do often. "I'm usually much faster than them and get to the door first."

"Does that mean if I get to the door faster you won't get upset if I open it for you?"

We stare at each other for a moment long enough that the automatic lights go off. His eyes almost glow from the reflection of the streetlights and my mind, ever so, helpful reminds me of his body pressed up against mine earlier.

I look away. "Actually, I'd probably get mad. I'm an independent woman capable of handling a car door. I guess that's what makes me undatable."

"You're not undatable," he whispers just over the twangs of an old school country song playing in the background. His right hand caresses the steering wheel as he turns the truck into traffic. "The assholes who didn't value you are the undatable ones."

I have to sit on my hands to not reach for him and—what? Kiss him? As if.

Ugh, but I want to. I really do. I just don't know how. I guess I could straight up ask him if he'd be willing to switch roles from dating coach to date, but I don't trust myself to not act like an absolute twerp if he says yes *or* no.

I need a clue that he may be open to that idea, but he's like a freaking vault. In fact, we drive the rest of the way back to the ballpark with only the music to fill the silence. Not hearing his voice, even if it's to tease me and annoy me, makes me increasingly more nervous. Somehow I'm much more aware of him when he's quiet, like the need to know what he's thinking—about me, let's be honest—grows hungrier in his silence.

I break when we're two blocks away from the facilities. "So... Are you doing okay after the whole mess yesterday?"

Wow, way to ease into a casual conversation.

He does the chin stroke thing. "I suppose so, but I'm kinda dreading going home now."

I jerk. "Because you don't want to be alone now?"

"Well." He flashes a glance at me before focusing on the road again. "I recognized one of them, she's followed me around my neighborhood before."

I suck in all the air in the cabin. "Wait, Cade. You had a stalker and you didn't tell anyone?"

"Lou knows now—my agent."

"Cade..."

"I just don't want to make a big deal about this."

I bite my lip. I can imagine how anyone in his situation would want to pretend like nothing's wrong, hoping that makes it all go away. But that's not usually how it happens, and yet I can't badger him about this and make him even more uncomfortable than he already is. Especially not when the minds of baseball pitchers are famous for being delicate.

He's not the most fragile guy around, considering everything he has gone through, but I can't believe that this hasn't affected him.

I soften my voice. "Cade, I want you to know that if you need me I'll be there, okay?" And I mean it as a friend for life if that's how he'll have me.

He's badging us in through the parking lot gate and when he's done, he tosses a little smirk my way. "You'll beat the women off me?"

"If I have to." I shrug. "Maybe I'll just order a T-shirt that says SECURITY at the back and keep it around at all times."

"Hmm, how should I compensate you for your services?"

Erm, I can think of a few ways and none of them would keep things friendly between us.

"Trail mix," I blurt out without thought. Cade drives his truck into a parking spot two spaces removed from my yellow Jeep, giving me some time to form an explanation. "You ate all of mine, so you owe me for that."

"Don't I owe you way bigger time for what you did yesterday?" he asks as he turns off the engine.

"Nope. You paid that off today, remember?"

His face starts turning my way and I don't know. My flight reflex kicks in because both my logical brain and my amygdala know that if I stay in his car for too long, I'm going to do something I'll regret. I open the door and jump out like it's an Olympic sport. Palming my joggers, I produce my car keys and click it open. There's some noise behind me as I open my car door and climb in.

But before I can even grab my door handle to close it, he's there. And by there I mean here.

Cade leans into my door, arm propped up at the top as he bends lower to look at my face. "Hey, Hope?"

I swallow hard.

"Yes, Cade?"

"Before you run all the way home, can I close your car door without you getting mad at me?" How dare he ask this and then give me this slow, cheeky grin that makes him look absolutely adorable?

And of course my breath hitches, and my voice sounds all weird when I speak. "Fine, if it's you I'll allow it."

Without another word, he leans away and shuts my door, stepping back with his hands on his pockets. The smile in his eyes keeps me company as I drive home on my own.

CHAPTER 36
CADE

'm maybe two miles away from home when a call connects to my sound system. Rolling to a stop at a red light, I check the screen and my body reacts even before my mind can process. It's embarrassing, really, and I even clear my throat trying to act all macho when there's actually no one here to witness this. But my heart rate skyrockets, my skin heats up to the point where my clothes feel uncomfortable, and a goofy grin takes over my face.

Pressing the call button, I say, "Hey, darlin'. Miss me already?"

Please say yes, because I will turn right around.

"Pfff." As she recovers, the light turns green and I keep driving. "It's just that I'm still worried about what you said earlier."

"What did I say?" My brain was in knots while we were alone in my truck, stuck in the real life version of so close yet so far.

"That you're dreading going home."

I cringe hard, wishing to turn smaller and smaller until I disappear. "Uh, yeah. Maybe I exaggerated."

"I don't think you did," she says softly, skewering me with her concern. I have to put a paw against my mouth to keep back the wounded animal sound that wants to come out. "So anyway," she continues, louder, "I'm going to keep you company on the phone until you make it home safe."

"How chivalrous of you," I joke even though I'm stunned by her offer.

"Lady in shining armor and all that, right?"

Shit, she has no idea what she's doing to me.

I've never had anyone genuinely worry about me so much, let alone a woman I'm so damn attracted to. Most people have wanted something from me—for me to be a quiet and good boy, or for me to play well, or my money, or just a good time—but here's Hope, willing to wrestle stalkers from me.

I sigh. "I feel like I'm not fulfilling my role as a guy too well."

"If I had a stalker who broke into my workplace to grope me you'd probably get worried too."

"Worried?" The question comes out with a hell of an emphasis. "You're wrong, Hope. I wouldn't be worried."

"No?" She sounds almost disappointed.

"I'd be freaking feral. And I wouldn't stop until I found who was harassing you to take care of them."

She gives a light laugh. "Atta boy. But anyway, it shouldn't surprise you that I'm the same. I'm a tomboy after all."

"Listen, I have no issue with this role allocation." And who cares about the tomboy label? I'm convinced that everyone who assigned it to her was just intimidated by the fact that she's strong physically and mentally, and that it's just part of what makes her so wildly beautiful that it's intimidating.

My mind plucks the memory of the first time I saw her. We were all lined up around the clubhouse while she was introduced by Steve, Beau, and Charlie Cox, the owner. She stood firm, almost soldier like, feet apart and holding her hands behind her. And she glared at each of us in turn while Beau warned us about what would happen if any of them acted disrespectful to the team's first female trainer. But there was no need, each stare down she did established a very clear *or else*, and fortunately the vast majority of our lineup was made of smart guys. No one would dare mess with a woman with the energy of a wild animal.

It's why lightly teasing her is so fun. Nothing like someone who can dish it back to keep things entertaining.

"Good," she says with finality. "Anyway, how far are you?"

"Pulling into my street now, two blocks from my house."

"Good thing you live in a bunker, huh?" She pauses. "Actually, how come you built your house that way? Have you been stalked before?"

"Technically no," I mumble, uncomfortable not by her questions but by the memories. "It's just—I was always under scrutiny growing up, by adults waiting for me to screw up or by other judgy kids. And I just didn't want to live like that anymore."

"How does that work with baseball now, though?"

"It's different. That attention I genuinely enjoy. It's how I get to show people I'm worth a damn."

"Cade… you're worth a damn even if you weren't a professional pitcher."

My voice is kinda choked up as I speak. "Careful, darlin'. You're gonna make me swoon here." Too late, though, pretty sure I'm in the Hope Garcia fan club forever.

She splutters. "I wasn't—I didn't mean to—Ahem."

I bite my lip and release it to grin. It's even better if it came naturally out of her, and not in a flirty way. She cares about me and likes what she sees, and I'm almost high from this feeling, from the hope I have that when I ask her out, she might really say yes.

Speaking of my bunker of a house, there are a few cars

parked by my sidewalk and one is almost blocking my garage entry, forcing me to slow down to measure well. But then I catch some movement from inside that car from the corner of my eye. Someone's there, and they just lowered themselves so I wouldn't see them.

Instinct kicks in. Instead of pulling in, I reverse and click the button to shut down my garage door right just as it was starting to rise.

"Uhh, Hope?"

"Yes?" She squeaks out, probably still embarrassed.

"I think the stalker's outside my house."

Her sharp inhale echoes in the quiet of my car. "Crap."

"I'm driving away," I say in a clipped tone. "No way I'm going in."

"Good call. Are you being followed?"

I check the rearview mirror and sag in relief. There are no cars behind me, but I'm still not far away enough that it's impossible to catch up.

"Not right now."

"Keep driving and don't disconnect the call, but give me a second." Some rustling is followed by tapping sounds. While she does whatever she needs, I take the winding way out of my neighborhood, keeping an eye on the rearview mirror for any weird signs. I almost forget that the call is still connected until Hope talks once more. "All right, I cleared it with my dad. He's good with you staying the night at his place."

"Huh?"

"I mean it's not like you can circle the whole night waiting for the stalker to leave, right? And the other option would be to call the police."

"No thanks to both of those."

"I figured. Do you remember how to get to Dad's place?"

"I think so."

A different kind of noise comes from her end of the call,

and it takes me a second to realize it's the engine of her car. "What are you doing?" I ask, confused.

"I'm going to meet you there because Dad is out with his pickleball buddies. Man can't play because he's injured but he sure can go out for drinks with them, huh?" I can picture her shaking her head right now.

I tense at the first sign of a car behind me, until it passes me and turns left and I see that it was a SUV, and not the sedan that was parked outside my house.

Hope's voice keeps my shit together as I drive down to the neighborhood between Audubon Park and the less affluent areas of Baldwin Park where her dad lives. I get there first and park by the curb of her childhood home, a bungalow with blue shiplap and white trim, an oak tree sprouting from the back-yard and palms lining the front.

My eyes are trained on the rearview mirror until another car drives into the street, but it has distinct round headlights and I know it's Hope. Turning off my engine, I get out of my truck to wait for her. She stops right behind me, barely leaving enough clearance for her dad to pull into his driveway later.

Hope jumps out of her car, leaving the door open as she marches up to me. She stops right in front of me, grabbing my arms and inspecting me. "Are you okay?"

My lips twitch. "I'm fine."

Then she rises to her tippy toes and grabs my face until my lips pucker out. "How about in here?"

"Eh. It'll be fine." Especially now that she's here. I grab her wrists and she allows me to remove her hands. "Did you see anything weird behind you?"

"No. You?" I shake my head and Hope presses her lips tight. "Cade, you do know this means you won't be able to leave it alone and hope it goes away by itself, right?"

"I know. I'll figure it out," I whisper.

"Sooner rather than later, okay?" She worries her lip and I feel it in every fiber of my being.

Of course, that's when I notice I still have her wrists in my hands and that she hasn't pulled away. Would it spook her if I slide my hands down to hers, if I sneak my fingers between hers?

Probably. Especially considering how stiff she was all through dinner earlier. So I let her go for now.

I clear my throat. "Right. Yes."

She jerks a nod. "Then, follow me."

"Yes, ma'am."

Her ponytail swishes as she strides to close her car. I wait just down the steps while she unlocks the front door of her dad's house and flips on the lights. It's really strange because nothing about tonight has gone the way I thought it would—dinner wasn't just the two of us, I certainly wasn't expecting the stalker to come back, and yet here we are. Alone anyway.

She shuts the front door behind me and I have to consciously remind myself to freaking behave.

My eyes travel around the living room, with the comfy brown furniture, potted plants, and picture frames hanging on every wall depicting the family history. Some of them are crooked and rather than looking shabby, it gives me the feeling that those are the favorite pics, the ones her dad or maybe Hope herself love on with their hands.

"So, this is it." Her hands smack against her thighs. "It's not a McMansion but this is where I grew up with my dad and an annoying older brother."

I smile. "It's a great home."

"Wait till you hear the creaky pipes," she says, but her eyes are bright as she guides me to the kitchen. "Kitchen should be pretty well stocked, but don't let me catch your hands in the Cheetos bag."

"Stay away from the Cheetos, gotcha. Is beer okay?"

She slides an openly unfriendly look at me before manhandling me toward the hallway. "Here's the bathroom. You'll have to share with Dad but I suppose you're used to worse."

"Did you have to share growing up?"

"Oh yes." Her voice darkens. "Don't reming me, it was a tough and very stinky time."

That makes me chuckle. No wonder she doesn't give a shit about what guys do or don't do in the clubhouse. She grew up knowing the absolutely foul smells that come out of men. Almost makes me want to check my armpits to confirm I washed them well.

Opening another door, she declares, "And here's my bedroom. It's better that you stay here and not my brother's because I visit more often, so I know the sheets are clean."

My eyebrows rise. "Wow, so I'll have the privilege of seeing where you grew up?"

"There are no dolls inside, if that's what you're expecting."

She lets me through and flips on a switch that turns on the light and the overhead fan. The walls are a pastel blue, furniture also brown in contrast to the yellow bedding. But just like in the living room, her walls are littered with snapshots of her life and also posters of… muscle groups, of course.

"Were you a muscle nerd since childhood?"

"Yes." Her expression is grumpy, cheeks pinking. "It didn't exactly make me too popular in school."

"Nerd."

"Jock," she spits right back out.

"Fair." I tuck my hands in my pockets and glance around at the pictures, spotting a few that no doubt are from elementary. I can't help but smiling at one where she's in pigtails and a toothy grin with a gap. But then I keep perusing until I land on one tacked on the wall above her desk.

Bypassing her, I march to it and remove it from the wall, setting the tack down to inspect it. "So this is the douchebag?"

"What?"

"Your ex." I flip the pic to her, knowing it shows her kissing some blond guy's cheek while he smiles for the camera.

A million emotions flash through her face. Surprise. Disgust. Embarrassment. Some other more unpleasant ones too.

She makes a grab for it. "Give me that."

"No, I want to inspect it."

"Cade." She glares as I lift the picture well above my head where she has no chance of reaching it. "I'm not above getting a step ladder."

I shrug. "I'd just move out of reach again." Looking up, I try to inspect the guy's face as if that could tell me what she even saw in him. But all I glean is that he's some random surfer-dude looking type and she's way too stunning beside him, her hair about her bare shoulder, except for what looks like a strappy swimsuit. Makes me grind my molars. "What did you even see in this guy? He doesn't seem any special."

Huffing, she takes a step away that allows me to lower the picture. She folds her arms and glares at it. "I don't know. I guess it was the fact that he was the only guy eager to kiss me."

"Wait, what?"

Her dark eyes lift to mine. "What do you mean what?"

"Only—" I shake my head. "So you've only ever kissed this asshole here?"

Like magic, red rises up her throat and to her forehead, and she avoids my eyes.

"As you're well aware, I haven't had a line of guys fighting to make out with me." She rolls her eyes but by the way her arms tighten around her, I know this really hurts her.

Slowly, I release air between my lips and toss the damn picture to the desk. Facing her again, I say, "Then let's change that."

"Change what?" Her eyebrows tighten.

This is it, the go big or go home moment. The moment we see if this turns into a home run or an out for me.

"Let me show you that all of that is bullshit." I make a point of looking at her lips. What happens subconsciously is that it makes me run my tongue across mine. Lifting my eyes to hers again, I say, "Let me kiss you, Hope."

CHAPTER 37
HOPE

"W—What?" The simply question comes out breathless, full of yearning but disbelief.

Cade tilts his head back, eyelids half mast and about to give me a heart attack. His voice grows even deeper as he repeats, "Let me kiss you." It must be so obvious that I'm still not computing because he adds, "Let me show you that you're worth being fully kissed. Until there's no doubt of how freaking hot you are."

My jaw drops.

My ears start buzzing.

My vision brightens, narrowing on his face and the fact that there's no teasing there. The cowboy is as serious as when he steps on the mound. As if this was a game where he's facing a big slugger with full bases and a full count.

I guess I've been frozen for so long that he takes a step back and says, "Of course, if you don't want to—"

Oh, no. There's no way I'm letting him takebacksies.

Grabbing a handful of his T-shirt and the open flap of his over shirt, I pull him down until his lips crash on mine.

I figure that maybe this wasn't the best approach when both of our eyes stay wide as saucers.

"Sorry," I say against his lips and pull away. "I don't know what I was—"

But then the corner of his lips rises, and next thing I know one of his hands circles my waist slowly, making sure I feel the firm touch, until it finds the small of my back and pulls me against him. Air rushes out of my lungs and I balance myself with my hands against his chest.

The index finger of his free hand curls under my chin and lifts it. There is something so hot about that little move that I melt against him, and that's even before meeting his molten blue eyes. My heart trips because they're focused on the lower half of my face, and then the pad of his thumb touches my lower lip.

I can't believe it but that's enough to completely disconnect my logical brain. I'm all feeling after that, all emotion, my entire being focused on the friction of his finger as it caresses my lower lip slowly, carefully, feather-like. I'm sure he can feel my heart violently punching his ribs through my chest, and I'm not even sure I'm breathing right now.

"Not like that, darlin'," Cade whispers, his deep voice wrapping around my skin like velvet. "I was thinking more like this."

This time my eyes flutter closed. I feel his breathing fan my face, his heat closer until we touch.

My soul sighs a little *oh* as his lips find mine, like a little eureka moment when you first figure something out. And what he's teaching me right now is that I've never been kissed properly before. It's not just about lips touching, tongues brushing. A proper kiss is so much more—it's two souls coming together for the first time.

His hand shifts to hold my jaw, getting out of the way as his lips close around my upper one. Cade savors it without a rush, his moist and hot branding my skin. My legs turn to jelly as he shifts his head, our noses brushing just like they accidentally did earlier, after he caught me from the step ladder. Maybe the same memory dances in his mind because he holds me tighter, and I appreciate the excuse to slide my hands up, palming the hard muscles of his chest and shoulders until I find his neck. The feel of his warm skin tears a little sound out of my throat that changes everything.

Cade's tongue runs over my lower lip, the shock of it making me open my mouth. His jaw works under my hand as his lips press against mine, opening to deepen the kiss. This time he's the one groaning.

I cinch my arms around his neck, bending him lower to remove the space left between us. Even though the kiss is deeper, our tongues brushing without shame, Cade doesn't let me hurry the pace. His hand tangles in my hair, fingers closing around the strands to hold me in place. The soft scrape of his fingers against my scalp almost makes me see stars.

Wow, so this is what kissing Cade Starr feels like. Life changing.

Sensing my need to oxygenate my brain, Cade slows way down to release my lips with a little pop that echoes in the silence. He doesn't move an inch though, keeping an arm around me like he knows I wouldn't be able to stay upright if he lets go.

Slowly, I open my eyes and almost die, because he's watching me intently through half mast eyes. "Do you get it now?" he asks, voice husky and thick and so, so damn hot that I moan.

"Get what? I don't even know what my name is right now," I admit, my voice completely alien to me.

His hold around my hair shifts, and that's when I realize that he messed my ponytail and I probably look like I have a bird's nest on my hair. But I don't think he cares. I don't think I do either.

"That's how you deserve to be kissed. Slow, thorough, and on purpose."

"On purpose?" I parrot, my brain not quite revving up yet.

"Isn't it obvious?" His nose brushes with mine again, and my heart hammers even harder as he speaks against my lips. "Can't you see you're making me wild, Hope?"

I gasp.

And then we're kissing again, and this time it's different. I grab fistfuls of his hair for dear life because I can feel myself falling, and this is the only way I can stop myself from crashing down. Except my feet are firm on the floor, and his hands still hold me safe.

Or as safe as I can be while they roam, while his mouth devours mine. A shiver racks my body when one of his hands travels down my spine, lower to my waist. I wait to see if he'll find the hem of my shirt and sneak past it, craving the touch of his skin on mine—but no. It keeps going. Thrill raises goosebumps on my skin as his hand finds my butt.

And he squeezes.

His lips stretch into a smile against mine. "I've been dying to feel you against my hand."

"Oh yeah?" I ask all breathy. "Is my butt living up to the hype?"

"It's even better." Something like a growl comes out of his throat as he squeezes.

"Cade!"

"You can grab my ass any time you want, darlin'."

That makes me chuckle, but then that sneaky hand of his keeps moving. I tense in a weird mix of anticipation and embarrassment as he finds the edge between my butt and my thigh, his hand closing tighter when it slides to my thigh and lifts it, forcing my leg to wrap around him.

Cade groans, hiding his face in the crook of my neck. "Shit. Don't let me keep going."

"Why not?" I ask, morbidly curious even though I can feel the self-restraint tightening his muscles.

He opens his mouth and scrapes his teeth softly against the skin at the crook of my neck and shoulder. A violent shudder reveals just how much I liked that.

"Hope, if you don't stop me I'll lift you up onto that bed and have my way with you in your childhood bedroom, while your dad could arrive any time. You deserve much better than that."

I gasp in his ear. The words *your dad* are a necessary bucket of cold water.

"Okay, good point." I loosen the hold on his hair, wondering if it hurt him. I pet his head all sweet in comparison, trying to soothe him. "Maybe we should put some distance."

"You first," he says against my neck. "I don't think I can move."

Snorting, I lower my leg. The issue is that the friction tears a little sound from him, and I'm not sure if it's a complaint or the opposite. For a moment he holds me tighter, one hand back on my butt, the other at the back of my neck, until I wedge my hands between us against his chest.

But then I can't move either.

"You feel amazing," I admit in a little whisper.

Sighing, he says, "Trust me, you feel even better."

"Good to know." My voice trembles, every cell complaining as we slowly take a step back.

Glad to see that his chest rises and falls with the same difficulty as mine, and that his face is just as flaming red. He runs his tongue across his swollen lips, and I almost complain that it's unfair. He shouldn't make me want to jump him again.

That's when it hits me. I just kissed Cade Starr. *Me.*

I cover my mouth with my hands, absolutely shocked at my own behavior.

"Don't do that." Cade runs his hand through his hair, reminding me of the state of mine. "Don't hide what we just did."

If anything, that makes my embarrassment grow until I can barely stand. I swivel away from him, busying my hands by redoing my ponytail. "It's not that I'm trying to hide it. I just don't know how to face you right now."

"Why?"

"Cade. We just kissed," I hiss, glancing over my shoulder as I work the hair tie around my hair. "Scratch that, I just jumped at you after you've had a pretty crappy night."

"Did you forget that I'm the one who pitched the idea at you?"

"Well, no but—"

"No buts, we both definitely wanted that."

"Well yes, but—"

His eyes sparkle. "I said no buts."

Mierda, qué bello es. This man is completely unreal. I can't believe he just made out with me and in my childhood bedroom.

"Fine, no buts." I sigh in almost dreamy way. "I'm just struggling right now."

He tucks his tongue against his cheek. "With what?"

"With the fact that I don't know how I'll stop myself from wanting to kiss you every time I see you now, and I'm not sure that's what you had in mind with this." I bite my lip.

We both know exactly what I'm asking. Was this just a one off, a consequence of being alone after a night of adrenaline? If so, then I'm really gonna have a shit time seeing him at work from now on, because that's not how I feel. Not for a second. This kiss fed the crush I have for him to turn it into a monster that's oppressing my chest and making it hard to breathe.

Cade's lips make a little smacking sound as they part to speak, but that's when the sound of jingling keys at the front door reach us.

Our eyes widen. If my dad had arrived some five minutes ago he would've caught his baby daughter all but wrapped around a random guy, eating his face in her room. I'd have been in need of moving to a different continent after that.

"Um, your shirt," Cade whispers.

I look down at myself. The fabric's twisted around my torso and risen over one hip. As I fix it, I tell him, "Yours too."

He straightens out his clothes. "Is my hair okay?"

"One second." I reach for him, and Cade bends lower without any prompting. I ignore how his eyes pin on my face, using my fingers as a comb through his soft hair to fix it. "There."

Swallowing hard, I move back to inspect him. The blush has gone down on his face, and if Dad doesn't pay any attention to Cade's mouth he'll never guess what we were up to.

Good timing, because Dad calls, "Hope? Is the baseball player here already?"

"Yes, Dad! We're coming," I respond loudly.

"After you." Cade tips his head at the door.

I turn to lead the way but right before I'm out of the door, I pause and glance back. The sneaky little jerk is watching my ass like he has a permit to do so. His eyes rise to mine and rather than looking chagrinned, he smirks.

I almost trip. I have to hold myself against the door frame so I don't waste all the money my dad invested in my orthodontics as a kid. Casting one last glare at the man behind me, I finally step out into the hallway.

CHAPTER 38
CADE

don't know how I manage to sleep in Hope's childhood bed. Not only is it way too small, half of my legs below the knee dangle out and at some point in the night, I almost roll over to the floor. But also, I keep catching glimpses in my sleep of what Hope and I could've ended up doing on her bed if her dad hadn't come home. I wish I could say that I'm a gentleman and would've restrained myself even without her dad in the picture, but I don't know. There's a visceral need for her that I've never felt before. Things would've turned dangerous if she'd let me.

My cellphone alarm goes off at five something and my groaning echoes in the quiet. I was getting to the good part in the dream. Reality is so drastically worse because she's not in my arms.

Sighing, I toss an arm over my face. Hope's not the only one who will have issues acting normal at work. For one, Lucky and Kim will look at us once and their clever, sneaky little brains will immediately deduce what's up. But just like them, there are other guys in the team and staff who may notice.

Especially because it'll be impossible to hide that she makes me salivate.

"Pull your shit together, Starr," I whisper to myself and run my hands down my face. With a not so friendly slap to my cheeks, I finally force myself to get up and fix the bed.

We did explain to her dad—who told me to call him Humberto—that I was gonna have to leave criminally early, but I still don't put on my shoes and trod on the floors as softly as I possibly can.

That's until I open the bedroom door and the smell of coffee hits me in the nose, followed by the sound of pots and pans in the kitchen. I perk up even more, wondering if it's Hope. My rational brain reminds me that she went back to her place, where she lives with Winters and Mena, and it's way too early for her to have driven back here.

Obviously, the one making breakfast is her dad. "Buenos días," he tosses over his shoulder before focusing on the pan once more. It smells like scrambled eggs, bacon, and something else that I can't identify but makes my stomach roar. "I hope you like arepas."

I give the word a try but I've never sounded more Texan than until this moment.

The older man laughs. "Don't even try again, son. You're giving me secondhand embarrassment."

"Sorry." I cringe before bending down to put on my shoes. "Well, thank you so much for your hospitality. I'll get out of your hair now."

"Nonsense, what kind of host would I be if I don't feed you?" He points at the stool by the counter. "Sit."

"Yes, sir." I do as I'm told. A second later I realize I'm being a terrible guest. "Um, sorry. Can I help you with anything?"

"Yes, with not pronouncing the word *arepa* in my presence again." He laughs all by himself, and I don't mind that it's at my expense. His English is pretty damn awesome, whereas I only speak the one language with a very heavy accent. As his amusement ebbs, he straightens and asks, "Wait, any dietary restrictions?"

"None."

"Good, good."

Grabbing a plate, he preps something on it with his back to me. Last he heaps eggs and bacon on it. And when I say heaps I mean it, the man limps a little before setting a mountain of food before me.

I gape.

"That—" he points at the white, flat bread-looking-but-not-quite thing, "is an arepa. It's made of cornflour and I filled it with cheese."

My stomach throws off a creaking sound straight out of a horror movie. "Wow, thank you. This looks amazing."

"Tuck in." Grunting, he turns away and limps back to the kitchen to fix himself a plate.

I pick up a fork and ask, "Is your ankle doing better, sir?"

He snorts. "It's just doing. I can't wait to get back to the game—pickleball, though. Nothing professional."

"But it's important to you, right? Your daughter mentions her dad's pickleball games all the time."

"Does she?" He's done fixing his plate and walks back around, relying on the full cast around his leg. I wait for any sign that he needs help, figuring that helping unprompted would tick him off. He has the same stubborn set to his face as his daughter.

Once he's safely sitting beside me is when I finally put a forkful of food in my mouth. I don't know what he put on these eggs, but the taste is better than any I've had before. I watch him pick up the bread-look-alike in his hand and I do the same.

"So, what's going on between you and my daughter?"

I choke.

Calmly, he slides a glass of orange juice toward me. Ruthless.

The juice unfortunately helps loosen my throat way too quick, and I'm forced to answer a question I don't have clarity on. "I'm not sure," I admit.

As he chews, he watches my face like he's looking for something. "But it's not nothing. My daughter wouldn't bring any random guy to my home, no matter how many stalkers are behind him."

Right, she did fill him in on the reason to get his permission in the first place.

"I can't speak for her," I start carefully, "but I really like her."

"Like her?"

"*Like* like her," I confirm.

"And does she know that?"

I drink some more of the juice, hoping it cools my face down because I really shouldn't be thinking about how I essentially ate her mouth under his roof.

"I haven't had the chance to tell her yet."

He jerks back in surprise. "Then what the hell are you waiting for? I mean, I'm sure you're a really popular guy, but no other woman can compare to my Hope."

"I know that." I nod in full agreement. "And I'm working on it."

"Well hurry, before a better guy snaps her up." He takes a gigantic bite out of his arepa after voicing my new biggest fear. He then speaks with his mouth full, "And just so we're clear, if you hurt her I'll hurt you back." Basically, kicking me while I'm already down.

But he's not wrong at all. "Understood," I say and grab a strip of bacon.

"Coffee?"

"Please let me get it."

He nods and points with his mouth at the pot of coffee. After bringing two mugs for him and for me, we settle into a pleasant quiet as we finish our plates. I insist in loading the dishwasher and letting him rest, and he shares that even though he can't play right now, he still goes to hang out with his retired friends while they play and then catch lunch together.

"Remember," he says at the door once I'm leaving. "You better treat my little girl like a gentleman or I'll use my machete to leave you permanently walking funny."

I'd laugh if it wasn't so graphic. "You own a machete?"

"Two. How do you think those plantain trees at the front stay nice and pretty?"

Well, I guess they weren't palms like I thought.

"Roger that," I mumble, resisting the urge to bodily protect my threatened parts.

Humberto offers his hand and I shake it. He's as strong as any young buck in the pros. "This time it's not a threat: good luck making my daughter happy."

"Um, thank you, sir."

With a final nod, he dismisses me and goes back in his house. I stand for a moment, staring dazed at the brown door, until I manage to drag myself to my truck.

Halfway to my house is when it clicks that he basically gave me permission to pursue his daughter in between the open threats and over the hearty breakfast. I sag in my seat, because I have no intention of hurting Hope at all. I don't know how the hell I'll manage to turn myself into boyfriend material, but I will—for her I will. With just the same frenzied zeal that took me all the way to the starter pitcher position of a professional baseball team.

The first rays of sunlight are hitting the sky by the time I roll into my street. The sedan is gone, along with most of the cars in the street. I pull into my garage and dial Lou as I get out of my car.

"What?" he snaps. "I was in the middle of sleep, you absolute—"

I interrupt him. "The stalker was outside my house last night. I had to spend the night somewhere else." I walk into the house through the garage door, checking the vast space in case the stalker found the way to walk through walls. Nothing but silence greets me, both in my house and also on the line. "Lou?"

"You gotta press charges," he spits out.

"I know, it's why I'm calling. I need your help to start the process."

"Right on. And maybe you should consider hiring security personnel for a while."

I scrunch up my face. "What if I stay at a hotel for a while instead?"

"Or that. Call me again if something happens." He grumbles, "Even if it's in the middle of the night."

"Wow, I appreciate the thought."

"Lay off the sarcasm, kid." While I chuckle, he asks, "Can I go back to sleep now?"

"Sure—and hey?"

"What?" he snaps again.

"Thanks."

"Don't get sappy again, it's too early." With that he disconnects the call.

I pocket my phone and hurry to my room. If it hadn't been for the stalker, I would've come home to replace the stuff in my suitcase and duffel bag, dirty clothes for clean. We have a road trip this morning and a flight right after that, so I need to pack now. It's why I had to get up so early.

My head spins with everything that's happened in the past twenty four hours, but as I turn into a tornado in my room around the luggage I have splayed open on the floor, I choose to focus on the best parts. All of them are about Hope and what this turning point means for us.

One thing is for sure, I'm not going back to being her dating coach or just another player in the roster.

The coast is still clear once I drive out of my house, but I wait to make sure the garage door is fully closed before taking off. My eyes bounce all around the neighborhood because right around this time is when the stalker started following me around while jogging. I know home ownership is public records in the state of Florida, but I can't help wondering if maybe the stalker lives nearby. Otherwise it'd feel even more unhinged for someone to drive a long way just to stalk some random guy.

I've never been more relieved to merge into heavy Orlando morning traffic than I do after leaving my neighborhood. The clock is ticking a bit too close to rendezvous time at the ballpark, and I'd really like to not get written off by Beau just when I'm starting to make a place for myself on the team.

"Whew," I say once I'm the very last one to the bus, finding a spot next to Lucky. "Made it right in the nick of time."

His eyebrows rise as he runs his eyes up and down my frame. "Bro, why are you wearing the same clothes as last night?"

"It's a long story."

"Is it juicy?"

I cut a sharp look at him. "Now would be a great time for you to choose maturity."

"Bo-o-ring." His eyes deviate to the front. "Oh, incoming."

"Incoming wha…" I'm unable to get the last letter out when Hope climbs aboard, carrying the bags full of snacks and drinks. I know it's part of her job but I hate how none of her coworkers pick up some of the slack.

I guess the good news is that her lips aren't swollen anymore.

"Dude, wipe that look from your face if you don't want anyone to figure out you were with her last night," Lucky whispers to me.

"What look?"

He points at my face. "That starving man look."

I duck my face because I have no defense. That's exactly how I'm feeling right now.

Clearing my throat, I reach around and tap Kim's arm, since he's sitting by himself right in front of me. He twists toward the aisle and takes off his Beats headphones. "What?"

"Got a piece of paper and pen I can borrow?" I ask.

His face twists, probably about to tear me a new one for bothering him, when he reasons that the quickest way to go back to listening to his tunes is to simply do me the solid. Grunting, he disappears for a moment until his hand pokes out, offering a small notepad and a pencil.

"Thanks," I chirp with exaggerated joy. It earns me a few choice words.

I rip a blank sheet out and jot down a quick note before returning the implements to Kim. Lucky watches in silence as I fold over the paper, and even as Hope finally reaches us to offer our snacks.

I admire her professionalism for keep a perfectly straight face as she hands over a little snack and drink pouch to Lucky, and then one to me. That is, until I grab her wrist. That finally makes her look down and meet my eye, and her breath hitches as I slide the folded up note into her hand. For a wild second I debate whether to bend over and kiss her hand, but that would get us in trouble.

Instead, I let my grip slide and release her. Her throat works with a heavy swallow and she moves on without further ado, carrying the note that says *Let's talk somewhere quiet when we can*, and leaving me to remember the taste of the skin at the base of her neck.

Settling with his snackies, Lucky says, "I expect a full report of whatever happened."

I lean back and close my eyes, eager to pick where my dreams left off instead.

CHAPTER 39
HOPE

Somewhere quiet ends up being this random bar we escape to after dinner at the hotel. It's lined up with pool tables, dartboards, and old school arcade machines that make a hell of a lot of noise. Rose, who was cleared to travel with us for the next stretch of games, found this place after a quick search of local spots for a night out.

The plan was simple: gather a group, come to this joint, and find some corner where Cade and I could finally have our talk.

The result was anything but: the second a bunch of Orlando Wild baseball players walked in, the locals pounced to take selfies, get autographs, try to get any info they can use for betting, or to get them to join their tables. O'Brian and Miller are in the middle of a pool game with an older couple. Logan is at the bar casually trying to ignore two women who have been trying to flirt with him for the past hour. Lucky Rivera is tearing up the dance floor, even though I wouldn't have pegged the Boricua for someone who jams to '80s hair metal. Rose is next to him, exchanging dance partners halfway through every song—there's actually a line of men waiting for their turn.

And then there's Cade.

First, he got caught by a group of elderly men who wanted to talk about ball grips in detail. Then, when Cade managed to excuse himself, he fell in the grip of a small bachelorette party of five very tipsy women. He hasn't made eye contact with me in a *help* type of way, and the women have only been chatty, so there's nothing I can do but sit in my corner at the bar, nursing a glass of lemonade.

My straw makes the gurgling sounds that indicate I'm now trying to suck the bottom of an empty glass. Perfect timing to set it down and take a restroom break. That's what I get for drinking like three glasses while waiting for Cade to be free.

I also wash my face because the place is hot and stuffy from being so packed, and a couple of women from the bachelorette party walk in right then.

"Do you think Jeff would get mad if I cancel the wedding because I want to propose to Cade freaking Starr right now?" the bride asks her friend with a laugh. They both take the sinks adjacent to mine.

The other woman shakes her head. "No, I think Jeff would abandon his bachelor party and come propose to Cade instead."

I nod to myself, but the motions of washing my face camouflage it. Cade's pretty damn lovable so yep.

"Oh my gosh, and did you see his eyes?"

"Did you hear his voice?"

"Did you see his *hands*?"

"Do you think his—"

I rise abruptly, water dripping from my face to my grey T-shirt, and blink at the women through the mirror. The chagrinned looks on their faces tell me that yes, their minds were going in the gutter.

"Ahem." I turn the faucet off and walk around the presumably bridesmaid to get some paper towels.

"Anyway. Stacy, you should go for him," the bride suggests.

Stacy sighs so big she deflates. "I already tried. He said he has someone he's interested in already."

I trip on my literal own two feet.

Obviously, the attention of the two women turns to me. Credit to the bridesmaid because she makes a move to steady me until it's clear I'm not really at risk of body injury here.

"Sorry." I give an awkward laugh. "Maybe I had too much to drink." Of lemonade but whatever.

"No worries, hun. Love your top, by the way."

My T-shirt from Target? Sure. Smiling I say, "Thanks, and congrats on the wedding, Jeff's a lucky guy."

"He really is." The bride's expression grows genuinely content. "But then so am I."

"Aww. One day I want to have what you guys have," Stacy says, finally forgetting about me.

The bride begins a pretty speech about how her friend's special man is surely out there, and this is when I slip out of the restroom.

Until a hand pulls me into a dark threshold right next to it.

My squeak is drowned by Cade's voice. "It's me. Sorry. I just couldn't find another way."

No complaints from me, especially when he's got me pressed up against him. Both of his hands are wrapped around my wrists gently—in fact, I don't even know if he notices how they're lightly caressing my forearms. I splay my hands on his chest and feel the steady beat of his heart underneath.

My eyes are getting used to the weak light and I start to make out the curl of his hair that's fallen on his forehead as he looks down at me. Somehow his eyes stay brilliant even in the dark.

"Hey," he says like a sigh.

"Hey," I return in just the same way. I bite my lip for a

second and release it to add, "I heard that you apparently have someone you're interested in. Is that so?"

"Who said that?" I can't suppress the little shiver that the grave timbre of his voice causes with just those words. He shifts his hands to slide up my arms and behind my shoulders, until they're splayed at my back and pushing me closer.

I open my mouth to respond but that's precisely when the two women walk out of the restroom, chitchatting about something wedding related. Impulsively, I use my hands to cover Cade's mouth while they pass, and I feel his lips stretch into a smile against the palm of my hand.

And here I am, jealous of my own hand.

Once the coast feels clear, I start moving my hands until Cade grabs hold of one again, the one against his mouth, and he presses a deliberate kiss into my palm.

My breath hitches.

"This is what I wanted to talk about." His thighs push against mine and next thing I know, he's walking me backward into a wall. My back flips on a light switch and I blink hard against the harsh white lighting, but at least thanks to that I now know we're in a cleaning storage room.

"Cade," I whisper. "We can't be here. Staff will kick us out of the bar when they find us."

"So you think we'll be here long?" His eyebrows rise and he gives me a hot little smirk.

I splutter. "Well, no—I mean—It's just—"

I freeze when he leans down, but it's not to kiss me. His lips brush the shell of my ear as he whispers, "Relax. I actually got permission from the bar owner to be here." Then he flips the light off again, leans an arm against the wall behind me, and...

Doesn't move.

He doesn't need to know that this is making my mouth water or anything, if that's what he's targeting, and it feels more imperative than ever that I teach him a lesson.

My hands search in the narrow space between us for the waistband of his jeans. I find the belt loops and pull him to me. "Talk, you said?"

"Ngh."

"Those aren't words, Cowboy."

His snort brushes my hair, but just when I think I won the game, he turns his face and softly, tortuously, scrapes his teeth around the upper part of my ear. The violent shudder that leads me to hide against his chest confirms who won.

Chuckling, Cade cinches his arms around me, this time in a hug that feels ever so sweet in comparison. I sigh into his T-shirt and bring my arms around his waist, settling my cheek against his heart and drinking in the scent of aftershave on his clean skin. A day's worth of travel among noisy, stinky men makes this so worth it.

Too soon he starts pulling away, and the areas of my body no longer in contact with his feel cold. As I collapse back against the wall, Cade leans his arm on it again to look down at me.

"So, we need to talk, darlin'."

"So you said," I grumble, annoyed that I'm no longer wrapped around him like velcro.

"About that kiss…" he starts but the silence stretches for too long.

"Don't tell me you regret it," I blurt out.

I catch the silhouette of his head tilting. "Not for a second. I've been trying really hard to not do it again right here and now."

I would definitely not mind that, but… "Then?"

"Did you see the guy sitting two chairs away from you at the bar?"

"Huh?" My nose scrunches up in confusion at the abrupt topic change. "What guy and why does he matter right now?"

"He matters very much." Cade's voice is soft, serious,

increasing my confusion. "He's been checking you out all night, trying to gather his nerve to talk to you."

I shake my head. "In case it's not obvious because it's way too dark in here, I'm going to verbalize that I'm confused as hell."

"Hope, do you know how freaking annoying it feels to see guys salivating over you and not knowing if I should try to protect you—if I even have the right—or if I should tell you to go for it because I'm supposed to be your dating coach, but actually feeling greener than The Hulk on the inside?"

I suck in air. "Jealous?"

"Out of my damn mind," Cade says in a growl, leaning into me again and this time lowering his forehead to mine. His free hand grips my hip. "But—" he says with difficulty. "It doesn't matter what I want—what you want is what matters. So who do you want me to be, Hope?"

My eyes widen. My pulse has been a flutter of butterflies at my throat from the beginning, but now turns positively violent. "What—What do you mean?" Something like the sound of waves crash into my ears, and my chest rises and falls rapidly.

Slowly, his hand shifts until his fingers find my jeans's belt loop. "Do you want me to turn back to being just one more player you sometimes have to ice? Or to keep being your dating coach until you find someone better?"

"Someone better?" I hiss.

"Or..." He swallows so hard that I can hear it over the crashing waves. "Do you want me to change roles from dating coach to dating you?"

"That's unfair," I all but wheeze out with what's left of my voice. "You should also say what you want."

"Oh, I'm sorry. I thought it was obvious," Cade says, laughter laced in his voice. But then he removes his arm from the wall and digs his fingers in my loose hair, arching my neck back as he bends lower. His lips stop a millimeter from mine, I can feel the gentlest brush as he speaks, "I want you, Hope. I don't want to hand you off to some other asshole, even though I'm definitely not good enough either."

"Hmm." The admission imbues me with a boldness I never knew I possessed, and I bring my arms up over his shoulders and around his neck. He stills as I give him a little kiss, just the softest suction of his lips, and say, "So if I choose option two you'll be my wingman with the bar guy?"

His other hand grabs my hip tighter. "Sure." The word comes out through gritted teeth.

Chuckling, I rise on my tip toes to press my lips against his. I mean it to be a brief kiss, something sweet, but I guess I should know better than to challenge a professional athlete.

Next thing, we're up against the wall making out as hard as if our lives depended on it. As if each other's mouths were the oxygen we need to stay alive. For the first time since we arrived to this bar, I'm really thankful for how noisy it is outside because Cade and I aren't being exactly discreet. Between moans and the sounds of lips sucking, it's a wonder we really don't get kicked out of the bar.

Somewhere in there, I remember that I haven't really answered his main question. Gathering all my willpower, I push at his chest with enough strength that he gets the hint. The loud kissy sound as we separate is almost embarrassing, but not more than our harsh breathing.

"To answer your question," I say while panting like a dog, "I don't want to go back to how things were. I can't." I close my mouth and shake my head, trying to clear it. But my lips tingle and my whole body's flared to life. "I can't go back to being near strangers, or to also feeling like She-Hulk because you're getting someone else's attention."

"Wait, wait." My eyes are now used to the lack of lighting and I can see his teeth through his smile. "You also get jealous?"

I shift my weight to the other leg. "Maybe. Is that gonna be a problem?"

"Oh, not at all."

"Good." I lift my chin and look him dead in the eye. "Because you're fired as my dating coach, and hired as my da —Eek!"

The man lifts me up. Straight up cinches his arms under my butt, making me grab onto his shoulders. And he's laughing like he just won the freaking lottery, instead of scoring the most awkward girl in all of the land.

CHAPTER 40
CADE

have a huge, massive problem now.

Every time Hope walks by, I can't help but notice.

She just had to border the pitching practice area for my peripheral vision to pick her up. I catch the ball from Kim and raise my glove to my face, just in case I'm making that silly grin I've been catching on my face in the mirror since I officially graduated from being the world's worst dating coach. Hope's back is to me as she talks with Socci about who knows what. I burn through my timer by pretending to turn the ball to find the best grip, when in truth I'm staring at her thighs.

Whew.

I'm not an eloquent guy but I could write poetry about her thighs. She's in black leggings today, the really sporty kind that are sewn around the thigh rather than just the sides of the legs. And whoa, shit. They're thick with muscle and so strong that I can't keep my mind from imagining things.

"Hey, dipshit."

I startle when I find Logan Kim's face an inch from mine. "Whoa, dude. Do you even brush your teeth?"

"My dental hygiene isn't the issue here." He smacks my

chest with his mitt. "Are you getting paid to throw a damn ball or to stare at your new girlfriend?"

"She's not my girlfriend," I spit out from behind my glove. "Yet."

Kim gives me an incredulous look. "Do I look like that's the point I'm trying to make?"

I grin. "No need to be so jealous that I swept her away from you."

"We both know I actually helped the two of you stop fooling around and get together."

"True. Do you wanna be my best man?"

He blows a raspberry. "You're thinking about marriage already? Are you off your freaking rockers?"

"You're right, it's way too early." I bring my eyebrows together in a frown. "Besides, Lucky would kill me if I make you best man."

"Starr, focus, for goodness's sake."

Hmm, I think I'm starting to learn how to play him back like he does to me, especially seeing how he genuinely grinds his molars in annoyance.

Grunting, he throws an arm around my shoulders and turns me away. "Listen, if you throw fifteen strikes in a row I'll let you go early to get iced or massaged by your beloved."

"Ten."

We look at each other from way too close, but we're in a battle I can't back down from now that he has presented the possibility of Hope putting her hands on my skin ASAP.

"Fourteen."

"Thirteen."

"Twelve, final offer."

I pin my glove between my elbow and ribs to free my right hand to offer it for a shake. Slowly, narrowing his eyes even more like he's full of nothing but distrust for me, he deigns return the gesture.

"Twelve. All cutters," he says, tightening his hand around mine.

Sure, my left is stronger, but c'mon—I work both halves of my body out. I squeeze tight enough to hurt too.

"Has anyone told you that you're an asshole?"

Kim smirks. "Oh, yeah. I tattooed it as my tramp stamp."

I make a face. The only tattoo I think he has on his back is a massive tiger, but I also don't spend any of my time inspecting his behind.

Before he walks away too far, I declare, "One day, Logan Kim, you're going to be so whipped that you also can't focus at practice. Mark my words."

He stops and turns over his shoulder. "You're gonna grow old waiting for that." Then he puts on his cage of a mask and stomps back to his spot.

Unfortunately, Logan Kim bests me. I manage to throw ten strikes in a row and screw up at the eleventh, which is when he decides to include a new clause in our handshake agreement: start over. I'm pretty sure this is pitcher abuse but Socci backs up the catcher, and that's when I realize Kim was two steps ahead of me—again—and had previously got Socci on board with the twelve strikes little test.

By the time I'm done with practice, Hope's already busy working with two of the younger catchers at the same time. It's puzzling how she can't see that the two of them look at her like she descended straight from heaven to grace them with her presence. Then again, she also didn't notice the guy at the bar last night who kept eating her up with his beady eyes.

Like yesterday, though, I can't do shit about it. People can't know we're starting to date, not when this is safer for her. Which means I can't give us away by socking the two young bucks for the way they look at her.

Day one and it's already this hard, man.

"Looking real good out there, Starr." I turn to Otto Berger as he heads toward me with an ice pack in his hands.

Well, this is a downgrade.

I straighten up as I start unbuttoning my uniform shirt. "Thanks, Berger. I appreciate that."

"You've really come a long way from last summer," he says as he stops beside me, using the bench to undo the straps of the ice pack.

"Sure have," I mumble, my eyes straying to Hope again.

This time she's also got her attention on me. And she doesn't look away. Interesting.

I keep my attention pinned on her as I finish unbuttoning my shirt all the way and take it off, dropping it behind me on the bench. I prefer to have full contact with the ice pack because I tend to run really hot. I dig into my pants for the hem of my undershirt and peel it off slowly.

Hope's still watching.

Well, shit. My skin breaks into goosebumps—just from her watching me half undress.

How the heck did I do this in front of her before?

But then Berger puts his hands on my shoulders and I do my very best to not grimace.

"Any pain?" He frowns.

I clear my throat. "Not at all."

I have to behave after that because I really don't need Berger or anyone to know my engine's revving right now. He fits me with the ice pack in a businesslike way and runs a checklist of questions through me, noting answers on an iPad.

When he's done, I lean back against the bench to wait for the ice to do its thing. Practice is still going for the fielders and the coaching staff's attention isn't as intent on Otto resting pitchers anymore. I grab my shirts, make quick eye contact with Hope, and walk over to the tunnel. Hopefully my hint was strong enough.

I take my sweet time sorting through a cooler with drinks in the middle of the clubhouse, and end up taking an allegedly strawberry flavored one. I'm uncapping it when light steps sound behind me.

"What?" Hope asks, breathless.

Slowly, I turn to her. "Hey, darlin'."

"Cowboy." She folds her arms. "Didn't we agree to keep it professional at work?"

"Yes?" I bob my head.

"Then why are you flirting with your eyes?"

"I am?" I bring the bottle to my mouth and she zeroes in on it, making me smile into my drink. After swallowing it down, I say, "Because just so we're clear, you're the one undressing me with your eyes."

"Ugh. I'm not the one who literally undressed in front of you."

"Well, thank goodness for that or I'd have to beat up the whole team." I think about it and shrug. "Starting by myself, actually. I'd be the first one to lose his mind."

"Cade."

I grin at the clear tone of warning behind my name. "Anyway, what are you doing tonight?"

"I—Nothing, I guess. Going home after work."

"How about we try a date instead?" And just to be very clear, I add, "With me, I mean. No PitchCom. No swiping. No pressure. Just good ol' Cade Starr."

Her jaw slackens. For a good moment all she can do is blink.

"No pressure?" Her voice shakes and she takes a step closer to me. "All the pressure, Cade. I really don't want to screw this up with you."

Well, shit. How is that simultaneously softening me up and increasing my body temperature?

"Trust me, there's no way that's happening." I lift my hand

and hold her chin, freeing my thumb to lightly touch the border of her bottom lip. Somehow this makes her lose her balance and she leans into me, her hands on my bare stomach.

"Oh."

My eyebrows rise. "Well, well, well. Aren't you a bit sensitive?"

Sucking in air, she pushes me away until there's plenty of distance between us again, and folds her arms. "At what time?"

"Seven?" A corner of my lips rises.

"I'll give you my address so you can pick me up."

"Yes, ma'am."

She bites the lip I touched, her eyes drifting low to where her hands were a second ago, burning my skin just from their intensity alone. If only she knew that I'm sensitive too, and if she keeps looking at me like that I'm going to get us in a world of trouble right in the middle of the empty clubhouse.

Sensing this, she finally returns her gaze somewhere more PG. "Dress code?"

"Comfortable."

"Very well," she says in an extremely professional way. "See you later, Cowboy."

I salute because it's all I can do to keep my free hand from reaching for her. How the tables turned, huh?

CHAPTER 41
HOPE

"Yas, girl!" Rose snaps her fingers as I walk by my two roomies in the living room. "*This* is when you know it's right."

"You mean because I'm going on a date in leggings and a sweatshirt?" I ask, not even pretending to hide the grin slowly taking over my face. "He did say comfortable after all."

From her arm chair, Audrey glances up from her iPad and says, "Wow, you almost make me want to try dating. Almost."

"Right? Too bad the whole scene is a shitshow." Rose shrugs from her spot in the middle of the couch, her arms thrown over the backrest as she faces me.

"Ya don't say?" I mumble. They know my misadventures better than anyone, so I have no need to elaborate. Instead, I take my phone from the pocket of my leggings and check the screen. Some texts from Kelly await, but no news from a certain cowboy yet.

The three of us jump in our skins as the doorbell rings. My heart rate increases not because of the surprise but because I bet I know who's behind the front door. I make for it.

"Wait!" Rose springs to her feet, fluffy socks making her skid on the hardwood floors as she rushes around the living room toward me. Her hands rest on my shoulders for a moment. "Let big sis handle it."

"Big sis? You're just a year older." I scoff.

"Oh, good idea." Audrey sets aside her device and also comes over to the door, rubbing her hands. That's when I figure whatever they're up to is no bueno.

Rose whips open the door and Cade's head appears over theirs. His eyes set on them, then on me, a question making his eyebrow cock. All I can do is shrug in response.

"Hello, Cowboy," Rose starts with an overly serious voice. "We hear you intend to date our precious little Hope."

"Precious I'll give you, but little?" I fold my arms.

All of them ignore me.

"That's right, ma'am," he responds back in kind.

"And is this with serious intentions or just for funsies?"

"Oh my word." I grab the back of their shirts, trying to pull my roommates away from Cade, but this is when they both decide to become stronger than me. They plant their feet wide and hold their ground.

"And by the way," Audrey says in a deceptively friendly way, "depending on your answer you may or not walk out alive."

"Geez. What's gotten into you, guys?"

Audrey bats my hand away. "We're tired of seeing you suffer because of men. We want you to only be with a good one from now on."

"And don't you dream about lying." Rose points at the much taller guy's face. "Your answer has to be as true tonight as in the undetermined future."

He lifts those killer blue eyes of his to me. "You have good friends, Hope."

"I know, but they're embarrassing me right now." I huff and pretend like heat isn't settling on my face right now.

"To answer your questions," he says, redirecting his focus to the two wannabe murderesses. "Yes, my intentions with Hope are serious. Although I want both of us to have fun too. And I don't know how to be 'a good one' but I'm more than willing to learn for her."

Silence.

A little mewl like squeal ensues, and it can only come from Rose.

Audrey throws her hands in the air and whirls around. "Sorry, Hope. I'm defeated."

Rose collapses against the door frame. "Listen, Starr. Any chance you have a clone hanging around?"

"Sorry, not that I know of." He stuffs his hands in the pockets of his joggers and that's when I realize he has chosen the exact same level of comfortable as me. Black joggers that cinch around his ankles and show off his powerful calves and thighs, a blue sports T-shirt that is going to retain most of my attention because it doesn't really hide the shape of his body, and some sneakers that match both pieces like he actually put some thought to the outfit.

I press my lips tight not to squeal too.

"Bummer." Rose drags her feet back to the living room, declaring, "All yours, Garcia."

"Thank you." I shake my head and quickly step out of the house, closing the door behind me because I'm sure the roomies will snoop. Before Cade can react, I grab his hand and pull him away. "Hurry, before they start taking pics paparazzi style."

He snorts but falls into step easily, and for a second everything's perfect until he shifts his hand, lacing his fingers with mine. His are so big that the way they stretch mine apart feels uncomfortable at first, and I stop to admire the phenomenon with my very eyes.

"What?" Cade asks.

I mutter, "I think this is the first time we hold hands."

"Verdict?"

"Takes some used to. Your hand is huge." I clear my throat when I remember the random women at a bar yesterday were talking about his hands, precisely.

"Hmm." Cade lifts them up for an inspection, twisting my arm slightly as he observes my smaller hand. "How about this, then?" Slowly, almost like he really wants me to feel the friction between his calloused palm and mine, he changes the grip again so that my fingers are free and his hand is wrapped around mine. It strikes me as the couple version of a handshake, still close contact but way less…

Intimate.

Heat rises up my throat. I never would've guessed that just holding hands with a guy could get me going, but here we are.

Taking a deep breath, I stretch my hand open forcing him to loosen his hold, and turn it so I can lace my fingers through his again.

Yep, this is what I want with him. The intimate version. The gives-me-so-many-butterflies-I'm-at-risk-of-barfing version.

"Nah, this is better," I say boldly, lowering our hands again.

Cade's expression is serious, intense, eyelids half mast like when we're kissing. My tongue turns into lead just from this alone. And then he brings my hand up and presses his hot lips on my skin, eyes still fixed on mine.

I deserve an award for keeping upright after that.

Wordlessly, he tugs gently and we keep going. His truck is parked right by our curb and he recovers verbal ability before me. "So I have a suggestion regarding the door conundrum."

"Door conundrum?" I sound sleepy already but not from

boredom. All of this just feels like a beautiful dream I don't want to wake up from.

"For you to open it, or for me to open it, therein lies the conundrum." He turns slightly to lean his hip against the door behind the passenger's, our joined arms extending like a hammock. "How about you open your own door and I wait right outside to make sure you go in safe?"

These damn butterflies in my belly are so annoying. I need them to let me think straight.

"Hmm, I'm not discarding this suggestion but I'm perfectly able to get into a car without banging my head."

"Certainly, but hear me out. What if an alligator pops out behind you as you're climbing into the car? Wouldn't you rather it jump me instead?" He punctuates the question with a cheeky grin that shows all pearly whites.

I give him a deadpanned stare. "What are the odds of that?"

"Hey, this is Florida. Anything can happen."

"Far be it for me to kill your chivalry, so I'll accept your suggestion." I try to free my right hand so I can open the door, but the lovable jerk doesn't let me. I open the door with my left and the wide motion of the opening door finally frees my hand. I grab onto the handles to hoist myself into his Texas size truck, and he's still smiling like a goof as he shuts the door for me.

The truth is that his smell in the truck completely shuts my brain off. I'm trying to figure out how to reproduce his scent into candles when he climbs into the driver's seat.

"So, where are we going?" I ask in an attempt to keep my hormones under control.

After we buckle up, Cade starts the truck and grabs the steering wheel to pull out of the spot. "Don't worry, I know for a fact that you like this place."

"Oh?"

The first five minutes of the drive are anyone's guess until I notice the obvious fact that I can still recognize the streets. We're still in my neighborhood, in an area that the girls and I hang out at all the time, which means that yes, I'll definitely like our destination.

I snort as the truth reveals itself while he's pulling into a parking spot. "Yes, this date is starting really, really well already."

Cade grins at me with so much joy it, strikes me as the very first time I've seen the phenomenon. "After you, ma'am."

Shaking my head, I get out of the truck and meet him halfway at the front. He presents his right hand to me, giving me the option of taking it or not, but now that I know what that feels like, I have no intent to squander my opportunities for skin to skin contact. I slide my fingers between his and we walk into the yogurt ice cream shop together, the same one we met at almost two months ago when I was desperate to get dating advice.

He leads the way weaving through some empty tables and some busy ones, back to the same spot at the bar by the front window. Freeing his hand, he grabs me by the shoulders and gently pushes me to sit. Then his breath nears my face and he whispers in my ear.

"Wait for me right here."

"Okay." I'm embarrassed to admit that it comes out like a squeak.

Gosh, is this what dating's really like? The teasing, the butterflies, the sweet and sexy mingling together? Or had I never really dated until Cade? And I don't just mean about the dates stemming from apps—but also with my ex. We did hold hands and joked with each other, but it never felt like this. Like just one look is enough to melt me down. Like every gesture is intentional and clear.

Like maybe the problem in that relationship was never

whether I was hot or not, but that I had no idea what I needed from my so-called boyfriend, and like he didn't care to give it to me in the first place.

I mean, Dawson never asked if it was all right to open doors for me or not.

Watching Cade head to the counter, I have to tell my heart to take a chill pill. It's way, way too early to be falling in love with the man already.

I stay stoic while releasing a little groan when he retraces his steps back to me, because I recognize the treats in his hands right away. "You're something else," I say when he places a cup, this time small, in front of me. It's a swirl with strawberries, bananas, chocolate syrup, and he didn't even forget the caramel.

He then sets down another small swirl cup only topped by chopped peanuts and takes his seat beside me. "What can I say, I have really good eyes and I use them to pay attention."

"Huh. What else have you paid attention to?" I scoop a strawberry and place it on his cup. It makes his lips curl and my toes do the same.

"For example, I've noticed how you don't freeze in front of me at all, compared to your other dates. Still trying to figure out if that's a good thing or not."

My mouth opens. We talked about that in precisely this same spot. Same chairs. Eating the same frozen treats. I guess that conversation made turns in his brain.

"It's a good thing," I say, expelling air. "A *really* good thing. It means I'm comfortable around you." And honestly until this moment I hadn't stopped to think about how important that is. It was the biggest missing piece in all those online dates, and in my one relationship in the past.

"Hmm?" Cade lets the spoon hang between his lips even as a smile blooms. "Truly an honor."

"That's right."

He places his right hand on the table, palm up, and opens and closes his fingers. "My hand is cold without yours."

"Pfff." I slap my palm against his, but I certainly don't mind.

By the time we climb back into his truck, I already know it's the best date I've ever had, even when he declares that we're only getting started.

CHAPTER 42
CADE

"How the hell are you so good at this?"

I don't allow myself to laugh because it would break my concentration. Instead, I wait for the machine to pitch a baseball at me and let my muscle memory take over. It's funny how as a batter I'm on my tippy toes just the same way I am as a pitcher, but it works. I get enough momentum as I turn, and connect the bat right on the sweet spot to send the ball flying into the tarp, hitting the home run zone.

Dropping the tip of the bat on the floor, I look up at Hope. She's in the lane beside mine, separated by a chainlink fence that she grabs onto with her fingers.

"I may not be a designated batter now, but I did have to bat when I was in school."

"Seems like a waste." She's frowning like she's annoyed. "You're pretty damn good."

"Wow, you truly know the way to a man's heart."

Hope points somewhere low with her lips. "However, you should use your hips more." I refrain from pointing out what those words can do to a man. "You're relying too much on your shoulders and I don't want you getting hurt on my watch."

I touch my hand to the bill of my protective helmet. "Yes, ma'am. How about this?" I get back in positing, swinging the bat at the air and more aware of what my hips are doing than ever in my life.

"Much better."

Yeah, not sure about that.

Fortunately, she rescues me from my own fog by resuming her batting. This place has brand new machines that you can just pause with a button, rather than having to wait for a predetermined number of balls to be pitched in succession and eat up all your coins if you're not ready. Credit to Lucky for suggesting it when I was researching first date ideas.

I wanted to do fun stuff that Hope would appreciate, rather than sit across each other at some table in a swanky restaurant, where nerves could get the best of her again.

Although apparently I didn't need to worry about that. She's comfortable around me.

If I polled the team about that half of them would say that's a bad thing, that it means I'm boring and predictable. The other half—probably consisting mostly of the married guys—would say it's entirely the opposite. That it means she knows I'm not a dirtbag who is going to hurt her.

When she confirmed it's the latter for her, I felt like the luckiest guy alive. Like somehow, in all my many shortcomings, I managed to prove that I'm not one such a dirtbag. And maybe twenty seven years of treading this world alone were worth it if it means they shaped me into a decent enough person to be worthy of Hope Garcia's time.

Goner. That's what I am.

I take a step back and bump my elbow with the button that stops my pitching machine, just so I can go hang out by the chainlink fence to stare as she gets in position for batting.

Listen, I may be a decent guy but the operating word in there is actually *guy*. I'm hard wired to admire how she spreads her legs apart into a firm stance, her butt facing me as she bends her knees loosely. Her sweatshirt has bunched above said butt, framing it perfectly for inspection. My eyes travel lower, down the length of one of her thighs. I collapse into the fence and have to grab onto it so I don't double over.

Shit, she's so freaking hot. I can't deal with myself.

Her hips swing as she connects the bat with the ball, a perfect clang echoing from the impact. I don't care where the ball goes, not when I'm fantasizing about her legs.

"Did you see?" She whirls around, her loose hair fanning around her torso, and bounces a little. "Home run, baby!"

"Come here."

Hope tilts her head. "Why?"

"Just come here."

I can tell she's warring with the desire to rebel just because it's in her nature, but she relents. Pausing her machine, she takes another side step to stand in front of me. "What?"

"So," I start in a casual tone of voice. "Has anyone ever told you just how mind bendingly hot you are?"

"What?" Her whole body springs in surprise.

Somewhere in the distance, other people bat more balls and voices mix with the faint arcade noises from the front of the establishment. All of that fades as I look at her.

"I'm trying really hard to be a gentleman here, Hope. But my eyes keep straying."

"Is that so?" She smiles while her teeth scrape over her bottom lip and, ah, shit. I feel that everywhere. "Well, where do they stray?"

Breathing out roughly, I respond factually, "I'm very, very weak for your thighs."

She bends forward to look down at herself. "What about them?"

"Hmm." I tuck my tongue against my cheek as she straightens up again. "I'm not sure I can answer that honestly with so many families nearby."

Hope gasps. "Oh my gosh, Cade!"

"I'll just say this…" I grin. "They're a work of art that I'm really glad they're not in a museum, because that way I get to touch them."

"Cade." She smacks the fence as if it was me. "You're bananas."

"So, what's your favorite part of me? Surely there's something that makes you, er, bananas."

Narrowing her eyes, she asks, "What do you intend to do with that knowledge?"

"To show off, of course." I shrug.

A corner of her lips lifts into a little smirk. "I appreciate the honesty. However, the issue is that it's not just one part."

I retreat one step to put my hands up. "Okay, don't get me wrong. I don't salivate *just* over your thighs either—they just happen to make me putty. But I assure you the rest of you makes my blood boil too."

Hope throws her head back and laughs from her belly. The gorgeous, gorgeous sound floats me from the ground and maybe I start losing oxygen from the altitude, because I keep running my big mouth.

"I'm very partial to how your butt fits in my hands too, but honestly I almost lose it at the dip in the small of your back. And you know I love your hair too." I demonstrate with my hands. "Next time I kiss you I intend to wrap it around my hand like this."

Her breath hitches.

My face splits into a grin. "And let's not even talk about your lips because it'll get me kicked out of this family friendly place."

"I'm sure you can come up with ways to keep it PG."

I curl my finger and she steps closer. I lean down until we're more level and I can whisper. "I can't stop staring at them and remembering what they taste like. The fact that I have this knowledge now feels like a miracle."

"See? That's pretty safe for work," Hope says slowly, sounding out of air.

"But my favorite part is your eyes." I lean my helmet into the fence, observing precisely those brown eyes deeper than an ocean, just as alluring in the uneven lighting of a batting cage in the nighttime as they are when the sunlight hits them directly, making them transform into spun gold. I don't know how to translate that feeling into words that give them any justice, so all I say is, "I don't want to stop staring at them."

She sighs long and hard, one of her hands rising to curl her fingers around the chainlink fence but right below mine. "Geez, no need for so many compliments."

"On contrary. This is nowhere near enough."

Her eyes shift down, cheeks pink enough that I know she's embarrassed. Clearing her throat, she admits, "I like your butt."

My eyebrows take off. "Huh?"

"It's just—baseball boys's butts are the most perfect butts in sports. This is a hill I'm willing to die on."

I choke back a laugh. "Wait, baseball boys's or my butt?"

"Yours is pretty superior, not gonna lie." Slowly, she lifts an almost shy grin. "I can't wait for your *SPORTY* issue to come out so I can study it in detail."

"Why wait?" I shrug. "You can visually and tactfully inspect it any time."

Her jaw drops. "You're kidding?"

"Am I laughing?" I pause. "At least on the outside, I mean. This is really tickling me on the inside."

"Fine, let's see if you mean it. Come here." She lifts her chin in a blatant challenge I have zero interest in turning down.

I remove my gloves and stuff them in one pocket, then take off my helmet and leave it on the floor before walking out of my cage. Hope watches me intently as I shoulder the door of her cage open, eyes roaming up and down my body in a way that is most definitely not PG.

Finally, I stop one step from her and spread my arms wide. "Frisk me, officer."

She blows a raspberry. "Cade Starr, I can't just grab your butt in public. But points for the willingness."

"How about…" I grab the bill of her helmet and take it off. Some strands of her hair catch on the foam inside the helmet, and I run my fingers through her hair to comb it back down. "How about you just kiss me and casually let your hands travel?"

"Just like that?"

"I may or not intend to do the same. Deal?"

Hope bites her lip until she allows the smile to break free. "Deal. But first…" She rips her gloves off and tosses them where they fall.

Then she grabs my face, forcing me to lower down to her and I'm a willing participant. My arms cinch around her waist and I bring her closer until there's literally only the fabric of our clothes between us.

For a moment she focuses too much on the movement of our mouths, her hands only going as far as my jaw where she can no doubt feel my muscles working. But finally she remembers that this kiss is just an excuse for her to feel me up and she gets with the program. I already have to fight off a groan when her hands are just at my neck. Something about her firm touch, the deliberateness of it, is already making me lose my grip on reality.

Before I lose the last of my presence of mind, I turn us slightly so her back faces the rest of the battling lanes. Behind me is only my empty one, which is the very last one on the corner. And beyond there's only a wall to witness her hands brushing over my shoulders, sneaking down to my chest.

I'm unable to feel so many things at once while in public, and I release her lips so I can process how her hands run down my chest to my stomach. Yesterday, we were in this same position for a second, except my skin was bare. I blame that for how high my pulse rises as she carefully feels every ridge of muscle against the pads of her fingers.

"I have to admit," she whispers against my lips, "I also like this a lot."

"Making a mental note to flash my abs more often," I joke, though we both know by my voice that I'm more turned on than the Olympic torch.

My breath hitches as she reaches the waistband of my joggers, but instead of keeping in that dangerous direction, she circles her hands around my waist to my back, and then they're on my cheeks. The posterior ones.

"Wow," she marvels against my mouth. "It's like marble."

"Yeah, I don't skip leg day."

"I'm proud of you." She gives a little squeeze that turns the rest of my body into marble. "Too much?"

"Not really, but an attendant is giving us a funny look." Unfortunately this is true. I can see the sour look on his face from over Hope's head.

Sighing, she drops her face into my chest. "Just when it was getting good."

I chuckle and place a kiss at the top of her head. "Don't worry, darlin'. My marble behind is going to be there for you any time."

"I'm creating a monster," she says muffled against my chest before raising her head again, and bringing her hands up to my back. "Should we behave for a bit and put a food court table between us for a bit?"

I scrunch up my face. "Ugh, fine."

The attendant's demeanor relaxes the hell down as Hope and I clean up our cages and return the equipment to the shelves. He pretends not to see us as we walk by him back into the building, hand in hand.

We join a line for cheap hot dogs and order enough to almost shut the place down. Each one of them is tiny, though, so Hope and I take seats at a table near the air hockey area, and get to work on our food.

Her phone on the table vibrates and Hope sets down a halfway eaten dog to unzip it and retrieve the device. Something about how her lips twists prompts me to ask, "Everything okay?"

"Yeah…" She drags the word as she sets the phone back down, without responding to either call or text, I don't know.

"That doesn't sound like a firm yes. Is it your dad?"

"No." She picks up her hot dog again. "It's a little blast from the past that I had almost forgotten about these days." Seeing my confusion, she decides to elaborate. "My friend Kelly reminded me that the freaking engagement party is this weekend. She wants to know if I'm going."

"Oh shit." I set down my sweet ice tea. "What are you gonna do?"

"Nothing." She takes a ginormous bite of the hot dog and I look down at my tray. Maybe they're not so small after all, and it's just that I'm big.

Shaking my head, I put my attention back on her. "But wasn't that what we were doing the whole dating coach thing for?"

Her shoulders rise. "I've changed my mind. I was definitely looking for someone to date more out of pettiness than any real desire to find a good person to share my life with. You're way better than I ever dreamed of, Cade. I'm not going to use you for my pride's sake."

I hang tight in the exact same position, bite of hot dog

against my cheek like a squirrel, glass of tea in one hand and new hot dog in my other hand. All that outside calm hides how hard my heart beats in my throat.

Slowly, I set everything down and wipe my hands. I resume chewing until there's no food in my mouth and I can talk like a civilized human.

"I have a story to share," I start, speaking low enough that she leans closer, though the confusion is evident on her face. "I've only ever done the boyfriend gig once and it didn't go well."

Her eyes widen but she doesn't interrupt.

"It was in high school. This girl I had a huge crush on finally gave me the time of the day for all of two weeks."

She shakes her head. "You don't have to…"

But I nod that yes, I have to, and continue, "She said she couldn't date an orphan, it was just too weird because I didn't even have an allowance to take her out on dates. And the very next day she showed up to school as the arm accessory of this asshole who was bullying me."

"Oh, Cade." The sympathy in her face melts almost as fast as it comes. "You just say the name and I'll find her."

"I have no doubt she'd regret meeting you." I clear my throat. "But anyway, my point is that I have plenty of experience with the casual thing, but not the real thing. I've never really been proudly presented as someone's boyfriend."

"Ohh." She leans back, understanding dawning. "So you *want* to do this? Like, genuinely?"

"Hell yeah. I want you to show me off like a freaking trophy. Not to make me feel better than that douchebag ex of yours, but so *you* show him you could replace him at the drop of a hat."

"But—"

Calmly, I take one of the hot dogs from my tray and take it to her mouth. She cooperates by biting into it. "I just don't want to make you uncomfortable," she mumbles while chewing.

"Trust me, there's nothing I want to see more than that dipshit's face when we show up hand in hand."

Her eyebrows rise while she swallows. "So, we're doing this?"

"We're in this together, darlin'." In *this* and anything she ever wants.

CHAPTER 43
HOPE

You know things are turning serious with a guy when the playlists get combined.

To no one's surprise, Cade's contributions are a medley of country from real classics harkening to as far back as seventy years ago, to pop country and the latest. He seems to bob his head a little harder at Beyoncé and honestly, I can't fault the boy's taste.

Meanwhile, I offer an eclectic mix of Latin songs from all decades and almost all Caribbean genres. At some point I'm singing along to a reggaeton song from Chino y Nacho, a duo from my parents' home country, and just listening to my off tune singing makes Cade grin. He can only spare me a few glances while driving through the horrible I-4 afternoon traffic.

The closer we get to the Lake Alfred venue, the less I sing though. We pull into a narrow country road lined by Florida oaks that are covered in hanging moss, shading the road and swaying with the wind, but the idyllic scene tells me we're close. My hands close tight around the little purse in a nude color that I borrowed from Rosalina.

"Nervous?" Cade asks while turning down the volume with the controls in the steering wheel.

I take a deep breath. "I'm not in the business of lying so… yes. Very."

"But why? You're not alone." He flashes those brilliant eyes of his. "We're even matching obnoxiously."

That was an idea from Rose too. Her words were, "I've always wished I had a boyfriend I could match my clothes to. Someone so obnoxiously in love with me that he doesn't mind if I mark my territory in such an obvious way, and the other way around."

A FaceTime call with Cade ensued after that, where we went through our wardrobes—mine included also both of my roommates's closets—until we found the perfect matches.

I check Cade out again. He's in a white linen button shirt that settles around his muscular body easily, not hiding any of his fitness, the top two buttons undone tastefully. At the bottom, he's in a pair of terracotta chinos—Audrey was the one who taught those two words to me—and some frat boy boat shoes that match. His hair is perfectly combed with wax and in fact, I think he even trimmed it for this occasion, and he's freshly shaved and smelling delicious.

Meanwhile, I have nearly the opposite ensemble. Rose had a pair of white jeans she described as obscenely tight on her, but they're decent on me. Still form fitting, but I'm not flashing anyone. And Audrey produced this terracotta color top I'm wearing. It's shoulderless but three-quarter sleeves, very tight—not hiding anything here—and cropped. I never in a million years would've chosen it from a store rack, but it's a special occasion.

The occasion of showing my ex boyfriend and my ex friend that I'm beyond fine. That I'm hot and happy and unafraid to show it.

"It's just…" I bite my lip as Cade turns into a dirt road

with the guidance of the GPS. "I'm still not sure this is the right thing."

"We can turn around any time," he says with an easy shrug.

"Well, no. *I* would get upset if I made you drive an hour and a half back just when we're arriving."

And we are. Up ahead in the horizon we can see a sprawling mansion by the shore of Lake Alfred, the venue for Dawson and Amy's engagement party. If only the sky would grow overcast so we could have an excuse to not hang out outdoors by a gorgeous lake surrounded by greenery and flowers. Alas.

"Then what's the hesitation?"

I shift as far as my seatbelt allows me so I can look at his profile. "I barely got any sleep last night thinking about something."

"Really?" He inspects my face. "You look perfect though, not tired at all."

I press my lips tight. "Trust me, it's the power of makeup. Anyway, I keep worrying about you."

"Me?" Cade blows a raspberry. "Those people won't heckle me any harder than Denver Riders fans will tomorrow."

"Not that. I really don't want you to think I'm just using you and that I don't have any real feelings for you."

Cade slows way down and brakes in the middle of the dirt road. I guess it's fine, since there are no cars behind us, but I turn back to him in confusion. "So what are those very real feelings you have for me, then?"

I clamp my mouth shut. Tingly heat rises up my chest to my face. Wriggling, I sit facing the front again and fold my arms. "I'm not gonna admit shit before you do."

"Hmm." After a moment, he gets the car going again and mumbles, "Fair."

The silence is way too embarrassing so I reach for the

sound system and crank up the volume to how it was before. We drive maybe one more mile up to the house and find a spot to park on the grass. Cade walks around his truck in the time it takes me to get out and finagle the purse strap so that it stays firmly on my shoulder. He offers his hand and I hold onto it for dear life.

"Do you still remember pitches eight and nine?" Cade asks as we walk up to the house.

For a second I actually have no idea what he's talking about, until I remember what feels like a year ago, when I went on my very last disastrous date and Cade fit me with a PitchCom so he and the guys could watch out over me.

A slow grin comes to my face. "Oh yeah, those were the *help me* pitch calls."

Grabbing both of my hands, he turns me to face him entirely. "We're changing them to a single one. Just whisper the words *wild pitch* in my ear and I'm bailing us out mid sentence if I have to."

"Good idea."

"And one more thing." He tilts his head back, my attention diverting to his thick neck for a second. "How much PDA are we doing?"

"Huh?" I blink hard.

"The whole idea with the outfits was to mark territory but nothing's more effective than a little public grabbing or kissing, or both."

I don't have to mull it over too hard, especially at the thrill wrapping around my heart and pumping it harder just from the idea of his hands on me.

"Both," I declare with a boldness I'd never have thought myself capable of. "Anything that doesn't land us in jail goes."

A corner of his lips lifts. "All right, darlin'. Let's go."

Nodding, I pull him to resume the walk toward the string music. We border the massive house following arrow signs decorated in fresh flowers that must've cost un ojo de la cara, as my dad would say.

The backyard is a massive grassy patch right by a private harbor. A couple of tents protect food and drink tables, and a temporary dance floor has been placed on the grass before the tents. A real string quartet plays from a stage by the harbor, and people in pretty clothes mingle all around with their little champagne flutes.

Cade and I are super late because there was no way of excusing ourselves from work together without anyone suspecting anything, which is great because it means we'll be in the presence of these people the least amount of time possible. Unfortunately, it also means that the moment we walk in, every pair of eyes turns to us.

"Show time," whispers Cade.

"Hope!"

I almost melt in relief at the only friendly face. Kelly rushes over, pushing one of our college friends out of the way. Her arms wrap around me with the same familiarity of years of friendship, and I return the favor because she's the one I'm genuinely glad to see.

"Oh my gosh, I'm so happy you came for your sweet, sweet revenge." She pulls away, inspects me with a grin, and turns to Cade. "And you must be the new boyfriend."

Cade drops my hand and for a horrible moment I fear he's going to declare that he's not my boyfriend. But instead, he offers that very hand to her for a shake. "Cade Starr, at your service, ma'am."

"He ma'am-ed me," she says to me while shaking his hand. "So nice to meet you, Cade. I'm Kelly, Hope and I went to college together."

"Aren't you that baseball player?" another familiar voice says and I relax because it's Mitch. He and I may not be the besties, but I guess he's the other friendly face in this vipers's nest.

"That's right." Cade glances at me like he's checking whether Mitch is a hostile or not. I smile a little and it puts him at ease. Freeing his hand from Kelly's grip, he offers it to Mitch. "And you are?"

"Mitch Geller, Kelly's husband." Mitch does one of those tight manly macho handshakes but gives up the alpha act when he asks, "Any chance we could take a selfie at some point? The guys at work won't believe I met you otherwise."

"Uh, sure."

I very openly explain to Cade, "Kelly and Mitch are the only people we can be normal with around here. Everyone else is no longer a friend."

"Gotcha." Cade frowns as if standing on the mound in the middle of a game.

But then he slides his arm around my waist, his hand falling perfectly on the patch of skin between my top and jeans, and he slides his thumb and index finger beneath my top to touch even more skin.

I swallow hard, trying to process how the relatively tame contact is making my entire body flare up.

The thing is, I'm very competitive. I can't really let Cade think I'm the only one who can get affected in this relationship. Leaning against his side, I slide my hand in the back pocket of his chinos, splaying my hand as wide across his butt cheek as the confines of the pocket allow. It might not be noticeable to the trained eye, but I sure feel his body tense.

The heated look he flashes at me makes me unsure of who won this little game. But it doesn't matter when we're both enjoying it, huh?

Kelly's eyes sparkle, having noticed everything. I have no interest in feeling embarrassed though, so I just offer a little shrug to her.

"Anyone want a drink?" Mitch glances at Cade and I, then at his wife. "Babe?"

"The booziest thing possible for me, babe," Kelly responds.

"Same." I grin.

Cade makes an attempt at freeing himself. "I can go with you."

"No need, man." Mitch shakes his head. "You have a very important role to play here as Hope's arm accessory."

Kelly nods. "That's right."

Cade clears his throat to tame a laugh. "Right. Then a sweet iced tea if they have it, please."

"Right on." Mitch takes the less disruptive approach of bordering the dance floor toward the tents at the back.

And that clears my view of the party to land squarely on the lovebirds. Amy with her short hair I know Dawson prefers —he used to nag me to chop all of mine off—and the pastel pink dress that shows enough cleavage and leg to be this side of spicy. She hangs from her fiancé's arm and I'm amused to note that he's matching her with a pastel pink button shirt and light grey slacks. In fact, a glance around confirms that all the decoration is done in these colors. Pink flowers, whites, and touches of silver.

Well, I guess Rose's dreams of matching with a guy aren't farfetched at all. Seems like this is a couple thing I had no idea about while I was with the groom-to-be.

Speaking of, he and his bride-to-be are heading over.

"Here they come," Kelly warns in case I haven't noticed.

Dawson's eyes are fixed on Cade's face. Funny enough, Amy's are too. Like I'm fully invisible to them and they're both just annoyed that someone who is somewhat famous is stealing their thunder.

"Hi," Dawson says, planting himself in front of Cade. "I don't believe we've met before. Do you have an invitation?"

Sighing, I say, "Of course he does. He's my plus one and I sure got an invitation."

Both of them jerk in surprise at my voice, and this is when I realize that the reason they hadn't paid any attention is because they simply didn't recognize me.

The cowboy, sharp eyes that he has, picks up on it right away and ramps the PDA just a notch. We definitely won't get kicked out of the party for it. But him squeezing my side just a bit tighter with his hand is enough to attract notice. I bite my lips not to react at the fact that Cade freaking Starr's hand spans almost from the bottom of my bra to the start of my hip.

"Oh. Um." Amy shifts her eyes from my face to Cade's, back and forth a few times. "Hope, so glad you could drop by. Is this…"

"Her boyfriend, yes." Kelly nods, smiling placidly. "Don't they look absolutely perfect for each other?"

Laying it a bit too thick, Kelly, but okay.

"Boyfriend?" Dawson lifts his eyebrows. "This is a new development. When did you start dating, Hope?" Something about his eyes is too shrewd, like he suspects me of doing exactly what I did. Date around until I found literally anyone I could bring here.

Cade runs his thumb back and forth, warming up my skin and reminding me that I'm not fighting this battle alone.

I fully lean into him, tucking my head against his chest. "Cade and I have known each other for a long, long time, but I guess we finally figured things out, huh?"

"A long time?" Dawson presses.

"What, three years?" Cade wonders aloud, looking down at me in earnest.

I make a sound from my throat. It's true that as of this year, it has been three since I started working for the team. "Exactly."

Dawson's expression tightens and in contrast, Kelly stuffs

her hand against her mouth to stop from laughing. It takes me another moment to connect the dots.

Wait, does Dawson think I might've cheated on him with Cade? Solely because Cade and I met while Dawson and I were still together?

Only someone who has considered something like that, or done it, would make that leap of assumption. Maybe his whole thing with Amy goes back farther than when Dawson broke up with me, and if she was entertaining something with my back-then-boyfriend they can both screw off together to another galaxy. I'll be way too glad if this is the very last time I see them.

"Here you go, everyone." Mitch approaches, hugging different drinks against his chest because he doesn't have enough hands.

As we reach over to help him, Cade and I have no choice but separating for a quick moment. But he doesn't pull away without first squeezing my side in such an intimate way that I transform into tingles personified. My skin breaks into goose-bumps that I can't hide because of the damn shoulderless top, and Amy notices right away.

"Thanks, babe." Kelly gives her husband a peck on his lips and it strikes me that now I can do the same.

I have someone I can show affection to whenever the heck I want.

Cade offers his hand to me with a little smile that I can't help but returning. I slide my fingers between his, deliberately trying to create as much friction between us as possible. He closes his hand around mine tight. It's a much more family friendly form of possession, but I'm sure the same pink that is on Cade's cheeks is on mine.

"Oh, excuse me," he says all of a sudden, handing me his drink to rummage in his left pocket.

That's when I remember we still have an audience. As

Cade check's the caller ID in his phone, I turn to the to-be-newlyweds and say, "Anyway, you two are made for each other and you have our congratulations."

I mean it too, if they're both cheaters then they're with no one better but each other. And now I can recognize that both did me a favor by hurting me. Otherwise I'd still be hanging around them, none the wiser, and I never would've been in need of recruiting Cade to help get me unstuck.

"My apologies, I have to pick up this call," Cade says to the audience with his usual politeness before leaning to me. "Come with?"

"Always."

I don't even pay the others any heed as Cade and I retreat as a unit, heading together toward the shore of the lake, as far from the quartet as we can. I feel laser beams trained on my back a while longer, until we stop under an oak.

"Hey, Lou," Cade greets to the phone and retrieves his drink from me. I'm glad, because my hand was starting to get cold. "Uh huh." He nods even though his agent can't see him, his eyes trained on my hand as I dry it against my jeans.

Then Cade straightens. "For real?"

I widen my eyes and mouth a *what?*

Whatever it is, it's good news going by the smile spreading on Cade's face. "Thanks, man. This is great. Yeah, you deserve a raise." He snorts. "'Kay, I gotta go tell the news to my girlfriend."

A pause in which my jaw drops.

Cade winks at me, making me wish I could touch the cold glass of his drink against my face. I down my champagne in one swig instead.

Finally, he clicks off the call and pockets his phone again. "What did he—" The rest of my question dies off as Cade takes my champagne glass and sets it on the dirt between some tree roots along with his glass.

"I have great news." He grins and spreads his arms wide. "The temporary injunction against my stalker is approved, if she doesn't contest it in fifteen days it turns permanent and I'm officially free of the weird fan."

Gasping, I drop the silly purse where it falls and jump in his arms, crashing into his chest. "Aleluya!" I say in Spanish, wrapping my arms around his neck. "This is the best freaking news ever."

"Right?" He curls into me, his face falling on my bare shoulder and he presses kisses against my skin. Wait, the kisses climb up my neck. His hand shifts to hold the back of my head as he arcs me back, his lips softly tracing my jaw until they find my lips.

But he doesn't kiss me. His lips just hover over mine.

"Thank you, Hope."

My eyes flutter open. "What for?"

"Caring about me as much as I care about you." His smile touches my lips. "Now, shall we give them a show?"

"Give who a show? We're all alone here," I tease.

"Oh yeah?"

At long last, his lips crash on mine and I groan in victory. Who needs revenge when something much better, something as pure as this feeling between Cade and I comes along?

We hang out with Kelly and Mitch for one hour and some change, enough to watch the sunset over Lake Alfred together while we make plans for this year's Friendsgiving. The four of us decide to leave together, and Kelly's tipsy enough that she proclaims to be Team Cape—Cade and Hope—*loudly* on the way out.

"At least Friendsgiving won't absolutely suck thanks to Kelly and Mitch, huh?" Cade says as he drives us back through the dirt road.

I snort. "Oh yeah, they'll make it worth it. I also can't wait to meet their little one. It's a shame I missed the birth."

"You have plenty of time to be an auntie."

"Who would've thought?" I say in a light tone, watching him from the corner of my eye. "That this year I'd earn two brand new titles. Auntie and girlfriend."

Unlike how any other guy could possibly react, Cade smiles.

"Is that okay?" he asks.

"Are you sure?" I ask pointedly. "We've only had like two dates and some minimal PDA."

He shoots narrow eyes at me for a short stretch of the road. "Challenge accepted, then." He stretches his right arm toward me and I watch as if in slow motion, only lit by the dim lights from the dashboard, as his big hand falls over my left thigh.

But that's not all, he slides it slowly to my inner thigh, pressing firmer until his fingers are wedged between my thigh and the seat, his thumb pressing into my muscle.

"Is that boyfriendy enough?"

Oh, yes. Especially how it's making me lose my mind.

I squeeze my thighs together and trap his hand. "Girlfriendy enough?"

Groaning, Cade shakes his head and focuses on the road more intently. "Woman, do you want me to crash this truck?"

I laugh. "Well, you started it."

Slowly, he releases his breath. Some old country singer crones in the background and I watch as Cade relaxes against his seat again, but keeps his right hand exactly where it is.

"There's something you have to know in case it's not clear enough," Cade whispers. "Do you remember that viral video your roommate put on social media? When I said that my ideal type is a woman who keeps it real?"

"Oh yeah." I bite my lip, my pulse spiking in anticipation.

"It was you." His words seem to echo in my head, but then he's speaking again. "At that moment, when Mena was recording me, you ran across the field behind her and caught my attention, and those words blurted out of my mouth. I might've been crushing on you before I even knew it."

"For… for real?"

"Yeah." His hand squeezes my thigh a little more. "I also distinctly remember checking out your thighs while you ran. Sorry."

"No apologies necessary." I chuckle. "I'm just glad I never skip leg day."

"But that's not the reason why I'm wild over you," Cade continues saying, effectively shutting me up. "You give it to me straight, the good and the bad. And when you show that you care, I have no reason to doubt it's a lie. That's all I've ever wanted." He glances at me, his expression serious. "You're all I've ever wanted, Hope."

My breath hitches. "C—Cade…" Heat pricks behind my eyes but rather than crying, I pluck his hand between my thighs and lift it toward my lips, dropping a little kiss on his palm. "You're more than I ever wanted," I whisper, truthfully.

Pulling at my hand, he also brings it toward him for a little peck. "So, boyfriend and girlfriend?"

"Sounds perfect."

And I mean it, I wish this moment would last forever.

But of course it doesn't.

CHAPTER 44
CADE

"Starr, come here."

I lower the water bottle I'm drinking from and swallow. First check: Beau's face is normal, therefore I must not have done something wrong. Second check: everybody in this damn dugout is watching, so they're probably wondering what I did wrong, which means literally no one could've given me a warning.

"Yes, sir." I set the water bottle down on the bench. There are enough people between the barrier and the bench that walking through is a struggle. I twist this way and that, and might not be super deliberate in avoiding my girlfriend who stands by the bench.

"Sorry, sorry," I mumble, lowering my face to give her a lightning quick wink that means I am not sorry at all. Kudos to her for remaining impassive.

Finally, I stand before the team manager and he says, "I'm subbing you out after this inning. Do you know what that means?"

My eyebrows rise. I may not be the brightest tool in the

shed but I catch the hint right away—it's actually what I was thinking about before he called me over.

"This is the team's last chance to get Miguel Machado out?"

"That's right." He nods while chewing mint bubblegum. "If you succeed in keeping Machado to no runs this inning, the pressure on Williams is going to get to him and cause a mistake or two."

Which would mean either *he* gets subbed out in defeat right away, or he hangs on for the rest of the game and gives us more opportunities to score on him. We're currently up by a single run in a game that has felt more like a season game against the Denver Riders, than the last game of Spring Training that it actually is.

What Beau is asking of me is huge, though. I have no idea if I can do it, but I sure as hell want to try.

"Key words *if you succeed*," Kim says from somewhere behind me, making me roll my eyes.

"Cade's got this," Lucky argues. "You can't tell me he doesn't deserve pizza with the way he's playing today."

Straightening up, I whirl around and point at Kim's annoying face. "If I strike Machado out you buy me pizza for the rest of the year."

"One month," he shoots back.

"You guys are kidding, right?" Larry Socci, the main pitching coach, asks with a frown. "Starr shouldn't eat that many carbs as the season's about to begin. He's our starter pitcher."

It's funny how somehow life gives you exactly what you wanted but with such little fanfare that it's hard to celebrate it. I've dreamed of the starter pitcher position my entire life, and this is how I get it? Because of pizza?

I tilt my head slightly to make eye contact with Hope. Her

barely contained grin confirms I did just hear what I thought I heard.

Clearing my throat, I ask, "One week?"

"Deal." Kim nods.

But Socci shakes his head. "Only tonight."

"Fine." I sigh and all Kim does is shrug.

The umpire calls for the last out of the inning, so it's time to switch. I wish I could get a kiss good luck from Hope—our pizza dinner is at risk here—but I can't do that with all these sharp eyes around.

Grabbing my glove from the cubbies, I nod at Beau before stepping back out. O'Brian returns from his at bat and he gives me a fist bump as we pass. Kim catches up to me and walks in eerie silence.

I break it. "What's your deal? Aren't you gonna tell me something that will piss me off so I get to the mound all fired up?"

"You don't need it this time." He bumps his glove against my chest and veers left where I have to go right.

Only being a professional baseball player with six years in my belt allows me to keep a straight face, when all I really want to do is gape. Who the hell is this guy and what did he do with the real Logan Kim?

Whatever. I head over to a gross, messy mound. Williams is progressively leaving it more uneven with every inning. I don't know if it's because he's getting tired, or just actively trying to get in my head.

While I even it out with my foot, I lift my eyes to the Riders' dugout and spot him right away, the former starter pitcher of the Orlando Wild. His attention is trained solely on me and I have no doubt that in this whole stadium filled mostly with Rider's fans, Ben Williams is still the person most interested in me screwing up. His sense of superiority is riding on the line.

Joke's on him, though. I don't think he ever cared to know me enough to understand that I thrive under pressure. And I don't know any other definition of it but this moment.

The fans go absolutely feral as Miguel Machado steps up to the plate. You'd think he's Babe Ruth come back to life or something.

He's not as big a guy as my own catcher is, for example, but Machado is still a wall of muscle capable of batting the ball out of the stadium with the wooden bats he prefers. I don't know a single pitcher who isn't terrified of him, and there are actually at least two who have developed the Unmentionable Illness, the one that finishes professional baseball players from time immemorial and starts with the letter Y.

Am I scared of him?

Sure. The same way I'm scared of getting into a traffic accident in this damn city packed with terrible drivers. I still get in my car everyday and drive, though. This is no different.

Especially when I have Logan Kim in *my* arsenal.

He signs for a fastball close to Machado's chest, which is basically a declaration of war against the top slugger of the league.

I'm in.

I nod and raise my glove, twisting the ball to grip it in a basic four seam. Sometimes you don't even have to be fancy. And sure, Machado could bat it, but as close to his chest as I'm gonna throw it this will be a hit at most.

For the pizza, I think to myself and wind up.

The ball flies out of my hand in such a satisfying way, I'm already closing my fist in victory before I land. Kim's glove makes the loudest thud as the ball connects with it, and Machado doesn't move a millimeter.

"Ball!"

I press my lips tighter. That should've been a strike, but whatever.

I check the bench. Beau touches his nose and then his chin, the sign for *calm your man boobs, son.* His words, not mine. I nod at him, my man boobs are very calm. The calmest they've ever been.

Kim throws the ball back at me and gives me a look I can't interpret, especially because it's not followed by any man-boob-calming signs. He crouches back down and calls for another fastball, this time by Machado's knees.

It should be an easy strike and I throw to the precise spot his glove waits at. But… "Ball!"

What the—Is this umpire drunk?

Now both Beau and Socci touch their noses and their chins. I do the same, telling *them* to stop freaking out.

There's no damn way I'm walking Machado. He's going on three outs no matter what.

"Do it for the pizza!" Lucky screams behind me, and more voices rise from the in- and outfield to remind me that pizza is at stake.

That actually more than pizza is. That our revenge on Ben Williams is in my hands—or well, in Kim's until he throws the ball back. That the public's attention depends on this at bat. That this game will set the tone of our season much more than the opening game will.

And that it's all on me.

I raise my glove so I can hide the savage grin on my face. Kim lifts his mask and narrows his eyes at me like he knows exactly what's going through my unhinged head. He shakes his and finally tosses the ball back to me.

In a fraction of second, I drop my expression back to blank and catch the ball. Kim crouches down and signals for a run off the mill curve at level with Machado's waist, close enough to him that it will still be annoying. I like the idea. I still wait until the pitching count almost runs out to throw it.

This time Machado reacts. I grow tunnel vision as his bat

swings. My leading foot lands. The ball dips inward. He whiffs it.

"Strike!"

"That's what I'm talking about," I mutter to myself when I catch the ball back from Kim. And because I enjoy being a little shit, I make direct eye contact with Williams as I raise one finger so the fielders know we have one strike.

His molars grind, and that makes me feel so warm and fuzzy.

The next one is another ball that should've been a strike if the umpire hadn't partied too hard last night. If I throw one more ball, I'm going to walk Machado. And if one of the next batters gets him home, I'm not getting pizza on Kim's dime tonight.

Speaking of him, he makes the sign for me to throw another curve at the lower corner by Machado's knees. That's a risky spot. The umpire hasn't liked any of the pitches we've thrown too close to Machado, but he's choking up on the bat like he expects one of the fastballs that the umpire called as balls.

My heart rate is high, like it would be after pitching six full innings and starting a seventh. But it's not exceptionally high like it would be if I was truly afraid of the batter, or if I was gassed.

I'm gonna trust Kim's call and give it my all.

Nodding, I wind up, my body acting like a whip that draws force from motion. The ball slides off my fingers and follows the right path.

Machado connects with it.

As I land, I turn to watch the trajectory and my eyebrows rise. It goes up into the blue sky of the early afternoon. Fans rise from their seats to catch it—but they're all in the foul post section.

"Foul!"

"Wow," I mutter, watching Kim under a new light. That asshole orchestrated a strike via a foul. He knew Machado would bat it to that exact position the second he choked up on the bat and played him like a fiddle.

This is why Williams made the wrong call by moving to the Riders. No matter how many more millions they pay him, he just doesn't shine without a catcher that polishes him. A catcher that is now going to buy *me* pizza.

I raise my index and pinky fingers for the fielders. Two outs, baby.

Also three strikes so… full count, I guess. Full pressure.

My blood boils in excitement. This is the moment I've been preparing for my whole freaking life. Since I started playing in the street in front of the orphanage with the other kids. Since I was officially allowed to join the pee wees because they played in a ballpark literally a block from the orphanage. Since my middle school coach started teaching me different ball grips. Since my high school coach told me that I had what it took to go all the way. Since I rubbed two neurons together and figured Williams' departure was my opportunity.

And of course, this is when Kim signals for the cutter. Straight to the center.

I agree that we should go for broke. We're not a battery of cowards.

I turn my face to the Orlando Wild dugout and fully ignore the manager. My eyes fall on Hope's face as it pokes from over the barrier. She nods at me, also telling me to challenge the batter.

What else can I do but obey my woman, huh?

Facing Kim again, I nod and this time I don't wait out the pitching count. That's not the mind game we're playing on Machado here. He's in for a lil treat.

I've never compared my wind ups in much detail but I have the feeling like this is the best one in my life. When the ball releases from my hand, I already know it's going to follow the perfect course, even considering the warm wind that blows against it. Machado swings, twisting his bat low like he knows this is a curve of some type. My lips start stretching. His bat rotates. The ball keeps spinning. The bat moves in perfect timing.

And then the ball drops sharply.

The thud echoes in the quiet. My feet land, left hand fisting. I grit my teeth but the word still escapes.

"*Yeehaw!*"

The umpire calls, "Strike, batter out!"

My infielders yell. "Yeah!"

The dugouts shout. Complaints from one side. Cheers from the other.

And the stands are quiet.

Machado stops to give me a look, tilting his head like he's figured something out about me for the first time. I don't know if about my cutter or if he's just realized I'm not the worst pitcher in the league, and I don't care.

"I'm getting pizza!" I shout.

Kim stands up and lifts his mask. "Yeah, okay. Focus on getting the next batters out too, you piece of work."

His PG rated choice of words for the umpire's sake makes me grin.

It's not like getting the next batters out is that much easier. Each one requires a series of chess moves I'm really thankful that I don't have to make all by myself. But we make it, and I'm floating on air as we return to the dugout.

My teammates jostle me around, congratulating me on the best inning of my life. I'm drenched in sweat and achy, but none of that matters as Beau nods at me. "Good job. Go get iced."

I'll frame those words and hang them in my living room.

For now, I respond with, "Yes, sir," and duck into the tunnel, enjoying the booing and jeers from Riders' fans behind me.

I'm still vibrating with energy as I take off my shirt and toss it on a chair. While ripping off my soaked through undershirt, I start calculating how much the bill will be at my fave Italian restaurant after Hope and I are done later tonight. We're going to bankrupt Kim and I can't wait.

"They sent me to ice you."

I lower my arms, the undershirt still caught in them. A grin takes over my face. "Well, isn't this my lucky day."

Hope folds her arms but is smiling. "Stop thinking whatever it is you're thinking. I'm here on a professional capacity only."

Gasping in mock outrage, I finish ripping out my undershirt and dropping it wherever. "Excuse me, I was going over the menu at the pizza place in my head. Come here, darlin'."

"Nope. I have to go get your ice pack from storage." She pivots away from me and I follow. Hope gives me a glance over her shoulder, probably about to give me another warning, but then her attention drifts lower down my body, and she doesn't say anything further as I follow her into the storage room.

Inside, she whirls toward me. "Okay, I can't help myself."

"Great, neither can I."

We meet exactly in the middle, our mouths hungry for each other. Her hands grip my wet hair, pulling me lower for a deeper kiss I'm only too glad to deliver. I eat her mouth like it's ice cream, my hands roaming down her sides, her hips, until I find her incredible thighs.

Disconnecting the kiss, I bend lower to pick her up. Hope cinches her arms around my neck and I walk a few steps to sit her on the table.

"That was amazing," she breathes out against my mouth.

"What? Lifting you up?"

"That too but I actually meant your cutter."

"Oh so you like me more for what my body does on the field than what it does for you?"

"I cannot believe those words just came out of your mouth." She blows a raspberry. "Of course I like your body for both. Please."

"Good. Then I guess I can do this." I look down and grab her knees, pulling them apart with no resistance. Like she's fully on board with this. Smiling, I look back up into her molten eyes. "And this?" Slowly, I slide my hands to her outer thighs, pressing tight so she knows I mean it, until I get to her hips.

"Hmm." She bites her lip. "Yes, that's all okay."

"How about this?" Grabbing her behind, I push her to the edge of the table so she's pressed against me. My lips hover over hers as I ask, "That okay?"

"More than okay," she responds in a raspy voice that makes me shudder. Her hands rise up my arms, kneading as she reaches my shoulders and wraps her legs around my waist. "I guess I could massage you first, right?"

"Yes, please."

I kiss her again and she keeps kneading my shoulders even as our tongues brush, and it's almost too much. Almost too perfect. Like maybe I forgot that life doesn't quite like me this much.

Because that's when someone clears their throat behind us.

Gasping, Hope and I pull away. Instinct kicks in and I bring her face against my chest, trying to hide her. But then I remember that many people know she was sent to ice me.

Swallowing hard, I turn to find Otto Berger behind me. He takes one look at the legs wrapped around me, puts two and two, and says, "I was coming for some Icy Hot but wasn't expecting to find this hot little scene instead. You do know I'll have to report it, right?"

The higher the harder the fall and all that, because I come crashing back down to earth violently right there and then.

CHAPTER 45
HOPE

manage to find the willpower to extricate myself from Cade, but there's no hiding the tremors racking my body. Or the way my chin trembles.

This is my worst nightmare come to life and I wish I could grab Cade's hand and run away with him to a Caribbean island, never to be seen again.

But I can't do that. Running would be a tacit admission of wrongdoing. And yeah, maybe we shouldn't have been making out like teen hornballs at work, but how is this a crime?

Pressing my hands against the scalding hot skin of Cade's chest, I offer a nod to him to let me go. His hands slide off me and he steps away, allowing me to hop from the table and face the intruder.

"Go ahead," I say, folding my arms. "Report us. I guess it was time HR and everyone knew we were dating, right, Cade?"

Cade recovers from the shock quickly. A shake of his head makes a smirk fall in place instead and he reaches for my hand. "My thoughts exactly."

Otto sputters for a bit before pointing at both of us. "This is not gonna go well for either of you. Especially you, Garcia."

"Are you threatening her? Because I could report you for *that*." Cade's voice turns low, dangerous. Even chock full of cortisol like I am, it still gives me butterflies. And sensing my eyes on him, Cade holds my hand a little tighter.

"What? No, I—This is up to Steve." Otto points at the door. "I'm going to talk with him right now, you two stay put and don't—don't get frisky again."

"He's a real peach," mutters Cade, glaring as my mean coworker walks out of the storage room.

And that's when I collapse back on the table behind me, pulling my hand free from his grasp so I can cover my face. Muffled, I say, "I am so screwed. I'm gonna get fired and I'm never gonna be able to pay off my student loans."

"Hey, Hope. That's not gonna happen." His hands wrap around my wrists, gently freeing my face. Something in it makes his breath hitch. "I'm so sorry to have caused this." One of his hands shakes slightly as it rises to my face. When his thumb swipes softly at my cheek is when I realize I'm crying.

"I'm sorry too," I whisper. "You just had the most amazing game and I just ruined it."

"You didn't. Whatshisface did." Cade tilts his head. "Then again, who knows what would've happened if he didn't interrupt when he did."

I give a weak smile. "You're right, I guess it could've been worse."

"Listen." He lifts my chin so I'm forced to meet his intent eyes. The blue in them is as comforting as it spikes my pulse. "I'm not gonna let them hurt you or your job in any way, do you understand?"

"But—"

"No buts." Leaning forward, Cade places a soft kiss on my

forehead, his lips lingering on my skin for a second too long until he pulls away. "I'll figure something out."

I sigh. I almost wish I could somehow undo the past ten minutes and yet, I don't. At some point, the team was going to find out that Cade and I are together, and I never intended to date him in secret for the whole season or more. Maybe this isn't the absolute worst that could've happened.

"C'mon," I say without much energy, grabbing his forearms to guide him backward. Standing on my own two feet again, I say, "Let's get you iced for real this time."

*

The whole thing results in a suspension. For me.

And without pay.

I'm not at all saying that Cade should've been suspended too, but that a suspension is a completely disproportionate reaction to this. But I don't know what Otto Bergman said in my boss's ear, because Steve found me after I was even done icing Cade, and Cade was back out in the dugout, and sent me home suspended until further notice.

When I tried to defend myself, Steve spoke over me. "I will kick off an HR investigation and if you're found to not have acted wrongfully, you'll be reinstated with backpay. But right now I can't hear any details from you before the investigation, okay?"

Not okay, but humiliation clamped a hand around my throat and choked me up. I basically gathered my stuff and ran off to my car in tears.

But the drive home has started to help me regain my senses.

Why the hell are they treating me like I'm on par with a stalker?

I park all crooked in the driveway but I don't really care.

Rushing to the house, I only let renewed tears fall when I'm confined by the familiar four walls. I toe off my sneakers angrily and stomp to my bedroom like someone's chasing me.

Shutting the door, I find myself reflected in the full body mirror behind it. One look at the team logo on my chest and I get angry all over again. Grunting like a cavewoman, I rip the shirt off me, ball it up and violently throw it on the floor.

That felt nice. I do the same with the annoying white pants I have to wear for most games. Last but not least, I pull the hair tie off and free my hair to be as wild and as in the way as it damn well pleases. In fact, I even mess it all up with my hands to drive the point home.

I've been doing the same thing at work that I did during my unfortunate relationship with my ex.

I've been confining myself into a little box, just making myself smaller and smaller until I fit in with the rest. When in truth, I was never going to fit in. I was always going to be a girl in a boys club, no matter how much I tried to act like the boys. And now, because I'm different, because I dared to step out of my little box, they're gonna can me. Because I have no doubt that's how the so-called investigation is gonna go. Their own biases will be judge, jury, and executioner. Especially if Otto freaking Berger is the only testimony they'll care to listen to.

Yanking open my closet, I grab the nearest T-shirt from the shelf but it turns out to be a team one, and I toss it behind me. The next one is from my college so I put it on. And I don't know if it sets me back to a time when I was smart and wanted to eat the whole world, but a lightbulb goes off in my head.

What does my damn employee contract say?

After rummaging in my closet for a bit, I locate the shoebox where I stored it in and take it to the living room, where I sit for the next hour reading every minutia.

And find exactly zero clauses expressly forbidding me from dating a colleague. Literally the only such mention is to say that *relationships outside of the professional realm between leaders and subordinates are frowned upon.* And I'm not Cade's boss nor is he my boss, so what gives?

I'm drafting a text message about this to the cowboy when the front door bursts open.

"Thank goodness you're here!" Rosalina says as greeting, barging into the living room.

Audrey shuts the door behind her. "We heard what happened. Are you okay? Is there anything we can do?"

"Is there anyone we can kill?"

I snort. "No need for that, but I may have just found the tools I need to defend myself right here, in my contract." I smack the piece of paper in my hand. "Gather around kids, we're going to brainstorm how to bring down the pearl-clutching men of the Orlando Wild organization."

CHAPTER 46
CADE

I return a saluting emoji and pocket my phone.

"You really want to do all this for a woman?" Lou asks beside me, his hands above the table in a manner I can only describe as businesslike.

"All this and more." I lean back on my chair and fold my arms like Hope does. "I'd do anything for her."

He hums while deep in thought with who knows what. Probably doing the math about when he can drop me as a client because I've clearly gone off the deep end.

Unbothered by that, I check my watch. I have to start practice in forty minutes so I guess this will be quick. The problem is that the big wigs have kept us waiting for twenty minutes already, further increasing my desire to sock each one of them the second they walk in the door.

Speaking of. The door finally opens and in comes the jury panel. It consists of Rob Beau, team manager and surprising choice for something not related to the team's performance; Steve Franklin, Hope's boss; Michael Watson, head of HR; and none other than Charlie Cox, the team owner. I'm not clear on whether this is a good or bad ensemble.

What I do know for sure is that I'm freaking fuming. Lou rises to his feet to shake hands and I cannot bring myself to do the same.

"We all know why we're here so let's get started," Watson begins, lacing his fingers in front of his face. "Starr, it has come to our attention that a female staff member has engaged in a non professional relationship with you. Is that correct?"

"Her name is Hope Garcia, not female staff member, and yes, she's my girlfriend," I respond through a smile of gritted teeth.

He scribbles some notes on an old school notepad with yellow paper sheets, and is smart enough to angle it away from my eyes. "You can relax, Starr. This isn't a trial on your character."

"Why not?" I lean forward, elbows on the table, and look at each one of them in turn. "Hope and I are two consenting adults who happened to fall in love. Why is this a trial on *her* character but not on mine? It would probably be a bad idea for this organization to engage in double standards, right?"

Cox takes a big, deep breath and releases it slowly. He slouches back in his chair and runs a hand down his tie to smoothen it. "I figured something like this would happen the moment I allowed hiring a woman into the staff. But it was good for publicity, and now we can't let it turn into bad publicity. So how do we prevent that, gentlemen?"

Watson ducks his face but says, "Well, in my opinion the first step to that is ensuring player safety so—"

"Man, I can assure you. Hope is the best thing that's ever happened in my life," I say in earnest, scooting even closer to the table in hopes that, by seeing my face and my eyes from closer, they'll find the truth behind my words. "Better than baseball or my paycheck. Did you all forget how she was the only person who even had the balls to pry those stalkers off me?

"Steve." I turn to the head of the trainers. "Do you even know how hard she works? That she does all the menial tasks that you and your other guys refuse to do because you think it's beneath y'all?

"And Beau." I face our manager. "Did you know Hope knows absolutely everything about every player? Down to what they're allergic to, to exactly which muscle group is affecting their play or quality of life?

"Like, I'm sorry." I shake my head. "She's not just the best thing that's happened to me, the woman I eventually want to start a family with, or someone I'd go to war for even in front of four powerful men biased against her. She's the best damn employee in the wider medical team and deserves a freaking raise, not to get fired because she dares to be happy with me."

In the ensuing silence after my rant, where I breathe harder than after striking out Machado in the seventh inning, Lou clears his throat to speak very clearly.

"May I also remind you that nowhere in Cade's or Hope's contract is it stated that they're not allowed to date a colleague?" He points at Steve. "She only can't date you and thank goodness, because *that* would be a power dynamic that would really interest the press."

Steve's face reddens but he says absolutely nothing.

"Three," Beau says out of the blue, resting his hands on his belly. As we all turn to him in confusion, he adds, "Three men in power biased against her. Not me. I see everything she does and have no intention of losing her to another organization."

My mouth opens.

"I don't particularly care about her," Cox says with his whole chest. "I just want to make sure we spin this favorably for our image. If we decide to fire her, we need a NDA strong enough to keep her quiet. And if we decide to keep her, we have to spin this positively."

My hands curl and I open my mouth to spit out some fire at this asshole, when Steve finally interjects.

"We're not firing her." We all zero in on him but his attention sets on me. "I also refreshed my mind by rereading her contract, and nothing in there would construe this as a breach. But we do have guidelines about appropriate conduct and there is a clause about decorum."

"Decorum?" I deadpan, as if we weren't talking about an environment where players are regularly naked.

"My suggestion would be…" He has the nerve to drag this out until I glare hard enough. "That we establish some clear, professional boundaries for the two of you. For example, I may permanently assign another trainer to you to prevent any bias that may cloud her judgement of your performance. And we definitely can't walk into another scene like yesterday's."

"Oh." I lean back, pretending like my heart isn't thumping like a drum. "That's reasonable."

"But that would be uncomfortable for the rest of the team," Watson says with a frown. "Which is distracting and potentially harmful to *their* performance."

"I can assure you the team doesn't care, and I have solid proof of this," I say, and this is when I search for my phone and bring it up.

Swiping the screen, I tap a few times until I find the video our social media manager, one Rosalina Mena, posted just a few minutes ago. The staggering numbers it has already amassed make me smirk. I place the phone on the table, screen up, and slide it over to them.

"Just watch that." I tip my chin at the device.

Cox is the one who picks it up and the others huddle around him.

My own voice sounds tinny as the video plays. "*A lot of you may remember a video from a couple of months ago where I talked about my ideal woman. Well, I finally found her and I want to ask my team-mates what they think about it.*"

It cuts to me asking in the background, "*What would you say if you found out I'm dating someone from the staff?*"

And O'Brian responds with, "*Oh, good for you. You're lucky to have her.*"

Brown. "*Lucky dog, you get to see each other every day.*"

Thomason. "*For real? Who? Spill the tea.*"

Lucky. "*You guys are so cute it gives me cavities.*"

Miller. "*What? Man, I kinda had a crush on her.*"

Kim. "*Finally. Took you long enough.*"

The video goes on with a few more players, none of whom seem to care one whit. Maybe except for the guys who are now coming out of the woodwork to say they were into Hope all along. Too bad for them.

"These are really good numbers," is what Cox says as he looks at the screen. He taps on it and moves it away from his face, eyes shifting side to side as he reads. "The comments are overwhelmingly positive, too."

"Isn't that all you were concerned about?" Beau asks with a semblance of sarcasm.

"As long as the team doesn't suffer for this, I don't care." Cox sets my phone down and without further ado, he pushes away from the table and stands up. "And Starr?"

"Yes, sir?"

"Just make sure this also doesn't negatively affect your

performance. Or then I might put a new clause in your next contract."

I shrug because I've only pitched better and better since the moment my Hope-era started. "Sure."

Watson splutters but no one's paying attention, Steve and Beau are also getting up.

"I will call her and discuss what was agreed," Steve says with a nod to me and one to Lou.

Then Beau points at me. "See you at practice and bring your A game. You also don't want to get in trouble with me."

I guess Watson must not want to be left alone with my manager and I, because he scrambles out of the room right behind them. The door shuts and I collapse on my chair.

"Happy now?" Lou asks with a grunt.

"As can be." I sound drunk as the adrenaline starts draining out of me. I roll my head to face him. "You didn't have to come in person to deliver one line, you know? There's something called a teleconference now, I don't know if you've heard about it."

"Don't get cheeky with me, boy." He also gets up and avoids my eye. "It seemed very important to you, so I didn't want you to get screwed over."

I grin. "So you do care about me, you big ol' softie."

Ignoring that, he says, "Go call your woman with the news and let me off now. I have to fly to Miami to deal with a much more annoying client."

Finally, I also get up and offer my hand to him. "Thank you. For everything."

He harrumphs but shakes my hand, and I'm happy that for the first time in my life, I realize that I'm not truly alone.

CHAPTER 47
HOPE

My health really takes a nosedive in the thirty-some hours after the incident. There was little sleep last night—for my roomies, for Cade and for me. I hate that instead of getting proper rest after finishing Spring Training, Cade spent so many hours on FaceTime with us while we plotted how to solve this. Unfortunately he was a key component and the only reason why a panel was assembled to discuss the matter just a day later. Otherwise I could've been suspended for a month or more, who knows.

It was near two in the morning when the plan was finished, all related parties were asked for help, and everyone departed for bed. Except I couldn't sleep at all.

I kept tossing and turning, uncomfortable in my soft bed that normally sucks me into its embrace without trouble. Which I guess is what happens when you're too pissed off to relax into sleep.

As the morning rolls in, the sun rays feel extra offensive on my dry eyes. I lay face up on my hot bed and kick the sheets away from me. There's some noise outside the door, which means the girls must be getting ready for work. I shouldn't be surprised that they immediately jumped on the cause and moved mountains in the course of a few hours to come up with ways to help me, but I really don't have the strength to see them off to work while I have to stay home all day.

So I wait locked up in my room, staring at the beams of light that filter through the blinds behind me, painting the darkened ceiling like a zebra. When the front door has been closed twice is when I finally allow myself to sit up. I rub my face but that doesn't get rid of the cocktail of acid emotions in my belly.

After five minutes in the bathroom, I return to my bedroom to put on some training clothes and literally the only thing I take with me is my house key. I want to go on a run so punishing that I forget about everything but the pain in my legs, the burning in my lungs, and the sweat dripping down my face. Maybe then I'll be able to at least nap.

I run around my neighborhood and into a nearby park only being used by young moms with baby strollers and people walking dogs. A few heads turn my way because in comparison, it's like I'm training for a marathon. Eventually, I circle my way back home when the sun is bright enough to make the skin of my shoulders itch.

I stop in the townhouse's foyer for a moment, leaning a hand against the wall as I fight to recover my breath. My eyes slide to the couch and I can see my name written all over it. That's where I'll dwell the rest of the day. But first, a protein shake and a shower.

Call me Speedy Gonzalez because I do all these things quickly, they're part of my routine. I towel dry my hair and apply some product the girls recommended a while ago, after they discovered I didn't use to put on anything. Marching back to my room, I select my comfiest training bra and boy shorts, and put on my rattiest T-shirt from one of the amusement parks.

As I tidy my bed up, I spot my phone on the bedside table and pick it up. Maybe I have texts from Cade or the girls. The screen doesn't light up, though, and pressing on the buttons does nothing. The battery must be kaput. It makes sense though, what with the late night FaceTiming and all. I pick up the charging cable from the floor and plug it in before heading out.

My stomach makes a gurgling noise and instead of veering right to the living room, I turn left to the kitchen to fix myself a plate with chopped fruit, nuts, chia seeds and a healthy dollop of honey that borders on unhealthy. I don't care.

The nuts provide some stress relief with the crunch. Grabbing the remote, I flip on the TV and change channels from HGTV to ESPN. They're talking about professional women's basketball and even though I'm not super versed in the sport, it's enough to suck my attention in and make me forget my bearings. Soon the food is nice and safe in my belly and the focus has shifted to professional hockey. I probably know even less about it but the compilation of the week's best fights sure is damn cathartic.

The clock on the wall tells me it's about time for the audience with Cade to start. I can't fool myself into thinking that my body temperature is dropping due to my damp hair. In truth I'm terrified.

I know Cade will do everything in his power to clarify the situation, but who knows what will happen in the end? The signs haven't been in my favor, even if I'm not in breach of contract.

I reach for the fluffy blanket that matches the cream color decorations in the living room, and wrap myself with it. The only thing that pokes out is my hand to grab the remote and crank up the volume. Every few minutes my eyes drift from the screen to the clock, and after a while of doing this, my eyelids start growing heavy.

I don't fight it too hard. In fact, I'd rather put off knowing what my sentence is for a bit longer. Tumbling on the couch, I turn the TV off and drop the remote where it falls. Snuggling against the cushions, I fully close my eyes and drift off.

*

The sound of keys at the door snaps me awake.

I only have enough time to sit up before my roomies burst into the door.

"Hope! You're alive!"

"We thought something happened to you. Why aren't you answering your phone?"

"Ngh." I rub my eyes and check the clock. It's past noon but I feel like I could've slept well into dinner if I wasn't interrupted.

"You look pretty bad, are you okay?" Rose lifts up my feet so she can take a seat at the end of the couch. Meanwhile, Audrey takes her armchair facing me.

"What are you guys doing here?" I squint at them.

"I got suspended too." Rose shrugs.

I sit upright. "What?"

"I didn't," Audrey clarifies. "But I'm protesting."

"Wha—" I shake my head.

"Apparently posting an unapproved video to the team's social media merits a suspension," Rose explains with a pensive expression on her face. "I mean, I can see why. Someone untrustworthy could post something that tarnishes the team's brand. But if they didn't want something like this to happen, maybe they should've put it in my contract, huh?" She smirks.

"Besides, it's been great for the team from a PR perspective," Audrey adds, reclining back. "That's why I'm protesting. A video that has accrued one million views in the course of a single morning, with overwhelmingly positive comments, and that is being shared all across other social media platforms, shouldn't merit a suspension. That's just my opinion as a PR specialist."

Shaking my head, I'm about to ask what video they're even talking about until it finally clicks. It was part of the master plan we orchestrated as a group last night.

"Oh." I gape at them. "So people are taking it well?"

"Don't get me wrong, there's some griping that the hottest baseball player of Spring Training has found his lady and it's none of the singles online, but it's a smashing success." Rose pats my leg over the fluffy blanket.

"In fact, everyone online is asking who this woman who keeps it real is that managed to capture Cade Starr's heart." Audrey leans forward again. "Would you be open to revealing your identity? I'm sure we can make you a celebrity of your own, and maybe that confers you an extra layer of protection."

"Or brings out the stalkers, no thanks." I wrinkle my nose.

"Okay, fair."

"Anyway, now that we're gonna have some free time in our hands, should we book a trip to the beach or something?" Rose asks, glancing at us in turns.

I'm about to remind her that I have a brand new boyfriend who isn't suspended and has a pool in his house, when the doorbell goes off and makes us jump.

"Um, is anyone waiting for someone?"

"No?"

"What if it's Cade?" I ask, making a move to pull off the blanket.

Audrey raises a hand. "You stay comfy. I'll get it." She leaves her chair and marches on her socks toward the door.

"Pizza delivery," a familiar voice says, just not the one I'm really waiting for.

Rose jerks in surprise even before our other roommate at the door asks, "Logan?"

"And me," someone else says, and Rose's frame relaxes at Lucky Rivera's voice.

"Plus me."

That's when I spring from the couch. My legs tangle with the fluffy blanket and I almost crash on the hardwood floor, but I manage not to break my face on athleticism alone. My bare feet give me enough purchase not to skid as I rush to the front door.

"Excuse me," I declare and Audrey has enough wit to step aside quickly. Logan takes one look at the bull charging toward him, he raises pizza boxes above his head and also moves aside. Rivera yelps as he tosses himself out of the way.

But Cade doesn't move an inch. Or I guess he does, but it's only to spread his arms wide.

I barrel into him at top speed. His arms close around me and lift me off the ground. With my arms over his shoulders and around his neck working as a pillow for his head, I crash my mouth on his for a kiss I mean to convey all my gratitude with, no matter what happened.

Except someone clears their throat behind me, and when that doesn't work in making us put some distance between us, Logan Kim says, "Hey, no one here has any issues with your PDA and all that, but you may want to do that inside the house where the neighbors can't see Hope's underwear."

Squeaking, I release Cade's mouth and watch his eyebrows rise. "What is he talking about?" he asks softly.

"I might not be wearing any pants."

"Ah." Slowly, Cade sets me back on my feet and leans back to look. I try pulling the hem of my T-Shirt lower but unfortunately it's a short one and there's nothing that can be done.

Amusement lights up my boyfriend's eyes. "And no shoes either."

"Yeah, kinda didn't think about putting any on the way."

He snorts, but next thing, he's bending lower to slide his arms under me. The whole world tilts and I grab onto his neck.

"Cade! What if you get hurt?"

"If the cowboy gets hurt from just that, I'd be real shocked," Rivera says as we pass him by.

Cade crosses the threshold into the house and still doesn't set me down. "Everyone look away from my girl," he commands.

From the living room, with his back to us, Logan waves a hand and says, "Trust me, I'm far more interested on this pizza." He turns to Rose. "Should we get plates or go rogue?"

"Always rogue," she responds while making space on the coffee table for him to set down the boxes.

"Any fun drinks around here?" Rivera's in the kitchen, opening the fridge like it's his house. "Ew, protein shakes? Gross."

Behind us, Audrey closes the front door. "Put her on the couch, there's a blanket there."

Turning my head to glance back, I ask, "Can you please find me some leggings?" She salutes and keeps going to my bedroom.

Cade maneuvers to the living room—narrowly avoiding maiming Logan with my legs—but instead of setting me down on the couch, he sits down on it with me on his lap. At least he sets the blanket on my legs so I can stop flashing other people. But he keeps a hand casually under the blanket.

I cock an eyebrow at him and he just smirks.

From the corner of my eye I catch Audrey emerging from the hallway, a pair of rolled up leggings in her hand. I have no doubt that she's the smartest cookie in the room because she takes one look at Cade's and my positions, and chucks my leggings at a random shelf.

"Anyway." I clear my throat. "Why are you all here? Not that I'm complaining." Especially not about using Cade as my personal chair. He pushes me against his chest and even though his body's like marble, we mold together so perfectly that I could nap here.

Well, in theory. I'm certainly not sleepy with his hand on my bare thigh.

"Your phone was off," he says, his voice rumbling in his chest and against me.

"Plus, I owed a certain annoying pitcher his damn pizza." Logan looks huge in our living room even as he sits on the floor across from the couch. He has a pepperoni slice in his hand and tucks in before everyone else, as if he too wanted some pie.

I lean back to use Cade's shoulder as a pillow and also slide my hand under the blanket to stop his. It'd be too weird to feel all bothered for whatever news they have for me.

As if reading my mind, Rose asks, "So, Cowboy, what's the verdict? Do we have to sue the Orlando Wild for wrongful termination or not?"

Rivera returns with a tower of glasses on one hand, and a two-liter bottle of soda that lives in Audrey's shelf in the fridge. She frowns a little but lets it go, preferring to sit at her armchair instead.

Cade turns his head and places a kiss on my temple and I look up at him. "Well…"

I bite my lip. "Well?"

"Sorry, what was the question?" Cade shakes his head.

Sighing, Logan says, "Put your hands where we can see them so you can focus."

"Stop sounding so jealous, Kim." Rivera chuckles as he sits on the floor at one end of the coffee table.

"Let them be, they're still on the honeymoon phase," Rose says as she puts one pizza box aside to explore the others.

It's funny how I can start making out the smell of bread and tomato sauce much better when Cade complies and puts his hands visibly around me instead.

"Right." He clears his throat and then speaks in a deadpan so sharp it could cut steel. "So, a panel of six men basically were responsible for deciding your fate."

Rose hisses.

Audrey expels a sharp breath like she's doing breathing exercises.

"Fortunately," Cade continues, looking down at me. "Four ended up being on your side."

My jaw slacks.

Rose freezes halfway to pulling a cheese slice from the pie. "Does that mean…"

"Two of them were my agent and I," Cade explains, his eyes softening. "Plus Beau." Someone gasps. "And your own boss."

"What?" I shriek.

"Yeah, he was pretty reasonable. Just wants us to keep professional boundaries at work."

"Who were the two against?" Audrey asks sharply.

"Watson from HR." Cade stops to roll his eyes and Logan drops an *of course* with a harsh word in between. "And the owner. Although he wasn't so much against it, as he didn't want any bad publicity."

Audrey sneers and leans back on her chair, saying nothing further.

"Let me get this straight." I grab Cade's chin and turn his head to me. "I can keep my job?"

His cheek pushes against my hand as he smiles. "Yeah, you get to keep what was rightfully yours all along."

"Woohoo! The job and the man!" Rose pumps the air with, er, a pizza slice.

"Salud!" Rivera lifts a glass of Coke. "To love's victory!"

Audrey scoots toward the coffee table and grabs one of the soda glasses that Rivera poured. She lifts it up ceremoniously. "Cheers to any future such panels having women in them."

"I can toast to that." Rose clinks her glass with Audrey's.

Kim adds nothing verbally but lifts his nearly finished slice as toast.

And Cade and I? We celebrate with a kiss.

CHAPTER 48
CADE

Once I step out of the men's restroom, I'm faced with Hope Garcia leaning against the opposite wall while she scrolls through her phone. She's much more blatant now than the one time she pretended not to be waiting for me so she could ask me not to tell anyone that she had a humiliating date.

I stuff my hands in the pockets of my uniform pants and clear my throat.

Hope lifts her eyes to my face but doesn't stop there too long. Slowly, she inspects me down to my feet. I'm about to tell her that she can inspect me with much more detail any time she wants, when she suddenly lifts her phone in the air like she's comparing me with something else.

"Hmm." Her eyebrows tighten in pensiveness.

"What?" I ask, thoroughly confused.

"Your *SPORTY* photoshoot is out," she explains, still looking at the phone. "I'm just comparing the photoshopped version to the real one."

"And?" I fold my arms and stand straighter. "Don't tell me you prefer the oiled up and touched up version?"

"Pfff. Of course not." Clicking the screen off, she pockets the phone back and adds, "Although I have to do a more thorough inspection in privacy."

A corner of my lips lifts and I'm amused that she could read my mind. However, I want to clarify something. "Of the real version, I assume?"

This evil woman looks at me like the power of her gaze is enough to singe the clothes off my body, complete with licking her full lips like she can already taste mine. Just the gesture alone is enough to send electricity down my spine.

"Both," she declares boldly before turning around. "Anyway, I was sent over to fetch you because the game's starting soon."

"Just to fetch me?" I catch up to her easily and slide an arm around her waist. A little squeak comes out of her throat as I press her against me, before lowering my face to nuzzle her hair. The scent of vanilla immediately eases my pre-opening game nerves, but does nothing to cool my blood.

"Hey, this crosses professional lines." She grabs my arm and if she tries to push me off, I will. Yet she doesn't. If anything, she melts into me even more.

"Eh, I think they know I need this." I drop a kiss on her neck. "Otherwise they'd have sent literally anyone else."

"That hypothesis has merit." Stretching, she twists enough to glance up at me. "What exactly do you need, though?"

"This." With my free hand, I support her chin so I can kiss her lips from behind. It's not the most comfortable position and I definitely can't deepen the kiss as much as I want to, but that's probably for the better. I can't get this kind of engine too fired up before the game, when I'm supposed to be revving up the starter pitcher engine instead.

All I manage is a brief taste of her lips, a graze of our tongues, before I convince myself to be responsible and pull away.

"If we win today's game you may have to wish me good luck like this before every future game, you know? You'll become my jinx," I whisper against her smile.

"Oh, no. What a terrible hardship," she returns with sarcasm.

We both chuckle until I pull away to offer my right hand to her. She slides her fingers between mine and we grip each other's hands tight as we walk through the clubhouse, only pulling away when we're at the tunnel. Hope motions at me to go first and I only obey because I do have to get my glove and get going.

"There he is." Lucky smirks as I emerge into the dugout. "The man of the hour." He tilts his head, spots Hope behind me, and winks at her.

"Ready?" Kim asks from the side as two guys help fit him with his catcher gear.

"As can be," I respond.

"Bro, you got this."

"This team has nothing on you."

"Get them with your nastiest cutter."

Rolling my shoulders, I head over to the cubbies to grab my glove. That's where Rob Beau, the manager, waits for me. He doesn't call me over like usual, just looks for some sort of sign on my face.

He must find it because he nods at me and all he says is, "I trust you, Starr. Go wild out there."

My breath hitches.

A slow grin blooms on my face, buoyed by the warmth that's expanding inside of me. "Yes, sir."

"Let's go, boys." Kim walks over to the exit. "Let's have a wild season."

Amidst hollers and yelling, we rush to the field right behind him. The rest of the team runs to their spots on the field, and the catcher follows me to the mound.

"Stop looking so damn happy, it's not intimidating for the opponent," he grouches and bumps his glove against my chest.

"You too would be this happy if you had an amazing woman who just gave you the most epic kiss of your life before a game."

He grimaces. "Are you going to focus on the game or on your girlfriend?"

"Both," I chirp back.

"If you stare at her more than once per inning, I will burn down your favorite pizza joint."

"I believe you." I smack my left hand into my glove. "But trust me, having Hope only makes me want to play harder. I got this."

With one last harrumph, he offers his glove and I bump it with mine. Kim really didn't need to worry though, the umpire calls *play ball* and I throw the first strike of the season—a nasty one that sets the tone for the new Orlando Wild.

EPILOGUE

HOPE: NEXT NOVEMBER

I'm glad we decided to drive my Jeep down to Miami. The top is off and the warm wind whips at us, the sun blasting from above. I'm sure my hair looks like black flames behind me and that I'm going to have a hand shaped tan line on my thigh by the time we get to Kelly and Mitch's McMansion, but I have no complaints. The weight of Cade's hand has become my favorite feeling.

There's no doubt it's also his, especially because I'm wearing really short jean shorts for the trip.

We're off the big highways at last and into suburban traffic when we roll to a stop at a red light, and he turns his head to me. His brown hair's also a beautiful mess, and I'm equal parts annoyed that I can't see his brilliant eyes behind the dark aviators, as I'm thrilled that I can't tell where he's looking.

"Hey," he says in a raspy voice that could be from the wind, from the off tune karaoke session we had a few miles behind, or from something else. I hope it's the latter.

I cross my legs, imprisoning his hand. "Hey."

"You look beautiful a little wild like this."

My heart skips.

I try to fix up my hair and straighten out the open Orlando Wild jersey that shows his last name and number one on my back, and my yellow bikini top. "Better?" I ask.

"Still you, and I like all versions of you." Cade reaches over the console in the middle and I fully turn into the kiss. The last time we kissed was as we were leaving Orlando, and I've missed his lips so freaking much.

Honking behind us forces us to separate. Sighing, Cade gets the car going again.

I don't move one bit, though, drinking him with my eyes instead. He's also wearing some shorts that ride high enough to show the defined cuts of his quads around his knees, plus an Orlando Wild shirt he custom made with my last name that he also kept open the whole way For Reasons. Them being that I really enjoy looking at his abs and the hint of V at his hips.

"Do you think the shirts are overkill?" I ask, propping my elbow on the middle console and my chin on my hand.

"Why would they be overkill?"

Has anyone told him that the way he turns the steering wheel with one hand is supremely mouth-watering?

Oh, right. I have. Multiple times.

I force my brain to get back to work with a deep breath that brings in the familiar scent of his aftershave. "Erm. I'm just wondering if it's too on the nose. Too middle school."

Cade shrugs. "I have no problem telling the whole world that I'm yours and you're mine. I'm making up for almost three decades of not belonging anywhere."

I reach for his knee and give it a squeeze—and I don't remove it. Cade flashes me a quick look, but the GPS instructs him to take a right turn and he focuses back on the road.

"Listen, if this Friendsgiving is in any way uncomfortable

for you, you call for a wild pitch and I'll bail us out of here," I say in all seriousness.

"Ditto. I may or may not have looked up some hotel alternatives already."

That might actually be preferable to this. I'm debating whether to just tell him that we should ditch, but too soon we're pulling to Kelly and Mitch's street and it feels like too late.

We're a bit earlier than I would've arrived normally, and there's still plenty of room by the curb of their house. I instruct Cade to park under the shade of a massive oak lining the street, and we get out of the car to put the top back up and secure it. After getting our overnighter bags from the back, Cade locks the car and pockets the key so he can offer me his hand.

A new development is that he's learned to rub the back of my hand with his thumb even as I grab his hand in a vise. I can't do the same in return because of the sheer size of his hands, but also because I'm not hypermobile and with fingers nimble enough to hold a baseball with a million different grips.

Taking a deep breath, I ring the doorbell and wait.

A few seconds pass. Setting my bag down, I tug Cade lower and start combing his hair back into order.

That's when the door opens. "Hey guys." Mitch smiles at us—although it turns into a grimace as his baby girl pulls at his ear. "Come on in."

"You doing okay, man?" Cade's lips curl in amusement as the baby keeps pulling and papa keeps grimacing.

"Living the life." Mitch grins though, like he means it. "You can leave your bags here and head to the back. We got drinks and food already."

"Great, I'm starving." I try to smile but the truth is that just setting a foot inside their house has my stomach turning already.

The literal last thing I want to do is see the judgy faces of the other people I went to college with. I debated whether to come at all or just excise myself from that toxicity forever, but Kelly and Mitch don't deserve that. They're probably the reason I even hung out with this clique in the first place, because Kelly—and whatsherface—were my OG friends I thought would always be my ride-or-dies.

"Wild pitch?" Cade whispers to me.

I steel myself. "Not yet. I'm not a coward."

He runs his thumb across my skin again and the little spark there fires up my engine, so I keep going.

Their previously picture perfect house is now much homier, with colorful toys and cushions strewn all over the place, and some curious stains on a wall that can only be the masterpiece of a toddler with some markers. It reminds me, like Cade's hand in mine, that sometimes things do change for the better.

This house isn't the same and neither am I, so what happened last year has no damn chance of repeating itself today. Whatever my ex friends do, it won't faze me.

But then we walk out to the terrace, and aside from Kelly working on the grill, and some gigantic floaties on the pristine pool, there is literally no one else.

"Wha…" I babble.

"Welcome!" Kelly abandons the grill and rushes over to engulf both Cade and I in a single hug. Her face is brighter than the sun as she says, "Mitch and I decided to change things up a bit and only have Friendsgiving with real friends from now on."

I blink a few times before sweeping my eyes around her. But other people don't jump out of the woodworks to scream *surprise* at us. Slowly, my pea brain figures it out.

"You mean…"

"That's right." She pulls away, hooking her arm with mine and Cade's in her other one. "It's just the five of us this year."

My jaw drops. Even Cade does a double take.

Nonplussed, Mitch carries the baby around the pool toward the smoking grill. "Hey, Cade. One patty or two?"

"Two?" my boyfriend responds like it's a question.

"Drinks?" Kelly adds. "I make a mean mojito."

"She does," I say in a breathless way.

"Sure…" Cade drags the word and Kelly hops over to the outdoor bar that I know is stocked with any flavor of booze under the sun.

Pulled by the same string, Cade and I turn to each other and just ponder about what just happened for a quiet moment. Until he tugs me closer.

"Aren't you glad you didn't use your wild pitch?" he mutters into my ear.

"So glad." I dig my face into his bare chest, where he no doubt can feel the tears springing from my eyes. I wrap my free hand around his waist from under his shirt. "Thank you for giving me strength."

Cade presses a kiss on top of my head. "It's the least I could do, when you give me strength every day."

"I love you."

The way he grows rigid makes me wonder if it was way too soon to say those words, but we've been dating since March and there's no denying that that's how I feel.

Cade frees his hand, sending my heart to a plummet, but then he sneaks both under my shirt to find my bare back, and he nuzzles my hair before speaking.

"I was waiting for the perfect moment to say it and now I feel like a fool."

"I'm sorry. I—"

"No." He runs his hands up and down my skin. "The perfect moment is every time I'm with you, and I'm a fool for not recognizing that until now. Hey, Hope?"

"Yeah?" My voice is but a thread.

"I love you more."

I sniffle against his skin and turn slightly to kiss his chest, the fuzz of hair tingling my nose. "Good, because I have no plans to let you go."

"That's great, because I'm not going anywhere."

We probably would've kissed indecently after that if it wasn't for Kelly returning to booze us up. Cade keeps his arm around me as we join my friend on the way back to the grill, officially kicking off the best Friendsgiving ever.

THE END

*

Turn to the next page to read a bonus scene from Cade's point of view!

BONUS SCENE

CADE: AUGUST

’m hiding a big secret from my girlfriend.

She definitely knows something's up from the moment I said I was taking her on a date but not where.

Oh, she's definitely tried getting it out of me. I could barely hear anything from our playlist while she came up with one idea after the next, more outrageous each time.

"I got it," she says as we walk up Park Avenue hand in hand, dodging people who speak all languages under the sun. "We're going bungee jumping."

I just toss her a raised eyebrow. We wouldn't be anywhere in the middle of busy Winter Park to do that, so I know she's kidding.

"No?" Her eyes narrow, turned golden by the bright sun above us. As she travels them up and down my body, I can't help but wonder if the sun turned hotter all of a sudden or why am I sweating.

But who am I kidding? It's her. She lights me on fire.

"No." I lick my lips. The movement distracts her from her surroundings.

Some guy in a skateboard comes at her from behind and I see him from the corner of my eye. I pull Hope toward me and she doesn't resist. In fact, she rests her chin against my chest and I zero in on her nose, all cute and easily accessible.

I boop it. "Stop trying to guess and just come along."

"But I want to know." Her face scrunches up. "I want to know everything about you."

The thumping organ in my chest trips on itself.

A slow grin forms on my face. "Stop flirting with me, woman. I'm already yours."

Her body tenses in surprise, it's only a microsecond, but enough to start making me panic.

Is that like an admission that I'm in love with her? Because I am. Severely. I've never in my life felt the connection *and* the desire I feel for her. There's only been some of the latter, and never this all consuming.

And it's not like I think about Hope every single second of my waking moment, but I'll hear something and want to share it with her. Or I'll look at something and immediately know it's so her. And I've even started developing a curious mind-reading super-power, especially around food. Somehow I've managed to guess that she's hungry and what she may want to eat more than once.

Right now I can't read her at all.

Did I screw up?

But then she releases a feminine little laugh that makes me want to preen like a prize stallion.

"That's good to know. However, I'm never gonna stop flirting. It took me forever to get the handle of it and I intend to show off my newfound skills regularly."

I roll my eyes dramatically. "Fine. Flirt away. Can we walk at the same time, though?"

"Of course. I'm really good at multitasking." She motions at me to lead the way.

I resume our pace, joining the heavy pedestrian traffic on the side of Park Avenue that has all the shops and eateries. Hope grabs my arm into something of a hug, even with our hands holding in between.

I… really enjoy when she does that. For reasons. I keep my eyes fixed on the path in front of us, face neutral, breathing even, because I'm a mature guy and—

Nope. I love feeling her curves pressed up against me. Drives me wild every time.

Breathing stops being even and face is probably turning red while I navigate her to one of the side streets. There are less people around here and my brain is officially overridden by hormones.

I walk her against a wall and lean her against it, lowering my mouth to her ear. "That wasn't flirting. That was an overt attack."

Hope frees her hand to sneak both of them under my T-shirt. My muscles tense, which is precisely what she's looking for. She turns a radiant smile up at me. Sweet, even.

"No, *this* is an attack, and I'm gonna keep it up until you tell me where we're going."

I steel myself as her hands rise another notch, her finger pads very diligent in mapping my stomach. This is going to get very, very dangerous if I don't stop her right here.

But first, I swoop down for a quick kiss, wrapping my lips around hers like it's a bite. And I pull away just as quickly.

The way a million emotions flash in her face makes me smirk. There's no hiding her annoyance or her need for more than a little nibble. But she's clearly not seeing the elderly couple watching us like they're about to call the cops on us.

Sneaking my hands into my clothes, I pull hers back to full

visibility and tug her to keep walking. "C'mon, we're gonna be late."

Grouching, she drags her feet behind me until finally there's a single establishment left in the street before the next block turns fully residential. She turns her eyes between the locale and me like it's a tennis match.

"No way."

"Way."

Her eyes narrow. "I thought you said I didn't need a makeover."

"And you don't. This is for me." I shrug and add, "And also for you if you want to join me. I did make a reservation for two."

She scratches her head. "I admit I'm very confused right now—and don't get me wrong, I'm not judging. Men can definitely also do this. Or anything they want, really. I just—it's unexpected, that's all."

I bite my lip even though I'm smiling. I love it when she gets all flustered and babbles.

"Why is it so surprising?" I challenge back, lifting our joined hands and my free one to her eye level. "My paycheck strongly depends on the health of my nails. If a pitch breaks one because it's too long and I start bleeding, I'm pretty much done for the game."

She coughs to hide a laugh. "Yes, that makes sense. So what are you getting? French? Dip? Or a standard manicure?"

I've been coming to this little establishment enough to know what those terms mean. Deadpanned, I respond, "A nice buff, exfoliation, massage, a pedi, and a glass of sweet iced tea. Are you in or not?"

She opens and closes her mouth a few times until asking, "Does the pedi also include a massage?"

"Always."

"Oh, then I'm so in. Let's go!" Now she's the one dragging

me across the street, and I'm the one leaving a trail of laughter behind.

I'm not sure this is quite what she had in mind when she said that she wants to learn everything about me, but we sure talk about everything and nothing while getting couple manis and pedis. And I don't know if it's because she's never been pampered by anyone, but the sheer joy on her face tells me this is going to become a thing we do together from now on.

I love that. So damn much. Just like I love her.

Now I just need to figure out the best way to tell her.

*

*Thank you for reading **Wild Pitch**! I hope you can take a brief moment to leave a review on Amazon.*

*Preorder **Wild Catch**, book two in the Wild Baseball Romance series featuring Rosalina and Logan.*

Turn to the next page to see my other works.

MORE FROM THE AUTHOR

WILD BASEBALL ROMANCE

Wild Pitch
Wild Catch*

SPORTY CHRISTMAS ROMANCE

Mistlefoe

ST. CLOUD HOCKEY SERIES

Faceoff
Overtime
Shutout

VOLLEYBALL ROMANCE NOVELLA

Set Me Up**

*Coming soon.
**Newsletter exclusive.

GLOSSARY OF SPANISH VOCABS

Chapter 1

- Mamacita: The equivalent of 'hot mama.'

Chapter 5

- Hijo de su madre: Son of his mother (see also Chapter 23).
- No bueno: 'Not good' in incorrect grammar (see also Chapter 41).

Chapter 6

- Estás dura: A Puerto Rican way of saying 'you're hot.'

Chapter 7

- ¿Qué diantres fue eso?: What the heck was that?

Chapter 9

- ¿Me estás diciendo que no sabes hablar con los manes?: Are you telling me that you don't know how to talk with men?
- Ay, bendito: Oh, blessed.

Chapter 11

- Ahora sí he perdido la cabeza: I really have lost my head now.
- Cojones: Men's dangly bits (see also Chapter 18, 29).

Chapter 14

- Es lo que hay: It is what it is.

Chapter 15

- Qué carajo: Colloquial way of saying 'what the heck.'
- Tía: Aunt.
- Mija: Colloquial way of saying 'my daughter.'

Chapter 17

- Mami: Literally translates to Mom, but in this case it's being used just as mamacita, 'hot mama.'

Chapter 21

- Mierda: Shit (see also Chapter 25).

- ¿Qué carajo me pasa?: What the heck is happening to me?

Chapter 22

- Gringo: Colloquial way of referring to anyone who isn't Latin American, most often used to refer to Americans.

Chapter 23

- Está bueno: Could mean 'he's good' but in this case refers to 'he's hot.'

Chapter 25

- Mondongo: Traditional Venezuelan soup that is basically everything but the kitchen sink.

Chapter 27

- Mi Papá: My dad.
- Está bien, quedará en tu conciencia: Fine, it'll stay in your conscience.
- Xfa: Chatspeak way of saying 'por favor,' which means please.
- Me muero: I'm dying.

Chapter 33

- Trágame tierra: Earth, swallow me.

Chapter 35

- Sí: Yes.

Chapter 37

- Mierda, qué bello es: Shit, he's so beautiful.

Chapter 38

- Buenos días: Good morning.
- Arepas: Arepa is one of the national dishes of Venezuela and has no English translation. It's a corn flour "bread" that can be filled with basically anything.

Chapter 43

- Un ojo de la cara: An eye from the face (yes, that's where eyes are but this is how the saying goes).

Chapter 47

- Salud: Cheers.

ACKNOWLEDGMENTS

As always, I first have to thank the Lord. Contigo todo, sin ti nada.

Thank you so much to my ride or dies Avery Keelan and Tamara Lush for helping me stay goodlulu.

To Enni at Yummy Book Covers who is the MVP of this operation. I keep saying that you saved my behind but what can I say, it's tradition now.

One thousand gajillion thanks to all my readers, ARC team (especially Lindsey), and to my cheerleaders for being the best of all. I said it and I didn't stutter, you're the best readers and the best part of this author journey.

Last but not least, I want to thank my mom, my sister, and my dad up in heaven. Thank you for encouraging me to never give up. Los amo con todo.

ABOUT THE AUTHOR

Mari Loyal was born and raised in Venezuela, a baseball country that only cared about another sport, football soccer, every four years. As such, she decided to make hockey her whole personality because she had to make a point of being different. These days she no longer suffers from Not Like Other Girls syndrome and is very happy to be in the sports romance fandom. She writes closed door romance with a Latin American flair and an abundance of cinnamon rolls heroes. She also enjoys eating cinnamon rolls (the confections), in her spare time.

Find her:
Website & Newsletter mariloyal.com
Instagram mariloyalauthor
Threads mariloyalauthor